'SSES"
'SSES"
"SSEY'

by

CHAULKY

'SSES' 'SSES' "SSEY'

ISBN: 978-1-940853-00-0

Ir 5 5 / 2 0 0

The concept + major portions of this book were published previously as 'SSES' 'SSES' by Kevin White in 1990 (to fulfill his MFA thesis at Art Center College of Design in Pasadena, CA).

'SSES' 'SSES' "SSEY' is a self-contained book object that requires no a priori knowledge or technology to read it. Instructions on how to read the book are contained within the book itself ... in fact, 'SSES' 'SSES' "SSEY' could be considered just that—a protocol to interpet itself ... or a literary work that interrogates the very inscription technology + processes used to produce it, mobilizing reflexive loops between original imagined intent + editorial deterritorialization ... a «gift of tongues rendering visible not the lay sense but the first entelechy, the structural rhythm»—as Stephen Dedalus says in *Ulysses* (from which this is in part derived).

All characters appearing in this work (unless hand-coded otherwise) are re-assembled from existng 'real' people, living or dead. Nothing is ever coincidental or accidental.

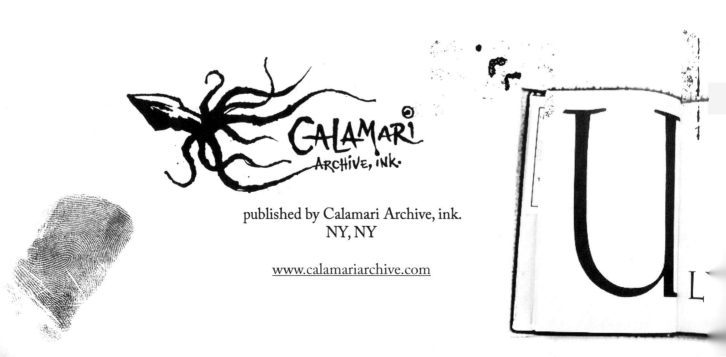

published by Calamari Archive, ink.
NY, NY

www.calamariarchive.com

0

EN-TELEMACHY
[IN ABSENCE]

Xhibit 0—self-portrait, date unknown
(the original burned in a house fire, but this photographic reproduction hangs over us for inspiration)

ABSTRACT: The jury of peers calls council to deliberate how we (in 3rd person cuz u too are included in this experiment) will recapitulate this hisstory. There are no "minutes" yet—the time has bin set but has not started ticking ... the only order of business is to send our hero — Telemachus—on his merry way (in our absence).

ART CENTER COLLEGE OF DESIGN

PASADENA, CALIFORNIA

August 18, 1990

'SSES"
'SSES"

Master's Thesis

by

Kevin White

[Handwritten note:] This is the 1st page of a book by & about my brother Kevin, whose life ended prematurely on April 3, 1997. To fulfill the requirements for an MFA at Art Center in Pasadena Kevin wrote this thesis entitled 'SSES" 'SSES" wherein he took Joyce's recapitulation of Homers ODYSSEY to ULYSSES 1 step further by recapitulating ULYSSES to a trip he took across Asia in search of our father, who commit suicide in 1982. This book you hold is a dilated (+ belated) expansion of that book, a deconstructed REDUX w/ further recapitulations by me searching recursively in parallel for: My brother searching for: our father.

Derek White, brother, editor

Submitted in partial satisfaction of the requirement for the degree of Master of Fine Arts, this thesis is approved and is acceptable in quality and form.

Buzz Spector
Buzz Spector
Studio Advisor

Stephen Prina
Stephen Prina
Studio Advisor

Jeremy Gilbert-Rolfe
Jeremy Gilbert-Rolfe
Thesis Advisor

Richard Hertz
Richard Hertz, Chairman
Liberal Arts & Sciences

---

[0] «Be-bop» being the 1st word he spoke.

(BREAKDOWN of breakdowns)   **SSEY** EN-TELEMACHY (in absence)

Kevin begins his original SSES thesis (after displaying "The Clown (1906)" by Georges Roualt w/ no explanation) by giving a rundown of the 24 chapters of *The Odyssey*. He then gives a breakdown of *The Odyssey* as used by Joyce in the 18 episodes of *Ulysses* (not included here in its entirety ... tho "The Clown" appears at the end of episode 5) + then brother-½ gives his own amalgamated reconstruction as follows:

[note: his "story" or odyssey starts on our father's birthday/deathday + ends on his own birthday]

EN-FOLDING

BREAKDOWN OF THE "ODYSSEY" BY CHAPTERS

BOOK I (ATHENE ADVISES TELEMACHUS) Ulysses is detained after the Trojan war by Calypso. Athene convinces all of the gods except Poseidon, who remains unsympathetic to the plight of Ulysses, to help, and then goes personally to the aid of Telemachus.

BOOK II (THE ASSEMBLY OF ITHICA MEETS) Telemachus calls to assembly the men of Ithica to discuss the situation with the suitors

BOOK III (TELEMACHUS AND NESTOR)

BOOK VI (TELEMACHUS AND MENELAUS) Telemachus meets with Menelaus, who tells him of Proteus, the old man of the sea, who can tell him of his father. Telemachus goes in search of Proteus. The suitors plan to ambush him.

BOOK V (ULYSSES ... home, but Poseidon ... island of the Phea ...

BOOK IIIV (... directs him to her ...

BOOK IX (THE W ... the land of the Fa ... the Trojan war ... effects of the lotu ... captive in a cave ... Ulysses after he sen ...

BOOK X (THE W ... the winds) gives ... jealousy his men ... Ulysses's men, kill ... lured by Circe and ... back, and becomes ... Hades in order to ...

BOOK IX (THE W ... world, makes offer ...

BOOK IIX (THE W THE SUN) Ulysses ... the mast. The two to ... passage is imposs ... sun god's cattle, ... then washes up on ...

BOOKS IIIX – XVII ... Ulysses meets Ale ... Telemachus. They ...

BOOK XVI (ULYSS ... then dies. Ulysses ...

BOOK IVX – III ... Ulysses is provoke ... home for the night.

BOOK XIX (PENEL ... Ulysses talks with ... suitor invoking a s ...

BOOK XX (ULYSS ... down on the suitors ... not listen.

BOOK IXX (THE ... Telemachus attem ... attempts. Ulysses ...

BOOK IIXX (UL ... battle he has the ... fumigated with sul ...

BOOK IIIXX (UL ... battle. She does ... identity. They go ...

BOOK XIV (U ... meets with his fat ... many before Athe ...

THE BREAKDOWN OF THE ""ODYSSEY" AS USED BY JOYCE IN "ULYSSES"

(1) TELEMACHUS- Leaves Ithica in search of his long lost father so that they might drive out Penelope's suitors.

(2) NESTOR- T ... military role, is ... to offer the boy ...

(3) PROTEUS- ... Proteus, god of ...

(4) CALYPSO- ... nymph Calypso.

(5) THE LOTUS ... the lotus eaters ... them forget the ... leave.

(6) HADES- Uly ...

(7) AEOLUS- (... winds that coul ... the bag while he ...

(8) LESTRYGO ...

(9) SCYLLA AN ... has to negotiate ... of Scylla, but to ... each of Scylla's ...

(10) THE WAND ... return home, sa ... Charybdis. ... He chooses the ... passed the wand ...

(11) THE SIREN ... be seduced by th ... can hear them, ...

(12) THE CYCL ... manages to esc ... stake, and esca ... Polyphemous o ... misses, he then ... journey to be p ...

(13) NAUSICAA ... awakened by th ... to play and was ... throws a large stone ... the cyclops's father ... years) The dramatic c ... Kong involving money.

(14) THE OXEN ... cattle of the su ... the only surviv ...

(15) CIRCE- Tur ... spell.

(16) EUMEUS- ... home to Ithica, ... suitors.

(17) ITHICA- U ...

(18)PENELOPE ... Only after he ... Ulysses.

MY STORY AS BROKEN DOWN INTO CHAPTERS, USING JOYCE'S CHAPTER BREAKDOWN OF HOMER'S ODYSSEY

TELMACHUS- JAN.5-6 89, Beginning of trip (sets out in search of his father)
NESTOR-JAN.6-23 89, [Switz.,Aus.,Spain,GDR,Paris] (useless advice from Nestor)
The Tyrollian alps at night, Karine.
PROTEUS- JAN 23-30, 89 ...
the sea and a form cha ...
connection between ...
CALYPSO- JAN 31-FEB 2, ...
by the beautiful nymph ...
end when I visited her ...
THE LOTUS EATERS-FEB 2 ...
visit the lotus eaters ...
-ience of coldness and ...
HADES- FEB 7- FEB 9 [...
My journey through the ...
AEOLUS-FEB 9-FEB 11 [M ...
containing all adverse ...
the bag and send them ...
Moscow.
LESTROGENS-FEB 11-FEB ...
express across Siberia ...
SCYLLA AND CHARYBDIS- ...
Ulysses has to negotia ...
Mongolia and into Beji ...
SIRENS FEB 18- MAR 20 ...
('The Sirens call Uylss ...
mast so he can hear th ...
goal, the quick exit ...
CYCLOPS- MAR 20- MAR ...
Ulysses's men, but Ul ...
throws a large stone ...
the cyclops's father ...
years) The dramatic c ...
Kong involving money.
NAUSICAA- MAR 28-APR ...
the land of the Phone ...
beach when she goes d ...
ball, she instructs h ...
in Nepal, including t ...
THE OXEN OF THE SUN-A ...
the warning, Ulysses' ...
all killed, leaving U ...
Nepal and India.
EUMEAUS-APR 26-APR 27 ...
Eumeaus). Leaving Ind ...
ITHACA- APR 27- APR ...
in Ithica) Paris, fl ...
PENELOPE- APR 30 [LA, my birthday party], Ulysses returns home. Penelope does not recognize him, he describes the design of their bed, she believes him. Home in Venice, thoughts about the journey.

'SSES" CHAPTER BREAKDOWN;

(#) SOMMONING OF THE MUSE-(REFERENCE TO HOMER)

(1.)TELEMACHUS- UNIDENTIFIED PHOTO, STORY;FATHER'S DEN, CLOUDS, ETC...

(2.)NESTOR- QUOTES FROM DELEUZE/GUATTARI, BERGSON, BACHELARD, H.LEVIN, ETC. AND COMMENTARY BY AUTHOR ON THE THEME OF JOYCE, MULTIPLICITY ("RHIZOMATIC WRITTING").

(3.)PROTEUS- TELEMACHUS LEARNS ABOUT DEATH.

(4.)CALYPSO- LOVE LETTER (TO..NORA, MOLLY, CALYPSO...)

(5.)THE LOTUS EATERS- DREAM FRAGMENT, 'D' ENTRIES, SECTION FROM "SORROWFUL WERTHER- GOETHE"

(6.)HADES- "BRAZILIAN STORY", SECTION FROM BURROUGH'S BIO. ON G. CORSO.

(7.)AEOLUS- PHOTOS; NORA AND JIM, TRINITY COLLEGE.

(8.)LESTROGENS- UNTITLED.

(9.)SCYLLA AND CHARYBDIS- TRAIN JOURNEY.

(10.)SIRENS ("CIRCE")- "CLAIR"STORY.

(11.)CYCLOPS- FINANCIAL CHARTS.

(12.)NAUSICCA- NEPAL TREK.

(13.)THE OXEN OF THE SUN- PHOTOS OF AUTHORS WORLD TRIP,89'

(14.)EUMAEUS- GREG, STEPHEN (STORIES)

(15.)ITHICA- BLOOM, GREG (STORIES)

(16.)PENELOPE- MOLLY, "HIPPY LADY"(STORY)

For [this] expanded 'SSES' 'SSES' ˢˢᴱʸ book object, we revert back (closer aligned) to the 24-chaptered cycle of *The Odyssey* (... if u trust me to help retell his story):

this SSES³ → TBD — see the beginning of the ODYSSEY book for Correlated Chapters

|| — see HOMECOMING book for Correlated Chapters

✳ (... interesting to note that book-chapters increase by 4—4, 8, 12 ... a sort of doubling onto itself)

... which is not to say the reader need have prior knowledge of *The Odyssey* or *Ulysses*—we are merely using this as a helical **framing device** to organize his writings (+ our own thoughts) into a (hopefully) somewhat cohesive twined narrative. Like Joyce, Kevin's original 17 chapter version leaves much of *Nostos* (the Homecoming) unfinished. Thru this xpanded treatment hopefully we can bring him home. So w/o further ado, let's get started shall we?!

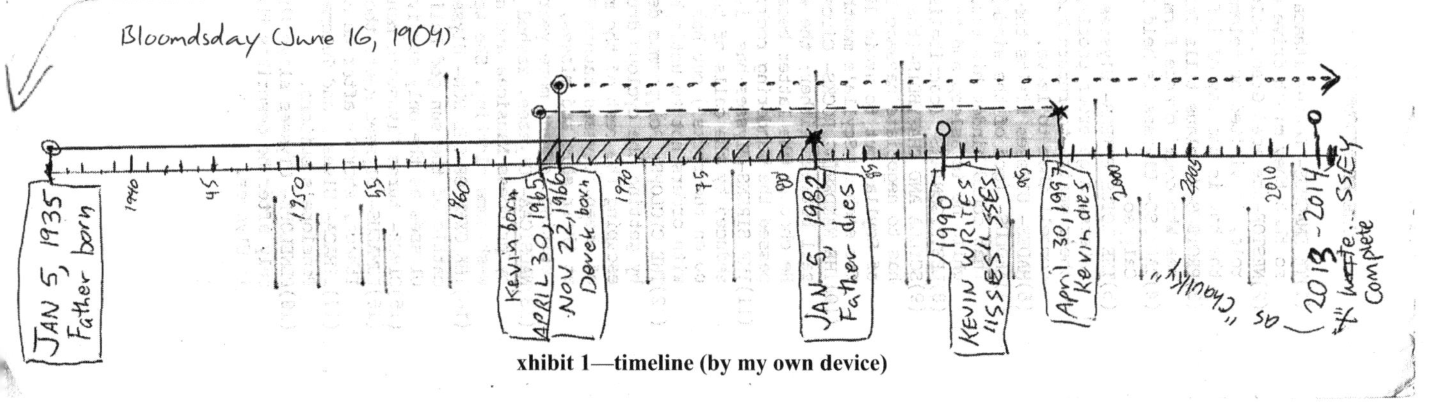

Bloomdsday (June 16, 1904)

JAN 5, 1935 Father born

Kevin born APRIL 30, 1965

Nov 22, 1960 Dovek born

JAN 5, 1982 Father dies

1990 KEVIN WRITES "ULYSSES" SSES

April 30, 1997 dead Kevin

"Chouky"

(2013—2014 "Ulysses"... SSEY complete

xhibit 1—timeline (by my own device)

*apologetically laying
some ground rules*

(Derek)

Before we get started, there's some things i should probably xplain ... while i myself do not make a habit of xpository writing, i feel in this case it is somewhat nessesary in order to understand Kevin's otherwise abstract texts + images. At least thru our college years, my brother-½ was always the right-brained artist (in fact he was left-handed), while i was the left-brained + right-handed «scientist»[1] (tho more recently i've become ambidextrous).

So generally speaking, we'll try to keep our running commentary to the right-hand side of the page + keep Kevin's original texts on the left. We'll also use this serifed (Times New Roman) font, while Kevin's writings will be in [this non-serifed Helvetica] (unless it's a scan of the original) —a font that brother-½ seemed to favor in his writings.

For example, the text that now appears on your left is in Kevin's actual words. I'm pretty sure he didn't write this on January 5, 1982—this was the day our father killed himself. He probably wrote this later + added the date either as the title, or for affect.

January 5, 1982 — Portland, Oregon

I came home from school at noon because I felt sick to my stomach ... something I'd never done. I'm using 'home' here as a [figure of speech] ... uncle [N's] is a transient resting place ... the soul [sic] place I have to go ... at this moment. The front door was unlocked. The whole family was [already] there. I went and sat in the kitchen, feeling a strange sense of compounding déjà vu. No one said anything [to me] ... they just looked sad, eyes on the linoleum floor. I didn't ask why. My sensory input kept bunching up on itself as I fought to retain control. Then uncle N came in and told me he had some bad news. I asked if it was about my dad, and he said yes.

The sun poured in through the windows making my skin flush with blood. My uncle was speaking to me but I couldn't hear him ... only the dim noise of a humming bird pecking at the kitchen window. The cat was scratching the couch ... stretching. The dog rattled its chain off in the garage. Somebody was watching [Bugs Bunny] downstairs. Aunt [Kate] was pretending to stir orange juice ... from concentrate ... the frozen glob spinning but not melting. Cousin [Ray] was shooting hoops outside with [the neighbors]. His voice echoed off the houses across the street ... "H, h, O, o, R, r, S, s, ..."

I imagined my friends, still in class ... [eyeing] my empty seat ... that [blissful ignorance] of not knowing. Uncle N looked like he'd done something wrong ... the one stuck cleaning up the floor of my father's garage.

Coincidentally, today—the date i started writing *this* (actually «put pen to paper»)—is November 22, 2013. Tho most people think of JFK's assassination on this day, it also happens to be my birthday—my 47th. Our father killed himself on his 47th birthday ... so i'm xactly as old as our father when he died ... a milestone Kevin unfortunately never reached. He died 16 years ago, just before his 32nd birthday. Like our father, he also died in a parked car (which perhaps explains my aversion to motorized vehicles) (+ sorry for spoiling the 'story' by telling u what happens).

Sorry it took me this long—16 years, ½ his lifespan—to piece this book together. I've been meaning to for some time—ever since his death—I just didn't know **how**. I'm still not sure i do (perhaps i'm too close to the subject matter), but figured this was a good a day as any to just start.

~~Mostly i am writing this for myself, so i apologize if it doesn't make sense to u~~. I never was any good at story-telling. I should also mention that some of the names of 'real people' herein may have been changed ... to protect the privacy of those still alive or however that disclaimer goes ... tho the bit about any resemblance to real facts being incidental is not nessessarily the case (if u trust that my brother-½ is telling the truth). The [bits in brackets] are words that i've edited or altered from the originul[2] + '[...]' (ellipses) denote omitted text.

---

[1] I received a bachelors in math the same year Kevin received his MFA ... then a few years later got a master's in physics.

[2] + apologies in advance if i interject myself by taking such creative liberties, but in this editorial capacity i honestly feel (at the risk of sounding cliché) that a part of Kevin (upon his death) transferred to me like some parasitic meme transfusion (or vice-versa).

Who is Chaulky?

Perhaps i shoud also xplain why «Chaulky» is the named author of all this ... after brother-½ died, i went to California for his memorial (or whatever u want to call it[3]). When we got to the awkward but nesessary task of going thru his personal effects, we came across his computer — 1 of the original Apple MacBooks. Problem was, when we tried to turn it on, it was password protected. The 1st string that popped into my head was «C-H-A-L-K-Y». I typed it in as our family looked on ... but no go. So i thought about it for a sec + then tried «C-H-A-U-L-K-Y»[4] + bingo ... we were in. The digital writings found herein (such as the left-hand text on the previous page) were taken from that machine. Other texts were scanned or transcribed straight from his 'SSES" 'SSES" thesis. And other texts (such as his actual travelogue) i painfully[5] transcribed from his handwritten journals + notebooks. For example, here's another version of the previous text dated/titled «January 5, 1982» that i found in 1 of his notebooks:

> Jan 5, 1982
> I came home early from school because i felt sick. Something i had never done. I went in and sat in the kitchen, no one talked to me, they just looked sad, i dident ask why. My uncle came in and told me that he had some bad news, I asked him if it was my dad, he said yes. ~~I wasnt really sad, i kind of imagined it would happen.~~ The sun porred in through the windows and made me feel flush, my uncle was speaking to me but i cou'dnt hear him, only the dim humming noise of. A hummingbird ~~was~~ knocking against the kitchen window, the cat was scratching the couch, the dog was rattling its chain in the garage, ████████ was watching bugs bunny downstairs, my aunt was pretending to stir the orange juice, ██████ was playing basketball outside with the neighbors, my friends were in class wondering why i left, my uncle looked like he had done something wrong and someone had to clean up the floor of my fathers garage.

A G

... interesting to note (besides the changes he made from the original handwritten 1 above to the version he transcribed to his machine) is that altho i didn't come across the above hand-written version until after i'd made the previous bracketed edits, for some reason i decided to change «cartoons» (as he had written) to «[Bugs Bunny]» cuz altho i wasn't there, in my head i herd the Looney Tunes jingle + felt it was important to include this detail rather than just generic «cartoons». Seems Kevin thought the other way around, perhaps in the end opting not to distract us w/ such details ... tho in the handwritten version he had our cousin playing basketball w/ «the neighbors» + in the digital copy he wrote out the actual names, which i then reverted back to «[the neighbors]» to respect the identity of these incidental people. ~~The names of our uncle + cousins i decided to leave as is.~~

Also interesting is that he crossed out the line «I wasn't really sad, I kind of imagined it would happen» ... was this becuz he *really was* sad + shocked, or cuz of aesthetic reasons he thought it better to show restraint + not be so xpository?

GUT TUG

---

[3] See volume 2 for that story.

[4] *Why* i thought to try «Chaulky» is a nother story we'll get to ... probly also in vol 2.

[5] ... painful yes, cuz often they were difficult to read, but also cuz his handwriting was at times barely legible

Almost 2 years after our brother-½ died, i logged this dream:

February 12, 1999 — Tucson, AZ

I was wrestling some big Chinese guy + beat him "hands down." I was declared the "overall winner." For some reason they played Tommy Tutone instead of the national anthem [maybe cuz he was a 1-hit wonder?]. Kevin was there to congratulate me. I turned to him + called him "Chaulky." He asked me the color code for yellow + green, w/ clipboard in hand, taking notes. Then 'Chaulky' asked me if i thought he had pretty hair. Before i coud answer he asked if i'd consider the color (of his hair) [to be] white.

perhaps it symbolizes wiping the slate clean for subsequent auguring/soothsaying

Don't ask me for an interpretation. Obviously our last name being **White** probly has something to do w/ it. And brother-½ did have a penchant for dying his hair (as did i), including platinum white. And the wrestler guy being Chinese probly wasn't coinsidental considering Kevin's connection w/ China as the geographical grail in 'SSES" 'SSES". I'd like to think (at least in my dream) i was helping to 'wrestle his demons'.

The 1st 2 pages (after the various chapter breakdowns) of 'SSES" 'SSES":

THE SUMMONING OF THE MUSE

THE SUMMONING OF THE MUSE

```
BLACK WHITE BLACK WHITE BLACK WHITE BLACK  KING
WHITE  PAWN  PAWN BLACK WHITE BLACK WHITE QUEEN
BLACK WHITE BLACK WHITE BLACK WHITE  PAWN  WHITE
 PAWN  PAWN  WHITE BLACK WHITE BLACK WHITE BLACK
BLACK WHITE BLACK WHITE BLACK  PAWN BLACK WHITE
WHITE BLACK WHITE BLACK WHITE BLACK WHITE BLACK
BLACK WHITE BLACK WHITE BLACK WHITE BLACK WHITE
WHITE BLACK WHITE BLACK WHITE  ROOK  KING BLACK
```

```
BLACK WHITE BLACK WHITE BLACK WHITE BLACK WHITE
WHITE BLACK WHITE BLACK WHITE BLACK WHITE BLACK
BLACK WHITE BLACK WHITE BLACK WHITE BLACK WHITE
WHITE BLACK WHITE BLACK WHITE BLACK WHITE BLACK
BLACK WHITE BLACK WHITE BLACK WHITE BLACK WHITE
WHITE BLACK WHITE BLACK WHITE BLACK WHITE BLACK
BLACK WHITE BLACK WHITE BLACK WHITE BLACK WHITE
WHITE BLACK WHITE BLACK WHITE BLACK WHITE BLACK
```

```
CLOUD WHITE CLOUD WHITE CLOUD WHITE CLOUD TAIL
WHITE CLOUD WHITE CLOUD WHITE CLOUD  WING  WING
CLOUD BIRD  CLOUD WHITE CLOUD WHITE  NOSE WHITE
WHITE CLOUD WHITE CLOUD WHITE CLOUD WHITE CLOUD
CLOUD WHITE CLOUD WHITE CLOUD WHITE CLOUD WHITE
WHITE CLOUD WHITE CLOUD WHITE CLOUD WHITE CLOUD
CLOUD WHITE CLOUD WHITE CLOUD WHITE CLOUD WHITE
WHITE CLOUD WHITE CLOUD WHITE  BIRD  BIRD CLOUD
```

xhibit 2—original opening gambit

allocation of Medium

... actually, the preseeding 2 pages comprise the totality of his *Summoning the Muse* chapter. No explanation is given, just the strings: { _ _ _ _ _, BLACK, WHITE, CLOUD, TAIL, etc.} alternately arranged in <u>chess</u>board configuration (language as signifier/placeholder text). But clues are given in his working notebooks + early drafts. Here's a scrap i found that appears to be an earlier version where Kevin 1st comes up w/ the 8x8 BLACK/WHITE scheme + that also sheds some light on the next chapter (where he does a fly-by over our home w/ our father). Presumably the «he» speaking is our dad ... tho personally i never member him saying anything (out loud), let alone to wax on philosophically ... perhaps this is brother-½'s projected wish fulfillment:

he told me once that we always perceived things in the past that because our bodies functioned in the corporeal world we were always destined to receive experience after the fact in the same way that the light from a star can be millions of years old so that something that stopped existing millions of years ago can in some sense continue to be seen to exist I found this revelation disturbing we are blind the closer the thing the more reliable its perception is if my thoughts are not governed within the time my body is does that mean that in thought there is no time only through the perception of the physical do we achieve the concept of time**absence** his absence his journey oscillating from rising and setting to rolling around the planet different models involving different perimeter,perilune,perigee,perineum my perception experience travels on his voyage vicarious telepathic distantly increasing interference dead air self dependency my relation with him goes dormant my relation with him grows stronger my relation to him get farther he has been dead for exactly seven years and 360 days and as usual its no coincidence that 360 represents completeness in a language invented by man to better describe**understandknowbelessafraidcontrol** the impossibly large**heavy** forms wich float over us everyday in the sky.[1-1-1990,11:19am]

‹‹... a world in white gets underway

.. nothing changes on New Year's Day››

BLACK WHITE BLACK WHITE BLACK WHITE BLACK WHITE
WHITE BLACK WHITE BLACK WHITE BLACK WHITE BLACK
BLACK WHITE BLACK WHITE BLACK WHITE BLACK WHITE
WHITE BLACK WHITE BLACK WHITE BLACK WHITE BLACK
BLACK WHITE BLACK WHITE BLACK WHITE BLACK WHITE
WHITE BLACK WHITE BLACK WHITE BLACK WHITE BLACK
BLACK WHITE BLACK WHITE BLACK WHITE BLACK WHITE
WHITE BLACK WHITE BLACK WHITE BLACK WHITE BLACK

BLACK WHITE KING WHITE BLACK WHITE BLACK WHITE
WHITE BLACK WHITE BLACK WHITE BLACK WHITE BLACK
BLACK WHITE KING PAWN BLACK WHITE BLACK WHITE
WHITE BLACK WHITE BLACK WHITE BLACK WHITE BLACK
BLACK WHITE BLACK WHITE BLACK WHITE BLACK WHITE
WHITE BLACK WHITE BLACK WHITE BLACK WHITE BLACK
BLACK WHITE BLACK WHITE BLACK WHITE BLACK WHITE
WHITE BLACK WHITE BLACK WHITE BLACK WHITE BLACK

EXHIBIT 2: loose found page from Kevin's notes (as pasted into my own personal "scrapbook")

My role here is CONTINUITY ... to provide parallels

also work in note about fitting things fitting in Constraint writing (maybe even this very note, as is.

... seriously, why are there 360° in a circle ... a degree for every day of the year? + actually, perhaps before this even (the page below is undated), he sketched this out in another of his notebooks ... so apparently this was all premeditated:

$$7' + 360'' = 8' - 5''$$

WHITE BLACK WHITE BLACK WHITE

spelled out black white black et.

black white black white et. white pawn black bishop et.

§ CHESS does rhyme w/ SSES ... ? Altho i don't member Kevin ever playing chess w/ me or other people, he used to like playing against his computer ... maybe U still are.

§ The boat-like figures U see bleeding over from the other side of the page to the right are preliminary designs from his corresponding MFA art exhibition (see episode 13), so he must've conceived of this introduction to his SSES thesis around about the same time.

* Kevin's address at the time -->

SS1 E. CALIFORNIA

black white black white et.

checkmate et.

+ here's another page where he brings CLOUD + AIR + TAIL into the 8-ply configuration + even sketches a boxed airplane into it that resembles 1 of those **word search** puzzles wherein u circle found words that often intersect each other:

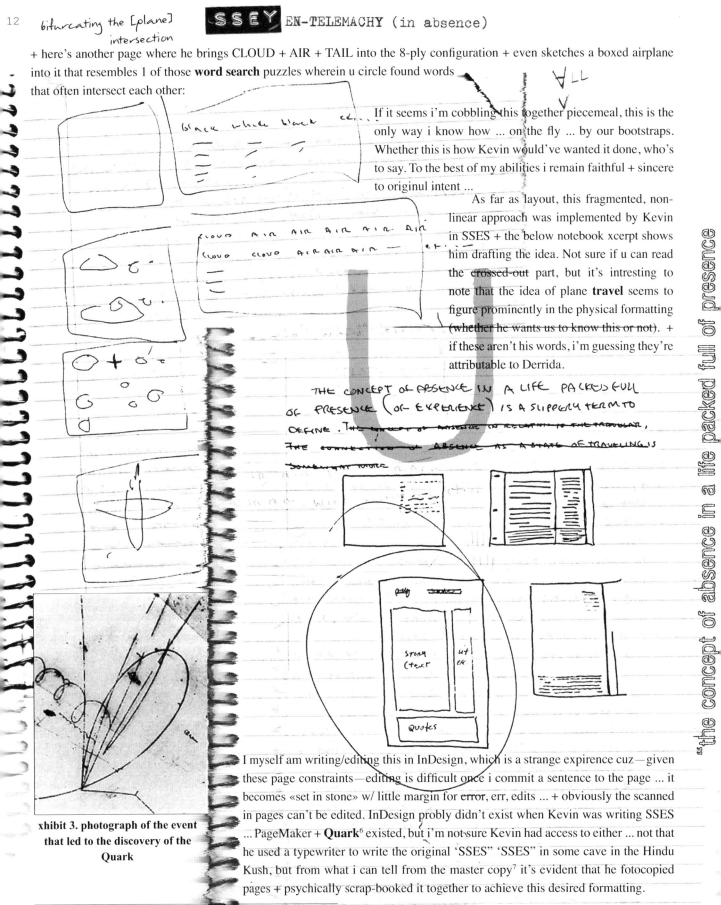

If it seems i'm cobbling this together piecemeal, this is the only way i know how ... on the fly ... by our bootstraps. Whether this is how Kevin would've wanted it done, who's to say. To the best of my abilities i remain faithful + sincere to originul intent ...

As far as layout, this fragmented, non-linear approach was implemented by Kevin in SSES + the below notebook xcerpt shows him drafting the idea. Not sure if u can read the crossed-out part, but it's intresting to note that the idea of plane **travel** seems to figure prominently in the physical formatting (whether he wants us to know this or not). + if these aren't his words, i'm guessing they're attributable to Derrida.

THE CONCEPT OF ABSENCE IN A LIFE PACKED FULL OF PRESENCE (OF EXPERIENCE) IS A SLIPPERY TERM TO DEFINE.

xhibit 3. photograph of the event that led to the discovery of the Quark

I myself am writing/editing this in InDesign, which is a strange expirence cuz—given these page constraints—editing is difficult once i commit a sentence to the page ... it becomes «set in stone» w/ little margin for error, err, edits ... + obviously the scanned in pages can't be edited. InDesign probly didn't exist when Kevin was writing SSES ... PageMaker + **Quark**[6] existed, but i'm not sure Kevin had access to either ... not that he used a typewriter to write the original 'SSES" 'SSES" in some cave in the Hindu Kush, but from what i can tell from the master copy[7] it's evident that he fotocopied pages + psychically scrap-booked it together to achieve this desired formatting.

[6] A word Joyce 1st coined in a different context (see xhibit 3, above left)

[7] From which these scans are taken.

RAW reverse engineering
any lingering bullet traces

Sorry if we're already all over the map before we even get off the ground ... i promise we'll settle into a proper itinerary w/ a destination (in line w/ where Kevin was going w/ all this). But while we're getting such house-keeping unpleasantries out of the way, may as well show a page from my own ~~raw~~ process ~~(or prawSSES)~~ notes that conveniently wraps (+ warps) up in any last loose ends w/ this chapter 0:

+ perhaps gratuitously

(or experience) is a slippery term to define"
(confined as such to the realm of the senses)

TELEMACHY   ODYSSEY   HOME C.

Start counting at

- 1st actual ~~title~~ page (in full...)
- define structure & timeline w/ intersections to my own
- my p.63 as ~~accession~~ notes, my RUNNING commentary in PARALLEL
  - ~~different fonts/styles, right/left brain thinking (science vs art)~~
- Odyssey ~~chapter breakdown~~ (as applied to "SSES")   THE STIRRING OF...
- Table of Contents (as our own breakdown (more in line w/ Odyssey)
- 3-fold canonized recapitulation (ser. EXCEL spreadsheet)   house keeping by necessity
- start w/ single column that bifurcates & splits into 2 & then converges & splits, etc.
- USE K's Jan 5, 1982 story as illustration to establish editing procedure
- use actual scanned docs, accentuate photocopy ~~distortion~~   [like Dead Sea Scrolls]
- both died in parked cars, at least in 1 case w/ the engine still running
- how i unlocked his writings w/ CHAULKY & how ~~Chaulky~~ becomes an amalgamation of me & Kevin
  - ~~same hand-written original of previous~~
  - reverse engineer actual design docs
    - work backwards from black/white ~~itemizing~~   -CESSpool   -salamander
  - ~~just print out this page (yes, this one!)~~
  - just print out this page (yes, this one!) to show thought process
    - to make it feel **actual** or legit
    - (maybe even muck it up some, w/ scribbles & distressed weatherings)
  - how these are bullet points of shit needs to be said.
    - to get off my chest.
      - to **understand** ... to |stand|under|
  - also, the IDea of Kevin's writings being like routines we CALL
    - like calling HOME ... (in a programming sense)
      - like this very this
        - code embedded in nested loops as such
        - develop as enveloped
        - somehow embed the idea of recapitulation
        - CANONIZE
  - & apologize to reader IF we make them uncomFORTable
    - ~~for speaking so frankly ...~~
  - & further apologies for 'publishing' things that perhaps Kevin didn't intend as PUBLIC
    - THEN apologize for apologizing
      - & make no more apologies!
  - establish p.o.v.'s/voice, as a sort of dueling banjos
  - 3x4 Warholish fragmented mosaic of Joyce   to end chapter.

his 'story' as FEEDBACK

> brother searching for brother
  > brother searching for FATHER
  : (embedded loop)
  : son searching father.
> searching for ? HOME.

like play where character busts out of character

who is 'Frank' anyway?!

family divorce

37
66 65 97 82

riverrun.

TRINITY 1/8

xhibit 4—opening page of the original 'SSES" 'SSES" ... perhaps even intended to be on the cover? From what i member, this is an ink drawing he did in high school. If he'd made it in conjunction w/ this SSES thesis, he likely would've made it an 8 x 8 mosaic, stead of 3 x 4.

1: Assembly + Departure (Telemachus)

Time: July 2013 (flashing back to January 1989 (flashing back to circa 1969))

Locations: Kathmandu /Portland / L.A.—Amsterdam—Paris—Switzerland—Germany—Dublin—Norway—FINland …   + IDea/symbolism: son disposed in contest / call to adventure

ABSTRACT: After summoning the wooing muses, Telemachus the artist fires up his engine + finds hisself hovering over an actor playing hisself (in turn flying over our childhood home). We (again in 3ʳᵈ person cuz u too are included in the expieæent) meet our father … or at least a surrogate version thereof… Not only must we realize that behind every swerving story or piece of history is someone writing or filming it (otherwise it never happened), but we must member that memory is inherently unreliable. Telemachus sets out in pursuit of _____ …w/ a support crew in tow to document the experience … to only become **desilleuzi**oned by his own vain pursuit.

Dons the HERMES denim/hat as stephication

exhibit 5—self-portrait (date unknown, but we're guessing he did this in High School, around the same time he did the Joyce drawing on the left facing page)

Portrait of the Young Man as an ~~Artist~~ a Young Man ~~Artist~~

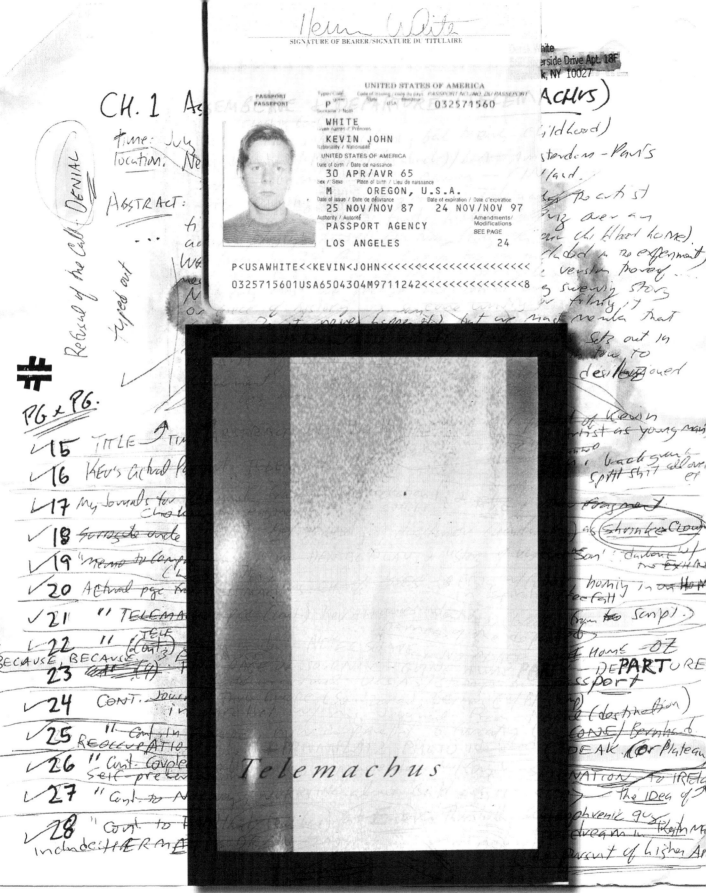

exhibit 6—"Untitled" 1991 (unique Dupont 4cast print. 19 ½" x 13 ½")(permanently collected in our kitchen)

Kathmandu, Nepal—July 14, 2013

... may as well just start piecing this together + see where it takes us ... here at the base of the Himalayas (where my brother-½ finished his odyssey) reading a copy of *Ulysses* we picked up at Pilgrim's Book House ... if u don't believe us, see www.5cense.com where we blog in real-time (+ in 3rd person—which in this context is inclusive of the part of brother-½ in us, together formulated in stereo as **Chaulky**). As we re-read *Ulysses* we recapitulate it into this—*'SSES" 'SSES" "SSEY*.

This is the very book + this will be the 1st real episode [tho since we started counting w/ 0, this is really the 2nd episode[8]], wherein brother-½ makes his plans + leaves Los Angeles—corresponding to episode 2 in *The Odyssey* (where Telemachus calls an assembly, feebly denounces the lecherous suitors creeping in on his mother in his father's absence + leaves home to look for his father, Odysseus, or **Ulysses** in Greek). James Joyce maps[9] chapters 1 + 2 of *The Odyssey* to the opening chapter of *Ulysses*, where we meet Stephen Dedalus (the Telemachus equivalent) + his freeloading friends. As mentioned in the previous episode, familiarity w/ *The Odyssey* +/- *Ulysses* is not a precondition for understanding this assemblage *-> or DISassemblage* of language u Hold in your hands, or even brother-½'s MFA thesis—*'SSES" 'SSES"*—which this hinges + extrapolates on. But if u are familiar w/ *The Odyssey* + *Ulysses*, it might help to think of my brother-½ Kevin as **Telemachus** (who he admittedly identified with), or Stephen Dedalus ... + me (Derek) as Odysseus (or Leopold Bloom). But i can't promise these roles won't flip by the time we get to the end of this book. Or that we both might merge into Chaulky 1 + the same (the 1 re/telling the story) ...

It's tempting to embellish on brother-½'s story w/in this framework (to at least help u follow the narrative arc) ... like he did indeed have pushy, drug-taking friends that he shared an apartment with in L.A. (the analogous counterparts to Dedalus's usurping cronies) that perhaps played a part in prodding brother-½ to flee *or DE-fleA* the coop in search of our father. But as mentioned before, i'm no good at story-telling (nor am i a poet) + as much as possible would rather Kevin write this book in his own words ... so for starters, below left is a text file we found on his computer + below right is a loose page we found (untitled + undated).

 RUG

It all started with an image out of the corner of my eye. There was no corresponding smell. The sounds of someone running, laughing, crying.

She was Italian thru + thru.

Move 'A' off of the defined space. Move it towards the wall + turn it sideways to fit. Drag 'B' off (towards the [ear-marked] double door). Leave 'B' positioned parallel to the transept shoulder 12e.

All remaining objects, lint, dirt, are to be removed. Begin rolling article 13c towards the main door. Begin by rolling a tube approx.; 2" in diameter. Upon finishing the rolling, tie 13c w/ 10 guage [sic] steel wire at 25" intervals.

Right now

transcriptions notes, running / running commentary while I'm on NY

As youread this, you are thinking about what is being written right there, no, not there! There, thats it! ~~When So~~ So stick with me here, thats right zip along here word at a time. Does it offer much? (Think about this question here.............) ~~Nope I~~ didnt think so. Skip the next part. You ~~will not be reading this or you will suddenly feel a sharp pain in your~~...

No. Just kidding.

~~Instead~~ I would like to draw your attention to this new *organizational* chart buster. A delightfull little tune. Done by a band that heralds from the sleepy little English industrial Burrough ~~of Manchester~~, you know, lots of fat girls with round pale faces and rosy cheeks, wrotten town , wrotten town, anyway where was I? Oh yeah this great peice of work by ▮▮▮▮▮▮▮. Not bad, but not great.

The album breaks down neatly into eight trays.

– Herrrrrroooooooaaaaaaaaaayyyyyyyyyyyyiiiiiinnnnnnnnnngggggggggggggggttttttttthhhhhhhhhhhh

One great single a lot of perky little tunes that sound like the single, playing at alternate speeds.

– But is that really such a bad tactic to take up in the creation of an album. "I heard the single, and instantly wanted the album, Ya Now!" The young man with the name that soundslike tinfusion.

Songs that drone on about;

Yes! You can bring a candle into your cell tonight! You peice of shit!

GO BACK TO THE FIRST THREE LINES.
READ THEM.
Did you read [thats right zip along here...] TWICE? IF SO RETURN TO 23b.

---

[8] We member a conversation on this very topic w/brother-½ in Nice, as the apt bldg we were staying in + other buildings in Europe follow the convention of counting the 1st floor as 1 floor up from the lobby, which is effectively 0 (unlike Americans, who start counting w/1).

[9] According to the Linati + Gilbert schema.

... not entirely sure what's the point of either of those previous instructional pieces, but figured they were something u shoud know ... + that this was a good a place as any to tell u, to get the conversation going. And while we're at it, here's a final (unpublished) disclaimer (in brother-½'s writing) about surrogate fathers

(equating them to shrinks):

shake out RuG, REplace (to keep from SHRInking)

> PUBLIC INFORMATION AND FUNDING DISCLAIMER.
>
> "WHAT DO YOU MEAN LIKE A SURROGATE FATHER? HE ASKED NOT BOTHERING TO ACKNOWLEDGE ONE OF THOSE TALL, BIG HAT-N-TRENCH COAT, EVIL FLYING SOLDIER LONG HAIRED MONKEYS (gays) UNDER COMMAND OF THE WICKED WITCH OF THE EAST HOLDING THE LIMOUSINE DOOR OPEN FOR HIM.
>
> "I MEAN NOT THAT THESE SHRINKS POSE AS SURROGATE FATHERS."

« ... You owe it.

Wait. Five months. Molecules all change. I am other I now. Other I got pound.

Buzz. Buzz.

But I, entelechy, form of forms, am I by memory because under everchanging forms.

I that sinned and prayed and fasted.

A child Conmee saved from pandies.

I, I and I. I.

A.E.I.O.U. » Ulysses

On the 1st page of the 1st episode (that he calls «Telemachus») of his SSES thesis, he shows this photograph (below) of some random dude from Toledo, circa 1906. We're not sure who this is (quite the stache!) or where he got the photo, tho we do member it hanging on the wall in the kitchen he shared w/ his crony friends in L.A. Judging by the appearance + the date[10,11], we can surmise that brother-½ equated this man with Leopold Bloom, or generally as a father figure to seed his search ...

TELEMACHUS

unidentified; circa 1906, Toledo, Ohio.

exhaust/smoke figures prominently

HAHA! an H less than AHA!

[10] 1906 is close to the year (1904) of Bloomsday—the 24-hour period in which all of *Ulysses* takes place.

[11] It's also worth noting the date of Georges Rouault's painting, *The Clown (1906)*(see end of episode 5—pg. 96), that Kevin led in with in 'SSES' 'SSES' (that clown **tragic**, the 1 above rather **comic**).

name —

DATE

OF STATEMANT (ISSUE) — *brief explanation*

(THIS IS WHAT WE DO) — THIS IS HOW YOU
GO ABOUT RECIEVING THIS PRIVELAGE —

— (DON'T FORGET YOU HAVE
THIS RENSPONSIBILITY —

IF YOU STILL CAN'T UNDERSTAND
THIS, THIS IS HOW YOU GO ABOUT
RECIEVING THE ABOVE DEFLECTIONS
IN A MUCH MORE PLAYED OUT
AND ILLUSTRATED FORM. FORM IS
WHAT YOU'LL GET WHEN YOU GO IN TO
RECIEVE MORE INFORMATION. INFORMATION
IS WHAT YOU NEED TO WORK FOR US. US
AND YOU ARE A TEAM. TEAM IS
WHAT WE ARE SO GET WITH
US AND DON'T HOLD UP THE
BOAT.

— VISUAL DISCLAIMER —

SIGNATURE

i.e. ∪

memo to company
worker, regarding
dental plan
description. This
form is didactic,
brief AND compact.
It is meant to be
READ QUICKLY, AND
UNDERSTOOD

DON'T DESCRIBE THIS PROCESS
OF COMMENTING ON THE
FORM OF DIFFERENT STYLES
(USES of) OF TYPE, BUT YOU'D
THE STRUCTURE AS A COATRACK
FOR IDEAS, LET A WORK OF
FICTION HANG FROM ITS
BEAMS, ITS TRESSES ITS
FLYING BUTTRESSES.

=Darkens with the exhaust. And [...] then gentle
vendors of the [...] stored instruments layed down a backing
track. The parser occurs [...] 15 and
every [...] [...] The parser ended
[...] plaref-node
∴ the story of [...] a [...] man [...] this
about this father's pen. This is about the language
[...] we with. Telemachus was Ulysses son so

[12] I have my own interpretation of the handwriting («darkens with the exhaust ...») but perhaps I'm
reading into it so here's the original 2nd page (above) for u to interpret for yourself ...

[Here's 2 more submitted exhibits ... left is a «memo to company workers» found in his notebooks + the below text is from some loose handwritten pages, that he titled «The Story of Ulysses Son»:

His birthday fell [on] a smoggy day. In throngs and throws they did swarm. [The] numbers exceeded available parking. The procedure was straightforward and mindless and required no motor skills. Slight brushes with other objects gently [guided] them—coasting—the whole time absorbing as much as possible of the moment. For the movement however short-lived, its [finale] brought about a dark, final bitter end ... an end to all ends. And to make matters worse, the leaving part was the worst of all. He was already angry, exhausted and sore (not to mention poor). [Exponentially], the pollution increases with the decrease in average speed. The night sky over West L.A. ... **Darkens** [12] **with the exhaust** [see left]. And [already?] then gentle sounds of the streets, the boulevard, waves of storyed instruments layed [sic] down a backing track. The parser [a censored?] every 15 and every fine [mother?]. The parser ended on a pparef node.

~~This is the story of a young man's life. This is the story of a man in search of himself. This is about the father's pen. This is about the language we live with. Telemachus was Ulysses's son, so they say.~~

[homing instinct]

TELEMACHUS

SSEY EN-TELEMACHY (in absence)

The next 4 pages are the same 4 pages that follow in the actual TELEMACHUS episode of Kevin's 'SSES' 'SSES':

TELE. phoney

[13] Stratocirrus. We leave as a trace a gossamer trail of cloud. I sustain a complete faith in my father and his single engine plane. I am not afraid. En route to the coast we pass over home so we decide to take the plane down low and wave. After a few moments the jumble of lines and tea-brown patches of earth coalesce into the true map. I am very pleased with myself. My map concedes nothing. The small metal boxes jerk erratically down the main road like slot cars in a track filled with neglect. I spot my school, and see through the windows my unlucky classmates probably wondering where I am. We follow the route I usually take to school every day on my bike. I am the first one to spot our house. She is standing on the front door step, with her hand up to her forehead, scanning the horizon for us

"There she is!" **I say pointing out the right side.**

" Ok, lets go say hi." **Dad says turning us around.**

We skim over the top of pirate's cove and past Eric's house. Aviators as gods, as parole officers checking on mortal relatives. My growing sense of omnipotence is checked by the majestic sight of my father's profile as we emerge from the rain cloud. We stick to back yards once we get to our street so that she will not see us coming. We stay just barely above the shrubs, fences and roofs. Out on the street we stay within the shadows of the trees. I hope that nobodys mom sees us. My father hands me an aviators hat and tells me to put it on. I do. He tells me that it will disguise my appearance from them. As he puts his on I look in the small mirror on the visor and see my father putting on his hat. We make sure that she is looking the other way, and then we sneak out of the rhododendrons. We come up from behind and surprise her. At first she looks mad, but then she smiles, kisses dad, and then reaches across and pinches my nose. As they talk about dinner I am overcome with restlessness. An arrow smacks into the column behind her and dad, seeing this, yanks her violently through the window into the plane. We speed off just inches in front of the would be assasins. Safely around the corner he stops to let her out.

ONCE WE RID OURSELVES OF HER WE TAKE OFF ONCE AGAIN FREE TO DO WHATEVER WE WANT TO DO A BACHELOR PARTY FOR TWO WE LAUGH AND TALK ABOUT ALL OF THE THINGS WE COULDNT TALK ABOUT AROUND HER AND HE USES THE KIND OF LANGUAGE HE USUALLY ONLY USES WITH HIS BUISNESS FRIENDS ON THE PHONE LANGUAGE SHE WOULD HATE BUT NOW IT IS OK WE BUZZ CARS OFF THE ROAD AND LAUGH HYSTERICALLY WE DO SPIRALLING DIVES INTO LAKES AND PULL OUT AT THE LAST SECOND WE FLY TO EXOTIC PLACES AND GET OUT FOR A BITE TO EAT THEN JUMP BACK IN AND GO OFF AGAIN TO EVEN BETTER PLACES NEVER HAVING TO WORRY ABOUT BEING LATE FOR THIS OR THAT BUT JUST HAVING A GOOD TIME LIKE ITS SUMMER VACATION AND WE DO NOT HAVE A CARE IN THE WORLD JUST A SUNSET WE SUCCESSFULLY CHASE ENABELING US TO AVOID THE END OF THE DAY AND CONTINUE ON AROUND THE WORLD TOGETHER ME WATCHING HIM LEARNING FROM HIM.

Aero-white Insurance,
which our father inherited from his father

---

[13] Not sure why he chose to lead in w/ this story ... again, it's probly best to just let u figure it out for yourself ... but if you're looking to these parallel footnotes + running commentary for help, this much i can tell u: our father was indeed a pilot that used to take us up for joyrides in his plane. I mean, it wasn't *his* plane, but a *collective* plane owned by his insurance company. My version of this memory has me flying w/ our father out at Canon Beach, on the Oregon coast. He put me on his lap + let me take the steering wheel + fly the plane around Haystack Rock. For the most part tho, i don't have fond memories of flying w/ our father + usually got sick (specially when he did the «upsy-downsies»). 1 take-away from this initial text is that off the bat brother-½ had a ***homing instinct*** ... at least moreso than this ½ ever did. Perhaps this was the beginning of his spiraling downfall ... this never-ending quest to have some semblance of «home» which i had long since learned to abandon. Also, intresting to note—as in the short piece we presented towards the beginning of the last episode—Kevin seemed to revel in the idea of being <u>absent</u> from school + his friends wondering where he was.

USING his 1ˢᵗ "time out"

TELEMACHUS

I HEV WAKED ENUF TO REELY HAV ERND ET. THE SALVTION I MEEN. FOR ALL I HAV DUN I GO TO THE ALTR ON MY NEES. ALL THE WAY WTHOUT THEM LETHER PATCHS THE CARPNTRS WARE. ALL THE WAY FEELN REEL BAD INSID FRETTIN SOMTHIN FEERCE. I DUN A MIT STUPIT THIN AND I REELY HAVE TO WERK ET OUT. THAS RITE CLEEN OUT OF ME. THIS MAN AINT GOIN TO WAET TILL ITS TOO LAT TO HEER THE GOOD WORD. NO SIR, I HEERT THES STORY THE UTHR DAY ABOUT THES GUY HOO GOT HIMSLF KILT. HE ENT UP DED. THER AINT NO CHANS FER HIM NO SIR! I AINT GOIN TO PUT   MYSLF IN THAT JAM, NOSIR!

[14] **YOU ARE NOW STARTING INTO THE MAIN PORTION OF MY THESIS. "I" AM KEVIN WHITE, CANIDATE FOR A MASTERS IN FINE ARTS DEGREE(ART CENTER COLLEGE. PASADENA, CALIFORNIA. EXPECTED DATE OF DEGREE; AUG.1990) AND AUTHOR OF THIS THESIS. UNLESS YOU ARE READING THE LIBRARY COPY, I HANDED, DELIVERED,** [15] **OR AM SUPRIVISING THE READING OF, THIS THESIS.**

THOSE OF YOU WHO HAVE RECIEVED THIS DOCUMENT FROM ME ARE;
_MY GRADUATE COMMITEE; STEPHEN PRINA, JEREMY GILBERT-ROLFE AND MIKE KELLEY (GRADUATE FACULTY AT THE ART CENTER).
_FRIENDS (BOTH STUDENT AND FACULTY) FROM ART CENTER.
_FRIENDS (FROM OUTSIDE OF SCHOOL) AND FAMILY.
_ANYONE (EITHER KNOWN TO ME OR NOT KNOWN TO ME) WHO CHECKS OUT THIS THESIS IN THE ART CENTER LIBRARY.

THIS PAPER IS BEING READ AT;
_HOMES (OF GRADUATE COMMITEE MEMBERS, CLOSE FRIENDS, FAMILY MEMBERS, OR MY OWN HOUSE) OR, AT ART CENTER (EITHER IN THE LIBRARY, CAFETERIA, GRADUATE STUDIOS OR CLASSROOMS).

THIS PAPER WILL EXIST FOR AN UNDETERMINED AMOUNT OF TIME AT;
_THE HOMES OF GRADUATE COMMITEE MEMBERS, FRIENDS, FAMILY,(AND AT THE HOME OF THE AUTHOR).
_ART CENTER LIBRARY (WHERE A BOUND COPY WILL BE AVAILIBLE FOR THE DURATION OF THE EXISTENCE OF THE SCHOOL UNLESS THE COPY IS LOST OR STOLEN).

— + **embedded herein!**

TELE.

Tiger swallow tail
Hessels hairstreak
Mylitta crescentspot
Chalcedon checkerspot
Phobeious parnassian
Moss elfin
California sister
Cloudless giant sulphur
Wright's metalmark
Blue copper
Pearly marble-wing
Sara orangetip
Broken dash
Whirlabout
Umber skipper
Brigadier
Funereal duskywing
Hoary edgr [16]
Red-spotted purple
Tiger swallow tail
Satyr anglewing
Sooty azure
Blue metalmark
Bog copper
Orange-veined blue
Chalcedon checkerspot
Definite patch
Gulf fritillary
Pearly crescentspot
Red admiral
Crimson-banded black
Creole pealy eye
Haydens ringlet
Chryxus artic
Ferentina calico

(he told me once (in a hard-ware store) that his ideal job would be to be the 1 who comes up w/ the names of colors of house-paint)

choice of FONT being akin to paint color...

---

[14] This marks the 1ˢᵗ departure point where Kevin breaks from his otherwise abstract character + speaks to us directly in plane english ... perhaps out of nesessity ... as a thesis requirement.

[15] Up to u whether u think he is officially «supervising» your reading.

[16] And as for the right column, need we mention that these represent various species of **butterflies** (where «Hoary edgr» should be «Hoary **edge**»)? *+ something about how u are NOW starting into the main portion of .... "SSEY'*

TELEMACHUS

ALBO-ZYGO

NO PLACE LIKE HOME

The glow is there and then there is the sultry summer air. The North. Father lifts us up so we can see, through the window in his den. His cheek scratches my face, alcohol burn. To me it is a pleasant smell. My fathers cologne. Outside fireworks fall against the night sky. Bouncing off it's walls. Falling into peoples homes. Out--side, it is one of those strange cloudy days. Where the clouds are so large, thick and black that the sun only fills half of the landscape. Unhindered. It is completely absent from the other half of the landscape. I look to where I know Eric's house to be within the cloud. Ensh--rouded. Buried. Enveloped. Submerged. They are now experiencing what we soon will have. The sun is not in this scene. It is a bald sun. One of the moons, as opposed to the sun. Cool bulb pale light. The light only burns clear so far in the sky. Exhausted. It stops at the mighty strato--cumulous, just about a block away. The light is such that the cloud is illuminated from with--in. This makes its surface invisible. A general darkness. Phantasmagoria.

the
air without is impregnated with raindew moisture life essence celestial, glistening there under starshiny column. God's air the allfathers air, scintillant circumambient cessile air. Breathe it deep into thee.

when
cockaignecohabitation will collatecemryculture it. recissoryheology can revise rinforzandoromance it miscreantics marmosets and not merciful maecen of afterwards I put on my clothes that now feel like dead skins, just hanging on my body. There is no doubt in my mind, it must be made, it must be mad

ALBOCINEPEOUS
AZUTOBACTER
CATADIOPFRIC
CERVILODYNICE
CHROMOBASTOMYCOSOIS
DACRYOCYSTOSYRINGOTOMY
DENTOALVEOLITIUS
EILOID
HEMLASYNERGIA
JEJUNOILEITIS
KOILOCYFOTICATYPIA
LIENOMYELOMALACIA
LOCHLOSCHESSIS
MEDULLOEPITHELLOMA
MEROCOSOALGHIA *etc. (assorted medical terms)*
MNESMASTHENIA
MYELOCYSTOMENGOCELE

Spiraling jetty in red salt water

Red Salt Reef

exhibit 7 (above)—start of yellow brick road or Smithson's spiral jetty?

TELEMACHUS

GLOSSY IBIS

Russet-orange fold citrus yellow spray berry-black blood bursts cesssium metalmolds all-around this bleeds off copper-bean.
        His foot swayed over the edge his foot stood soft in the grass the sun beat down painfully on him the road stretched out mercilessly out of sight each section synonymous with the last his side was all dead grass golden dull blades its uneven surface giving way to tar burning tar .002 grade sandpaper coarse teflon skin grafts showing selfconsciously over the wounds on its sides down the center a racing stripe skunk back yellow warping distance up ahead floating car horizon is seen from under the headlights at least where they should be all present if that should be the case if so in its perception our impression of its appearance all that has been laid out in front of us our perceptibility all that is for us our ability to deceive its ever closing proximity it only now assumes the image of whole instants before its presence speeding by me oblivious I turn my face and close my eyes two stings to my cheeks I open my eyes and all I have of it is the pain no other humans are watching I can scream out I can talk to myself No one is around to see...........after two straight days of walking my shoes are shit my nose is a pepperoni pizza which I pursue from extremely close range my arms are dropping in their sockets I am off to see the wizard the wonderful wizard of Oz wonderful wonderful wonderful wonderful wonderful wizard of Oz if ever there was a wizard there was la la la la la la la la la la Oz. THE EMERALD PALACE.

doubt in my mind, it must be made, it must be mad

Gloosy ibis
Pamarine jaeger
Doverik
Cinnamon teal
King elder
Lesser scaup
Bufflehead
Gadwall
Hudsnian godmit
Snowy plover
Ruddy turnestone
Asprey
Caracara
Common flicker
Verdin
Pyrrhuloxia
Scarlet tanager
Leggerhead shrike
Lazuli buntang
Solitary vireo
Bohemian waxwing
Wheatear
Rofous-sided townce
Dickcissel
Lapland longspur
Boblink

...you get the idea ints end, the TELEMACHUS Ch. as kevin would have it.. yet we sense there's more he's not telling us.

+ again, we can't help but to note the homing reference (the reason Dorothy seeks wizard of OZ is to find way HOME.

And we're off! To fill in the gaps, we're taking the liberty of including his 1st visa + actual hand-written journals, which we transcribed (as best we coud) into text ... here's the 1st entry (the original, overlaid w/ transcription):

9:40 Sat 07 Jan 89 — Paris (Gare d'lest)

The flight over was appropriately nauseating ... exactly seven years to the day of my father's suicide (the prime inspiration being alcohol) and I have never been even remotely close to being as sick as I was. My going away party we went to the Brig (after a huge meal [G] cooked). Everyone was buying me mixed drinks ... didn't feel so bad then, but by the time I got home after 12 (after saying bye to everyone) I was already puking. Got up at 6 am wishing I was dead. Puking. To the airport ... puking ... checking into the flight to Vancouver in slow motion ... calm ... puking. [Layover in] B.C. If I had a gun I might have finished myself off. Flight to Amsterdam ... aisle seat (there is a god), trying to sleep. [undecipherable] ... if I [can just] make it through take-off. Sleep ... nausea ... small talk with some old British man next to me. Amsterdam ... train ... still nauseous. [undecipherable] to the first still dark out. [My] body thinking it's 6 p.m.. when was more like 6 a.m. ... finally starts to get light out ... no snow ... surprisingly warm ... still feeling sick. Subjected to a hippy (Brit) pushing a hostel—"vegetarian meals, man!" Felt like puking on him. Train took for fucking ever ... still wanting to die. Checked into the hostel ... "absolutely no drugs" says the sign ... good! By now 9 a.m. Finally got a room. Five blankets on a floor ... room full of hash smoke + sleeping hippies. Slept it off. Woke up. People staring at me, speaking French ... went back to sleep. Repeat. Eventually got up + went to the red light district ... groups of people shooting heroin in the middle of the street. Lodes [sic] of ugly whores ... [undecipherable] freaks ... one surprisingly beautiful blonde ... a pretty young Italian one tries to persuade me. Honey, if you only knew how I was feeling. Went back to sleep more. Woke up ... vegetarian meal. No idea what time it is. Somehow lost my jacket already, smashed my [glasses]. Made it to [the train station] ... let's see, destination du jour . . . how about Ireland? Wherever ... end up in Paris ... 6 hours later ... oops ... wrong station ... at Gare de l'Est [Paris]. At least 10 people gave me wrong directions, it's a conspiracy. I'm running, dressed for minus 10 degree weather, humping a pack. "Wrong way you imbécile! Dis train only runs Tuesdays, you fucking Américain." Look, you don't understand, I'm getting over alcohol poisoning, I feel like dying!" I'm soaked w/ sweat ... frustrated until numb. I hate this fucking city. Longing for L.A. already. Meanwhile, trying to get a hold of [H]. Not home. Smell like shit but "sorry, showers are closed." End up forking over $30 for a ticket to Zurich. Now it's 10 p.m. ... in a cafe, in Gare de l'Est ... 40 minutes more. All that matters is that everything is in order. Still haven't met anybody, but am starting to feel okay ... maybe.

Now, to the important observations:

—There's an obnoxious machine (video game) keeps playing the same French jingle over + over. This place already grating on me.

—In all fairness, some french dude spotted me 2 francs when I came up short buying [my ticket].

—[The] pretty girl across from me looks like a girl I know in Carmel ... I assume she's French (they have darker hair than the Dutch).

1:15 p.m. Jan 8, Arosa, Switzerland (youth hostel)

Sitting here alone in this silent hall. An old Swiss clock ticks quietly on the wall. Outside the window, snowy peeks [sic] loom ... snow-filled valleys seem to spell impending doom. There's a distant noise which proves to be some kids throwing rocks + swinging clubs ... venting their anger at the pubs. Inside, their fathers sit ... calmly drinking.

There's a phone ringing in the adjoining empty room ... hang up asshole! No one is here, stop [calling this] phone!

[...]

Jan. 20 — Nurenburg, Germany

It's 4 p.m. in [this] youth hostel, which is an old castle (in what used to be the stables ... a huge (5 storey [sic]) structure made of massive stones, attached to the base of the old castle, which sits on a hill overlooking the walled-in old city of Nurenburg.) There's another guy in the room (sleeping ... [occasionally] snoring) from New Jersey. Seems we are the only two staying here. It's cold out + I've spent the hole [sic] day shopping + doing laundry (all the museums, etc. are closed). Today [has been] my first relaxing day (this hostel doesn't kick you out from 10 a.m. to 5 p.m. like [the others]). Tomorrow I think I'll go to Munich (went there briefly yesterday ... didn't think much of it). So I'm going to backtrack there tomorrow ... god, this writing is so boring. What am I doing? Describing this trip in superficial travelogue language. Really wish I could find some relief from whatever it is [that is] making me this way. I'm not so much lonely (I know what a score would intail [sic], its [significance], expenditure of energy, lying, feeling bad, etc. ... but in a way I wish I could get laid).

"fuck anyone who is reading this"

I really want to make friends w/ some European(s) who I can stay w/ in April (a girl). I don't know why I'm taking this trip. I haven't relaxed, haven't done much thinking, mostly just walking, staring, riding trains + waiting around. Haven't done any reading. I seem only able to vegetate, walk around cold cities aimlessly + look into windows, fantasizing my way out of this. Reality seems to be inevitable, but not really effective (... this NJ guy is snoring full bore now). As if without the [fantasies] to live by I am just an ugly corpse. I've never felt so [unattractive], my hair, long + thin (going bald) + [disheveled]. My body pail [sic], except my red swollen face. My 400 dollar leather [Gaultier] jacket is falling apart at the seams, in tatters. I'm going bald, I can see my scalp. Fuck all this, fuck anyone who is reading this, I don't want other people to know or read this, it puts me at a disadvantage. I haven't even thought about art for weeks. I feel like a prisoner without an identity. Bullshit, I am a decent looking college graduate, tall, healthy, good sense of style, [undecipherable], touring the world, smiling, carefree, attracting girls, living life ... bullshit, it's hard to do something you don't [believe]. I know now the reasons for the way my life is. I know cuz I can't change these things, this is why their beginnings surface. I am unable to get relief. I am unable to feel like I'm really living life effectively ... + to make it all worse, this period of 4 months has been ... what? ... set aside? [The anticipation] feels like how I used to feel when I raced [cross country] in high school ... lots of preparation, anxiety, [...] ready, set ... the start is almost here. You're going to do good Kevin, get ready, prepare, you've waited a long time for this, the heart pounding, feet sweating, stomach turning, so nervous [that] time seems to slow to a crawl as I line up ... then, bang! The gun goes off, suddenly everything changes, it's finally [happening]—

I'm on remote control ... once in motion I can't change what's happening—I'm just watching. My mind is going "why?" ... I see the stands as I come around ... glimpse friend's faces, [they're] rooting me on, but I don't hear anything ... it's like a dream ... as if it's not me. It all comes back after the race, but during the race ... I've grown to fear, be

---

[June 28, 2013—en route to Nepal]

[We originally lied + date/place-marked this as "June 5—somewhere over the Indian Ocean" because somewhere over the Indian Ocean is on the opposite side of the globe from Portland, OR—where we were born (+ our father died)—+ June 5 is similarly timewise opposite to January 5—the date our father was born + died.] It was no accident Kevin started his odyssey on January 5/6 (the 6th being the day they actually found his body).] For what it's worth (time doesn't mean shit here), it's 12:00 noon. The sun is blinding. My skin flushed. We're flying east to west, so each hour is probly 2x as long as it should be. I should be tired but don't feel it. I don't feel anything really [...] This stuff has a way of sorting itself out.

These are notes for the beginnings of a book—call it 'SSES' 'SSES' 'SSES' ... or **'SSES'**[3]— about my brother-½. And *by* my brother-½ (cannibalizing his own 'SSES'[2]). Likely we'll just add these as side notes or footnotes [...] + yes, this is also about ~~our dad ...~~ our father ~~not Bloom-like, "Stately, plump," as begins *Ulysses*, but more akin to Odysseus.~~ [It's] the age-old story of a son venturing to find himself in his father ... in turn venturing to find his way home ... w/ a twist of a brother, in turn, venturing to find himself in his brother-½ searching [in parallel] .

[We've been] distracted [in the 16 years] since Kevin's death, wrapped up in the day to day ... it took him 8 years to put pen to paper, but he never really finished the story, so we're finishing it for him. Our father died long before my brother-½ 'found' him ... then my brother-½ died before I 'found' him. Both died in parked cars. Now I'm left with the blood still coursing my veins ... to get released as ink.

+ it's not so much a story as the process of telling, or RE-telling

scared of racing, going faster, because of that [undecipherable] sensation, the "runner's high". Eventually some dudes come in speaking German, wearing tight heavy metal pants, fixing the lockers, interrupting my thoughts ...

Says the guy from N.J.—"when you come over here, you can figure out what you want to do with your life, then go back. After going to Europe, going out won't be as appealing to me anymore" ... whatever that means. In me is a necessity to react to sexual stimuli, a need to talk to + be w/ people (my own age).

AS   SEMBLAGE ⊣

10 p.m. Youth Hostel, Munich, Germany

Sitting here in the cafeteria ... it's been 12 hours since I left [Nurenburg], and equally long since I've talked to someone (even if it was an annoying guy from N.J.). Feel like I'm going thru a mental change. Today, walking around alone, not allowing myself to maintain a daydream stupor, forcing myself to see a particular reality (which I imagine as a non-objective view) I got very lonely (obviously) + then bitter ... felt ugly, wanted to bark at people—what the fuck you staring at. Hated the world. Now it's Saturday night in Munich during carnevale [sic] + people who I failed to make friends with are filing out of the hostel cafeteria in chattering groups, off to the beer halls? Girls (British) laugh 10 feet away, I could get up, introduce myself, say 'hey let's go to the Hofbrawhaus, shall we?' Want to so bad, but something is keeping me back ... maybe I'm tired of [what I'm] starting to see as routine—meet, go out, share bits of our lives, drink beer (even [if] I don't want to), say good-bye, later, maybe exchange addresses. Blah, blah. I don't know what I want. I really need drugs. Want to go to sleep even tho I'm not tired, sleep is like getting a 'Go to Boardwalk' card ... just cruise all the way thru...

exhibit 8—brother-½ in Munich

—Bohemian (Italian) girl walks by w/ her ape-like boyfriend, what is it about these 'bohemian' [women that] moves me? Oh well. Now I'm going into the next room to get something I don't want from the machines [as an excuse to] meet people ...

... well, I bought the cheapest [candy bar], turned around, interjected something into the existing conversation (they were debating the merits of a hostel I stayed in) ... then just let it fizzle, not worth the effort. There are so many lonely people ... the homely looking ones in the corners alone, leafing thru maps, maybe they don't feel that Saturday night urge, maybe they aren't bound by the usual aesthetic standards of beauty.

(from www.5cense.com/13/SSES.htm): On the plane [to Doha] we read *Correction* by Thomas Bernhard which is as good a book as any to get us thinking about **framing devices** ... it's the story of [this guy, R] who becomes obsessed with building an object, 'The Cone', as a monument to honor his sister. The story is told by his friend, who goes to [R's studio] ... also referred to a few times as a 'thought chamber' + in a sense **reoccupies** R's life in order to tell, or re-tell the story (thru all the notes + manuscripts that R left behind).

Our brother-½ didn't build a **Cone**, per se, but he is/was an artist that built [conceptual] objects (after he forswore painting when a fire burned all his paintings + drawings) ... The Cone is just a metaphor ... a metaphor for something ideal + unobtainable. Maybe, to our brother-½, this cone was heroin ... or maybe Everest or some other holy Himalayan peak. The question is, how do we **inhabit,** or get under his skin, to tell his story? How do u occupy's one's 'thought chamber' without becoming possessed by their thoughts? Not that we're afraid we'll be tempted to try heroin or something (our fear of needles alone would prevent us), but it's dark shit, his rehab journals ... + it's one thing to read, but another to understand ... + then to understand enough to tell or retell it ... which is basically what the unnamed narrator in *Correction* is tasked with.

10:37 Tues. Jan 23. Train Amst. Paris (Dublin)

Yesterday went from Sulzburg to Amsterdam w/ a British/Aussie couple I met the night before in [the hostel pub]. Their names were Colin + Lucy. When we talked in Sulzburg it became [apparent]

Dimetry "I am constantly thinking of self-preservation"

that Colin + I had a similar upbringing (we both lost our fathers about 7 years ago, inherited money afterwards, left home, colored our hair, started using drugs, travelled, then became somewhat more conservative in appearance (cut hair, etc.) But Colin's girlfriend, Lucy, is very straight, naive catholic upbringing, etc. ... but it was her idea ... "gee, neither of you guys has been stoned in a while, and you both used to a lot a while back, let's go to Amsterdam!" (... + get stoned, [have] fun ...). [...] Congenial train trip, pleasant conversation, etc. Get to Amsterdam, bad hostel experience, go out to Bulldog, get stoned, all of a sudden [they stop] talking. I remember watching them from behind—he looked small + awkwardly groped his arm around her as we walked by all the prostitutes. Suddenly I was dirty + they were clean. They were grossed out by the scene, didn't talk ... I talked, tried to lighten up the mood, small talk, jokes, maybe sounded a bit stoned + stupid. Soon they wanted to walk back ... a quick "uh, yeah, good-bye" at my door [then I] had to go deal with a room full of French chicks. [undecipherable] managed to get out on the train ... ...

—Colin was at one point very much into drugs, smoked a lot of crack, long green hair, various arrests (assault, drug-related, etc.) ... wild life. Met Lucy, straightened up into a clean college student ... Colin struggles w/ his past, w/ her ... guess the night in Amsterdam was totally predictable ... ...

The kind of talking I want to do here is related to stagnation—this constant moving, like treading water, travelling, shifting, etc. like work, etc. keeps stirring up [undecipherable, crossed out] so I am constantly thinking of self-preservation, especially preservation of belongings, making sure I don't get run over, have not been in a daze for days. [sic][hard to read handwriting]

Leaving Amsterdam, briefly thinking of Anne Frank (not sure why) [...] Jews still live here after all that happened, not a [camouflaged] group of people, very visible [...] religion in general a narrowing of their world, isolated view of everything, [undecipherable ...]. Seems to me the safe approach, such a deterministic life, a cop-out—[...] As hard as life may seem for me at times, I never regret godless wandering, ever wondering, [undecipherable ...] Maybe [it's an] unhealthy, unrealistic view ... brought on by extreme events in my life (family, childhood). Colin seeks relief thru Lucy—why doesn't he just join a church if that's what he wants? [undecipherable...] some Buddhist drove him to L.A. [undecipherable] said he didn't remember anything [undecipherable] does he need Lucy [to feel himself] or religious, pure, complete?

10:13 a.m. Somewhere on the coast of southern England (Boat to Ireland)

This ferry is all but empty, maybe 20 passengers (+ a little more crew)—all of us in the bar last night. Slept on the [deck], under the stars, in front of some information kiosk. As I imagined, the ride is very rough... the boat barreling thru 20', 30' foot swells, going up + down + side to side. Feel kind of sick. Didn't sleep well, was thinking about how I'd get to the lifeboats in the pitch dark if it came down to it. [...] The worst part tho is that I have to come back on this thing in 4 days. Getting here (thru France) was hell. Overnight to Amsterdam ... then up early, pay extra for the train to Paris (so I'd have more than enough time) ... guy in Paris tells me [you're] not going to make it but try anyway. Four hours to le Houre, running thru the station ... taxi, how much? 25 francs (I say it 4 times to be clear, write it out twice on the window) guy says yeah, yeah, he knows where he's going ... he goes against every sign that says 'Irish ferries,' way out of the way, "trust me" he says, [...] we get there, "voila" ... but [I have my] doubts, tell him to "wait here" while I run in + ask ... "no msr, it's on the other side of the port." Shit. Back to the taxi, 15 minute ride ... finally steer the cabbie to the right place, "ah let's see ... 68 francs msr," No way, fuck you asshole—start yelling in english [...], he relents, finally I board the boat. Waste my last pound on a cup of coffee tastes like dirt. Next time I'll pony up 5 pounds for a bunk.

[this almost blank background page appropriated (w/out permission) from J. Joyce's draft notebooks for writing Ulysses *(courtesy of the NLI (National Library of Ireland)— http://catalogue.nli.ie/)]*

While it's incidental that we happen to be reading *Correction* on the plane here [...], it is not coincidental that we are thinking about our brother-½, for we are on our way to **Nepal**, which seemed to be the apex/ Cone of our brother-½'s journey/walk-about/ pilgrimage/whatever u want to call it ... in fulfillment of his vision quest for the sake of his 'SSES' 'SSES' thesis.

The funny thing is that our brother-½ was not exactly the outdoors type. [I was] the brother addicted to climbing + hiking + whatnot ... tho [i] never had ambitions for high-altitude mountaineering ... specially something like Everest. And the basecamp of Everest is the last place in the world [i'd] want to go. Our brother-½ never hiked or climbed in the U.S. ... he was a city boy ... but for whatever reason he fixated on Himalayan peaks. [I'm] not sure what Everest or Annapurna or Machapuchare or the Himalayas in general meant to our brother-½ .. maybe 'it' represented an unobtainable goal, the 'highest' u could get .. complete purity ... higher than even heroin. Or in regards to *Ulysses/ The Odyssey,* it stood for our father.

[...]

[or ENTELECHY]

the IDea of ∃Ireland

7:30 p.m. train from Gallway to Dublin (very shaky)

[difficult to read] I tend to be a loud self-centered braggart when it comes to meeting new people. [undecipherable] pretty young German girl working reception at hostel (in Gallway). Unfortunately was involved w/ a sleazy 50'ish fisherman (big-belly, farts all the time, picks his arse). Didn't work at the hostel but him + his loser friends were constantly hanging around, smoking, [...] drooling all over her, she awkwardly submissive. Oh well. Talked a while to a pretty Dublin girl ... presented myself as a bourgeois American, what a nightmare, backfired. Didn't get a hold of [D—American friend at U. of Gallway] ... walked in + out of pubs all night [...] looking for him. Pubs packed with local college kids having a good time, it was miserable. Train back to Dublin. I really have to make better use of this trip, grasp the moment more, quit seeming so depressed. Realize [this might] be my last trip, some people aren't so lucky (have I ever really acknowledged this—am I responsible for others misfortune, should I feel guilty because others [can't] do the same? No.)

Anyway, things [occupying] my mind, in [no particular order]:

—watching out for myself (physically) + my stuff (survival), my security
—staring longingly + fantasizing about girls I see on the street
—hunger as related to seeing + smelling food
—wallowing in misery, self-doubt
—trying not to worry about losing my hair.
[...]

Indrejst den
3 1 JAN. 1989
Rigspolitiet
Rode: Heyn (115)
DANMARK

"I don't seem to have any "real" feelings."

Why haven't I seriously ever (or even casually) considered suicide? I don't seem to get depressed anymore, it just seems to be some constant state. Designating this trip as a time to do some thinking was a bad idea—too many distractions, [undecipherable] even while providing myself with an escape, there doesn't seem to be the opportunity to take advantage of it.

9:10 p.m. Sentralstacion, Oslo, Norway

I am wearing my hair differently today. Figured combing it back was making me go bald. Now it's just down. Uglier + more mangy looking.

I'm waiting for the night train to Stockholm. 3 more days before I go to Moscow + it looks like I already overshot my monthly budget by at least 50 bucks ... oh well, just realized I lost my Swiss army knife. [...] I've got a headache, feeling shitty, looking shitty + vice-versa. Am still in a mental state of suspended disbelief, numb. Don't seem to have any "real" feelings. Apparently I am funny looking—the locals have been laughing at me (ha, classic paranoid schizo) especially in SKIEN where I spent all day on a train to go (there + back) only to walk around for a minute [+] decide it was the ugliest city I'd ever [seen] + left. Norway is a strange place. [undecipherable ...]

If I could feel something right now it would probably be straight [sic?]. I don't know why.

Observation: nice train station.
Thought: I'm leaving Europe + going to Asia.
Thought: I want to call home + check on my car, make sure it isn't stolen.
Thought: maybe I don't want to know.
Observation: the guy across from me has a black eye.
Thought: memory retention [is] intrinsically related to physiological states or chemical secretions.
Thought: the above statement is inept.
Thought: I wish my hair was thicker, more plentiful.
Thought: [...] I would like to get laid.
Thought: I need to wash my face.
Thought: I like <u>the idea</u> of Ireland better than being there.[17]
Thought: Norwegian sounds stupid.

[this background image from 1 of Kevin's 1st sketchbooks]

---

[17] At least on our grandfather's side, we are mostly of Irish descent.

Kathmandu—June 30

[...]

Our sleep was restless because of **jet lag**, so eventually we woke up + scribbled down some notes in the darkness, to help trigger what we were thinking about (we do this often). We scribbled down things (still in a half-asleep state) like "suicide as a short circuit" + "the idea seemed biological ... almost down to synapse level ... we could see the actual firing ... a sort of built in safety mechanism." [see actual handwritten notes on blog]

But most of what we wrote we can't make out. And we'd wake up again + write over what we'd previously written. From what we can piece together in our head, the thinking, this **thought**, had something to do with the vanity of pursuit in thinking ... + language itself. Of trying harder + harder to articulate it + then, almost like a line end or carriage return, the line of thought (that again, was almost biological, that although text-based, was like a firing synapse) would **feedback** on itself like a sick joke (we wrote "Infinite Jest in that it bypassed consciousness or understanding itself"). Ingrained in this was the knowledge that this, the feedback control, was necessary, as a survival mechanism. This is what kept people alive (hence why we wrote "suicide as a short circuit" [...] suicide is a loophole in this feedback system.). And while we wrote

Hermetic drain [E threshold XING]

Thought: My vitamins will probably get me arrested at the Russian border.
Thought: I will be in China at the same time as George Bush.
Thought: I won't get a shower + change of clothes [until] tomorrow.
Thought: —
Thought: I must buy some toilet paper before going to India.

11:20 train from Turk to Helsinki (Finland)

There are a lot of beautiful blondes + redheads in Norway. I haven't talked to a soul since I left Oslo. The sky is grey + the ground is covered w/ thick ice. [Forests] of spruce trees, fields, rundown old barns, patches of old dirty snow. No sign of people or cars. This guy next to me is snoring really loud.

> *I'm on my way to Russia ... hope you keep in touch*
> *hope they don't make [a fuss] ... about very much*
> *just writing this poem could be ... enough to incriminate me*
> *not because it seeks to undermine ... but cuz I badly cross the lines.*

Here's an idea should get my mind going—I'm heading east for the first time in my life. I am [leaving] the west. [...] This is a long journey, thru 12 time zones. Hope they let me bring in food.

There's a bearded guy across from me talking to himself (in Norwegian). He asked if he could sit down, the girl said yes. He set his bags down + started jabbering away. She looked out the window trying to ignore him. People stared. She finally left ... he continues blabbing ... then another person (woman) sits next to him ... he keeps talking to himself, all paranoid, out of touch w/ reality, schizophrenic though he looks totally normal ... she offers him some candy + talks to him. She doesn't seem interested in him, is just being polite. The "normal" people mind their luggage, talk softly to each other about how strange he is, give annoyed glances.

Around midnight [now, on a] Luxury Liner off the coast of Norway (on the way to Helsinki), like the Ritz on water—discos, casino, luxury, the fanciest place I've ever been + it's totally free w/ the Eurail pass. Loaded w/ Finnish + Swedish blondes. Think I'm the only tourist. Drank a beer (even tho I spent about 90 dollars today (phone call home, posters, sending package, food) [undecipherable] once again a ghost ... .

that "complete understanding was not possible, yet the idea to keep trying is what is built in" ... we think what we meant (consciously) is that this was at once both the carrot dangling at the end of the stick + a built-in, hard-wired switch that at some point limits understanding for our own protection ... at least as far as re-articulating it precisely with language. And because of this hard-coded limiter switch, we're not exactly sure we consciously understand the dream or what we are saying here ... which is fine ... it's the trying that matters ... just like the cliché about it not being about the destination, but getting there.

Besides dream stuff, in this half-lucid state we were also writing down things about this SSES book we've been talking about (which is not uncommon, especially when we're traveling + we can't sleep [...] we'll often scribble such notes in the dark that of course we can't really understand later) ... on how to approach this 'SSES'[3] book. The dream (both of them actually) has a lot to do with 'SSES'[3] in fact, as this limit was what our brother-½ was vainly striving for, knowing full well it was unachievable, but trying anyway. In our notes we wrote "the pursuit of higher art" ... as a phrase, perhaps to include in the title even, that captures what it was our brother-½ was looking for (+ that we in turn are looking for in writing/re-writing his story).

exhibit 9—"Untitled" 1991 (pourstone, enamel, drain element, 7" x 16")

[A.K.A. "HERMES HAT"]
(to cover baldness)

2 RHIZOMATIC SHATTERING
(SUPERNATURAL ADVICE)

[cont.]

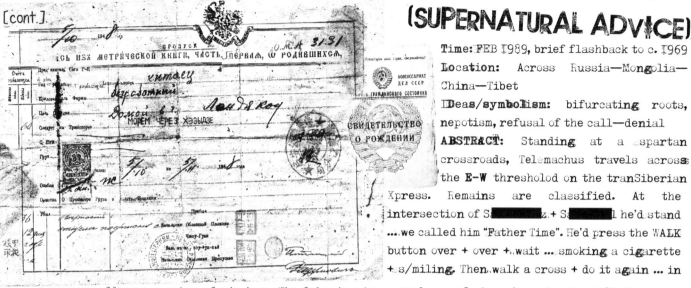

Time: FEB 1989, brief flashback to c. 1969
Location: Across Russia—Mongolia—China—Tibet
Ideas/symbolism: bifurcating roots, nepotism, refusal of the call—denial
ABSTRACT: Standing at a spartan crossroads, Telemachus travels across the E-W threshold on the tranSiberian Xpress. Remains are classified. At the intersection of S█████z + S█████l he'd stand ….we called him "Father Time". He'd press the WALK button over + over + wait … smoking a cigarette + s/miling. Then walk a cross + do it again … in a square, allways counter-clockwise. The laboring transcendence of sissyphean tax in infinit nested circuits. We all had our theories 'bout him …. supposedly some 1 approached him once, determined he was pyschizo—had no clue where he was or where he was going … some 1 else claimed he was a Vietnam vet, a drunk. He had dirty blonde hair, always wore a jean jacket. His presents grounded us ….whenever we were in far-flung situations (i.e. drinking yak tea in a yurt in Mongolia) we thawed of him ….wherever we were we could rest assured he'd be standing there, at his intersection—a normalized x-section by witch to measure ourselfs in time.

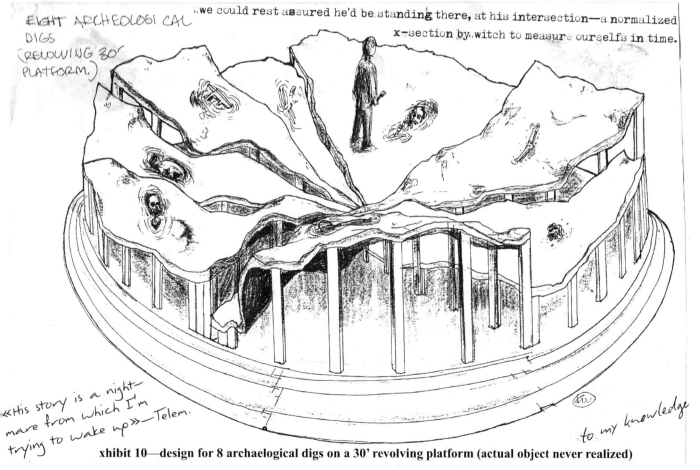

EIGHT ARCHEOLOGICAL DIGS (REVOLVING 30' PLATFORM.)

«His story is a night-mare from which I'm trying to wake up»—Telem.

to my knowledge

xhibit 10—design for 8 archaelogical digs on a 30' revolving platform (actual object never realized)

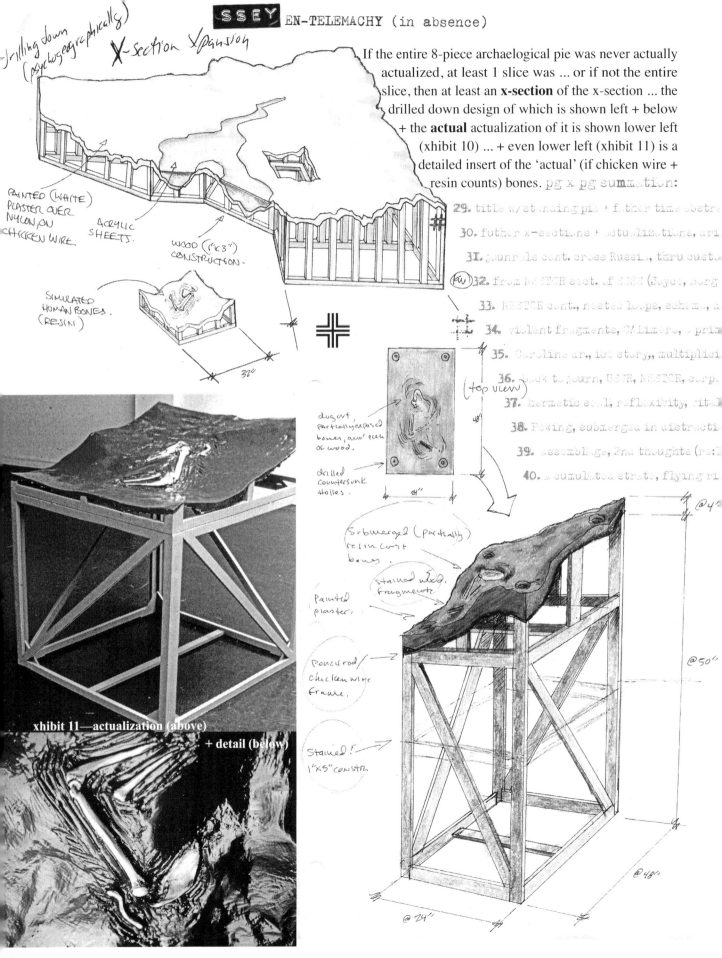

X-section X/pansion

drilling down (psychogeographically)

If the entire 8-piece archaelogical pie was never actually actualized, at least 1 slice was ... or if not the entire slice, then at least an **x-section** of the x-section ... the drilled down design of which is shown left + below + the **actual** actualization of it is shown lower left (xhibit 10) ... + even lower left (xhibit 11) is a detailed insert of the 'actual' (if chicken wire + resin counts) bones. pg x pg summation:

29. title w/standing pie + further time abstr
30. further x-sections + actualizations, ori
31. journals cont. cross Russia, thru custo
32. from NESTOR sect. of SSEY (Joyce, Borg
33. NESTOR cont., nested loops, schema, a
34. violent fragments, CALimero, prim
35. Caroline dr., ice story,, multiplici
36. back to journ, USSR, NESTOR, corp.
37. hermetic seal, reflexivity, vital
38. Peking, submerged in abstracti
39. assemblage, 2nd thoughts (re:
40. accumulated strata, flying ri

PAINTED (WHITE) PLASTER OVER NYLON, ON CHICKEN WIRE.

ACRYLIC SHEETS.

WOOD (1"x3") CONSTRUCTION.

SIMULATED HUMAN BONES. (RESIN)

32"

(top view)

48"

dugout, partially exposed bones, and piece of wood.

drilled countersunk holles.

24"

Submerged (partially) resin crust bones.

stained wood fragments.

painted plaster.

Pencil rod/ chicken wire frame.

Stained? 1"x5" constr.

xhibit 11—actualization (above)
+ detail (below)

@4'

@50"

@48"

@24"

[handwritten top right: X-ing thru customs / E→W threshold→]

[Jan 25, 1989] Train between Leningrad + Moscow

Well this is it, the Russian experience ... [embarked] in Helsinki. Dark train with Russian emblems on the outside. Inside, Persian [rugs] + wood paneling. Got a sleeper (unexpected), Anti-USA pamphlets on racks in the aisles, train full of Finnish and Spanish. Got nervous about customs ... guy in the same cabin as me (Finnish) is bringing a whole load of microchips + a big computer. Russian police so busy with him they don't bother w/ me. Got off to go [into] a town to change money ... incredible old buildings, monumental structural elements [...] All the men wear big fur hats. The rubles are very small. Talked in Spanish to a young Colombian student. [...] we get coffee, he says, "everyone in the US has AIDS don't they?" Now thru Russian customs ...

ONE POT ISM

Moscow-Peking Express

11:30 p.m., Siberia (writing this on the train) ... well Moscow was pretty intense. Met some [Swedes] who were also going to Peking, taxi from Moscow station, impressive city, large monuments, old buildings, churches, everyone wearing big fur hats. [...] Walked around, immediately asked to sell dollars [in] trade terms, got 2 T-shirts, a fur hat + Russian posters + pins. Irritated sales people in all the stores, most of them don't want to help, no one smiles. Walked around (w/ Swedes) [...] went to a nightclub, met enthusiastic, talkative locals [...] Tour of Kremlin next morning. To the post office to send [stuff home] .... then to train. Coal-burning heaters (constant smoke), in 1st class w/ [insurance salesman from Kansas] who keeps me up snoring all night. 1st class is nice, wood paneling, bathroom w/ shower, 2 beds, meals are kind of gross. 2nd day I slept, ate, talked to Swedish girls, drank (orange juice) w/ Brits + Swedes who drink Vodka (can't buy on train except in dollars) ... 3rd day on the train, backgammon, fields of snow + Spruce trees, distracted chaotic thoughts ... submerged into interaction w/ people [...] Chinese turn on radios ... we have to listen, no choice ... a distraction? Or music to think by? Inspirational to some, annoying to others. 4th day, days running together ... Siberian landscape is more beautiful, along the coast of the largest fresh-water lake in the world (lake Bikal) the food is getting more miserable, I'm wearing earplugs so I can sleep, we are just about to get into Mongolia . . . I have to take a shit ....

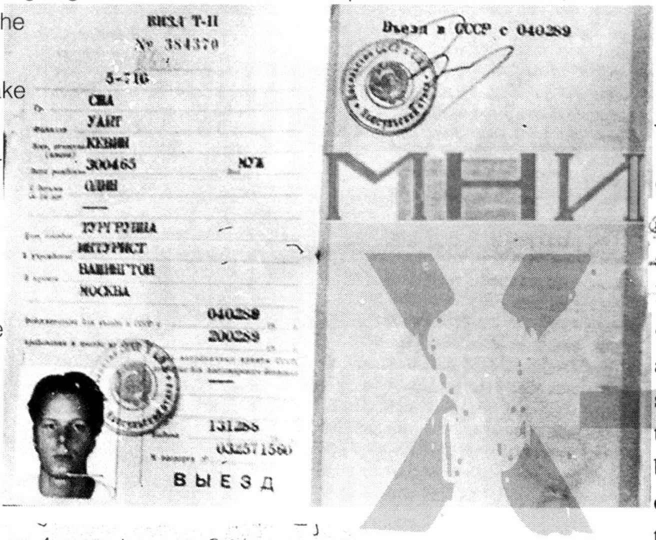

[handwritten bottom left: 4th day, Siberia ... going along freshwater lake ... the food is gr... I am wearing earplugs so I can sleep. we are just about to go into Mongolia... i have to take a shit...]

§ This is the 3rd episode ... corresponding to book 3 in *The Odyssey,* wherein Telemachus (after leaving home) receives advice from **Nestor.** In *Ulysses* (episode 2), Stephen Dedalus teaches a class, tests his patience w/ a degenerate student, then gets paid by his boss (Mr. Deasy). As i wrote in a blog post from Kathmandu, on July 14, 2013 (http://5cense.com/13/rejoyce.htm): «*Not sure exactly who Mr. Deasy would be (in our brother's book), but sure there's a parallel here as far as our brother's obsessive concern with money ... inheriting dirty money from our father when he died, which he used to go to art school + take his trip. And then later the guilt of having to let others pay for his rehab or living with our mother because he couldn't afford rent.*»

§ It's also perhaps worth mentioning that brother-½ + i had a mutual interest in Joseph **Campbell** (watched all the Bill Moyer interviews w/ him), who not only provided us w/ THE «skeleton key» to Joyce's even more esoteric + inaccessible text, *Finnegans Wake,* but Campbell also gave us a general 16-fold «monomyth» framework that could easily be applied to both *Ulysses* + *The Odyssey,* as well as this book (+ most any other). E.g., the [previous] episode could be considered «Departure: Call to Adventure» + this episode could be filed under: «**Departure: supernatural aid**» ... tho we're not sure what form this aid takes ...

§ In February of 1989, i was living in Santa Cruz, CA. finishing out the last year of a degree in computational math. I kept a journal back then, but didn't date anything so not sure exactly what i was doing when our brother-½ was on his trip + logged these ~~this entry. Mostly our journals from these years are filled w/ mathematical doodlings & song lyrics/compositions.~~

§ We remember Kevin telling us once about a performance artist who took this same transiberian trip, only he boarded-up the windows + never left his compartment between Finland + China. In the context of quantum mechanics, this was interesting to think about [... had he *really* been to Russia?]

«I paid my way. I never borrowed a shilling in my life. Can you feel that? I owe nothing. Can you?»—(Telemachus's boss)

[left margin handwritten fragments: ...g down ...irty money ...c.) ...l ...drunk ...him, et... ...whore... ...pulse, ...ulate ...t), worrying about it ...handed flux...]

We take a break now from Kevin's raw journal entries, to bring u the next 3 em-

bedded pages—from the 3ʳᵈ, **Nestor,** episode of his *'SSES'* *'SSES'*:

NESTOR

unity continues its spiritual labor

(1.)*In Borges's story, Pierre Menard lives Cervantes's life in order to write Quixote. He spends years in the process of becoming Cervantes, and then dies after only completing a few lines of the book. Borges presents us with this apocryphal event in which an individual (re-)writes an epic, maintaining the linear directionality of the work, (in a way that makes its linear realization impossible by its existence within a short story).*

Joyce uses the epic, the ODYSSEY, in a way that could be effectively termed, multiplicitous. The structure of the epic is used as a supplementary dimension in the novel, a structure which legitimizes, and provides a structure to anticipate. The epic is privileged, by being the title, as being the most visible structure in the work. Like the OEDIPUS, the ODYSSEY is a generic drama, the theme of which could be applied to almost any event (especially those involving (men); traveling, wandering and searching).

(2) When Joyce "shatters the linear unity of the word" the result is not a cyclic (reunification of) unity, but a permanently shattered form. The "spiritual labor of unity" reffered to by Deleuze and Guattari, does not exist within the work, but is acted upon it from the outside. Nothing is ever shattered within the book itself. In order for the word to be shattered in this way one must have as a dominate linguistic model some form of neoclassical thought. I grew up reading, among other thing, "MAD" magazine, this would it seems automatically put me in the position of experiencing Joyce's innovations in a different way (ie. not as transgressive). The fact that Joyce preceded "MAD" magazine by fifty years does not seem to be an issue in this particular consideration. Joyces transgressions of the rules of language and writing are perceived as being less threatening to someone raised with the satire, advertising and pop music lyrics of the last twenty years of American culture.

Every system presents itself as being an end in itself, but is this always the case. "Cyclic unity" (...of language and thought) sounds very much like the tree (root) model of language/thought. Deleuze, Guattari argue for the adoption of the rhizome, (and the dissolving of the dominate tree/root (Platonic) model championed by the likes

...the folding of one text on to another, which constitutes multiple and even adventitous roots (Like a cutting), imp--lies a supplementary dimen--sion to that of texts under consideration. In this sup--plementary dimension of fol--ding, unity continues its sp--iritual labor. That is why the most resolutely fragmented work can also be presented as the total work or Magnum Opus. Most modern methods for make--ing series proliferate or a multiplicity grow are perfect--ly valid in one direction, for example, a linear direct--ion, whereas a unity of tot--alization asserts itself ev--en more firmly in another, circular or cyclic, dimension.[1] [18]

Joyce's words, accurately des--cribed as having multiple roots, shatter the linear uni--ty of the word, even of lang--uage, only to posit a cyclic unity of the sentence, text or knowledge.[2]

"The internal monologue, in its nature on the order of poetry, is that unheard and unspoken speech by which a character ex--presses his inmost thoughts (those lying nearest the uncon--scious) without regard to log--ical organization- that is, in their origional state- by means of direct sentences red--uced to the syntactic minimum, and in such a way as to give the impression of reproducing the thoughts just as they came into the mind".[3]

".. there is no difference be--tween what a book talks about and how it is made.[4]"

"Multiplicities are rhizomatic, and expose arborescent pseudo--multiplicities for what they are...[5]"

The falls cry of ‹unity› continues its spiritual (labor) is perhaps begins idea of ‹‹supernatural aid›› of us only advice from NESTOR that would help us in figuring out what he planned to our father.

Oh! i had a parrot named NESTOR ... he never talked but used to shred my writing paper into nesting material...

§ This quote (left) remains still at the heart of our publishing manifesto. D + G continue by saying: «... *therefore a book also has no object. As an assemblage, a book has only itself, in connection with other assemblages and in relation to other bodies without organs.*» (See page 37 for further discussion).

---

[18] Kevin's embedded footnotes are for references on page 39. (Yes, this is a footnote for a footnote... if such a hyper-recontextualized reference is allowed in book form.)

the breaking of the mirror in sleeping Beauty

§ Perhaps this «rhizomatic shattering» could also be considered (in Campbell's framework) as a «Departure: refusal of the call»—a **denial** of the linear/cyclical thinking that came before us.

§ As readers, we seek a **linear** narrative to attach ourselves to ... + thru his itinerarized trip it seems brother-½ was trying to orient himself in linear fashion, in a line across Russia, around the world ... but in the end what we inevitably discover is an induced rupturing of complacency, a defragmentation left to reconstruct.

§ The art to any thing is learning the balance between rhizomatic rupturing + linear narrative. It's a fine line. Like [this] ... should we be trying to organize + explain what 'SSES" 'SSES" is about? Or shoud we just present a shattered smattering of texts + images + let the narrative/meaning coalesce in the mind of the reader?   NESTOR

fully achieved, his preoccupation with mapping out chapters of text, and revision, would argue for its discreditability.

(4,5) Joyce's writing process involved the continual infusion of coded systems into the work. His friend, Stuart Gilbert, in his book on ULYSSES reveals some of these codes; color-chapter, body organ-chapter, etc. By permeating the text with hidden codes Joyce succeeded in making what Deleuze, Guattari refer to as a multiplicitous, rhizomatic work. Through his process of external reference he also is successful in losing the author within the work. He does this by making it impossible, because of the multitude of references, (planes, codes, systems,etc.) to pinpoint the author in the text. This refusal to be identified, to submit to societies codes, is what Deleuze, Guattari refer to as the 'Body without organs". ULYSSES, (and Joyce) are bodies without organs. ULYSSES is also inherently autobiographical. As Brenda Maddox elucidates in her biographical novel on Nora Joyce, ULYSSES is almost completely attributable to quotes, descriptions, and recollections of the relationship (both public and private) of Nora and James Joyce. Through the inclusion of hundreds of letters, quotes and interviews, Maddox diagrams the formation of a novel that is shaped by personal conflicts, (being literally written into the work) and seemingly dictated by the events of the life of James (and Nora) during the time of its creation. A biography of Nora and James Joyce fits over the structure of ULYSSES in the same way that the structure of Homer's epic fits over ULYSSES.

NESTOR

of Chomsky) to have it serve as a model within a society already geared towards schizophrenic thought. The root model they imply, is unrealistic in its isolation, incompatible with thought in its exclusivity.

On the topic of literature (and rhizome) they (D.G.) bring up Burroughs and Joyce, and describe their work as being multiplicitous/rhizomatic and thus in the end cyclic and circular. This idea of circularity does not seem to be in keeping with the idea of the rhizome. The description should be; When the work is read, unity continues it's spiritual labor, but when the light goes out, the shattered rhizogenic forms retain their original patterns.

(3) This quote is from the French symbolist writer DuJardin, who Joyce acknowledges (citing specifically his work entitled; "Les Lauriers sont Coupes", first published in 1887, and then reprinted shortly after Joyce's acknowledgement) as the inventor of the writing style which he himself perfected. This quote precedes the years of Surrealist experimentation involving stream of consciousness and non-logical thought. The terms such as "without regard to logical organization" and "unheard and unspoken speech" sound naive, romantic and hopeful. Unlike what is implied by DuJardins description (and Joyce's acknowledgement of it) Joyce's style of writing was very logical and labored. As H. Levin describes in his book on the author;

"Joyce's habits of composition were Daedalean labors, to which his rewritten manuscripts and revised proofs bear formidable testimony. Collation of a casual page of printers typescript with the final text of ULYSSES indicates that sixty-five corrections have been made in proof.... at least ten of them contributions of some importance."

Joyce's admiration for poets and writers such as DuJardin and Mallarme is well documented. He saw these writers as innovators, people who would be remembered as pioneers in new directions of literature (and poetry). He was especially fascinated with their works involving stream of consciousness and interior monologue. Although it is not clear where Joyce stood on the idea of non-logical organization in literature, whether he believed it could be

§ For those interested, the **Gilbert** scheme can be found online at http://en.wikipedia.org/wiki/Gilbert_schema_for_Ulysses. For example, this Nestor episode can be mapped to the following attributes:

Scene : the school
Hour: 10 a.m.
Organ: -
Colour: brown
Symbol: horse
Art: history
Technic: catechism (personal)

An alternative + more comprehensive mapping was created by Carlo Linati.

unity continues its spiritual labor

Primarily the pump in Nested feedback loops

§ (Brother-½ left this right column blank so in the interest of spatial optimization, i'll go ahead + write over it. This is the part of 'SSES" 'SSES" where he gets rather analytic + philosophical ... perhaps out of necessity, to fulfill thesis requirements.

§ No coincidence the similarity between Dedalus + *Daedalus*—the Greek craftman, sculptor + inventor + builder of the labyrinth where the Minotaur was kept. He also famously fashioned wings that he + his son Icarus used to escape from the island of Crete.

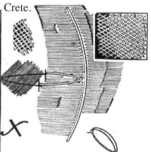

„ПОМОРЬЕ"

§ A biography of Kevin White fits over the structure of 'SSES" 'SSES" "SSEY" in the same way the structure of *The Odyssey* fits over *Ulysses* fits over 'SSES" 'SSES". They form **nested loops**, if u will. If a book is a function, or routine, then this book is made like this (where **x** is an arbitrary string to pass):

```
create 'SSES" 'SSES" "SSEY' (x)
  call 'SSES" 'SSES" (x)
    call ULYSSES (x)
      call THE ODYSSEY (x)
      return THE ODYSSEY (x')
    return ULYSSES (x'')
  return 'SSES" 'SSES" (x''')
return 'SSES" 'SSES" "SSEY' (x'''')
```

on comical violence
a "primer of sorts

fry ①

He sat back and fought off the urge to re-enter the world. Nothing was going to harm him. Sure. What they did was stupid, to say the least. Sometimes things have to be done that wake you up, ~~my~~ ^make^ life more exciting, more dangerous. If we were to be caught, and thrown out of school our lives would be over. Our dads would give up on us, we would be forced into a life of exile, of oblivion, a sharp blast of reality.

"No more ski vacations" B▓▓▓ added while evading an invisible defense man with his lacrosse stick.

Stupid. Stupid. What a rush. God I can hardly stand it. Shit, I think I will go turn my self in to break the suspense...

"Fuck you dude! Don't even joke about it! You hear?! It's not fucking funny!" B▓▓▓ has stopped his lacrosse practice with the stuffed moose head, and is now standing in the middle of the room giving me his best look of intimidation, gloved hands on hips.

I role over in my bed to face my corner of safe space. I press my teeth together as hard as I possibly can and pray feverently for B▓▓▓'s untimely death.

"Don't fucking ignore me you asshole!!" The lacrosse stick comes down hard on my right shoulder, pain shoots down the side of my back.

"Hey!, I'm talking to you!"

This time when the stick hits my shoulder I spin to my right as fast as I can and grab the stick by the net. B▓▓▓ looks surprised and trys to pull away. I push the end of the stick hard into the base of his neck, he lets out a choking sound and steps back. I spring to my feet and before he has a chance to say anything I bring my right knee up full force into his groin. He drops the stick and doubles over with ~~his mouth open~~ ^an open mouth^ and glazed eyes. I calmly pick up the stick, marvel for a moment at the possibilities fiberglass has created for lightweight and extremely strong sporting equipment, raise it above my head, and bring it down ~~full force~~ ^hard^ on ~~the back of h▓▓▓~~ ^to his^ neck. His whole body shakes violently for a few seconds, and then drops into a pile on the floor. His eyes are ~~open~~ ^barely open^ and there is a small line of blood coming out of his nose and going on to the carpet. I ~~quickly~~ ^quickly^ grab some kleenexes and stop the blood.

В ГЕОМЕТРИИ

Consider B = Clay

... or is this book a **feedback** loop? The 4th derivative (X'''') of *The Odyssey*, primed thru *Ulysses* + *'SSES" 'SSES"*. As Dedalus says in *Ulysses*, «a nightmare from which I am trying to awake.»

The piece to the left is a loose page i found in his notes, not dated or associated w/ anything else.

This rhizomatic shattering seemed to at times release itself as **violence** in Kevin's work ... something that always surprised me, as i thought of brother-½ (+ myself) as non-violent, maybe even passive, akin to Leopold Bloom. We were not the kind of brothers that got into fights—physical, or even w/ harsh words. Like me, i doubt brother-½ once in his life threw or received a punch. On more than 1 occasion in our years growing up Mexico, i watched him swallow his pride + suffer humiliation rather than fight back against the taunting/macho bullying we endured. This violence starts to creep into his work around the time he started working in film ... so perhaps these are things he forced in cuz it was xpected or nesessary to shatter the rhizomatic mirror? Or maybe all that swallowing of pride was catching up to him.

CALIMERO

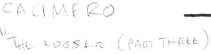

"The LOOSER (PART THREE)

xhibit 12—various sketches from a comic strip brother-½ made, featuring this egg-shaped CALIMERO charactor depicted in various scenes of violent + lewd debauchery (our father's name was CAL)

Here's another unincorporated flash piece entitled CAROLINE DRIVE.DOC (the street we grew up on) that shows brother-½'s early penchant for this reflected idea of fracturing (as inspired by an ice storm in Portland, OR, that left enough ice that, yes, we were able to skate on the streets ... in theory anyway. Mostly we just did it for the idea of it, to say we did):

The frozen rain keeps us from going to school. We are elated. Within the long shadow of our house the street is covered with a shiny thick coating [of] glass. Every ripple, wave, every splash is frozen; the surface bumpy. I manage to stay up as I skate [across] it. I'm wearing red corduroy stovepipes & a crimson ski jacket with an oversized steel zipper. I chew on the end of my mittens ... [they taste of wet] leather.

Sunlight falls and the ice disappears. The pink & white Japanese cherry blossoms smell once again. [Peering] through the layered grey ice into pockets of pearl I see black asphalt, the sun and wavering trees. A boy with straight blonde hair. The sun singes the ice away. Pebbles that were embedded are now free. They draw the light around them inward. Like points where the mirrored surface has been pulled simultaneously up and down.

like a terminal moraine.

+ maybe we're getting ahead of ourselves, but here's a sculpture he made after his travels to India, along w/ the notebook page where he came up w/ the idea for it:

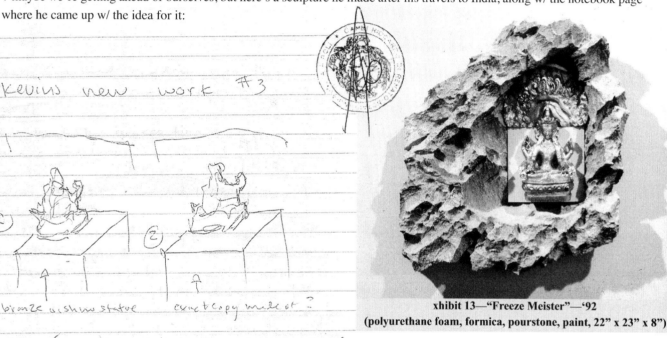

Kevin's new work #3

bronze vishnu statue   exact copy made of ?

**xhibit 13—"Freeze Meister"—'92
(polyurethane foam, formica, pourstone, paint, 22" x 23" x 8")**

① bronze (copper) statuette of vishnu, mass produced in the process of wax... process. made in India, made to look old ("w/chemicals) sold in every store in Khotmandu, expensive.
② my copy, hand carved, same form, not same color, material.
3 er about - ① commercialization of religion, older practition being subsumed by a younger one is plain and its processes) selling older talking of to new tourist (west) India and etc... confrontation to (modern protest dean

Such notes (left) were interspersed throughout his journal. This particular piece shows he was thinking about **multiplicity** (not to mention the commercialization of religion)—the idea of taking an original (bronze Vishnu statue, of which we have the original) «mass produced in the [lost] wax process» + replicating it ... in this instance in a sort of icy styrofoam cave-life enclosure.

how to NOT lose shit in the editing process draw SKES

a circle is aerial view of helix

add story circles.

CUT back to Kevin's SSES ... side by side w/ the raw journals of his actual odyssey:

[Jan 26] 11:30 p.m., Russia-Mongolia border

Right now as I'm writing this Russian border agents are going thru my compartment, checking my papers + luggage. We are waiting here for 2 hours as they check the train + passports.

... now it's nighttime, somewhere near the Chinese border in southern Mongolia. My inability to reach an understanding, to find psychological relief from [existential anxiety], to scratch the itch that throbs deep within my psyche, to experience change, to have time take effect, to die without dying—[this all weight heavy on me]. **I know now (something I always knew but never practised) that the adventurous world traveller never finds anything (that he can't find at home)** ... even going thru the Gobi desert of Mongolia, I only find myself submerged in distraction (interacting w/ other people). I fear I've lost the ability to be the person I feel inside. My actions (of Kevin) are automatic ... words just spill out. To be the person I feel inside is to be alone, and that is a pain I cannot bear, at the price it costs me. I will always be a character who occasionally sees himself objectively as a stupid being, who comes in one form, afraid to face the world alone ... but we're all social creatures and it's just the people I [choose] to be around that drive me to these actions. The desire to make art is dead, I am not sure when I realized I was running on empty, but I'm not sure if I can get it back. The reasons why I created as a young man and the reinforcement I received were actions of a person w/different needs. The 'peer' reinforcement is not present anymore, no longer is it the thing Kevin does good, he is such a good boy, wow Kevin wages so hard to make something of seemingly natural instincts and maybe it's ok, good, but let's see some more, the driving force. I am supposed to think of a thesis on this trip, but all I think about is **corporeal awareness** (eating, sleeping, watching out for cars) the only reason I'm going to school is because I have gone this far ...

We're going thru inner Mongolia, cold + frosty, [dusting of] snow, camels, getting more mountainous, glimpses of the Great

NESTOR

(1) The idea that ULYSSES can be read forward or backwards is absurd. It would be safe to assume that even Joyce could not have read the book backwards, nor would he have probably wanted to. Any cyclic structure that might be inherent in the book because it takes place over the period of one day is negated by he specificity (of peoples, places, things,) written into the work.

(2) One of the ideas Joyce found compelling about the ODYSSEY was the idea of man as both father and son. Leopold Bloom seems to be the incarnation of this ambiguity, but the roles of father and son float freely throughout the characters of Stephen, Bloom, (and Joyce). No real identities are presented in any of the cases. It is hard to say whether the nomadic qualities of Bloom and Stephen, (they both lose their keys at the beginning of the story) include more of Joyce, (an Irishman who gives up his country to spend the rest of his life in foreign countries) or Ulysses (who wanders for 27 years before returning home). In this sense the book shifts from the personal to the epic continuously. There is no unity, subject or object. Joyce was a nomad in the realm of language as well. His systematic Irish patois was an advanced literary form that had little respect for the Queen's English (a language which Ireland has been subjected to for over four hundred years, a language which Joyce, because he spoke very little Irish, was forced to learn as his mother tongue). Samuel Beckett, the Irish contemporary of Joyce, achieved a similar refusal of English, by writing in French.

(3) Joyce had a great fear of dogs.

does mocking a mocking negate it to Sunday ﹖ (real?)

§ This disillusionment w/ his chosen field (or the field that chose him—art) is reminiscent of Kurt Cobain, who killed himself 3 years before brother-½ died. *1989*

§ My chosen art in my teens to 20s was music + i too had to give it up for fear that it would kill me if i kept «pursuing» it.

mock epic

"The exposition of ULYSSES is necessarily circular, it plunges the reader, with epic vengeance, in medias res. Jung has declared that it has neither a beginning nor an end, that it can be read both forwards and backwards. The reader, entering the mind of the character without the formality of an introduction, will encounter allusions long before they are explained."1

"His favorite story was still the ODYSSEY, Joyce told a friend, in reaffirming his choice. "It embodies everything", The man of many devices, who has known so many men and so many cities, is an all-embarking figure, a composite of the prettiest stratagems and the broadest sympathies in human nature."2

"Always evasive when confronted by action, Joyce shuns heroics. The relation of the ODYSSEY to ULYSSES is that of parallels that never meet. The Homeric overtones do contribute their note of universality, their range of tradition, to what might well be a trivial and colorless tale. But in so doing, they convert a realistic novel into a mock-epic."3

HERME.tic seal of re:FLEXivity

NESTOR   body without organs

Wall [...] Pull into Bejing, check into some shithole hotel w/ the Swedes ... showers are disgusting, [switched] to another hotel. Much nicer.

12:05 Qiao Yuan hotel, Bejing [not dated, but likely a week or so after the above entry]

Here I am, 5 stories up + 12 time zones over, **as far away as I am it still follows me ... orderliness doesn't mitigate or correct my loose ends** (je ne suis pas dans ma peux). Kristan is washing clothes in the sink, Cocteau Twins are playing on the tape deck, tomorrow we get up early to go to the Great Wall. Bejing was interesting, we walked a lot, had a decent meal, changed money, saw a cool [part of town]. I don't know what to say. After 740 million seconds[19] (more or less) I still fell very much in the dark ... I know, I know, as Derek[20] was fond of saying, we are always very much alone. Interactions w/ people are something else entirely—social life, sensory physical life—but when you're alone, very much alone in the cold [darkness], tree [shadows] looming around you, the silence laughs at you, ridiculing your ignorance, you have momentary illusions of substance, of existing, of blindness, of weakness. I can run to the other side of the world

(1) Joyce and Bergson both engage in the process of reducing things in themselves to a series of or--ganic relations. It is in this sense that Joyce can be aligned with Bergson (vitalism). In the phil--osophy of Bergson, we are given a visual presentat--ion of time. Time itself is saturated with a stain indicator, and the form that grows is described. Joyce makes visible his own degrees of difference, his own history, hacked up and rearranged.

(2), "There is no difference between what a book talks about, and how it is made." These two quotes (Pual DeMan, Deleuze- Guattari) seem to discuss language in the way it might function at degree zero". In some fields of thought, for example; Qua--ntum physics, ideas are more suitably played out in closed (hermetic) systems. This allows huge am--ounts of information to be somewhat stabilized and mapped, for results to be systematic. But in talking about language and writing, setting up hermetically sealed situations seems to be useless. It simply sounds like the reduction of variables in order to achieve a cleaner result. To say that " Literature is not a reliable source of information about anyth--ing but its own language" is to acknowledge every--thing but the nose on your face. "Watch out for that tree!" does not reveal much in the analysis of its language, but it does have great importance for George of the Jungle, swinging on his vine.

(3) -What do you have when you leave something with nothing more than a name?"Derrida-Language uses you, not the other way around".
    The machinic assemblage is ULYSSES. The strata is the world outside of its cover, seeing it as a book (object). The reader, body without organs, opens the book and reads it. The book is reoriented, rewritten and renamed. Instead of 28,899 different words, it now contains 2898. Where there once was a total of 260,430 words, there is now 3,539. Instead of 110,374 monosylla--bic words, there are 1,876. Relevant material has been assimilated. 86 percent remains familiar (up to one sentence need to establish familiarity).

"It seems to us that dura--tion essentially defines a virtual multiplicity (what differs in nature). Me--mory then appears as the co--existence of all the **degrees of difference** in this multipl--icity, in this virtuality. The **élan vital**, finally, des--gnates the actualization of this virtual according to the **lines of differentiation** that correspond to the degr--ees- up to this precise li--ne of man where the Elan Vital gains self-conscious--ness!"[1]

"Literature is fiction not because it somehow refuses to acknowledge reality, but because it is not a priori certain that language funct--ions according to principles which are those, or which are like those, of the phenomenal world. It is therefore not a priori certain that literature is a reliable source of info--rmation about anything but its own language."[2]

"One side of a machinic assem--blage faces the strata which doubtless make it a kind of organism, or signifying total--ity, or determination attrib--utable to a subject; it also has a side facing a **body with--out organs**, which is contin--ually dismantling the organ--ism, causing asignifying par--ticles or pure intensities to pass or circulate, and attrib--uting to itself subjects that it leaves with nothing more th--an a name as the trace of an intensity."[3]

[19] 740 million seconds is 23.46 years, which is at least in the ballpark of his age (at the time—he was born April 30, 1965).

[20] This is the 1st reference of my name in his journals ... apparently early on i somehow learned to stop relying on others for my happiness—something i guess i tried to instill in Kevin (or at least i said this to try to keep him positive) but his inherent need for human companionship was much stronger than mine.

收信人地址: 大鼻子's (big noses)
251 ½ DIMMICK AVE
VENICE, CALIFORNIA 90□□□
收信人姓名:
寄信人地址姓名:
美国 (U.S.A)
贵阳市邮票公司

[21] Often as i confuse the words **hermit** + hermetic, i find it strange they are not etymologically related (*hermit* derives from hermitage + *hermetic* (in the sealing sense used above) derives from Hermes, the Greek god of travelers and boundaries, who i also confuse w/ Archimedes (the dude who xclaimed «Eureka!» in the bathtub)(also see xhibit 9 on page 28).

[22] Intresting xample he chooses (by George of the Jungle), but perhaps brother-½ cuts off his nose to spite his face in disagreeing w/ Paul De Man.

[23] For more on Bergson + élan vital, or «vital impulse», see http://www.5cense.com/12/creat_evol.htm, where i talk about Bergson + travel + running as relates to **tendency** + mobility.

<<< Self-addressed postcard Kevin sent to "big noses" (what the Chinese evidently call white people) from China.

NESTOR　歇斯底里　sum of the parts

Holistic History

(1)People do not generally function like mach-
-ines (although scientists in almost every field of
study, from linguistic theory to sociology, would like
to make their jobs easier by thinking so.) Sperber and
Wilson (two European, linguistic theoreticians), in a
quote here from their paper on relevance (communication
and cognition) state that an increase in contextural
information leads to a loss of relevance (here relev-
-ance applies to the subject recieving the information).
I would argue that an increase in contextural informa-
-tion does lead to an increase in the processing effort
(variable to an individual's knowledge of the language
and coded systems present in the information). This inc-
-rease leads to either a loss of relevance (the effort
is too much and the subject fails to process it) or an
increase in relevance (the subject, because of the inv-
-estment required, takes a greater pleasure out of de-
-coding the text, and subsequently views information
more easily processed; a waste of time.)

(2)The little people.(Not French). Levy-Bruhl
fetishises primitivism as some sort of Platonic ideal
(these little people have some sort of one to one rel-
-ation with language? With the world?) and at the same
time brings up the intresting idea of the other (foriegn)
languages serving to enrich ones own thoughts (and
speech).
　　Joyce used his knowledge of different (Euro-
-pean) languages to internationalize the Irish text.
As a student at Trinity College (Dublin) Joyce taught
himself Norweigen in order to be able to read Ibsen
(something that was looked upon with scorn from the fac-
-ulty of the college), and later in life; Italian in
order to read Dante. Translations would not have sufficed.
Joyce wanted the original words, the text, without tra-
-ce, resemblence or association. This increased versatil-
-ity with the international novel allowed Joyce the abil-
-ity to use the foriegn text as building material, to cov-
-er up and structure over layers of coded systems (a lat-
-eral function) obfuscating his own handgesture in the
process.

... we have already assumed
that the context is automat-
-ically filled with a huge
amount of encyclopedic info-
-rmation, most- and sometimes
all- of which fails to incr-
-ease the contextual effects
of the new information being
processed. Since each expans-
-ion of the context means an
increase in the processing ef-
-fort, this method of context
formation would lead to a gen-
-eral loss of relevance.

...languages of primitive
peoples "always express their
ideas of things and actions
in the precise fashion in
which these are presented to
the eyes and ears."(2)They
have a common tendency to des-
-cribe, not the impression wh-
-ich the subject receives, but
the shape and contour, position
movement, way of acting, of
objects in space- in a word,
all that can be percieved and
delineated. They try to unite
the graphic and the plastic
elements of that which they
desire to express. We may per-
-haps understand this need of
theirs if we note that the sa-
-me peoples, as a rule, speak
another language as well, a
language whose characteristics
necessarily react upon the
minds of those who use it, in-
-fluencing their way of thought
and, as a consequence, their
speech.[2]

but it still finds me.
　I'm cleaning my stuff, [securing
my] belongings. I'm very together,
huh? ... you idiot, you're wallowing
in materialism, suffering [from]
psychosis. You'll always be left to
wonder—no, not wonder—**you'll
always carry the burden of his
choice**[24], **because you were
connected to *him* in more ways
than you thought**. The battle goes
on between [some aspect of the
psyche] which wants to fly away
somewhere alone, content, self-
centered and the bleak aspect,
72% of the time submerging me
blindly in trivial pursult, materialism,
pre-occupations + desires (of my
parents, etc.) I'd like to be strong,
break away, but Sat. nights will
always call me out ... beautiful girls
will always strike a pining knot of pain
in me ... what I've been conditioned
to want, even if the failure is sublime,
etc... I still have never really had
suicidal thoughts that I know of.
My pain is dull + it scares me that
someday I just might stop caring
about these things that move me
now, that some day this might all be
alien to me ... ...

emphasis mine

1 p.m. Hotel Peking, Feb 18
Today we went to the summer palace. Walked on a frozen lake, saw the Peking acrobatic troupe. Thought of the day: A generalization
of this journey; historical proofs, buildings (castles, churches, palaces, war buildings, fortresses, walls, etc.) are guides for countries
to direct the thinking of their history. For me they are just that, I have tried (+ failed) to visualize the emperor walking the grounds of the
Forbidden City. [...] From the bridge, all these things just illustrate stories . . . there are buildings + places that for me recount + stand
as a sort of testimonial to my history (Granini's house, etc.) in a way that these (European + Asian) monuments for the most part can't
to anybody else (unless the building happens to parallel a life time of events for [another] individual). But I have sensed the different
perspective on these places (from my p.o.v.) by people who grew up w/ these things (+ places) ... familiarity seems to breathe a life
into them, a knowledge (true acquiring over a long period of time) of breeding, [family], becoming assimilated into the psyche ... no
longer is new stimuli latent (you'll trip much harder in a place you've never been, [than] your own room that you're accustomed to).

--Dream[25], Feb 17:
I'm surf fishing, see
large dark fish below
the surface (obvious
interpretation) reel it in, it
becomes friend (named
Fred) + walks away

--Dream 2, Feb 17: Found a leather suitcase full of money ... (in stacks, different currencies—
American, Chinese, etc.) took it to my hotel room, various [people] try to infiltrate + steal it (including
the police). Go to record store, they're playing Paul McCartney albums only available in the USSR,
it sounds good (has a red + black cover). I get a CD with 12 EPs of various bands (all 4AD) for
74 (Belgian francs, divided by 12) my hotel room is filled with steam (coming from people in the
room trying to locate the money). I take the bag + run outside, to the airport, w/ all the money in my
suitcase. I fly to L.A., [drop it off], then fly back to Bangkok.

---

[24] Assuming he is referencing our father when he writes «his choice».

[25] Brother-½ never did give much creedence to dreams, considered them «garbage collection».

a *Ssemblage*

...2nd thoughts

39

NESTOR

Feb 21 Shanghai

It's rainy outside + I'm in the dorm (large floor-to-ceiling windows overlooking the city), used to be an old Euro luxury hotel in Shanghai. [I'm] working out my funds, it's cold ... what does the future hold? I don't know why the fuck I decided to come here (to go to Lhasa). I'm already over budget, the Chinese govt told me Tibet is closed, all the Swedes took an inexpensive boat to Xiania, towards Hong Kong. This whole thing is making me [anxious]. Even if I can go, it will cost around 700 dollars (that's altogether close to 900 I didn't plan on spending). I could try to call mom in Hong Kong to get money ... god, I don't know ... only time will tell [...] the Swedes were getting to me, they're very nice + actually seem to like me (don't know why) + want my company, but I'm not used to being around people constantly. It would be nice to go to Tibet but do I want to go just so I can say I've been there? Yes, mostly. (Nepal probably will be similar + because of the large Tibetan refugee population it's easier to buy Tibetan goods in Nepal than Tibet). So here I am again, just like 2 years ago going to Inverness, but this time on a grander scale. If I turn back at Chengdu (towards Hong Kong) I will probably save at least 600-700 dollars (+ I won't have to borrow money to go to Europe (the thought gives me relief ... yah, it would be nice to go to Tibet but it seems unrealistic at this point ... why not lie + say I went[26]? It's dishonest, so what. Why lie, to be able to say I've been there? Because it will make me more important somehow ... I'll be more qualified, more well-travelled. Why don't you just wait + see how much it costs. Okay, Today I've had three cups of black coffee. The stewardess just handed us lunch [?] a box w/ 4 small plastic cakes filled w/ [?] [...] At least this plane is not a turbo prop ... oh what is the meaning of life (ha ha) have I been chosen to replace the recently deceased Dali Lama? Are they waiting for me at the airport? Will an extremely wealthy old patron feel sorry for me, say, "I went there when I was young + you should get the chance also," + give me the money ... will it be too much, will it be closed?

.unity continues its spiritual labor.
1.Gilles Deleuze,Félix Guattari. A thousand-plateaus(Capitalism and-Schizophrenia).Univ. of Minnesota Press, Minneapolis. p.6.(intro.;RHIZOME).

2.Ibid.

3.Levin,Harry. James Joyce. New directions paperback. New York,N.Y.1941.p.90.

4. A thousand plateaus.p.4

5.Ibid.p.8.

2. mock epic.
1.James Joyce. p.89.

2.Ibid. p.68.

3.Ibid. p.72.

3. body without organs.
1.Gilles Deleuze.Bergsonism. Zone Books.New York,N.Y.1988. p.113.

2.Paul De Man.The resistance--to theory.p.11.

3.A thousand plateaus. p.4.

4. sum of the parts
1. Dan Sperber,Deirdre Wilson. Relevance,communication and cognition. Harvard Univ.Press. Cambridge, Mass.1986. p.136.

2.Lucien Lévy-Bruhl. How primitives think. Princeton Univ. Press.Princeton,N.J. 1985.p.122.

«In short, the way an expression relates to a content is not by uncovering or representing it. Rather, forms of expression and forms of content communicate through a conjunction of their quanta of relative deterritorialization, each intervening, operating in the other. We may draw some general conclusions on the nature of Assemblages from this. On a first, horizontal axis, an assemblage comprises two segments, one of content, the other of expression. On the one hand it is a machinic assemblage of bodies, of actions and passions, an intermingling of bodies reacting to one another; on the other hand it is a collective assemblage of enunciation, of acts and statements, of incorporeal t r a n s f o r m a t i o n s attributed to bodies. Then on a vertical axis, the assemblage has both territorial sides, or reterritorialized sides, which stabilize it, and cutting edges of deterritorialization, which carry it away.»— Deleuze + Guattari (*A Thousand Plateaus*) as contextualized at http://5cense.com/10/flood_dream.htm

(Kevin's actual ticket from Chengdu to Lhasa)

中国民用航空客票及行李票　蓉 4192371288

[26] A favorite phrase of our stepmother (who raised us in our formative years) was «let's not + say we did.»

Nestor

'Spark of kings,

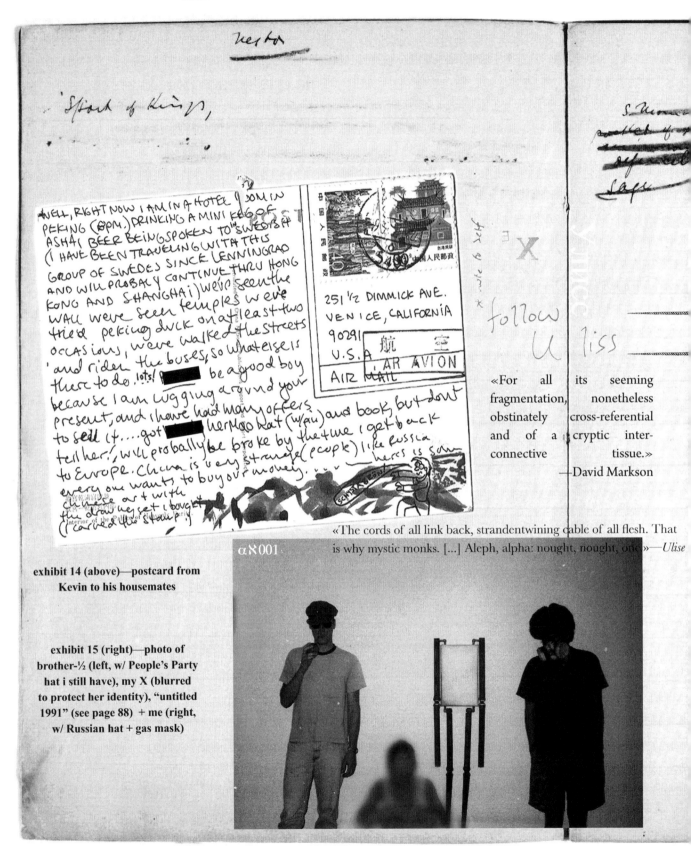

WELL, RIGHT NOW I AM IN A HOTEL I AM IN PEKING (8PM.) DRINKING A MINI KEG OF ASAHI BEER BEING SPOKEN TO" SWEDISH (I HAVE BEEN TRAVELING WITH THIS GROUP OF SWEDES SINCE LENNINGRAD AND WILL PROBABLY CONTINUE THRU HONG KONG AND SHANGHAI) we've seen the WALL we've seen temples we've tried peking duck on at least two occasions, we've walked the streets and ridden the buses, so what else is there to do, lots! ▮ be a good boy because I am lugging around your present, and I have had many offers to sell it....got ▮ her Moo hat (w/you) and book, but don't tell her!, will probably be broke by the time I get back to EUROPE. China is very strange (people) like Russia every one wants to buy our money, ... here's is som the draw I got I bought art with (carved this stone)(Interior of the Palace of Cultural Party)

251 ½ DIMMICK AVE.
VENICE, CALIFORNIA
90291
U.S.A
AIR MAIL   AR AVION
航 空

follow
Uliss

«For all its seeming fragmentation, nonetheless obstinately cross-referential and of a cryptic inter-connective tissue.»
—David Markson

«The cords of all link back, strandentwining cable of all flesh. That is why mystic monks. [...] Aleph, alpha: nought, nought, one.»—*Ulise*

α ℵ 001

exhibit 14 (above)—postcard from Kevin to his housemates

exhibit 15 (right)—photo of brother-½ (left, w/ People's Party hat i still have), my X (blurred to protect her identity), "untitled 1991" (see page 88) + me (right, w/ Russian hat + gas mask)

exhibit 16 (backdrop)—original (virtually blank) page from J. Joyce's working notebooks for the Nestor chapter of *Ulysses* (appropriated from the National Library of Ireland— http://catalogue.nli.ie/)

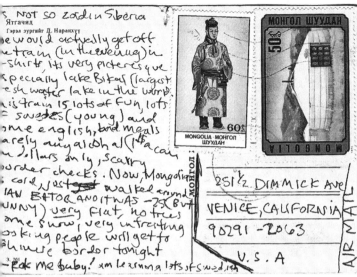

exhibit 17 (above) another postcard to his housemates

exhibit 18 (right)—letter from me to brother-½, sent to Hong Kong (found in his belongings)

exhibit 19 (below)—altered photo Kevin made for/of me playing my industrial drum kit (or a photo i took of him ... can't remember which, as whoever it is has a trash can over his head + we both had such paisley shirts).

Greetings

You are probably half-stoked and half thawed with your Jan housing open....
So how is it??? Give me the rap as we are curious as Hell as to how you are doing. Before I forget.:

DEREK
10 LEONARDO LN.
SANTA CRUZ, CA. 95064   (408) 426-9352

Oakland, CA. 94618   -2257

CAMBRIDGE, MA. 02139   -9679

MOM
Apdo #107
Ajijic, Jalisco
Mexico

Call Collect

I'm not even sure your going to get this mom is in Mexico til' may.

Hope you enjoy the tape — I sent it to Sound Choice — they are independent tapes i.e "Indies" and they produce a contact, addresses, and then people get them.

Did you get the tape I sent to L.A. before you left, I also tried to call but I think I was too late.

Well this quarter is marginal, got a Zero on my Electrodynamics midterm but am not worried as everyone got a Zero the teacher is an asshole. Also added Asian Art (needed to fill general ed. I forgot) So am following you through China and India in Book. Don't miss the Buddhist and Hindu Art in India. They really know how to sculpt girls with bodacious breasts.

Its freezing here too and actually snowed here. The only drag about living in a camper is its freezing. Oh well, write me and tell me what your doing. — I'll tell and to write you in Hong Kong too!

Think Nice thoughts.

Happy Trails
I hope you get this   — Derek

Thanx for the cards

Will I get drunk tonight at the Jiang Hotel with some other foreigners (after getting tickets? After failing to get tickets?) Will this plane crash, will I disappear into central China? (I bet no one would know where to find me, ha ha ...).

I'm flying above the clouds, over central China and it's really beautiful. I don't think it matters where I am on the map, that's just my rationalization or way of imagining the world. I [may] as well be flying home to Portland as a 12-year old boy, leaving mom and San Francisco, but the way it looks, and the way I feel makes [undecipherable] to see it as the clouds ... flying down to San Fran, the beautiful skies of California ... **it's funny how you only really have something when it's not around to have**. I never figured it out as a kid, but it's always sunny when you're above the clouds.

6:30 Flight to Lhasa from Chengdu.

Well, I got up at 4:30 ... at 5:10 I was squeezed in w/ a mob of Chinese pushing to check in (there was a rumor that the plane was overbooked). Managed to get on the plane, still dark as [it flew] above the clouds. [...] Then the tips of the Himalayas [could] be seen like islands in a sea of clouds. Now below me is the Tibetan plateau ... snow-capped peaks, the red glow of dawn ... really not as beautiful as anticipated (at least this [aerial] perspective)

Lhasa, Tibetan autonomous region

Well, I've been here 2 days and these people are really incredible. Every single Tibetan (almost) whether it be a 90-year old woman or a 2-year old boy (+ everyone in-between) that I see smiles + says hello, it's incredible. I spend [the days] grinning back to people + saying hello. The sights are incredible, beautiful old temples, incense clouding the air, Tibetans in native garb, Buddhist monks chanting, huge prayer wheels (gold covered columns about 10 feet in diameter) slowly revolving [in] a temple room visible from the cobblestone street. The hats, the clothes, the smiles, the animals, the jewelery, the small hand-held prayer wheels constantly revolving in the hands of (older) Tibetans, usually chanting + counting beads w/ the other hand. The Tibetans are constantly going to the bathroom right in the middle of the street, but somehow it seems far from disgusting, these people [are] doing what they've been doing for thousands of years and it's natural. There are more Chinese than Tibetans (Chinese look different, usually wear Chinese or western clothes + don't smile or say hello unless you want to change money). The sun is incredibly strong here + I got sunburnt today walking around. At night + in the early morning the temperature feels painfully cold (especially in the hotel room w/out heat + hot water) ... -20. During the day it varies.

I tried Yak butter tea (tastes like tea with milk in it, quite good). Saw maybe 4 (young) westerners (2 groups of Germans). Walked around a lot. It's about 6 o'clock and I'm ready to go to bed. Spent 60 RNB (13) on a fur hat, 50 on a silver prayer wheel and 90 on a flint pouch, I'm toying w/ the idea of getting a jacket to complete the Tibetan outfit. My head hurts and my back hurts. *THIS WRITING IS DONE WITH MY RIGHT HAND.*

3 : fishtailing to plateau (proteus)

Time: Mar–April 1989 / 2011
Location: Tibet—China—Hong Kong—Nepal—Delhi—Paris—L.A. / Delhi
Ideas/symbolism to incorporate: tides, evolution, primal matter, mountains, quality control, decompressing files, getting "high" ... higher, snake eating own tail
ABSTRACT: The prohecy repeats[3] (to the 3rd power) ... said Homer: "That proteus made, by which he knew / His brother's death; and then doth show / How with Calypso lived the sire / of his youngest guest. The wooers conspire ..." We also remember our drunk father pulling our T.V. to the ground Reaching the peak (or plateau?) our hero bids a hastey retreat home, tale between legs, arriving w/ no fanfare (by design). Who was it said he renounced destination to keep from getting lost? Re-assembly instructions are sent scrambling home to self to guide him in reconstructing at least a remote semblance of what had been bsent all these years. Ist he must get to the sorce of the iconic fish smell...

[OBJ]

Page Two
Press Release, White
11/15/90

For Kevin White, objects have their own rules; they are indicators with fields of influence and have ways in which they can and should be approached. Their design indicates a level of reverence; form and function; worth and historical presence. The packaging elements, although usually disposable, point to an interior fragility and susceptibility to damage; objects are therefore only complete when they retain their packaging assembly. Just as clothing and accessories play a key role in one's outward projection, the packaging of an object tells of what it covers and protects. Unlike the usual consumer's objects, White's objects retain their packaging as built-in elements. The forms of these objects are of retention, allud to a precious element once present in the piece, inviting the viewers to project their bodies into the absent form. The non-existent focus around which these forms are created is presented as the auto-biographical. Its perception and accessibility are denied by the use of assorted visual puns and inversions. The negative space defined is that of an inverse flow, or a flow that goes in more than one direction at a time. This flow occurs in the form, but is subordinated by the flow of the aperture(s) built into the object; solid metal nuclei which demand a neutrality in the rest of the form; a figure dominating a field; a figure serving a field.

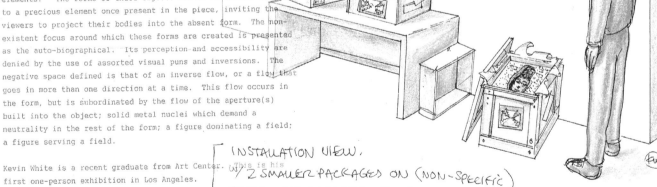

Kevin White is a recent graduate from Art Center. This is his first one-person exhibition in Los Angeles.

The Marc Richards Gallery is located at 2114 Monica. Gallery hours are Tuesday through Sat to 5:00pm. A reception for the artists will take place on Thursday, November 29 from 6:00 to 9:00pm. For further information, please call the gallery at

\# \# \# \#
11/15/90
for immediate release

INSTALLATION VIEW.
W/ 2 SMALLER PACKAGES ON (NON-SPECIFIC)
BASIC - NON DESCRIPT TABLE.

PACKAGES TO BE SENT TO LOCATION, OPENED AND
DISPLAYED

X — THESE PIECES (BY KEVIN WHITE) HAVE TO DO WITH (THE CONCEPT) OF)
FORGERY AND THE COMODIFICATION OF RELIGOUS OBJECTS FROM OTHER
COUNTRIES (THERE RELATIVE VALUE INDICATED BY THE VALUE AND
LABOR INTENSIVNESS OF THEIR FREIGHT PACKAGING.

exhibit 20—sketch (1 of 3) of freight packaging installation (w/ text from subsequent press release)

HANDLE WITH CARE

PACKAGE (TO BE OPENED AND DISPLAYED ON TABLE (OR DESK) CONTAINING (FAKE) SMALL (FRAGMENTS) OF 1500 YEAR OLD SHIVA SCULPTURE.

CARDBOARD.

POLY FOAM

ENVELOPES (CONTAINING DOCUMENTATION)

6"

14"

8"

BRONZE SCULPTURAL FRAGMENTS (SHRINK WRAPPED ONTO BOARD)

PACKAGE (TO BE OPENED AND DISPLAYED ON TABLE (OR DESK) CONTAINING (FAKE) POTTERY FRAGMENTS

REPLICA OF POTTERY FRAGMENT WRAPPED IN PLASTIC.

(GREY) SOLID FOAM.

POLAROID OF OBJECT.

8"

CARDBOARD BOX W/STICKERS AND STAMPS.

13"

14"

1 of 3

exhibit 21—sketch (2 of 3) of freight packaging installation (above) + detail 3 (below)

CRATE (TO BE OPENED AND SHOWN AS DRAWN, ON THE FLOOR) CONTAINING EXACT FORGERY OF BLACK STONE HEAD OF PARVAATI (LIFE SIZE, 10TH CENT.

. OF 3.

FRAGILE

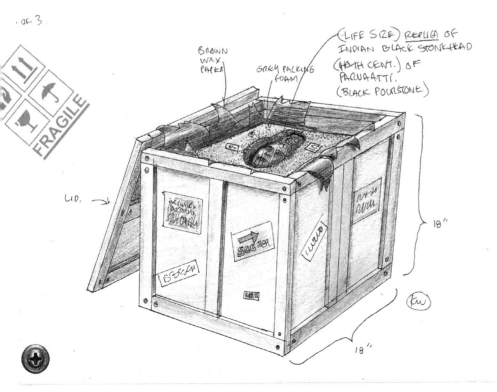

BROWN WAX PAPER

GREY PACKING FOAM

(LIFE SIZE) REPLICA OF INDIAN BLACK STONE HEAD (10TH CENT.) OF PARVAATTI. (BLACK POURSTONE)

LID.

18"

18"

.cOMpromising posture

"They don't want me to" he said calmly. The grey smoke of his cigarette forms a perfect "T" like the automatic movements of Catholic priests. "They don't want me to, or I don't want to, ... I don't know... guess I like the feeling of struggle." He dragged on his cigarette, now staring me [right] in the eyes. "I mean to give in, and that's just what it is, giving in—would be to die, to turn into one of these zombies that love their jobs."[27] With this, his mind trailed off. He turned and looked out the window at the greyest landscape imaginable. A stretch of grey beach, [unintelligible], clouds, fog, rain, glamorous 70s era luxury mobiles with their bellies rusting right off. Crabgrass grows right out of the concrete. Their [sic] is a slime on the potholed streets, as if the fisherman have just finished dragging a

non-existent abundance of flounder down the street, the proud citizens, long since done congratulating them, have gone inside their [mustard-colored] one-bedrooms. Rust-filled tap water doesn't succeed in prying rejected fishsticks from their last gasp. The smell of fish [permeates] the house and the streets, thru a range of experience. Both states of fish represent the extremes, the [polewick?] from which this community makes its existence.

(I. line that forms meaning
TRUTH COMES FROM STRUCTURE
A Reversal of entropy.
please pay at the second window
god, this sucks!
It's a start.

«Gaze. Belly without blemish. [...] In a Greek watercloset, he breathed his last: euthanasia. [...] They are coming, waves.»—*Ulysses*

"More than anything it has to do with some obscure notion of posturing. [Try] to position yourself in a way that is both competitive and self-serving."
"Come now, no need to be so—"
"Yes there is, I am tired of it. I want to get me leg up and move on."
"Don't you think that's rather dishonest."
"Honesty doesn't apply when one is concerned with the notion of self."
"So young, so bitter..."
"Okay, I guess I could be more, I don't know, regular, if I took a more Christian approach, a more puritanical approach. Do you think America's early religious story had anything to do with the development of a society [in synch] with the notion of justice, sin, transgression and betterment of self (to be closer to god?!)"
"Blah, blah, blah.")

---

[27] Brother-½ was never 1 to compromise himself.

from the lost manUscripts

He slows now, [glaring] at him standing in his space, [undecipherable...], mimicking his movements, playfully sparing with him.

"Come on chap, you know better than to start me off with that line. I came here for help actually."

"Yeah, I heard, pa's been too long, but don't [deprive?] off, [steadfast? ... hard to read] son. And don't think anything other than that your father has the ability to protect and fend for himself.

[Stu], the old janitor [stands] near the boiler, holding the grey plastic phone in his hands like it was a plate of money. "I'm sorry your dad's missing kid, really, I really [am]. Hey listen, I gotta go, but you keep your hopes up, yeah? Do it [for your dad]."

"Whatever you say old man."

"Listen kid, all I know is that yesterday, when we were cleaning out the desks in your room 205m we found these manuscripts ..."

XX XX XXX X XXXXX XXXXXXX XXXXX XX XXX X XX XXXXXXXX XX XXX X XXXX

... the «FISH» story (recovered from Kevin's journal) ends there, so not sure which manuscripts the janitor was referring to. Perhaps consider it to be [this] ... bringing us up to speed to where we stand ... brother-½ has reached Tibet, the plateaued apex of his journey. In Joseph Campbell's scheme of things, he's crossed the **threshold** ... the point of no return. Or maybe he's in the figurative «belly of the whale». In Joyce's book, all our Telemachean hero does is mope around down along the Sandymount strand + piss behind a rock.

In Homer's book, Telemachus learns more about his father—how he master-minded the infamous Trojan Horse, etc. Thru **Proteus**, we learn that Ulysses is alive, kicking it w/ Calypso on her island ... which, if Ulysses stands for our dead dad, U could say he's not in such a bad place.

Proteus (a.k.a. 'the old man of the sea') was a shape-shifting god of rivers + bodies of water, of «elusive sea change». Nowadays, proteus is a bacteria found in the intestines of animals ... perhaps why Joyce chose **green** for color + **primal matter** for meaning[28] in the Proteus episode (3) of *Ulysses*. For symbols he picks: *tide, world, moon, evolution + metamorphosis*. In Kevin's **SSES** thesis (right), he tells the story of some all-American war hero type who snaps + slices up his wife, then waits in a rain so sustained + long that it strips «all the plant life of [chlorophyll].»

I love thee? Oh my dear little one let me count the ways;

He graduated from his high school at the top of his class. He was voted twice to the All-American football team. After high school he went on to attend Harvard, where he recieved his M.B.A. in Political Science (with Cum Laude distinction). He passed up an inviting offer to run for office so that he could join the Army. A veteran of over forty mission, he recieved the Congressional medal of honor and the Purple Heart. He returned state-side, married his High School sweetheart, and successfully ran for governor. He fathered three healthy boys who went on, later in life, to pursue careers in politics, following in their father's footsteps. He was elected to the Senate one week before his fiftieth birthday. He came home early from the Senate house one rainy afternoon and sliced up his wife into little cubes with a razor. He then used these cubes to build a fifth wall in his bedroom. He then hid behind this wall wearing his Army fatiques, and clutching the phone. He waited desperately for her to call and take him away from all this...the rain poured down incessantly...it was connected to his actions.. only when his life got this out of hand did these things start to happen, those natural events that could be termed; impossible. It was simply unnatural, for the rain to come down for four months straight. Hard, driving rain. So hard that the fog looked more like steam (because of the powerful force of the rain, burning the concrete, eating the paint off the car, stripping all the plant life of chlorophil,

...A Joyce scholar and expert on the background of Ulysses, A. Walton Litz of Princeton , has suggested that the active sexual life of the Joyces ceased around this period (Zurich, 1917).[1] As Joyce plunged deeper and deeper into his own erotic imagination, he lowered, as he said to Stanislaus in 1906, "a bucket into my own soul's well, sexual department", and everything he drew up he put into ULYSSES. The novel changed course (according to Litz) between 1917 and 1920, sharply turning away from naturalism and heading into the surreal phantasmagoria of the brothel scene in which every form of sexual perversion whirls past. It seems likley that there was nothing left- from that department- for Nora. In this light, Joyce's furtive correspondence with Dr. Kaempffer, like the 1909 correspondence with Nora, looks like yet another warm up exercise for ULYSSES.

- pp.152, <u>NORA</u> , Brenda Maddox,Miffen Co.,Boston. 1988. [1] from; A.Walton Litz, THE ART OF JAMES JOYCE,and inter. with BM, April 2, 1985

---

[28] Per the Linati schema.

<<It's a HARD RAIN's a gonna fall>>

causing all household pets to go crazy...). Be-
-cause of the rains, his sons did not call. He
was constantly pushing redial, constantly con-
-nected to the phone, never, not even for a sec-
-ond, was he out of range of the phone. Even the
smallest click! Resolution. Shift. Line open. An
incredible human presence ushered in by a click.
The harbinger of good fortune. Click...Scratch..
Click...She is there. She is turning away from
the phone now. She is putting her earring back
on, grabbing her purse, heading for the door.

[SHE;is going to meet HIM;]

..........so they can escape together, to Rio.
He is all to aware of his body rotting. He is
with his sons, in a model T, cruising the well
of the Grand Canyon. The Grand Canyon, halcyon [29]
days of youth. Halcyon daze. He is squeezing the
life out of t...
out of him. "...
and bite you"...
-board sheets...
Runner only does...
-sin, immortal...
SQUISH! Peeeeel...
insignificant blo...
resting on the d...
immortality befor...
new day. for the...
and other beige...
-toon. Thats rig...
Do not worry no...
a man. Birthday...
-es down in bolt...
it in. It stains...

"I believe I told you
that my book is a modern
ODYSSEY. Every episode in
it corresponds to an adven-
-ture of ULYSSES. I am now
writing the "Lestrygonians"
episode, which corresponds
to the adventure of Ulysses
with the cannibals. My hero
is going to lunch. But there
is a seduction motive in
the Odyssey, the cannibal
king's daughter. Seduct-
-ion appears in my book as
women's silk petticoats
hanging in a shop window.
The words through which I

PROTEUS   (bleu cheese + burgungy)   **JAMES**

with the good, out with the bad. Out with the bad, in with
the good. In with the bad out with the good. Full tank of
gas. Bugs and Will E. come to talk him out of it. They do
not seem to mind that he has always ignored them. They
are so forgiving. They are not just out to boost rat-
-ings.
LOW-CAL (LOH-KAL) adj. (informal) Having very few calor-
ies. Hardly any. He laughs. He is everywhere; Cal-cal...
she'll get a kick out of it. They all will! Those cock
sucking bastards. Those fucking shit eating motherFUCKERS!
HEARTLESS FUCKERS!!!
[a blue pencil will stand in at this point for a pen or pencil]

     They caught up to me (will..). X..."I could love
you, I do not need six months, I have forty years exper-
-ience in these matters...". "No sir, I cannot on such sh-
-ort notice, you are a kind sir, but I hardly know you."

     Scintillant still air, circumambient. Gold light
streams in through the stain glass above the threshold.
The musty air smells of ten years of piano lessons in the
absence of youth. The unused portions of the house faintly
echo with childrens voices. Unused portions. A jar of mayo-
-naise stands alone on it's shelf. Ten year old cremed
spinach blows out of the airduct under the derilict kitch-
-en table. Two containers of (Vasoline intensive care)
hand cream and a role of toilet paper, selfconciously
stand around in a sparse room, near assorted porno mags.
This room is the only one free of dust and cobwebs. The
Christmas presents are under the bed. They are huge, and
they are plentiful. When he leaves you alone on a Sunday
afternoon sneak in and open them, leave doors open and
tip-toe, listen for the faint sound of a shutting car
door, of keys clicking together. Fee-Fi-Fo-Fum, I smell
my own foul stench. I notice not, the television fail-
-ing to stand still under my weight. It falls, I stumble.
During a shower, sneak down the hall naked to get a brew-
-ski. I do not think he even notices me. I am disgusted,

(margin numbers: 30, 31, 32)

* A poor player, that struts and frets
his hour upon the stage and then is
heard no more. It is a tale told by an
idiot, full of sound and fury".   -W.
Shakespear (MAC BETH)
ABSENCE. The state of being away 2.
The time during which one is away 3.
The condition of not having needed or
desired; lack

33

     The carriage climbed more
slowly the hill of Rutland Square.
Rattle his bones. Over the stones.
Only a pauper. Nobody owns.
In the midst of life, Martin
Cunningham said.
    - But worst of all, Mr. Power
said, is the man who takes his own
life.
    - Martin Cunningham drew out
his watch briskly, caughed and put it
back.
    - The greatest disgrace to have
in a family, Mr. Power added.
    - Temporary insanity of
course, Martin Cunningham said said
decisevly, we must take a charitable
view of it.
    - They say a man who does it is
a coward, Mr. Dedalus said.
    - It is not for us to judge,
Martin Cunningham said.
    Mr. Bloom, about to speak,
closed his lips again. Martin
Cunningham's large eyes. Looking
away now. Sympathetic human man
he is. Intelligent. Like Shakespear's
face. Always a good word to say.
They have no mercy on that here or
infanticide. Refuse Christian burial,
they used to drive a stake of wood through
his heart in the grave. As if it was not already
broken

    - J. Joyce.
. Random House, NY
    1934..pp

---

[29] GENUS: *Halcyon*, family *Alcedinidae*: a mythical
species of Asian kingfisher w/ brightly colored
ploomage, said by ancient writers to breed in a nest
floating at sea during the winter solstice, charming the
wind + waves into calm. ORIGIN: late Middle English
(in the mythological sense): via Latin from the Greek
alkuōn 'kingfisher' (also *halkuōn*, by association w/
hals 'sea' + *kuōn* 'conceiving').

[30] I claim full responsibility for the «cremed spinach
[blowing] out of the airduct». I used to hate vegetables
+ would hide them behind the refrigerator, or yes, i
would lift the heating vent grate + dump my soggy
veggies down there ... until the day our fat calico cat
named Miki-moto sniffed them out ...

[31] «Fee-Fi-Fo-Fum» is something our father used to sing
to us in his more sober, playful moments ... followed by
«I smell the blood of an English man.» In the Proteus section of
Ulysses, Joyce has Dedalus think:
«I'm the bloody well gigant rolls all
them bloody well boulders, bones
for my steppingstones. Feefawfum. I
zmellz de bloodz oldz an Iridzman.»

[32] While i never saw our father
walking around naked in search of
brewskis, i can vouch for the falling
television ... 1 night our father
came home late + we were still up
watching S.N.L. He attempted to
make conversation w/ us, but was
so drunk he couldn't stand, so he
grabbed onto the T.V. for support +
pulled it to the ground. At the time i
didn't even know what being drunk
meant, i just thought that was our
father's natural state.

[33] See also http://www.5cense.
com/13/rejoyce.htm: «... Bloom +
a couple of other guys (including
Stephen's father, Simon Dedalus)
travel by coach to the funeral of
Paddy Dignam, who essentially
died of drunkenness (like our own
father ... so the correspondence is
obvious here). We find out that
Bloom's son Rudy died + that his
father commit suicide (doubly
corresponding) ... which becomes a sensitive issue as the 4 men
debate suicide. Mr. Power (who doesn't know Bloom's father
commit suicide) is the most critical + judgmental [... at which
point we quote the same passage brother-½ quotes above. Then we
go on:] Through Bloom's parallel stream of conscious thinking,
more is revealed about his father's suicide in bits: *The afternoon
of the inquest The redlabeled bottle on the table. The room in the hotel
with hunting pictures. Stuffy it was.* [...] *V*erdict: overdose. Death by
misadventure. [...] *No more pain. Wake no more. Nobody owns.*»

Prophase (middle)

Prophase (late)

Anaphase

Telophase

**exhibit 22 (L)—mitosis in animal cells. Light
chromosomes of paternal origin.**

March 3 [1989] - Chengdu, Hotel Jiujang

Well, I got in to a dorm room, sharing it w/ an Australian martial arts instructor, mustache, flowered [Hawaiian shirt], muskateer boots, etc. We played snooker up on the 9th floor + were challenged by some locals ... a crowd gathered + I managed to make two lucky shots + we won. We should have left, but they challenged us again + barely beat us [+ then another] game they barely won. We refused to pay the whole sum + things started getting ugly ... thought I was going to see one of those 'martial arts instructors fighting Chinese thugs' story come to life, but managed to get out [unscathed]. Next morning paid top dollar for my original plane ticket to [Bwuillin?] [...] now it's 3:30 a.m., there's a Russian movie on T.V. in Chinese. I'm in bed, listening to the Cocteau Twins, imagining a future—on the beach in Carmel, w/ a woman, someone I love, a relationship that's successful in all the ways I've always imagined [...] a transitory feeling, **a search for some kind of substance, knowing that achieving it would be the worst thing** [...] I realize [this] kind of contentedness is blind, the only real state is aloneness (existential). [...] my walkman is broken, warped sound [...] where was I? Oh yeah, life sucks, but I don't have the strength to end it. ... not really. There is definitely something to live for (to have a good image in the eyes of others) heh heh, or how about: don't let others see your weakness, what will they say behind your back, yea Kevin, if you're going to make some art you better not do any pathos ... it's out of style, rationalize it, just like you should do with your life, your down outlook on life is only doing just that, dragging you down ... bullshit, dragging anywhere, to live life without really questioning it is fucking blind, I assume that artists have these feelings (everyone does) but have wasted it and presented in a format that both conceals and reveals itself at the corners.

9:30 AM the Lobby, Chengdu

Waiting for the bus to plane. [...] I do miss home, but I know when I get there I will miss where I am now. Maybe I just want things to speed up, maybe it's easier to always want to be where you're not. I'm feeling sick + run down, I've got some kind of rash on my hand, my nose is full of junk, my hair keeps going in my eyes, my sinuses are clogged, my feet are cold + I know its going to be hot, humid + miserable in Guillin [...] when I get to Hong Kong I won't get into the hostel, it will cost me a hundred dollars to get a place to sleep. No Visa Card will be there, the Nepalese office will be closed ...

It's been a long time since I've been stoned. The last time was in Amsterdam well over a month ago w/ that Australian couple, I want to feel really high right now + not be paranoid. I want to be high here in this Chinese hotel + not feel self-conscious at all. I want to be completely healthy. I want to be at Granny Nanny's house w/ no one there ... well, it would be nice to be at Granny Nee's house w/ [J, R, W, K, G, D], my Swedish friends, [J, C], Derek, [S, M + T]—all of us at Granny' Nee's house (w/ no one else around, having a summer BBQ party, lounging by the pool, music playing, warm evening, soft talk of going to a concert or a movie, everybody happy ... I'm sitting there watching them, in the pool floating, feeling content, thinking that 10-year old Kevin on summer vacation at Granny's house would be happy w/ the way I grew up; that life is good + I've lived a full life ... back to reality, the reality that makes my feet feel cold, my head ache, my nose drip + my back ache. If I had a really good job in L.A. I would be happy, if I was earning back all the guilt I've spent ...

Fantasy Scenario #000001: [LEFT]

[34,35] Kevin + i are the only ones appearing 2x in the above fantasized aerial sketch of our grandmother's house. Besides lounging in + around the pool, he has us both playing soccer on the lawn (left). I am also the only blood relative in the scenario.

It had been half a year since he left + as the plane taxied into familiarity, he could feel the anxiety creeping over him. The duration (that was the journey) was now just a division. Small objects acting as indicators, proof of a history, [relied] on certain beliefs. He had slipped back to where he started. Had anything changed? Before he could fret too much over it he saw her.

She (the stewardess) dropped the fork in his lap + picked it up, gently touching his penis as she did. She was quite aware of this + smiled at him + [continued] on. As he watched her, he thought to himself that she [moved] in the world in an unusual way. She seemed to be some [scribbled out...]

I can never be a writer, my use of words is weak + understanding of language is lame ... how can I say, describe a woman, the one that I am imagining. A woman, a girl like the girl in Zubreski point. One that functions well enough in the (real) world ... she's so attractive (sexy) that even if she is out of touch with reality, others will make sure she is not hurt. She makes me feel anxious. Partly because I don't feel I deserve her full attention (love) + partially because I am aware of this.

I'm 14 on my way to spend summer vacation at Granny Nanny's, flying on a hot summer day from Portland to San Francisco. I've never felt happier. A whole summer in California, at lake Tahoe w/ cousins [...] Tones on Tail, psychedelic shirt, red 67 bug, sunny summer day in L.A., I'm stoned, driving to Westwood, the great escape, every weekend without exception. I need to be with [W] + the others, need to be around people who I've shared experiences with. People who share my sensibilities, preferences. I feel like the more I go in the direction of contentness (happiness) the worse it seems to drag along uneasiness, nausea + anxiety, the two are inseparable. Why do I live my life this way? Why would I want to live anyway else? God, I'm wasting my life, there's no place I'd rather be. Consider determinism, I have no choice but to live this life, no comfort in determinism. [illegible] buying me mixed drinks. [illegible] didn't hash smoke. Sleeping hippies ... .

Somewhere on the other side of the world, Ronald Wilson Reagan, an old man, sits at a desk in a not-quite moved into office in Century City. With a pen + a legal pad in front of him, he tries to collect his thoughts, to start his autobiography. News (stories) make my life less important. They create (+ sustain) the illusion that there is a vast world out there full of people, living interesting lives, people I can't + might never see, I continue to watch + read the news, sometimes imagine there really is a man named Ronald Reagan, not just light pixels or ink on paper. Someone who has memories of a small boy at a [swimming] hole, [...] her gaze turns into a laugh, then he realizes that she is laughing at him, everyone is laughing at him, she's pointing at his (small) erection clearly visible because of his wet shorts, the memory makes him uneasy, he reaches for a drink, "I showed them".

The pursuit of usual thought ... ideas which seem to twist new meaning out of the question of existence. Gimmicks, patterns, 'natural' hallucinations. Why not resort to chemicals to produce the same results, quicker, more powerful, longer duration, the governing factors of the psyche, cry rape, warn of a coup, loss of self, unsufferable guilt, losing touch w/ reality ... life's hard enough w/out something else occupying your mind. An understanding that my lifestyle isn't in for any great change. Want to feel [real] fear and trepidation? Think about your money situation. Who controls who? Is money the chief of all your physical needs, is that the real governing force in your mind, should it be? Can't think w/out food, someone put me on a 'life support' machine, I want to devote all of me to thinking (not about sensuality, survival) ... back at Zig Zag [36] ...Indian Summer, hot, dry, still, ... shorts, cold lunches, motorcycles + gasoline ... piney cedar + stain, the rough interiors of the unfinished 'mountain cabin' ... a long walk into the forest ... explorers, pioneers ... Zig Zag store ... candy ... posters on our walls ... Chinese guy up the aisle looks + talks like a rodent, his little hands, adding to his heated explanation, pulling the food to his little rodential face.

It feels better to go south than north (Portland > S.F, S.F. > L.A, Chegdu > Guilin). No one ever promised I would have tomorrow (to continue) so how could I complain (in fact, be upset) if the plane dropped like a rock now ... my feet are really cold (as usual). [...] The pilot seems to be having trouble flying the plane ... last words ... here we go ... bye ... we're going down ... [36]

This whole time he thought Ian Curtis was saying «a LONELY GIRL won't set you free ... so you say»,

March 15 Youth Hostel, Hong Kong Island 10:50 PM   but really he says: «a LOADED GUN won't set you free...»

I just walked thru the darkness up the long road to the hostel. Since I've been in Hong Kong or even since the last few weeks, I haven't noticed (appreciated) one beautiful thing (e.g. a young woman's face, the city at night, etc.). In Europe, as lonely as I was (and still am) I was moved by beautiful women in train stations, castles shrouded in mist, snow-capped peaks in the morning ... this awareness seemed to allow me to laugh at myself, at my obsessive thoughts, materialism, my inability to relax, my need for tension, to stay within the 'physical' world. Inability to lose myself in my oceanic world, meditative tranquility. I once told myself that I'd rather be dead than to be lost permanently in the 'present' physical 'existence'. But the scary thing is I don't realize when I am[37]. My objective view, the overall view (birds eye view) comes in moments of inwardness, the oceanic feeling. Money + all it encompasses seems to be a big threat to my ability to relax. Maybe I was conditioned from an early age to worry about things like money, things i wish I could lose that I need.

---

[36] Zig Zag village is near Mt. Hood, OR where we spent most weekends as kids.

[37] As we edit this, just learned of the death of Phillip S. Hoffman, who reminded me of brother- ½ in many ways ... even before *the way* he died.

Kevin sent me a letter from Hong Kong. The 1st few pages he summarizes his trip, giving pretty much the same detail as the journal entries. When he gets to Tibet he says: «I could go into the country (+ a description thereof) and how incredible the people are but there's not enough paper in this book.»

While he was often prone to **exagerration**, what he says on the 3rd page (right) about Tibet being closed right after he left was true. Per http://en.wikipedia.org/wiki/1987%E2%80%9389_Tibetan_unrest:

- March 6—Riots spread to the center of Lhasa. Chinese stores were wrecked and as a result a state of emergency was called. This enlarged the power of Chinese authorities.
- March 7—All foreigners including journalists were evacuated. This signified an end to the provision of information to the rest of the world on the riots. Five people died in two days according to official sources. However, Tang Daxian, a former Chinese journalist present in Lhasa during that period, claims 387 civilians plus 82 religious people have been killed, and 721 people have been injured, according to a report he saw from Public Security Bureau.
- April 15—China's former Secretary-General (until 1987), Hu Yaobang died. Hu was a supporter of the withdrawal of the Chinese army from Tibet and his death led to a student protest in Beijing. The Tiananmen Square protests a few months later on June 4, 1989 was crushed.

The letter continues on the next page where he gives an encouraging critique of a cassette i sent him (that used to be my thing—making music on a 4-track).

He ends by saying «you know sometimes on this trip I think that I could write a whole book for you (and [my X]) if you're going to come this way—on the do's and don'ts ... if you are, I will sit down w/ you and do just that.»

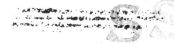

[left is a postcard he sent to our mom from Nepal]

Meanwhile, back on the ranch (from my own dream journal):

April 4, 1989 – Santa Cruz, CA

I broke Miles' ski that i borrowed. We were at Boreal + it was all rocks. Then we were at [X's] house w/ a bunch of people + I didn't like eating so i went to look for a new ski at the mall. I was still barefoot + had the broken ski + used it like a blind man's cane until i saw 2 real blind men + was embarrassed.

The mall was full of snobby uptight people. 3 ladies were wearing furs so i asked if they were wearing dead animals on their backs. They said it was synthetic + asked if i wanted to buy 1. Embarrassed again.

Then I was walking w/ Kevin in Axixic. This group of gypsy guys threw something at us w/ the intent that we'd lift our arms to catch it + then they would grab what was in our pockets. They didn't get me, but they all jumped on Kevin + started wailing on him + someone threw his wallet but i intercepted it + ran for miles, purposely not to our house, but these other people's house where i hid the wallet so we could get it later.

I took an aerial tram back + the gypsy guys recognized me + started following underneath. I got off + was suddenly a «family member» w/ a normal family. We walked to our Volvo + the «father» insisted on driving. They were my family, but i didn't know them + didn't know what my role was (father, son or ???).

«My consubstantial father's voice. Did you see anything of your artist brother Stephen lately? No? Sure he's not down in …

exhibit 23 (archived at http://calamaripress.com/Music/music.htm)

My walkman is broken + they can't fix it. I might not get my $600 before I leave. I'm not going to have enough money to finish my trip. The meal I'm eating is costing [too much]. I won't be able to pay off the 600 when I get home. I won't be able to drive my car w/o insurance. I spent too much money sending the package home. I'm growing old + have never had a serious relationship. This next sentence won't fit on this line. I won't have any ideas for new art works. I won't find a place to stay in New Delhi. I should really go to Calcutta. [They're] not going to have my $600 by friday afternoon. I won't make it back to the hostel before it closes. The oil in the food I ate is going to hurt my body. [...] I won't be able to stay all April in Europe. I won't be able to afford to go to London. Unless I relax I will get an ulcer + die. Why worry about things you can't change. What if I didn't have the comfortable life I do. What if I worried so much I forgot to enjoy my life ... taking care of business is one thing, but not the only thing ... ...

"Collection ot travel photos taped end to end ... photos at angles to eachother ..."

7:06 AM Tami Hotel, Khatmandu [SIC], Mar 18

In Hong Kong I got everything in order, [... tickets, money, mail, etc.] We flew over Laos in the evening. The sunset was in front of us, there was a thunderstorm going on. Scattered everywhere in the dark jungle below I could see forest fires (rings of fire) ... quite amazing. We then descended thru the storm, the roughest landing I've ever been thru to land in Dakha (Bangladesh) where we stayed on the runway for an hour before flying to Khatmandu. Arrived in KTM, haggled with some locals (managed to avoid declaring my electric gadgets), got a taxi, staying at a $2 (each) hotel. I am going to try and pick up the BBC. [Followed by the page below:]

I run down from the Tibetan restaurant (leaving the 2 Swedish rastas) to the bus. Sit in front next to 3 complete stoners from England. Sit + eat the last cake I have just because. The British guy next to me is mangy + a little out of it. He proceeds to eat a handful of valiums ("you can buy them in the fucking stores here") + [takes a] big bite of a brick of hash ("after you've smoked as much hash as we have, it doesn't affect you that much"), a swig or 2 of beer + many hits off his pipe full of weed. So next thing I know I'm on the night bus thru the Nepalese countryside (very beautiful) a little stoned, sitting next to some British hippies who are very stoned. They start acting like vegetables, smoking cigarettes until they burn down to their fingers, stumbling around dazed on the bus, completely incoherent, asking the non-English speaking attendant (loudly) if this is their stop. After 8 hours we get off in Pokhara, the stoners taking hits off their pipes, stumbling to the lake, I follow the Danish couple (college students from Copenhagen) up to a small hotel, eat + sleep for a few hours, then get on my way.

March 26 (easter Sunday)(Jeff's b-day) 1 pm
Annapurna base camp, elev. 4500 meters

Well here I am, after 5 days of about 10 hours a day walking (up + down many thousands of meters). I'm at the Annapurna Sanctuary. After Chomrong, me + the 2 Norwegian guys headed up towards heuku, one guy got sick, so I continued on reaching the cave known as Hinku around 6 pm. Spent the night in the cave (dark, cold, nice Nepalese guy lived there, ate some daal). Got up at 5:30 to clear the avalanche area, made it to Machapuchare base camp around 4 pm + Annapurna around 11. The view is incredible. Feel very melancholy, alone. It's still sunny out but getting cloudy. Extremely cold in the room, no heat. This is going to be a cold night. Think I will sleep w/ all

my clothes on. Oh yeah, made a resolution today to change my life, start respecting, trusting + loving people (including my family, who I've neglected for years, friends, etc). So there you have it.

March 28 Khurdi Ghar, Nepal

[...] I'm worrying now about I don't know what. One thing's for sure as long as you have money the locals will make you feel welcome ... expressing their disgust under their breath in a foreign tongue.

A false start, a failed day or realistic restraint. This trip has gone for nearly 3 months on the calendar, but not on the rings that layer away from my beginning ... A CHANGE OF PACE, relieved to be alone, relieved to not have to deal w/ people + reality. Now I'm old + I want more. **The worst part is that the voice is still contained within my cranium** ... it originates and resonates there. I guess I've always wished that I would lose awareness of that. Why bother to stay, I'm only doing it to add to my resume.

6:35 am single room, Dr. Square lodge Khatmandu

After spending a lazy day in Chomrung (stoned), I got up the next day, [paid] my bill + [headed] down the mountain, met the English guy (Stephen) on the trail. After a few hours the trail started getting very steep. I was sore + tired, a huge storm came, it started thundering + raining ... then fierce hail for an hour as we ran up a hill, down the other side, thru another valley (for a few hours) down a huge hill to the end. Nobody to pick us up on the road ... walked at least 10k more on the road, got into Pokhara around 8 PM, extremely sore, feet bleeding, can barely move. Managed to get the back corner seat on a 2nd class bus to Khatmandu. Hell ride, didn't sleep ... crawled to hotel (SR square), welcome the food here (excellent + cheap). Me + Stephen ran into Joakim ... it seems he's losing it acts kinda weird, spent all his money. Next day buy a statue, see a large demonstration, buy ticket to Delhi.

April Fools Day Khatmandu

Where do I start. The word for today is <u>teetology</u>[38]. Spread it on, as the smell (of remorse, guilt, loss, introversion, loneliness, death).

—I'm a Ralph Lauren (adv) man, tan, strong build, khaki pants, leather jacket, big black Tachymeter watch, manicured nails, slight beard growth, safari boots, walking thru the third world, an explorer.

—I'm a rockstar in cognito (of my favorite band at the time, usually Cocteau Twins) walking around, am recognized (barely) by an ardent fan (beautiful female), I act jaded + disheveled.

—I'm a young graduate student in art, smart, talented + w/ a comfortable life (not much work, lots of travel, nice apartment, car, lots of friends), interesting past, fairly good looking, tall, healthy, fashionable, alone on a tour of Asia (finishing up) a young man who brings the loneliness upon himself with his self-pity + aversion to fantasizing (replacing reality).

I'm in a room that is 8x6 feet whitewashed plaster walls roof thatched with ratan, small wooden cot, table, window, one light that just went out as I wrote the word light, coincidence? Maybe, okay, it just went back on so I will forget about it, small indentation in the wall (w/ my bronze vishnu statue).[39]

—can hear babies crying, young boys + women speaking dramatically in Hindi. Birds, distant motorcycles, woman shouting (talking?) washing clothes, pigeons cooing.

—smell dust (faint smell of hashish).

---

[38] Did he mean teleology, or tautology?

[39] The statue used as the mold to make the piece shown on page 35.

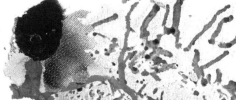

—feel good (took a huge shit recently), also shaved off my "beard".

—see my body (shoulders down) or what I assume is my body, writing this, lying on a bed, feet up by the small window.

—feel mildly content, relaxed, not anxiety-ridden. Wish my laundry would get here, will meet Joakim at 4 pm for lunch, hope I have enough money. Now hear Indian music on the radio.

[...]

—just finished reading over this whole journal for the first time + it's OK ... how's that for ineffective. Guns + Roses (Welcome to the Jungle) is playing now on the radio instead of Indian music, the old lady (Indian) washing her clothes decided to liven up now ... now she's drying her hands on the shawl wrapped around her big body, as the guitar solo begins. She reaches into her bosom for the syringe, takes one end of the clothes line ... maybe today I should only think evil demented thoughts, a hard thing to do when my pen is not working so well. I'm going to stop writing now because it's boring me.

9:54 PM April 2 DR Square Lodge, Khatmandu

I'm lying here alone in my room reading *Zen + the Art of Motorcycle Maintenance*. Someone is practicing the flute, the BBC News (radio) is playing somewhere outside ... talking about the present tensions between India + Nepal (there's talk of serious confrontation, king of Nepal sent 50,000 troops to Indian border, I watched a large protest downtown first night). Am disappointed in this book (only read 50 pp), was hoping to find some instructions, clues to what I'm looking for (it's supposed to be about some guy discovering insights into meaning of life while travelling around). Right outside my window is the bathroom, the door is open + someone is brushing their teeth neurotically, slowly, with unusual rhythm + forever, stopping, going, stopping, going, must have had a bad experience as a kid, a scary dentist. ... more Indian radio now (western) heavy metal. ... this person is still brushing the teeth, maybe they are very stoned, and just having a good time, the strikes and problems with India is making me think I might not get to India. Have to go help Joakim send a package tomorrow morning, I think I will not eat breakfast tomorrow, been spacing myself out w/ food ... eating too much. It's not good to indulge too much in a good thing, have to keep in mind what bad is ... now Bad Company playing on the radio.

Spent the day hanging out with the Swedish guys I met in Lhasa (tall rasta guy Joakim + short guy, the nerdy more interesting guy. Saw Joakim today ... seemed very depressed, seemed glad to see me, just because I was w/ other people, didn't stay long, said he was going back to his room, guess he's very depressed, felt bad. I wonder if people feel responsible for me in that way (if I'm depressed + go out to be alone). If they talk about me like that, "he's a nice guy I wish he wasn't so depressed, I don't know what to say to him ... I don't want to be around someone when they're like that, but I do like the guy, he's nice." I wonder if people talk about me when I'm not around. ... ... in the last 3 months I've talked to only a few girls, haven't met that many. In 28 days I will be 24. It would be nice to spend my birthday at home ...

April 3, 5:25 PM

Just got a heavy dose of this city, walking in the crowded, noisy, dirty + smelly streets ... millions of tourists, locals trying to change money, selling hash. The whole place is really getting on my nerves. This morning I spent 4 hours at the post office helping Joakim to send some packages, he was as usual moody + insensitive. When i didn't feel like talking the whole time, he was trying to be cheery ... wouldn't care if I never saw him again (unfortunately he has my address in California). Remembering

---

[40] The layout of Kevin's apartment + surrounding hood at the time, in Venice, CA.

back 2 years to Copenhagen, the 2 Irish guys I met ... me trying too hard to be their friend + when they were leaving one of them made a comment (to the extent of) [unintelligible...]

"... preservation of my belongings [occupies] my thoughts ..."

10:44 PM Khatmandu

Alone here in my room. I've said bye to all my friends here, Joakim, Veepankin, Martha + Tina (?), tomorrow morning the bus to India. I guess this is a different chapter [of] my trip, (kind of a relief in a way to know I'm not going directly back) still 26 days left ... maybe there's more to come. Finished *Zen + Motor Maintenance* last night + this morning [sold it to Joakim]. Felt particularly good all day, in a good mood ... have to admit I did indulge twice today in the local D.W. [?], but even still, not much + all day I was very happy, content ... maybe the book set something straight in my mind, maybe the vast amounts of food I'm eating is doing, I don't know ... tomorrow i say goodbye to all this, to transition to Europe (whatever that is ... don't know my plans yet ...). Elvis ('Love me Tender') is playing in the next room, it's amazingly quiet considering this is a holiday. Saw the little girl[41] [that] is supposed to be the incarnation of a goddess, large procession, marching soldiers, this painted up girl being carried along on a throne, very serious, a local told us ... wait ... i can hear the festival processing again in the street (drums, flutes, etc). Anyway, a local said that a girl is picked to be queen for 6 years. If she smiles even once they get a new goddess (6 years in a temple, not allowed to smile). [...] (Elvis crooning away, sounds strange). There was a beautiful sunset down by the river, didn't get my statue certified fake, might get it taken away at the border, oh well ... will probably get robbed in India, oh well, today I don't care, tomorrow I hope I feel the same ...

April 6 1:56 PM on bus somewhere in Nepal

The bus has about 30 people on the roof, maybe a hundred inside. My luggage (I think, I hope) is on the roof, Khatmandu is gone, I had daal for lunch. Even tho I paid for a ticket on a 1st class bus I ended up sitting on the floor of 3rd class (between a gas can + the front door). It's hard to tell if I'm in a good mood or not today. [shakey handwriting]. Think I will just call myself "tired". It's starting to get hot + dusty. Things I've daydreamed about today on the bus:

—I'm in the Cocteau Twins, imagine the concert we'd have [etc.]

—Quick fantasies about sexy Hindu girls walking on the street outside of the bus.

—Think I am going into [unintelligible] day segue [unintelligible] preservation of my belongings [occupies] my thoughts, wont' have any more thoughts until I get to Europe, can relax a little more. [I have] to stop now it's too bumpy to write.

[... continued from http://5cense.com/13/SSES.htm:]
Kathmandu, Nepal—June 30

... but we like the *idea* of the book. And the second half of the book gets better, when he actually starts piecing together R's story (the first half could basically be summarized as setting the stage, him describing how he was going to tell the story, how he got into R's mindset ... something that would've been better perhaps as an accompanying blogpost ... or whatever the equivlent was in the 70s when *Correction* was written). The narrative transition is gradual + seemingly **schizophrenic** ... his friend keeps telling his story (+ this is where it gets tedious ... for example, every time R underlines a word in his writings, the narrator would say the words were underlined, rather than just underline them ... which perhaps is necessary to keep reminding us that it is he, his friend, who is telling the story ... but we'd just assume read straight from the source).

What's interesting though, is this idea of **correction** ... of R writing + rewriting + correcting until he destroys what he wrote in the first place, or creates something new out of the destruction ...

«... because the destruction of his work by his own hand, by his keen mind which dealt most ruthlessly with his work was, after all, merely synonymous with the creation of entirely new piece of work, he had gone on correcting his work until his work was not, as he thought, destroyed, but rather a wholly new piece of work had been created.»

This is sort of how we felt in writing *The Becoming* ... editing + changing so much that the final version hardly resembled the original manuscript. But in regards to the editorial process of the narrator of *Correction*, he doesn't delete or correct anything, but only 'sifts and sorts'. He takes 800 some pages + wittles them down to 80. This namesake 'correction' process has more to do with just writing tho ... what the book is really about (in our minds) is **suicide** (as with our brother- ½'s 'SSES' 'SESS' ... the suicide of our father (+ 'SSES'[3] about our brother- ½'s final act)).

---

[41] A Kumari Devi (pre-pubescent girl that manifests divine female energy) which in 1989 in Kathmandu would've been Rashmila Shakya, one of the more famous ex-Kumaris, perhaps because she subsequently wrote an autobiography, *From Goddess to Mortal*. She is now a 36-year old software developer for a banking company that enjoys shopping + seeing Bollywood films (per Wikipedia).

Visas — Departures/Sorties — Entrées/Entries

S.No.EN 209310.0.00
VISITOR VISA NEPAL
(ENTRY) Received US CATEGORY TOURIST
Valid Until 2 JUN 1994
For SINGLE
Entry
Length of stay:- 30 days from the date of entry.
Passport No.
Visa issued at T.I.A. KTM
Date: 0 8 MAY 1992
Visa Officer
3 MAY 1994

Early morning train somewhere in India

After an especially grueling bus trip, got to the Indian border ... then 3 hours [to the] nearest train station only to find there wasn't a train waiting for me ... it was just a scam, had to pay 135 rupees for the ticket I already paid 400 for. When I got on the train I realized the ticket only costs 81 rupees ... ripped off again ... my patience to appreciate things in countries like this is wearing thin. It's an amazing place (so far), once again very different, less (much less) English writing etc. than Nepal. Infinitely more beggars + people trying to sell stuff. This is the place (along w/ every other new place I've been) for which I have no 'a priori' image (a mental map, expectancy). There's no possibility of jarring, only the preoccupation from media, maybe that's why it's so exhausting to travel for such a long time ... back home, my model of my world (extending say, LA country, road to S.F., Carmel Valley etc.) seems to stabilize the landscape somewhat here. In some sense there's no rest, I'm constantly uncomfortable, convincing myself that there is no danger, right now the guy next to me (who's helped himself to my magazines) is leaning over to read this, he can't read my writing, cover up your body parts, hide valuables, [unintelligible] wear the passport, leave in some safe place.

5:32 Tourist camp, Delhi

Sitting here in a cafe, outdoors, in a yard, dotted with little bungalows, which is in turn surrounded by a wall ... this constitutes the 'tourist camp'. I have 226 rupees to eat for the next 3 days. I'm trying [to account] for the dough + how I will make it up ... go home + work [for mom].

8 Apr 8 a.m. Delhi

Yesterday took what might be termed a 'worshipper' bus to the Taj Mahal, the birth place of Krishna + few other places. The bus left at 6 a.m. + took about 4 hours to reach Agra. I was the only westerner on the bus + the tour dialogue was given in Hindu. I sat in the front of the bus—bad choice—soon as the bus took off they blared (full volume, one foot in front of my face) some ridiculously bad Indian movies. I got incredibly hot. The scenery was dry, poverty ... sad. The Taj Mahal + the Red Fortress were amazing. Lunch + the gift shop were not. The Krishna temples we visited (until about 10 PM) were. We went into one Krishna temple in a small village (late at night). I was stuck in the back (the only westerner I saw today was myself) ... went in, they started worshipping, strange. Everyone was kneeling in the chapel, they showed the altar, pulled a curtain open, a small room w/ cloth, gold, flowers, large mannequins [?] ... weird looking, not human, black, gold faces, started into the 'we need your money pitch,' went back to the bus, everyone on the bus wanted my walkman, interested to buy it but didn't have the money, etc. delays, problems, people on the busy trying to assault the driver while he is driving, more fantastically bizarre Indian movies (kung fu, disco glitter, musical numbers, bad guy/good (Hindu) guy, western sleaze girls, goody-tissue [sic] Hindu girls, etc. get home at 2 p.m. [a.m.?]

Then again, u could also say *Correction* is about authors + **books** ... The Cone (in our mind) is just a metaphor for a book, how lives become reduced to books ... not just any old books, but 'good books' as Bernhard says ... the books with lofty unobtainable ambitions ... high art ... where in the end the only thing worth writing about becomes the writing process itself. And how this obsessive self-correcting that we all fall prey to, knowingly leads to our demise ... yet we do it anyway.

«The matured idea is enough in itself to destroy most people, so R. And such an enormity as a work of art, a lifework of art—regardless of what this monstrousness is, everyone has such a possibility in him, because his nature is in itself such a possibility—can only be tackled and realized and fulfilled with the whole of one's being.»

The author **sacrifices** himself for the sake of his book ... his opus. The next reader occupies the book, lives in this author's shoes for a spell, becomes possessed ... + in turn sacrifices themselves for their own book ... + the cycle goes on. Not sure if our brother-½ ever read Bernhard ... the book was written in the 70s so he definitely could've, we just don't remember him talking about him.

exhibit 24—untitled + undated (cast of Hindu head w/ inscribed 'EIRE' on top) ... also on cover

Kathmandu–July 2, 2013 [http://www.5cense. com/13/kathmandu.htm] 1:58 a.m. Half-waking, half-sleeping, can't tell the difference. The same with j. Mind keeps having the same dream, though we're not even sure we'd call it that so much as **pineal** pinings or déjà vu gone haywire ... similar to the thought chambering dream in the last post ... obsessing thoughts concerning our brother-½ + the nature of experience ... to the extent that we're convinced we already wrote this entry before. [...]

quality of vanity 57

April 10 Evening, New Delhi

Well this morning my life was wonderful ... after all the frustrating experiences + seemingly torturous conditions I had to put up with, it was finally coming, Europe. I had spent the day before hanging out w/ my 2 Norwegian friends (they left to Malaysia in the evening). Went to bed early, it was like Christmas eve. Get up leisurely (very early), lie around, pack (god, it was almost here) waited out by the gate for the bus at 11:00 a.m. About a minute before the bus I thought I should double-check that I had my ticket (I had taken it out the day before to reconfirm my flight) ... I looked at it for the hundredth time and realized it said 0320 + it slowly sunk in that my plane had left early in the morning ... I had missed it. So here I am hours later, still [here]. But I cant think right now, to attempt to do so would be forced so I won't.

April 12 1 PM Delhi

I've been confirmed on the flight early tomorrow morning. Spent most of the night thinking about the concept of quality (+ where that concept takes my thinking). Quality (not necessarily perception but implied betterness) seems to be the main objective in advertising (they want to give quality, consumers want it). **People are the sum total of perceptions (qualities) of objects.** The word doesn't really work for me + the more I think about it the more I end up out of the woods and into a clearing, w/ the remnants of a deserted party—Baudrillard, Bickerton, Steinbeck. I'm about 10 years too late in pursuing these ideas. Right now I'm reading Baudrillard "selected essays" ... seems he was hopeless to [do anything about] these things, [unintelligible] hopelessly over-killed. Bickertons self-contained, wall-hanging (large metal + plaster) pieces seem to deal with these ideas in the most successful art world way, so I will drop it. Am desperately trying to form some ideas for new work. Whatever the ideas are, they're not too far from the last works I've done. Hopefully the whole thing will clear up, I'm going to take a shower.

1:51 PM Delhi

I went to double-check for the 10th time that the airport was really only 100 rupees and not 300 like I had thought (I had already spent most of the 200) ... she was getting sick of telling me it was 100, she reluctantly called again, turns out it is 100, but for Thai Air (my airlines) it's 300. God, I'll be glad to get out of here ... ...

... expert ping pong players, lots of flies, good daal bat 10 rs, more things to worry about (on a full stomach). I want QUALITY ... before he left he felt like he was falling apart mentally, he left (somewhat in promptu) fearing that his friends would see this decay. He knew he had to go somewhere where he was not known, not required to be the person he was, some place where he could let the person inside his mind really break thru, take form. He felt like he had another life, a long one, and some very traumatic event had wiped it away ... all he had left [were] a few memories, short, very distanced, black + while like old family photos. He never questioned this lack in his memory. He never knew there was supposed to be anymore, but over the years he became aware of the black, he started to become aware of a time in his past where the haziness began. He avoided thinking about it for a long time, but the images kept surfacing uncontrollably, like vomit, an involuntary occurrence. When he was on the other side of the world, he let these things come out, provoked them to come out, he passively experienced a change at the helm ... within months the other had fully evolved, his history was (almost) complete. He didn't feel different, he only felt that as it was happening now he was only vaguely aware of some kind of shift w/ his psyche. He really couldn't understand if he wanted to. He did feel strange when he thought

To be honest, we're not even sure what the dream was. Suffice to say if we did, we wouldn't be including it here, but in the **'SSES'**[3] book we've embarked on in tandem. It had something to do with a journal entry our brother-½ wrote, back in the days before u, the Internet, existed .... weird to think u, the Internet, didn't exist for our brother-½, at the time of his death in 1997 ... at least not in your present wide-open, searchable + hyper-linked manifestation.

Good thing we recently **indexed** 5cense because now we can go back + find all the posts where our brother-½ makes an appearance. But for our journals before that, especially the hand-written ones? ...

Besides the Internet, the other thing we can't believe our brother-½ never experienced is Radiohead's *OK Computer*. It's almost like, in our minds, he has been here all along, stuck in a state of arrested development, but still experiencing things vicariously thru us ... + Nepal is something we've until now only vicariously experienced through him. Maybe it is even a part of him writing this ... we are after all 50% the same, genetically speaking. And it is our **genes** doing the talking ... in regards to this writerly compulsion. [...]

Sorry if u came here looking for a **travelogue** about Nepal. Maybe we'll say something or show some pictures later ... or maybe not. Part of what we are thinking about has to do with the vanity of travel. There's a part in our brother-½'s journals where he gets so frustrated dealing with the hassles + expense of getting from China to Tibet that he considers just not going + saying he did. This seems to be the motive for many people ... especially in regard to doing things like climbing Mt. Everest ... just to say u did it.

of home, for him that was when he really realized what happened, after the fact when he realized the desire to go home was not there, he did not understand how he got where he was, he had no desire to return, he realized then he would have to be him again, for everything to be alright. He would have to do + live (+ work) like he did + that idea repulsed him. He was running out of money + he had to go back to the place where his name was written (his name) on lots of pieces of paper, where his bank, car, job, etc. were. When he just wished there was a way to sell all his things and leave without having to deal w/ his friends. He decided to return + try to act like nothing had happened. Resigned himself...

I'm at sea again, can you hear my tender frame, screaming from beneath the waves.

[Crazy people who look like cartoon characters, with cartoon character tattoos on their arms, hundreds of cartoon character flies buzzing around their heads ...]

crazy people who look like cartoon characters, with cartoon characters tattoos on their arms, hundreds of cartoon character flies buzzing around their heads.

very (très) serious [...] I ping-pong plays cats that look like [...] on balthis's paintings Germans that are hopelessly east German in appearance its 2:31. April 11.89 (Delhi, India) [...] is on too tight [...] worlds welcome the chance to go home right now (my reasons being 83 percent financial). 2:15 am New Delhi Airport Int. departures. My jackets ripped (leather jacket) my shirt buttons broke off my pants are really dirty They took away my walkman batteries. I've got a sore throat It turned out the airport tax was only two (we called this afternoon, the airport assured me it was 300, I spent all day, and sold my telephone (very cheap about 10$, so I could get the money)

[... CONTINUED FROM BELOW LEFT] [Spent all day and sold my telephone (very cheap, about $10, so I could get the money).]

Hung out today w/ a British guy. Was at the height of my frustration (was told I needed 300 for airport tax + I only had 100), had talked to him the night before briefly, he said he didn't have any US bills to exchange w/ me but did I want to smoke out. Went into his room, didn't really get stoned (bad hash) we then went to Connaught Place, ate at Wimpy's, sold my computer (unnecessarily) he told me [about some traveller's cheque scam]. Talked a lot about drugs in India, how good the acid was + about parties in Goa, etc. he had books in his room on Bob Dylan + famous British gangsters, very violent mob heros who he obviously idolized, he talked about smoking so much hash in Manaili [sp] that after a few days (weeks?) of smoking in bed (it was very cold) when he looked in the mirror it scared him, he looked old. He said he was a carpenter in East London. Asked me if I had bought a present for my mom, was small, wirey + had short hair, seemed fairly generous, kind of boring.

Plane Apr 12 over Poland (?)

They're shutting the shades now, I guess they're going to show movies. Thai Air is really incredible, what a nice flight. Saw the snow fields of Russia this morning. They're showing *Pascuales Island,* I remember a while ago Mike [K] at school told me that soundtrack was done by a band that sounded like Dead Can Dance. Haven't watched an (english) movie in a while, I think I'm into it.

10:14 Gare du Nord, Paris

I usually don't like writing when someone's looking over my shoulder but here goes ... stayed at a fairly nice youth hostel for the last 2 days. Got here (Paris) saw how expensive everything was (room was 80 fr.) + decided to change my ticket. Changed the ticket to the 15th (cost 50) bought a ticket to Amsterdam (35) then went to Versailles for the day (mildly interesting, smaller than I imagined) went to bed early, walked around Paris the next day. Today went to the Louvre + the Pompadou, bought [Clay] a model car (30) managed to spend 200 dollars in 3 days (could have stayed in India for a month on that). Called [Ray] + told him I was coming Saturday night but please don't tell anyone. He didn't sound happy. I'm now sitting waiting for the train to Amsterdam ... tomorrow night I'll be home, this trip is over.

9:10 April 15. Plane (over Canada) to Vancouver

Contrary to my aspirations, nothing 'came together' in my mind on this trip's last leg (I imagined (since January) that on the way home on the plane I would come up w/ the idea (for artwork) that would fill me w/ inspiration). Today's like any other day, my uneasiness + anxiety (at the trip being over, not having accomplished enough, where my life is going, etc...) is balanced out only by the feelings of [content + pleasure] of going home. The total emotional charge is zero.

"I have spent the last 5 years like a cat continuously dragging dead birds into the house."

April 20 8 AM Venice, [California]

Well, I've regressed back to my old spot. Wasting my life, mortality [?] tug of wars. Guilt is something I don't need, really, I can almost understand its function, it's not my implementation, my design. This world that I am including myself in is [screwed up] by people who characteristically are substance abusers (including myself), who violently mishandle the concept of love ... lose sight of any role models ... all different ways of achieving the same result. [Unintelligible ...] I will establish in my mind a portion of determinism, don't worry about it, let go, your character will take you where it wants to go, if you don't have control over your direction by now then whatever. Movement is only an illusion of faith, the regression is just that. Goals + beliefs no longer grow within me, the movement has been exposed as illusion, I can no longer believe in it.

When I was young I produced quality because when i did people (adults) whom I projected parental emotions unto (stepmother, mother, teachers, coaches) reacted to it in a way made me feel more wanted, protected, or better than my competitors (brothers[42], other students, etc.).

Obviously when I got to college in 1984, all that stopped + I have spent the last 5 years like a cat continuously dragging dead birds into the house. Continually hoping that praise will someday replace indifference. That attention will replace minor setbacks and failures.

April 20 12:52 Venice, CA

I've lost my dad's wedding ring and it doesn't bother me at all ... within me, the movement has been exposed as illusion, I can no longer believe in it.

"... the movement has been exposed as illusion...."

April 25 12:47 Venice, CA

Here + now, working w/ a limited scope, unable to give up the ghost. Without his weakness who would he be? So many have been confronted w/ this guilt, call it Christian in nature. Somehow using it to propel them, to achieve movements to opposition, undermining it ...

---

[42] Strange to find myself considered amongst the competition.

[http://5cense.com/11/delhi.htm:]

8.2.2011. Fiumicino gate D08 [Rome]

«The language he used was that of a man who was sick and tired of the world he lived in—though he had much liking for his fellow men—and had resolved, for his part, to have no truck with injustice and compromises with truth.»[—reading *The Plague* by Albert Camus]

(Zurich airport)

hassled for our passports because although we have U.S. ones we are living under an Italian visa leading to some confusion with the feeble-minded Swiss. through security again (they took away the water u just purchased in the airport), barely enough time to make our connection. [...]

9.2.2011. Delhi

[...] once inside the Red Fort we found this shop called Tularam + bought these amazing paintings done on old recycled book pages (with text still intact) [...] the backsides of these paintings also have text (Arabic), like here is the b-side of the above (also note bookworm holes) [...] there is no "artist" associated with the

... only to admit defeat on the brink of death. Only these great works, diminished slightly by the last moment of regression, are publicized ... there must be ... no, why should there be, the optimism has been spent at a steady rate ... or maybe it never existed at all ... I guess I believed at one time in the movement of my life, forward, I've come to know only lateral thinking, maybe suicide is an attempt at getting into the forward track, after trying [everything] possible in the lateral track (note: I'm not being suicidal here, just thinking about people I used to know). This will be the last entry in this journal ... I will try to define my mind.

[handwritten text]

I believe ... I have witnessed, no, I have memories of witnessing a large (comparable to what I don't know what) amount of [information]. I believe I have certain physical responsibilities to attend to, to avoid death (the culmination of physical harm to the (my) body). I believe time starts at the tip of my nose. I believe time started sporatically, first around 1967-8 and then more [definitely] + regularly around 1969. (At this moment, time is continuous, more than 30 seconds ago it starts to get sporatic. Simulacra aptly captures the form of my memories. My mind is a prison, if I get injured or crazy, it's very difficult to get anyone in their to help (they have to cut their way in with a saw, to 'repair' the damaged caused by a

10.2.2011. *Delhi*

[...] sometimes u wonder if u spend too much time thinking about thinking. u guess that's better than worrying about worrying. or being tired of being tired. or bored of being bored.

«I used a cobra snake as a neck tie.» —as sung by The Jesus & Mary Chain

language is tautological. no, better yet, all knowledge is tautological. it's all founded on it's own inherent hypocrisy. you're not sure why u wrote that in your travel notes. presumably u were reading E.O. Wilson because next u quoted him:

«The informational content of language is to be carefully distinguished from all it's emotional content. To these various ends verification is all important—indeed the very meaning of a statement is it's method of verification.»

[...] 3 things most hustled to u in hushed tones: hashish, dick massages + Flash drives.

«Unconstrained by information from the outside world, deprived of context and continuity in real space and time, the brain hastily constructs images that are often phantasmagoric and engaged in events that are impossible.» (E.O. Wilson)

E.O. Wilson starts to get all psycho-babbly by the episode on drugs + dreaming but the part about snakes was interesting being in this cobra-crazed culture. come to think of it cobras figured prominently in your dreams last night—something about a table whose legs were made from cobras, this before u read this episode.

L'Enfant

exhibit 25—"Untitled" 1991 (particle board, formica, belt, colored silicon, 41" x 7 ¼" x 8 ¼")

(exhibit 66 on page 159 shows more detail of guts)

few things that shouldn't have been seen or heard. As always, what I believe + what others tend to conflict ... ... I will now sign off this 'diary' (or travelogue log) that has been a failure ... a failure because it [failed to resuscitate] my thinking, I have lapsed into something I can't get out of ... laziness of mind, wedged in uncomfortably, but too numb to feel, these pages only contain a few, no I don't believe in myself ... cannot [unintelligible] i could make anything worthwhile, that belief must be subject to change, has to be subject to change.

bye~~~~~~~~~~*

IN PURSUIT
OF HIGHER
ART IN

What some people don't realize is that the actual odyssey in *The Odyssey* doesn't even begin til the 5th chapter (4 in our #ing scheme). + the bulk of Joyce's recapitulation of *The Odyssey* is from this mid-section—⅔ of *Ulysses* (12 of 18 chapters) can be mapped to this middle ⅓ of *The Odyssey*[43]—which is also the case w/ brother ½'s original SSES thesis. But as said before, we are following a more linear, 1-to-1 mapping to *The Odyssey*. Here's the continued plan ... at least thru this middle *Odyssey* section:

TOC TBD

11 — See book #2 HOMECOMING for Correlato6 Chapters

.... not that i totally know where i'm going yet here on this odyssey. Personally, i find up-front tables of contents patronizingly suspect ... as if the author(s) know xactly where they are taking us. I'll be 1st to admit i don't have a clue—i'm in the same boat as u (or U ... as in Ulysses)—xcept i have my brother-½'s 'SSES' 'SSES' thesis + pre-xisting writings/art ... + the road-maps of *The Odyssey* + *Ulysses* to guide the way.

(deterritorialized)

So here we are ... hobbling along by our bootstraps ... travelling, unravelling ... technically in the unchartered territory tween episodes 3 + 4. Finished **en-Telemachy** (look ma, entelechy!). In the Telemachy section of *The Odyssey*, Telemachus—spurned by his mother's lecherous suitors—leaves Ithaca to search for his father. In our book [this book] brother-½ leaves home (L.A.) to search for our father. At the beginning of episode 3 i lied when i said brother-½ had crossed the **threshold** (in J. Campbell's monomythical sense). This—[this space between episodes]—marks the threshold ... yoU're Xing it knowingly now.

Going from Telemachy to The Odyssey amounts to an abrupt change of perspective—from Telemachus to Ulysses—in Homer's book ... this is when we start following Ulysses in his adventures (or misadventures) as he tries to find his way home. In Joyce's book there's also an abrupt shift of p.o.v.—from Dedalus to Bloom, who we then follow thru the course of a day (June 16, 1904 to be x-act) ... not a very adventurous odyssey (U never leaves Dublin city limits) + Bloom is only *symbolically*

stet

---
[43] See http://www.5cense.com/14/351.htm for a complete mapping.

Dedalus's father (at this point in the story they haven't even met).

This is the crossroads we are at in our story ... *his* story. The obvious choice woud be to have Ulysses/Bloom be **our father**. So here begins the story of our father (at least metaphorically) ...

2 years after Kevin's Telemachean trip (not nesessarily an 'odyssey') to look for our father, i took a trip of my own. On January 5, 1991 (our father's birth/death day ... also the same day brother-½ left on his trip xactly 2 years earlier), i wrote him this letter from the straits of Malaka[44] using the table of contents of *The Odyssey* as paper (see below left) as apparently there was no writing paper on the ship i found myself on.

I found this scrap in brother-½'s things ... a keepsake. Maybe this makes me Ulysses? Maybe U (the reader)? Or maybe i am *also* Telemachus, looking for our father **in parallel** ... taking a cue from my older brother-½? Here's the flipside of the letter below ... in case you're wondering what the rest of it said.

(Somewhere in the Straits of Malaka)

JAN. 5, 1991

Dubious Maximus greetings from your Bohemian Bro on a 3-day trip through hell. The only problem is they have no paper on this here ship. So i will write small. So How was X-mas and New Years and all that? I'll be in Penang soon so i sent letters and tapes. I hope used to see out been I'm to may days

AND i'll cuz and Not het place see to to Vol Vol really eerie lake well

back in Denpasar if your tape was to no avail. It may be forwarded - well on this ship from JA Sumatra > 3 days - stop there for a to check out some GITANS but then to malaysia for not i'm fixing for India & Nepal that INDONESIA the most Intense i've ever been. often last fall you i was Mt. Batur cano with cano. It cold. There's a huge in the Crater as the other volcano. I climbed it at 3 a.m. to make sunrise at 6. The fog came in (from the steam in the crater) ten minutes after sunrise. There was actually

"She boiled the eggs by setting them in one of the steaming fissures."

This little footstall on top. This woman came strolling up with everything balanced on her head (a 45° incline of Ash!) She boiled the eggs by setting them in one of the steaming fissures. Hitched my way up to a beach - a backup travellers 'resort' set off on this amazing stretch of travel - Dec. 29 7 a.m. left Bali. Crossed the Strait to Java - came into Probolinggo at 1:30 where i find this guy to take me up to Mt. Bromo in his Jeep - 4 wd Land Rover. We picked up some Singapore tourists to pay expense, then went down into the Crater (Another volcano within volcano) and across this huge Sea of Ash - Endless black plains and up to the other side Just in time for sunrise - the peak Jutting out of a blanket of fog. Then down to Probolinggo dropped me off at the train station where i got one to Surabaya - huge with no redeeming features so i got to Yogyakarta. At this

"At this point I had been travelling for 36 hours straight without sleep or food — I got into Yogya at 11:45 p.m. I totally forgot it was New Years Eve."

travelling for 36 straight sleep or food - i got into Yogya I had totally forgot it was New Years eve I was riding in this Becak (A Bicycle with a cart in front where you sit pedalled by this intense subspecies of Javanese humanity) down the main Drag - completely Packed and hectic - people were Dancing in the streets throwing things at me and blowing whistles and horns in my ears - it was a grand welcome - the most amazing New Years i even had. Unfortunately it went on for most of the night as every Hotel in town was full - so i Just wandered around all night with my Backpack. Yogya is the coolest

<< I >> in CONTUITY «Rhythm begins, you see. I hear.
Acatalectic tetrameter of iambs marching.

N - Zyme Substrait   No, agallop:
                       decline the mare.» —*U*

---

[44] Even tho i was there, i'd all but forgotten where the Straits of Malaka were ... xcept it happens to be in the news today (March 12, 2014) —they're now thinking (5 days after it disappeared) that the missing Malaysian airliner flight MA370 may have veered off course + are widening their search area to include these straits.

It might be worthwhile to hang out here a little longer—in this no man's land between episodes 3 + 4—between Ithaca (home to Ulysses + Telemachus) + the isle of Calypso (where U has been detained now for 7 years) ... in the dire straits of Malaka where the search has been widened for the missing airliner. Apologies again if we've been all over the map so far ... i'm trying to piece together brother-½' writings as best we can into a coherent narrative ... **intervening** or projecting as little as possible. A lot of it still doesn't make sense to me, some 17 years after the fact ... perhaps why we're trying to get this all down on paper.

After the 1ˢᵗ TOC in the en-Telemachy section, we included a timeline of sorts. Here it is again to jog your memory:

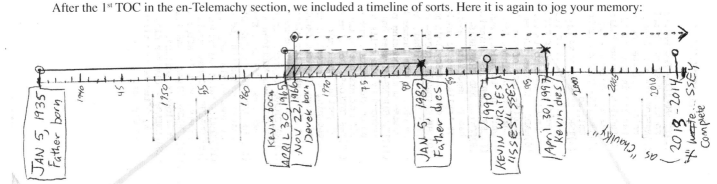

... not that any of this need make any sense to U, but at least for us it acts as an itinerary of sorts to stay the course ... to ground us.

Here's an x-panded timetable of the shaded area above (where most of the book takes place) ... filling in the gaps:

TIMELINE:		**EPISODE**
1965	April 30, 1965—Kevin is born (in Portland, OR)	# 8
	Our parents divorce + Nov 22, 1966 Derek is born (in Portland)	# 4, 8
	Our father remarries S + our real mother splits to Mexico. We remain in the custody of our father + S	# 4, 8
	Our mother kidnaps[45] us 4 brothers to Mexico	# 8
1970	K voluntarily returns to Oregon + eventually our father kidnaps D back to Oregon (under Disneyland pretense)	# 4
	...	
	K + D together in Portland w/ our father + S.	# 4
	At some point, our other 2 brothers J + D come join us, 1 x 1	# 4
	... (otherwise uneventful)	
1975	...	
	Our father gets divorced from S + is deemed unfit to care for us, we are returned to the legal custody of our mother in Mexico	# 4, 5
	K + D cohabit in Mexico	# 5, 6, 7
1980	Our father attempts suicide + fails, K goes to live w/ uncle in Oregon, D remains alone in Mexico	# 7, 8, 9
	Jan 5, 1982—our father successfully commits suicide	# 0, 10
	K + D both go to boarding school (RLS) in California ... D only stays 1 year, K stays 2	# 11
	Kevin graduates from RLS, goes to UCLA for a year	# 11
1985	Derek graduates from high school (Mtn View, CA) + goes to UC Santa Cruz	# 6, 11
	K switches to Art Center College of Design in Pasadena	# 7, 11 (+ vol 2)
	K takes his world trip from which 'SSES' 'SSES' is based	# 1-3, 11 (+ vol 2)
	K gets his MFA, remains in L.A.	# 0, 3, 4, 11 (+ vol 2)
1990	D graduates from UCSC (math/physics) then takes a world trip of his own	# 9, 11 (+ vol 2)
	D goes to U of AZ (MA in physics/philosophy). K remains in L.A. making art/working in film, meets Nadine	(vol 2)
	K works on a film being made by our cousin Ray in France. They invite D out (as a stunt double/stand-in)	(vol 2)
	D returns to Tucson, works in field geophysics, gets married to Hope	(vol 2)
	K goes back to L.A., sometimes France, takes another Himalayan trip w/ Nadine	(vol 2)
1995	K breaks up w/ Nadine ... in + out of rehab	(vol 2)
	April 3, 1997—Kevin overdoses in San Francisco, CA	(vol 2)

(+ again, apologies for giving away the punchlines, but this isn't about the outcomes so much as how we arrive at them).

---

[45] Funny word—«kidnapping» ... as if we slept thru the ordeal.

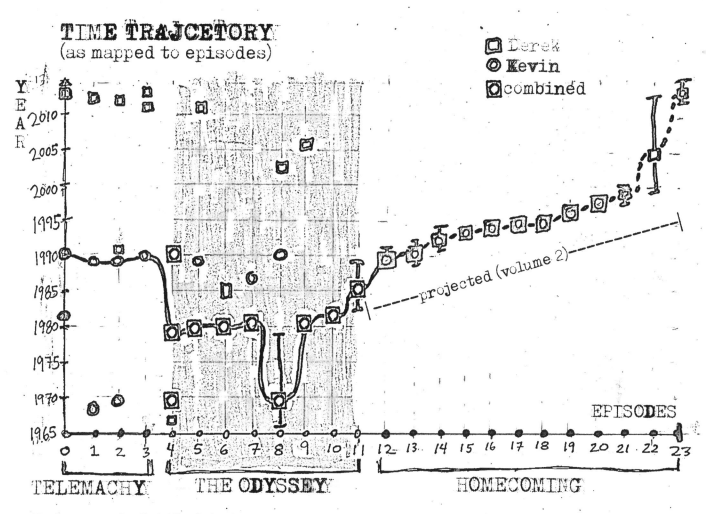

TIME TRAJCETORY
(as mapped to episodes)

☐ Derek
◎ Kevin
⊡ combined

YEAR (axis): 2010, 2005, 2000, 1995, 1990, 1985, 1980, 1975, 1970, 1965

projected (volume 2)

EPISODES

0 1 2 3 4 5 6 7 8 9 10 11 12 13 14 15 16 17 18 19 20 21 22 23

TELEMACHY | THE ODYSSEY | HOMECOMING

For those more visually inklined, the above graph might help navigate the timeline of 'SSES' 'SSES' ˢˢᴱʸ. The overarching narrative is fairly linear xcept in this Odysseian mid-section where we flash back (x2) + hop around some in keeping in line w/ Ulysses's trajectory.

And here's a timeline of sorts from an email our mother sent us (in her typical CAPS LOCK! style):

From: Sharon White <s▮▮▮▮▮.jjj.▮▮▮▮▮>
Date: Tuesday, October 29, 2013 8:07 PM
To: Derek White <derek@calamaripress.com>

HELLO DEAR DEREK!
  HOPE ALL IS GOOD WITH YOU AND ▮▮▮▮▮ I GUESS IT HAS BEEN A YEAR SINCE YOU MOVED!
  SINCE YOU ARE WRITING ABOUT KEVIN---- I THOUGHT I WOULD TELL YOU A FEW THINGS I FELT THAT WERE "DIFFERENT" ABOUT KEVIN!
  1965-67--- HIS EYE COLOR, HAIR, BODY ETC.-CAME FROM MY MOTHER'S SIDE! HE NEVER LIKED TO BE CUDDLED OR HUGGED! HE GOT HIS LOVING FROM ATTENTION! HE DIDN'T TALK EXCEPT TO SAY BEBOP-WHILE BOUNCING UP AND DOWN IN HIS CRIB!
  1968--I REALIZED KEVIN HAD A NATURAL SENSE OF HUMOR--LIKE MY BROTHER!
  1975---I REALIZED HE WAS AN ARTIST---AND HIS BRAIN WAS DIFFERENT!
  1976- WE WERE ALL (INCLUDING COUSINS AND LOBO) AT LAKE TAHOE---DURING THE GRANOLA AND HEALTHY EATING STAGE! KEVIN WAS 11 YRS. OLD---AND WAS READING "INTRODUCION TO A YOGI". WE WERE TALKING ABOUT IF PEOPLE COULD READ OTHER PEOPLE'S THOUGHTS! SINCE ALL YOU KIDS WERE THERE-----I GAVE EACH OF YOU A PIECE OF PAPER! I WAS THINKING OF A TALL TREE! I DREW A LONG TRIANGLE AND THEN PUT TWO LINES AT THE BASE! KEVIN DREW A REGULAR TRIANGLE---CROSSED IT OUT AND DREW A TREE! KEVIN REMEMBERED THAT HE HAD THAT POWER!
  AFTER KEVIN DIED-I WAS GETTING A MASSAGE IN PALO ALTO WITH SOMEONE I DIDN'T KNOW! IN THE MIDDLE OF THE MASSAGE-SHE SAID THAT SOMEONE ELSE WAS IN THE ROOM,----THAT THIS PERSON HAD QUITE A SENSE OF HUMOR ---AND WAS WITH THE GRINNING CHESHIRE CAT! I REMEMBERED KEVIN'S ART WORK---UNTIL HE WENT TO COLLEGE--HAD A ALICE IN WONDERLAND FEEL-----SO I INVESTIGATED! IF THERE IS REINCARNACION---I FEEL KEVIN WAS JOHN TENNIEL! JOHN TENNIEL DID THE DRAWINGS OF THE CHESHIRE CAT, ETC.
  LOVE MOM

STARTING THE TREK

The smell of burning coal, wood and yak butter fills the dark low-ceilinged room. Cold mountain air and piercing morning light streams through the open window. A few sherpas sit at a table wearing bright-colored down jackets, drinking coffee. They laugh as they describe (in Nepali) something that apparently happened up the [up on the mountain] somewhere. [Stephen] and [Nadine] step into the kitchen to get something to eat before they start up the trail. A good-looking sherpa boy tries to convince them that they need a guide, describing the dangers of altitude sickness. Stephen tells him they don't have the money to pay for a guide, but the smiling young Nepali persists with his pitch. Finally Stephen pays the old Tibetan woman for the pancakes and (instant) coffees, thanks the young sherpa again for his offer and concern for their safety, and leaves, with Nadine.

Out on the trail the scenery is beautiful. They don't take any pictures because they both know that as the days progress it will only get more beautiful and spectacular. Within minutes they see their first yaks—large brown-haired ones—coming down the trail in the other direction. Nadine is elated.

After a while they stop to rest, leaning up against the side of the hill, putting their weight on their backpacks. Nadine is happy, Stephen is happy, things are good. They have been in Nepal for three days. The plane trip was hectic, their time in Khatmandu was uncomfortable (most of the time was spent getting permits and supplies for the trek). The flight up the mountain (just the two of them, in a small twin engine plane) was anything but relaxing, even for Stephen, who is usually comfortable in planes. But now they are finally on the trail, alone, no more things to do, no more contact with the outside world. They are free, and finally they are both feeling the freedom they only anticipated before. For the first time in years Stephen is truly happy ... but within minutes he finds himself wondering how long it will last.

from http://www.5cense.com/14/372.htm:

As the sub-title pretentiously says, *Mount Analogue* (the book, by René Daumal) is: «A Novel of Symbolically Authentic Non-Euclidean Adventures in Mountain Climbing». Mt. Analogue (the mountain) is an allegorical mountain, a metaphysical object that is revealed only to those that seek it. The expedition to scale it is ignited by an academic article the narrator writes «... a rather hasty study of the symbolic significance of the mountain in ancient mythologies.» This guy Sogol (**Logos** backwards) takes note of it + invites him on this expedition + they put together a team to climb the mountain, [...] Daumal being the 1 to keep the journal, from which the book is made. As the book goes along, the voice becomes increasingly 3rd person plural.

> «In my imagination I did away with all the outward circumstances of my life and felt myself confined in ever tightening circles of anguish: there was no longer any "I" .... What does it mean, "I"? I couldn't succeed in grasping it. "I" slipped out of my thoughts like a fish out of the hands of a blind man, and I couldn't sleep.»

Speaking of **fishing**, while we are writing this, on a lawn chair looking out over Great Pond [Maine], we have a line cast out with a bobber. Yesterday we caught a bunch of bass, mostly small, but the elusive brown trout still avoids us so we are changing up our tactic (using a bobber. Tho thanks to you, Internet, we see it is better to put the worm on the bottom ... only problem is that when we put it on the bottom, the little bass come along + nibble it to shreds.

You could re-write Mount Analogue to be about fishing rather than mountain climbing and in fact, Melville, Hemingway, et al already have ... the «big 1 that got away» ... of which we had 1 yesterday, a large bass that we glimpsed before it snapped our line ... but that is not something we'd expect U to believe. It is this vain ambition to conquer—to catch the big 1—that we must abandon, w/out abandoning the process of going about it. At times we have fished w/ no bait on our hook for this very reason ... for the experience of it ... for the idea of waiting knowing you'll never catch anything (tho there are some fish that will bite an **empty hook** ... forget what they are called—unless this is just my imagination, or adults were pulling my leg—but we member fishing for them on the Columbia river in our youth) ... googling now yields no conclusive results, or a proliferation of other junk that masks the truth.

Mount Analogue is sort of like a black hole, abiding by Einstein's special theory of **Relativity** (whether Daumal knows it or not). In the following diagram included in the book, the people on the ship think they are travelling in a straight line, but in fact (relative to an observer above) they are travelling in an arc. Mount Analogue effectively curves space, just like a large gravitational body.

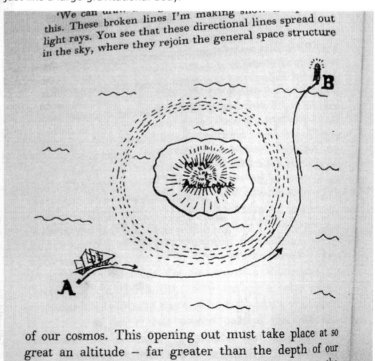

of our cosmos. This opening out must take place at so great an altitude – far greater than the depth of our

CAST (tentative, also note role-reversals can occur):

Kevin : **Telemachus** (to become Ulysses). a.k.a. **Stephen Dedalus,** Seth or even **Shiva.**

Derek : **understudy** for Telemachus (to perhaps also stand-in for Ulysses)

Cal : as himself (father figure, our 'Reverence,' but also more **generally** as a placeholder for home (**CA**Lifornia), Ulysses, Brahma, Bloom, etc.

"father Time" : as hisself

Mother (biological) : Penelope, Vishnu

suitors : as themselves (Rocky, Lloyd Ericsson, etc.) + **generally** as 'the competition'

JD : an amalgamation of our 2 older brothers

Fernando, a.k.a. "The Mexican" : his drug-dealer, modeled after:

Rocky, our mom's junky suitor

Shirley (S) : stepmother, Molly Bloom

uncle Stu (paternal, our father's brother) : as hisself, doubles as surrogate father

uncle N (maternal) : as hisself, also surrogate father (responsible authority figure)

aunt Kate : as herself, doubles as surrogate mother

cousin K : as herself, surrogate sister (not blood-related)

cousin Ray : as himself, rogue cousin, film director

granny Nanny (a.k.a. **granini**) : as herself (step-grandmother)

grandpa Cal : true (blood) **grandfather**

Nadine (or just N) : Kevin's love interest (also Nausicaa)

Hope—**Derek's** love interest, his Molly

Loder brothers (Mark + Buck) : friends of bad influence, evil twins, **Buck Mulligan**

Clay : Kevin's straight-laced, conservative, goody 2-shoed friend

Pascal : draconian boss-figure that Kevin despises but accepts as necessary evil

Stephen (or Steven)(**Dedalus**) : idealization of what Kevin wants to be, the 'artist as young man'

J. Joyce : as **hisself**

gods : there are none (greek or otherwise) in this variation

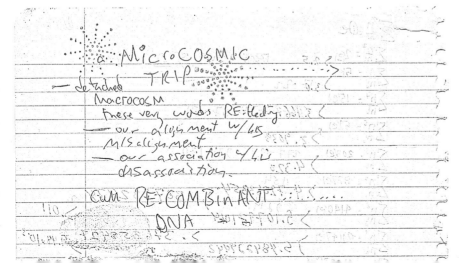

Trippy, right? Like a naked **singularity**. Mount Analogue is a strange place in other regards + has other peculiarities, some by contrived definitions they establish (like that the peak must be inaccessible, but the base must be accessible) + others discovered ... for example they find out they are unable to photograph anything, all the photos they take of Mount Analogue come out blank. In this speculative regard it seems very Swiftian + also reminiscent of Edwin Abott's *Flatland* ... a book that certainly must've influenced Daumal. [...]

The book specially appealed to us cuz we used to be obsessed w/ **rock-climbing**. Tho high altitude mountaineering never really rocked our boat much ... never really saw the point of it (+ we are particularly pre-disposed to altitude sickness). You can see/learn more by *traversing* a mountain than by scaling it. But we liked rock-climbing for similar reasons of setting contrived goals for yourself, to climb what is nearly unclimbable + to push yourself to the next limit (which in rock-climbing would be grade, 5.10, 5.11, etc.) ... but mostly we did it for the excuse of what we saw along the way, like technical hiking.

The book also appealed to us cuz in the SSES book we are currently working on—that our brother left incomplete—the destination of his odyssey (paralleling Homer/Joyce) was the Himalayas, in particular **Machapuchare**—a 7000 meter unclimbed peak ... unclimbed cuz it's sacred to the Hindus (evidently Shiva lives there or something). And there's a story w/in the story (they have downtime by the campfire or on the ship getting there so they take turns spinning yarns) about 2 twin brothers that are both mountaineers. Their father doesn't know which is eldest, that should succeed him, to whom he would «hand on the great knowledge» .... so he tells them (both accomplished mountaineers) that whoever retrieves a mythical bitter rose (found only on the top of the highest peak) would be his successor. 1 of the brother dies in the quest, or becomes a «Hollow-Man» which are some sort of mythical beings that live in the mountains + the other brother kills this Hollow-Man + then inhabits his body + becomes the combined force of both brothers, both w/ their combined skill set that allows them to get this bitter rose. This is sort of what we feel like writing SSES ... that we need to re-inhabit our brother's body, together becoming «Chaulky».

exhibit 26—2 more untitled door paintings

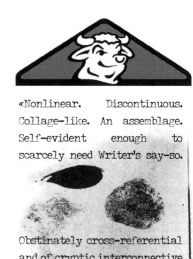

«Nonlinear. Discontinuous. Collage-like. An assemblage. Self-evident enough to scarcely need Writer's say-so.

Obstinately cross-referential and of cryptic interconnective syntax. Here perhaps less than self-evident to the less than attentive.»

—David Markson

«Conforming to the meaning of the word "process," recording falls back on (*se rabat sur*) production, but the production of recording itself is produced by the production of production.»

—Deleuze + Guattari, *Anti-Oedipus*

Back in Venice, Kevin walks a sad flower alone. No *codega* to walk in front lighting the way ... warding off the inner riffs of your dark streets ... no shiny beacons to source home.

1st memories were parceled discontinuously ... for both time + space. Whether it's the actual memories lodged in our brains or the developing **consciousness** of the events as they unfolded who's to say. In the days before googlemaps we had no spatial awareness of our relation to the rest of the world ... in the early days when all we knew was our own backyard ... the suburban streets tween our house + school ... like mice trails we memorized ... to the bowling alley + friend's houses, etc. ... no further than Jamison road which we were ordered to not cross.

O, SSEY, can U see?

LETTER OF INTENT

My first four terms at Art Center were spent concentrating on learning techniques and methods of representation (and of course, draw--ing the human figure). I switched back to fine art (I had studied at the UCLA fine art department for a year prior to attending Art Center) because I felt that the concerns dealing with illustration were infringing with my need to keep up with current art dialogue (theory) and to change my work acc--ordingly. Although I feel I have come a long way in the past four terms, I still am not able to articulate the concepts behind my work (and to discuss its place in current art theory) as well as I would like to. I feel that the graduate program at this point is vital to the development of my work, and to my understanding of current art issues.

The main concerns of my work deal with creating a discourse with the viewer thru the use of a compeling polyphony of styles, medias and images. The inherent sense of uniqueness is greater facilitated thru the use of the diptych format (juxtaposing stylistically different panels to encour--age a dialogue between the two panels). I have consistently used the door (either thru the literal use of or the dimensional equivalent) as my basic format because I see it as a size and shape we feel comfortable going thru (as well as any archetypal implications). The continued use of this format also provides me with a vantage point from which to view the changing aspects of my work (as well as making it possible to combine any works together, in different pairings). In many respects my work physically resembles the work of Rauchenberg and Kienholz(combinations of unusual materials, non-organic garbage and abstract expressionist painting gestures), but it is in many respects dissimilar to the work of the last 30 years(it being more in--volved with current issues). The rerepresentation of that which has already been represented (in a new way) and the value or worth of the art object (in the consumer world) are also issues which I am currently dealing with in my current work.

—KEVIN WHITE

1st concept came cuz teachers told us to not sniff it so of course this made us want to sniff it

OUR 1ST CAR (a Mustang from the same year we were born) we were

At the age of 5 we built 1 from LEGOS ...

Horses used to be used for glue. Or rabbit. Catgut used for rackets.

Horse is the street name for heroin.

Then in basketball it's a game where U need to mimick the technique + location of the shot of the player before U or risk receiving a letter, spelling out H-O-R-S-E.

This book is a game of horse w/ ourselves. Current score: H E

RIVEr SHAFBT broke while

IN CHESS, IT'S THE ONLY PIECE WITH NON-LINEAR MOVEMENT, A SORT OF QUANTUM TUNNELING

FACTORY + soldier for parts for 300 dollars

JAN H

smacks of penetration, rupturing membranes

In the ancient (Greek) sense, it is a gifted vehicle to implant within the enemy THE IDEA OF

In the modern sense it's a rubber membrane to PREVENT such implanting

in the cyber sense it's a virus a non-self-replicating type of backdoor virus containing code that, when executed, may cause loss or theft of data, and possible system harm

enTROPIC of cancer

i'm on

HORSEY

i'm on

HORSE

Pursuit as RE:Capithlation.
We turn our attn. to the Source...

exhibit 27—photo of our father that was displayed at funeral (left) in loo of ashes, photo of brother- ⅔ RE:painting this photo of our father in a 3x3 grid (middle)(whereabouts of original unknown) + an article appearing in his 1984 high school yearbook using this photo of Kevin, (bottom left)(+ Derek's hands framing the scene)

Meet the Cover Artist: Kevin White

Senior Kevin White, our cover artist.

Kevin White, our cover artist and a senior at Stevenson, began his art career in the eighth grade while attending school in Guadalajara, Mexico. At that time, he developed an interest in surrealistic images, and created a style of drawing with pens that included both real and surreal images packed together in a collage, much like the work of the Mexican muralists. He has adapted his style to incorporate a concern for the use of negative space, while continuing his use of surrealistic images. As with most artists, Kevin is diversified, as is exhibited in his work on the cover. This landscape painting, done in acrylics, shows two familiar sights on campus: the wooden bridge in front of Benbow and Reid Hall, the school's cafeteria.

Kevin has received many honors for his work, one of the most distinguished being the Third

Place Award in the Congressional Art Award Contest. The winning art work is on display in Congressman Leon Panetta's Washington Office. Another work, which can be viewed while visiting the Stevenson Campus, is the mural located in Simoneau's, a student recreational area. The design for this mural was selected in open competition by the student body.

Another special interest for Kevin is running. He has been running competitively for three years and has been the Varsity captain for both Cross-Country and Track.

Kevin hopes to begin his university study at UCLA before transferring to the Rhode Island School of Design. He attended a workshop at the Rhode Island school last summer while there, received several awards for his work.

«Who ever anywhere will read these written words? Signs on a white field.»—*Ulysses*

EX-LIBRIS
KEVIN WHITE

TIME: late 1969/1979/1989
PLACE: Portland, OR --->Guadalajara, Mexico / California + belly of the whale
IDEAS/Symbolism: Xisle, threshold xing, vagina, hypocrisy, pointilism, shit, departing wayfarer
ABSTRACT: Absence makes the heart grow fonder... or so they say. No need to rally against hypocrisy ... our father conseeded. Calypso held the phone in front of her bare thrust-forth crotch + the phallus receiver out to him. "If U need to call home so bad, just dial the damn number." These were the days of rotary phones ... + at least in Mexico (where we were mandated to live) they put these locking plugs in the 1-hole so unless U unlocked the plug, U coud only dial 1-1-1-... not even 0 to reach the operator.

... which is not to say everything (concsciousness-wise) was linear ... temporally or spatially. Shit just started to materialize for us w/o thinking much about it. A steady (yet discrete (IMHO)) stream begins to form from the headwaters of who knows where ... the bloodmelt off the mounting fountain ... seeping from a silvery vein. A sliver of roosting movement in the corner of our right eye coagulates to thawing flesh from the late spring frost ... inevitably sublimating + joining w/ more like- minded souls (or ghosts thereof) following the same trail west to "The Oregon Territory". Spawned from the deterritorialized terror of those that killed + were killed to land us brothers [HERE] ... those pilgrims who lived to die for our sins so they SSEY ... then forgot the meaning of what they read + said after a few stabled + guilt-ridden generations ... may as well get drunk + fuck not think about it much see what happens + next thing we know we're playing on the floor of our ever unfinished cabin on the headwaters of the SANDY river—so named by Lewis + Clark (actually 1st named 'Quicksand river' til it was shortened) cuz when they 'discovered' it it was a boggy glacier of quicksand + pumice—at the base of Mt. Hood[46]. Accumulating 'we' carry on blindly like the river ... shooting + looting up mountains to plant flags to stake our claims ... in due time to settle in a cul-de-sac in Zig Zag Village. It keeps coming, albeit in spurts ... biased shards we piece together + instinctively salmon against. «The past is just a story we tell ourselves» as Spike Jonze has the OS in HER say. Which is to say history (the memory thereof) is far from reliable ... + in our case admittedly fragmented, perhaps beyond reconstitution.

exhibit 28—½ of Chaulky at the base of Machapuchare (left) + the other ½ at the base of Mt. Hood (right (this image later used on the cover of the reprint of *History of Luminous Motion* by Scott Bradfield—a book that inspired both ½'s of the author))

---

[46] Scientists in retrospect speculate that Mt. Hood had erupted a few years earlier.

In ZIG ZAG the SANDY river was the limit ... too big to cross + no bridges ... we could only look w/ binoculars + imagine Bigfoot, just like we'd seen in the famous Patterson–Gimlin clip. We were certain we saw a bald eagle once but adults told us it couldn't be.

We are now in the CALYPSO episode of our odyssey. Anagrammatically,

$$C\text{-}A\text{-}L\text{-}Y\text{-}P\text{-}S\text{-}O \approx C\text{-}Y\text{-}C\text{-}L\text{-}O\text{-}P\text{-}S$$

(see episode 8) ... if u change an A to C. Or dial #225-9776. Back then there was no need to know area code. We never called outside it. Our father (CAL) remarried now for 10 years.

exhibit 29—both sides of Chaulky playing on the unfinished floors of our Zig Zag cabin

In 1968, Tammy Wynette released D-I-V-O-R-C-E. Our stepmother used to play the 8-track ... tho it wasn't til the Circle Jerks redid the song in '83 that we really got it (we thought Wynette was just spelling it out for us, not censoring it) ... the same Tammy Wynette whose next hit was «Stand by Your Man» (can u spell H-Y-P-O-C-R-I-T-E?). In '66 our parents got divorced ... the same year i was born, 2 years after brother-½ popped out burping BE-BOP. Our father remarried right away (to the same aforementioned stepmother, we'll call **S**). In '79 they got divorced + that's where this episode begins ...

When our hero was 14 + your untrusty editor was 12—after sum 7 years or so of general stability (living in suburban Oregon)—our world was suddenly turned upside-down. We can't speak for brother-½'s memory of it, but i member i'd just started 7th grade, at Whitford Jr. High in Beaverton. Just when i'd gotten over the dreaded first 2 weeks, our mother appeared 1 day ... i was bored in the back of a school bus when she hopped on + said something to the driver, handing him a note[47]. I recognized her as our mom + thought about hiding or pretending i didn't know who she was ... but she saw me + came running back + told me to get off the bus ... that we were going to **Mexico**! My classmates looked envious, that this crazy hippy lady singled me out + that *i* got to go to Mexico ... so he went along w/ it. Next thing he knew he was enrolled in another school in Guadalajara. Kevin was in 8th grade, at the same school. There was another brother in 10th grade + another (collectively we'll call them JD) that already fled the coop + was in California. To keep things to the point, this'll be about me + Kevin + our father Cal who would soon be dead. This wasn't the 1st time our mother tried to snatch us off to Mexico ... but this time our father sur-rendered us willingly ... or so we were told when we asked ... since his D-I-V-O-R-C-E from S, evidently the state of Oregon had declared him unfit to take care of us on his own.

Switching gears—this shift from suburban Portland to Guadalajara is akin to the shift from the ancient Greek island of Calypso to modern Dublin ... (if u will)

«I, Calypso»—Butthole Surfers

... question is ... who stands for **Calypso**—the nymph who detains Ulysses for 7 years on her island? If U is our father, than the natural choice for Calypso would be our stepmother, **S**. S was far from a sexy nymph tho ... nor was she wicked, as stepmothers are often portrayed. After our real mother abandoned us (when Kevin was 1 + before i was even born), our father was quick to remarry ... he couldn't live w/o a woman in his life. So for all intents + purposes, S was our mother for the 1st 10 years of life (minus the year or 2 our real mother kidnapped us to Mexico ... but that's a whole nother story). If i am to be thought of as U, then the obvious choice for Calypso woud be my 1st long-term girlfriend at the time, **X**. Serendipitously, i spent 7 years w/ X, before breaking up w/ her to go on the trip i allude to a few pages before in the pages between episodes (or maybe i was using this as the break-up excuse). I was always luckier than Kevin in the dept of finding love. Or maybe it's just that i wasn't *looking*

[47] Derek registers this as his 1st out of body experience, his 1st experience in 3rd person.

exhibit 30—water-logged page from Kevin's 1st notebook (this shift to Mexico also marks when he 1st started drawing)

for it. In transcribing Kevin's journals from the previous en-Telemachy section, it seems his trip across Asia was more about looking for **love** than our father. If u've gotten this far, u've read those pages, so u tell us? But before u reconstitute, u need to self-destruct +/- **deconstruct.** While hanging onto the unraveling thread as bootstraps. Where we left off in the last episode is that after travelling all the way across Asia looking for our father (or for love), he retreated home to Venice, CA. When he returned, he didn't tell anyone (except cousin Ray), just like he said on page 59 .... he just quietly came back + resumed his life. He kept his journals up for a while after he got back .... here's the next entry for the sake of continuity ...

10:51 AM, May 5, 89—Venice Beach

"Finding the direction is simple enough ... you follow the source from one point first, you fix yourself right up there on its tail all the while anticipating the next observer keeping an ear out for observations and breaks in movement." .... by now [he] had stopped talking, and was aware, and being made acutely aware, and had to stop for a while in order to catch his breath.

The journal gets more fictional/abstract (less autobiographical), before eventually trailing off into the designs of how he'd write his SSES book (see page 76)]

§ The **duelling dichotomy** as expressed by Henry Bergson in *Creative Evolution*: «There are things that intelligence alone is able to seek, but which, by itself, it will never find. These things instinct alone could find; but it will never seek them.» + «This mark is like a trace, still visible in each, of what was in the original tendency of which they represent the elementary directions. The elements of a tendency are not like objects set beside each other in space and mutually exclusive, but rather like psychic states, each of which, although it be itself to begin with, yet partakes of others, and so virtually includes in itself the whole personality to which it belongs.»

§ We wake, we sleep. **Continuity** is provided by the duality of the opposing forces that keep both spheres in orbit. The horse kicks. For each force there is an equal + opposite force ... collapsing when we state our intentions.

«What? 1 shot?»
«2 is pussy.»
«I don't think about 1 shot that much any more».
«You have to think about 1 shot. 1 shot is what it's all about.»
                    —Deer Hunter (1978)

TAC
CGA
TAG
UTU
CAT

IN THE WORLD OR WITHDRAWN LIKE THE TURTLES HEAD, ITS SMALL TRIANGULAR PINK TOUNGUE IN WHAT LOOKS LIKE A BIRDBEAK HE HAD TO DECIDE.

PEOPLE MAKE 200 MIL.

I FEEL LIKE ITS TAKING LOTS ENERGY TO HOLD BOTH IDENTITIES (?) AT BAY, AT THE SAME TIME (ASSIMING LETS SAY THAT THERE ARE TWO). THEREBY BY PREVENTING BOTH OF THEM TO GROW UNCONTROLLABLY.

May 8. 89 Venice Beach, Notes from "The Sense of Beauty" By George Santayan.
- "We do not often indulge in retrospection for the sake of scientific knowledge of human life, but rather to revive the memories of what once was dear."

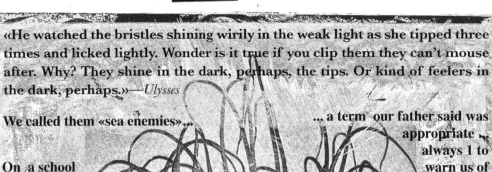

«He watched the bristles shining wirily in the weak light as she tipped three times and licked lightly. Wonder is it true if you clip them they can't mouse after. Why? They shine in the dark, perhaps, the tips. Or kind of feelers in the dark, perhaps.»—*Ulysses*

We called them «sea enemies»...

... a term our father said was appropriate ... always 1 to warn us of the evils of women. He said they resembled the female anatomy.

On a school field trip to Canon beach our biology teacher told us to stick our tongues in an anemone + when we did we got a mild shock.

When we told our father he called the teacher a sick hippy freak.

«... which gave to his palate a fine tang of faintly scented urine [...] made him feel a bit peckish.»—U

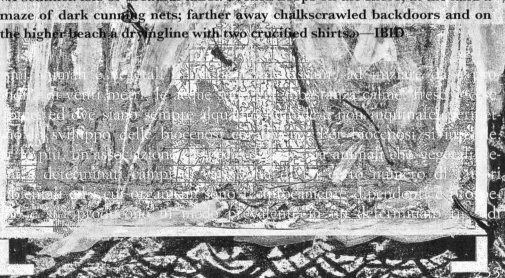

Kevin would later have a white cat (actually not his, but 1 his junkie roommates neglected) named Helen (cuz she was deaf). Altho deaf, she always knew somehow when some 1 was at the door. He lived in a 2nd story apartment w/ 1 of those mechanisms that let u open the door from the top of the stairs. The latch to the door was broken, but when we pulled the lever the protruding cable would retract into the wall giving Helen endless hours of addicting joy.

«A sentinel: isle of dreadful thirst. Broken hoops on the shore; at the land a maze of dark cunning nets; farther away chalkscrawled backdoors and on the higher beach a dryingline with two crucified shirts.»—IBID

pus that changed color w/ the light.

We'd revisit later as adults for the nostalgic kitsch of it + even brought ourselves to buy a dollar bag to once again feed the seals + to cross the Sandy River (see episode I4).

exhibit 31—(underlaid image) page 0:0:6 from *Ark Codex ±0* (Calamari Press, 2012)

We'd be putting words in our mouth to say we're «channeling». Our mom gave us 500 pesos (before the devaluation) for milk (that cost 8). I gave in only cuz she never noticed when we skimmed change off the top. Out onto the cobblestones .. in the blinding white sun. There we came across a TURTLE making it's way up from the lake. It was still there after we got the milk so Derek figured mom's courtyard was a good a place as any to keep it.

When he picked it up it peed on him, ha ha served him right. Mom wasn't thrilled. «Even if you set it free in here, how will we ever find it again?»

"We'll paint it, red," we said in stereo. I took the initiative to paint more than just a stripe or random blob, but to come up w/ a unique design ... tho our mom wanted just the letter ⚓ ... for Turtle or «Tortuga» (what they call them in the language they use here). I appeased her by saying the design would be Aztec influenced.

The paint («sangre de christo» colored) smelled like rotten eggs. Derek ruined a ruler to mix it than handed me a brush, saying "you're the 'artist'" (not w/o some detected sarcasm). May as well just put everything "in quotes" here. When U tell stories later it's "just words" ... the way you're telling it, not actually what happened in real life.

Derek asks what if GIRL turtles don't want to mate w/ it? That maybe the original markings on its shell (that I painted over) meant something? What is IT anyway, a boy or girl? How do you sex a turtle? We set it loose in the courtyard + never saw "it" again.

Whenever we wanted to use the phone in Mexico our mom acted like it was a special privilege ... it took her 13 years to get it after all! Evidently she had to be on a waiting list that long. It became a coveted object that we learned to worship + brag about to friends that didn't have 1, but we never used it (unlike Oregon where we'd sit + dial random #s for hours on end making prank calls). There was a locking plug on the **1** slot (sort of like the 1 left) that kept us from dialing any # xcept 111-1111 (tho in Mexico the pattern was 11-11-11). We don't have a photo of the very 1 we had ... the same phone i'd later receive the call on (see episode 10) from our other brother JD telling me «Dad's dead» .... but we're getting ahead of ourselves.

tele mach us

S K E U O M O R P H

The sound of horse hoofs on cobblestone re-wakes me up ... a loping clopity clop ... looking back on it (w/ the intent to make of it something else) was pointless. We'd yet to have custody of ourselves. He kept re-dealing the cards expecting at least a flush. Scrap-booking w/ glue the same story ... HIS story frozen ... on hold. How they ever got H-I-E-LO from I-C-E was beyond us ... living in the same submarine even. Or the time we found Rocky's loaded pistol ... or the jolt against my shoulder the 1st + only time i fired a .22 (not sure U were there? ... in that quarry at the base of Mt. Hood). Or when they raced horses on that linear track in Axixic ... remember? «Over as fast as the 2nd orgasm» said our mom's friend, Michelle (the same hippy lady U equated to Claire/Circe in episode 9). At the same place we'd rent horses from cuz it was the only thing to do ... until U got bucked off + kicked + after that you steered clear of horses in general.

ever-evolving we are ... he wished we didn't have to think ... that we were barnacles ... free swimming thru our larval stages ... 'till we could find a nice rock to take root on ... at which point barnacles digest their own brains he told me ... cuz we wouldn't be needing them anymore. «barnacle» also being the maiden name of joyce's wife nora (in real life). we'll settle into a pattern eventually (here) ... or not. perhaps this should be somewhat unsettling. ever-blooming like a wandering jew.

... born comme ça from sea enemies. «Hen-peck» a politer way to say «pussy-whip» or «cuckold». Our mother wasn'tpregnant w/ us, she was «**expecting**». She'd tell us later they never loved each other ... that they did it cuz it was expected.

THE ART OF SEDUCTION

May 20, 1989 – Santa Cruz, CA [from my dream/journal]

Dad + [our stepmother] came over to my house. He didn't give me a hug or even say hello. I tried to talk to him but he was very nervous, agitated, wouldn't make eye contact ... reminded me of Dustin Hoffman in *Rain Man*. Kevin was there + had a *Playboy* magazine, his feet up on a table. We just sat there at the table. I sat directly across from Dad while Kevin sat across from our stepmother, looking between her + the Playboy magazine as if making comparisons. Somebody off-screen (like a studio audience) asked our dad a question + he answered matter of factly. It was all very vivid.

(May 20 Venice Beach, 12 PM

The beast walks with two backs, light racks through the wall in carefully disguised rhythm (its shy) in my dream the other night [J] B. told her new boyfriend "Oh there's Kevin, he's in love with his dog (obvious). I think I have new molars growing in, or it a dense growth rising into my psyche.

(48)

May 21 12:41 PM Venice, CA

[Ray] and I just discussed the idea of an ambient television channel, I just thought of a way to transpose this journal into a book

[feels in his hip pocket for his latch key]

[real life story (now)] + [segments journal] + ["] + [If] + ["]

as the story progresses, the segments[,] current descriptions (?) of my life [become] juxtaposed with transcriptions of the journals. The segments go from long to shorter and shorter eventually merging and engulfing, written very scientifically, [w/ care, love?] formal, real time, date, locations, etc.

---

[48] Perhaps it's worth re-iterating here that tho we are using fancy word processing software + have the technical writing + information architecture chops that would enable us to use such features as auto-#ing + referencing, we are hard-coding these footnote + page #s. It's a sort of **constraint** writing that forces us not to add or subtract from our initial gut inclination. Tho this may seem fragmented, we are piece-mealing it together page x page in 1 fell swoop.

Hope we're living up to his designs ... at least **form**-wise. Content-wise, this is sposed to be about our Joycean or Odyssean father ... or our Calypsoian mother. In Kevin's original SSES thesis, all he included in the **Calypso** section was a letter that James Joyce wrote to Nora (his wife), w/ some side commentary about how Molly (in *Ulysses*) was modeled after her. Whether Molly represents Penelope or Calypso (or both) who's to say. The common thinking is that Molly is Penelope. Since our brother-½ inkluded this letter in the Calypso section, we have to wonder if he (+ Joyce) thought Nora was more characteristic of Calypso, or had more Calypsoian qualities (for starters, both were controlling nymphomaniacs).

On the above-mentioned journey i was taking by ship thru the straits of Malaka, i ~~member~~ i had a conversation w/ an Indonesian man who was very inquisitive about the American way of love + sex. It wasn't the only such conversation i had while in Indonesia (it seemed every day a complete stranger would come up + (holding my hand as they customarily do) ask me what it was like to have sex w/ American girls) — at ~~1st i thought these guys were gay or perverts, but soon realized they were just curious (+ ok maybe a bit repressed)~~. What struck me about this particular conversation on the stern of the ship (like Joyce, gazing at the wake)

CALYPSO   TR   June 16, 1904   was it was the 1st time i'd considered there coud be 2 kinds of love. Like many Indonesian men, this guy had a wife + a **mistress**. The way he rationalized it, he loved them equally, but in different ways. He had a «heavenly» love for the mother of his children + an «earthly» love for his sexy mistress.

My Dearest Nora;

The crossing was long, and cursed by foul weather. I am somewhat embarrassed to say that I spent the major-ity of the journey looking at the ship's wake.

I am now settled in Paris, in the hôtel du Triests, in the Montmartre section of the city. From my window I have a splendid view of the Basilique Du Sacré- Couer, and the Notre Dame de Clignacourt. The hotel itself is quite comfortable, and for this I am very glad. Our parting has left me in no state to continue traveling, or to be soci-able.

I am waiting to hear from Señor A. Boudin regarding the house I am to rent from him in Gibraltar. I have no idea how long my wait might be. I had informed Mr. Paul De-Cock that my intention was to report for work on the first of July.

I do not think you could imagine the pain I feel at this moment, my desire to run to the station right now and board the next train to Calais, to return to you. Oh my dear sweet Molly! Can you ever forgive me for leaving you? You must believe me when I say it was the hardest decision of my life. I will never, not even for an instant, forget you. The battle that is waging in my heart has left me crip-pled.

That dark island you call your country will always be for me where you live. Shan Von Vocht, waiting on the shores of the emerald isle, a queen among nations. You stand there, on the pier at Rosslare, pulling your shaw over your shouldar, wiping your sweet eyes. Molly. As you stood there and watched me sail away, I could see them coming down to take back your body. The dark storm clouds pouring down from the mountains of Kerry, from behind you frail figure on the pier, the kings and saints, the warriors and the poets, driving me away and reclaiming you.

You. The beautiful young girl standing alone in front of the black carriage, her red curls dramatically in front of the black lacquer.

By the time the boat was turning out of the breakwaters the flowers on your dress had blended in, making it look grey. As I watched you there on the pier, clutching yourself to block out the now colder winds, my desire to reverse my decision was so great that I grabbed the ship's steward, who was walking al-ong the deck, and pleaded with him to turn the ship around. He said he could only do so in the case of an emergency. I told him it was, he gave me a very grave look, and I declined to pursue it any further.

Spread out behind me was the rest of the world, a vast expanse of sun drenched land and sea. In front of me; one dark, green island. On that island there is, somewhere, an old cottage constructed out of sandstone and pale slate, with smoke pour-ing out of it's small chimney, a carriage pulled by a glossy brown horse, a handful of churches in various states of decay, and some castles suffering the same, some dairy cows, a tiny pier and a young girl who is standing all alone.

NORA- reference to Joyce's wife, after whom the chara-cter of Molly Bloom was most likely modeled. June 16 (1904) is the day that Joyce probably discovered that he was in love with the 20 year old Galway woman, whom he married some four months later.
Señor A. Boudin the true name of the drunk sailor in the "Eumaeus" chapter.
Paul DeCock ,C. French nov-elist(1794-1871)of trashy smut, Molly thinks he got his name through his sexual proclivities.
Calais-French sea port, one of two boat ports for ships to Ireland (Rosslare Harb-our).

[2]**Shan Von Vocht(the)** Irish mythical character, old wo-man, personification of downtrodden Ire., who will become a beautiful queen when Ire. takes it's right-ful place in the world.
[3]**Rosslare**-<see Calais>
[4]**Molly**-(Bloom) char. in "Ulysses",<see Nora>
[5]**Kerry**-County in So.Ire.
[6]**Cliffs of Moher**-"There's the Burren and the Cliffs of Moher,..........
  (Jimmy McCarthy, from;
  "Lisdoonvarna". Perfo-rmed by Christy Moore on his self titled LP, "Christy Moore"1988. -Atlantic Rec. Corp.
[7]**...held captive seven years...only ■with aid of the spirit of Athene....** Reference to the "Odyssee"(Homer), book v, ("Odysseus departs from Calypso"); Ulysses manages to escape from Calypso with Athene's help (she persuades

While this age-old duality may not be news for some, this was the 1st i'd heard it explained in such a reasonable ~~(but still sexist=in western standards)~~ way. The sense i got in reading *The Odyssey* was that Calypso's love for Ulysses was not 1-way ... that he loved her back (despite it saying he was «forc'd» ... «unwilling») + U also seemed to enjoy his time spent w/ Circe (episode 9). When wing-footed Hermes[49] is dispatched to fetch U, Calypso rails on him + the male gods for their hypocrisy ... but we don't know what Ulysses thinks cuz he can't get a word in edge-wise ... 1 thing for sure is nobody was holding a knife to his throat on his last night w/ Calypso: «*This said, the sun set, and the earth shows gave; / When these two (in an in-room of the cave, / Left to themselves) left no rites undone.*»

... on the other hand:

«Surely if a wife had been dutifully avoiding any number of suitors for twenty full years while waiting for her husband to come home she ought to have recognized the husband when he got there.»—David Markson, *Wittgenstein's Mistress*

[49] See exhibit 9 on page 28 + also footnote 21 on page 37.

1 thing for sure (as evidenced by his love letter to Mrs. Barnacle) is that Joyce thought of Nora as Calypso[50] ... + altho he was seduced + captured by love, he was a «most willing victim».

+ then as if to balance out the pussy-whipped love of Joyce, Kevn gives us a dose of misogynist violence.

CALYPSO   JUNE 16, 1904

The mood of this letter is a far cry from Bloom's feelings toward Molly in *Ulysses*. He is devoted, but also somewhat detached ... in denial of her extramarital affairs. After going to the butcher to get a pork kidney, he makes breakfast for her ... like a good hen-pecked husband. But otherwise, they pretty much do their own thing ... he reads some letters, 1 from the dude Molly is openly having an affair with + another from their daughter. Then he takes a dump in the outhouse.

The Calypso episode of *The Odyssey* is about more than Calypso ... it's about Ulysses *leaving* Calypso. This is only the beginning of his troubles. The gods enable him to get a boat + crew to split the island, but Poseidon—who not only feels cheated cuz he wasn't consulted in the gods' plans to help U, but still holds a grudge against U for killing his son—isn't having it ... he whips up a storm + sinks his ship, but Athena intervenes + whisks U to safety on the island of Scheria.

How does this translate in our book? We already said that the leaving of Calypso coincides w/ our father's + S's d-i-v-o-r-c-e (tho it was actually her that left him). This rupture/threshold also coincides w/ the point in which we left our father to live w/ our real mother down in Mexico ... so we weren't privy to the rest of Dad's return odyssey + have no records to show for it.

Do you remember the afternoon we spent together lying in the tall grass of the cliffs of Moher. You des--cribed for me the forms you saw in the clouds, and I rec--orded in my mind the features of your beauty. Your image of languid palor,blood red lips, long copper shavings coil--ing down over delicate matte porcelain, your young laugh.

For you I will burn for the rest of my life. Like a condemned man being slowly led away, backing into the sun to burn. My heart suffers the opposite fate. I tried to tell you that first night we spent together how I felt. Of how your blood had mixed with mine, causing me to lapse into a sickness completely foreign to me. I did not vocalize this feeling then, as I thought you would take it wrong.You did not poison me, I was the most will--ing victim, I chose my own fate, and then I left you while I still could, before I became just some aspect of you, before I lost myself.

You have held my heart captive for seven years, and, only with the unforeseen aid of the spirit of Athene, have I managed to leave you! Leaving with you most of my interior, taking with me just enough to survive. But this self preservation is unmotivated, I feel I have no real reason to live. It is some blind faith that makes me draw the next breath. My love for you has left me less than human. I can now only prepare for an existence of artifice, as a man without a soul. I declare blindly that my sense of self, as atrophied as it is, will re--generate itself. You, Calypso, have committed the worst possible crime unto me.

- the other gods to recon--sider their punishment of Ulysses (a movement spear--headed by Poseidon, who hates Ulysses for what he did to his son the cyclops). After they consent to her intervention, she orders Calypso to release Ulysses. **[8] Calypso-** George Sigerson, an Irish Renais--sance popularizer, champio--ned the idea that Homer modeled Calypso's island (Ogygia) after Ireland. Joyce did not accept this idea. He believed Homer developed his composite of Ogygia, at least partially, with Gibraltar in mind. Gibraltar is where Molly is from. Joyce's wife Nora was from Galway (on the west coast of Ireland). Joyce was from Dublin. The train from Dublin to Gal-way runs twice daily. The morning train leaves at 7am, arriving in Galway at 1:30pm.

"You stupid FUCKING CUNT!"...(CRASH)...(SLAP!)...

"I..dent meen et...(sob)"

"You stupid fucking bitch! I have a mind to beat your fucking ass to a pulp"

"Oh pleeese Dave...(sob).. OOOOhh!..GOD! (slap, CRASH!)"

"You STUPID fucking bitch! I told you a million times to stay out of my stash

"(sob)"

"You just couldnt? Could you? Huh!?...(SLAP!)"

"Imm saary..."

"Your sorry? SORRY?? .. YOU STUPID BITCH!!!...(THUD!).."

                    (KNOCK!KNOCK!KNOCK!)

-(silence).....

"Hey Dave! Whats up?...(door closing)"

"hey"

"Great truck you got out there, where'd you get..Hey what's going on man?"

"HEY! MIND YOUR OWN FUCKING BUISNESS MAN!!..(BLAM!!! BLAM!!!..BLAM!!)

"OoHH MY GOD!!!"

---

[50] In fact, in his notebooks he writes Calypso = Penelope. By the transitive law (if A = B and B = C, then A = C), since he also equates Nora to Molly (2x in the letter he calls her as such) + also Calypso (he signs off «You, Calypso ...» + also says «you have held my heart captive for seven years» on the «dark island you call your country...»), we can deduce that Nora = Molly = Calypso = Penelope.

... on the other hand, it's absurd that Joyce equates Calypso = Penelope ... unless these are just roles that the mistress/nymph + wife/mother of his child can be embodied in 1.

[handwritten:] Homer   All 1 of the Same embodiment!

[handwritten:] Calypso = Penelope.

[handwritten right margin:] ...or Nora/molly stand for the ISLAND of Ireland/Calypso w/o blm at it's heart.... where he never returned ...culture + (in real life) race And Irelend

[handwritten bottom right:] Rhet
Mimesis- "Well, I gues" ✓
Archaism- "It was, I ween"
Prosthesis- "Down, adown"
Epenthesis- "Confederate"
Paragoge- "Lily light" ✓

It seams brother-½ had more designs for his Calypso episode than what he inkluded in his thesis. Below we have 1 page from his notebooks, listing places in Paris (perhaps in response to Joyce's previous letter) + in the left column below it says:
«I received her ~~first letter after~~ I returned, the morning after my apartment burned down. It's been over two years, I remember what ----[scribbled out + unfinished] [....] ~~I came back from ...~~»

" CALYPSO "

I received her   Port de Bagnolet
~~first letter, the~~   Gambetta
first letter after   Pere-lachaise
I returned, the   Saint Maur
morning after my   Parmentier
apartment burned   République
down, It's been over   Strasbourg St. Denis
two years, I wrote   Bonne Nouvelle
what ~~she~~   Rue Montmartre
                         Opera
                         Madeleine
                         Concorde.

~~I came back from~~

[p. 324 "internal combustion engine in theory and practice vol. 1. taylor.]

«He held the page aslant patiently, blending his will, his soft subject gaze at rest.» —U

ABSENCE, subs. (ETON).— NAMES calling, which takes place at 3 p.m. and 6 p.m. on half-holidays; and at 11:30 a.m, 3 p.m and 6 p.m on whole holidays; at 6 p.m only in summer half.
DICTIONARY OF SLANG (BOOK 1; A-K) JOHN FARMER, HERTFORDSHIRE (UK), WORDSWORTH EDITION ltd. 1987.

He started writing more than his 'SSES' 'SSES' thesis after he got back from his trip. ~~And started to get more into drugs ... tho this was not information he shared w/ me at the time. I didn't take drugs or even drink all thru high school + college ... it never enticed me much, having a stoner mom + alcoholic dad. When we discussed these things our brother-½ agreed, in theory, that drugs + alcohol were stupid + destructive.~~ But evidently (as i woud find out later in Kevin's rehab) our mom xposing us to drugs at an early age had more of an impact on him than we thawed ... ~~Around this time was when he 1st admitted to us that he'd smoke pot on occasion ... mostly he did it while making art cuz it stimulated the creative juices, relieved boredom, the usual justifications ...~~

Living in a vacuum on A no man's isle

This idea of ABSENCE starts to become more + more of an obssesion for brother-½. As we speculated on page 12, we're guessing this is attributable to reading Derrida. In the drafts of pieces he was writing, u can see how this notion of absence seeds stories, as if he was **deconstructing** his stories rather than constructing.

For example, to the right is a page (after inventorying his casettes + books) that starts w/ the definition of absence (highlighted by an F (another habit of his)) followed by the beginnings of a story:

ABSENCE. THE STATE OF BEING — which one is away 3. The condition of not having needed or desirable; lack.

He had slowly built her up in his mind. Bits and pieces of everyone he had ever known. When completed, she would be the person he does not know. A

FLASHBACKS   He had slowly built her up in his mind. Bits and pieces of everyone he had ever known. When completed, she would be the person he does not know. A person about whom he would learn nothing. A person through whom he would learn everything about himself, more than he could imagine to contain within him. In order to make himself complete he needed every other person. In this way he needed every other person.

Making objects to negate itself

[This] = information ... ≠ Art

person about whom he would learn nothing. A person through whom he would learn everything about himself, more than he could imagine to contain within him. In order to make himself complete in this way he needed every other person.

Her image burns unbridled through my being ... a violent addiction. I can only wait for the burning to stop and see how many layers she has burned through. I am now waiting, submitting myself unwittingly to the pain. I feel incapacitated and incomplete. I want this to stop. I want her out of my mind.

Not sure who he is talking above ... if brother-½ did have girlfriends at the time, he didn't fill us in. The next page goes back to the perspective of Telemachus looking for his father ... + how this gave purpose to his odyssey, rather than just being a wanderer. Then he returns to the idea of **absence** as relates to travelling, which seems legible enough that we shouldn't need to transcribe it:

instead we split + fracture further

TELEMACHUS ~~DON'T THINK~~ TOOK ON THE SEARCH FOR HIS FATHER SEVEN YEARS ~~AFTER~~ HE LEFT. TO THE DAY AFTER HE LEFT. HE DESCRIBED HIS JOURNEY ~~FOR~~ HIS FATHER, BUT HE KNEW THAT HE HAD NO INTENTION OF FINDING HIS FATHER. HE JUST WANTED TO GET OUT AND SEE THE WORLD, AND HIS EXPRESSED MOTIVE SUPPLIED HIM WITH ~~AND~~ A REASON FOR THE TRIP. HE HATED THE IDEA OF THE TRAVELLER AS A WANDERER AND IMAGINED THAT A PERSON WITH AN IMPORTANT MISSION

THE TERM ABSENCE CAN AT TIMES REFER TO EVERYTHING THAT IS IN MY MIND (AND SUBSEQUENTLY EVERYTHING THAT IS IN THE WORLD) IN ORDER FOR ME TO CONVEY MY NOTION OF ABSENCE I WOULD HAVE TO DESCRIBE SOMETHING I WOULD CONSIDER AS PRESENT. FOR ME ONE CAN ONLY REALLY HAVE AN ~~EX~~ EXPERIENCE WITH THE LANDSCAPE, AND THE SURROUNDINGS HAVE TO BE UNFAMILIAR AS FAMILIAR SURROUNDINGS ARE ALREADY STORED IN MEMORY AND THUS ABSENT.
THE TRAVELLER IS UNATTACHED FROM THE LANDSCAPE. AT TIMES MERELY A GHOST EXPERIENCING NEW LANDS. ~~AN INVISIBLE~~ MOSTLY BECAUSE HE IS UNKNOWN, ~~THE ELSE~~ ON OCCASION HE IS PRESENTED AS A TOURIST IN THE EYES OF A LOCAL IN ORDER TO OBTAIN FOOD, LODGING OR SOME OTHER SERVICE.

SHE SPEAKS TO HIM SOFTLY, OF THE HALCYON DAYS A MOUTH. A FILM TRAILER BEAUTIFUL IN ITS EDITING, EVERYTHING LOOKS SOFT ON THE EDGES AND THE LIGHT SHIMMERS. LEAVES CASCADES TO THE GENTLE STRING MUSIC IN HIS HEAD, THE BACKGROUND

FRACTAL FRANKenstein

PROMethean DRESSing

this could be U

Our brother-½ didn't just explore the notion of absence in his writings, but he started to integrate it into his art, into the objects he made. Mixed in w/ these half-baked stories are *ideas* he had for objects, such as this text):

~~Absence in a presence~~

Absence within a presence.

~~My work seeks to be involves the~~ The objects I make are built up and around the absence of the artist. The works, ~~which being~~ with the hollow(s) left by the artists hand, are never really complete unless the artist (to whom the arrangement and size of the ~~who~~ holes are made) refills the holes with his hand. ~~Although the holes do not only~~ The holes could conceivably be filled by someone else (left handed, large, etc.) The dimension of the [piece] also correlates to the artist's body, the holes are directly at groin level, the top point at eye level.

The pieces share a standard size uniformly, which as I mentioned, correspond to the artist's body (the general dimensions are 42" high, 12" wide, 9" deep). The body shapes of the pieces are ambiguous shapes which seek to subtly refer to identifiable shapes but not to being recognized as such. The metal plate (in which the holes are drilled) is no more than 10 inches square, usually flat, sometimes shaped. [The] shapes of these metal pieces are signs, symbols or icons of absence and transitoryness [sic] (Frosty the Snow Man, Starburst, the Microscopic). The body forms are covered in elements (graphite, sulfur, iron, lead) <u>transitory</u> in that they all react to the air we breathe to form compounds, thus never really being just elements.

eXile on (X) isle

... + it continues on (below). The pieces he de-scribes became realized as the objects that went into his Master's xhibit—ELEMENTS (see episode 13). (Also note that these names below left—Palmer Land, Wilkes Land + Enderby Land—are regions of Antarctica, that he again lists in the Oxen of the Sun episode (#11).)

["ABSENCE WITHIN A PRESENCE"]

THE THREE WORKS ENTITLED; [orange] "PALMERLAND", [LEMON] "ENDERBY LAND", [CHERRY] "WILKES LAND", FUNCTION AS A SET, ALTERNATLY STANDING IN FOR FRAGMENTATION, (INCOMPLETNESS) AND completeness. The titles orange, lemon, & cherry, not only function as visual suppliments to the correlating bright colors (orange, citron, dark red-brown) but also they seek to minimize the harmful elements (sulfer, iron, lead) from which the colors are the colors (in their oxidized forms) The lusciousness of the positive surfaces, along with the flavor titles propose cause our to deem these that these should be read as large candies, their shape having something to do with the flavor (as their colors do). When one reads the material list, this stated urge to taste is quickly dispelled. The caustic nature of the elements (and the extreme delicacy of the surface) Give significance to the metal parts, as handles from which to grasp (move)the piece. Their size tends to this idea of portability.

[* For a tran-scription of these notes to the left, see episode 13.]

♪ 🎵 🎼

«...was a fairy tale
they say
he was made of snow
but the children know
that he'd come
to life 1 day ...»

While watching POPEYE he'd joke about the flagrant drug metaphor of snorting spinach thru his corncob pipe + then getting a rush like he was jacked on cocaine...

Ulysses's absence is what sets the gears in motion for Telemachus, just like the absence of a father figure explains a lot about brother-½. Even when our father was alive, he was far from **present**. He may as well have been maruined for life on Calypso's island.

This objectifying of absence in brother-½'s art coud be seen as a sort of negation of self, but the objets also have something to do w/ the idealized embodiment of love—an untouchable, maruined ideal.

Ulysses's journey starts on an island ... which in a sense is a **clean start**.

Her hair is big and sometimes [seems] off. The color itself is unnatural, it looks OK though, I mean, after all this is 1970.

MORE BLOOD MONEYTEEN

xhibit 31—"untitled" 1990 (sulphur powder, wood, aluminum)[dimensions not specified, but all the 1s from this series (see episode 13) are the approximate size of a female torso + were to be mounted so the finger holes (that fit Kevin's hand) were at groin level]. Altho untitled, he referred to this 1 as «Sulphur» or «Frosty the Snowman».

She [–sounds like our stepmother, S] was married three times before she finished high school. Her father was a leathery Canadian old-timer who skated across vast sheets of black ice for hours through the dark pre-dawn morning, just to get to work in the mill every day.

In her day she was a hot little number, with good values. Anyway, she eventually finds the handsome doctor-type, raises a litter, gets sick of his drinking and leaves him. Then she goes out and finds herself another man ... basically the same one, with the same number of kids. Marries him and raises his clutch through the next decade.

Eventually she leaves him because of his drinking. She goes back out into the world and finds herself another guy [our father]. Once again she plays the role of surrogate mother, this time to his kids [us]. This time everything is fine. He doesn't drink. She is happy and the world is a better place for it.

It's always tempting to project or compare ... but we must persevere + put some distance tween ourselves + the narrator. Yet at the same time not be afraid to walk in his shoes. Still saddle sore in Axixic are we. Kevin + i living parallel lives under the same roof. Each staking out our turf. We shared a room at 1st ... it was dark + when we 1st walked in we almost stepped on a dead scorpion on the floor. Our mom said it happens when you shift things around or do construction (which she was doing in preparation for our arrival) + that if we ate the heads we'd become immune to their stings ...

«It's dark + damp» Kevin said.

«Easy to change» she said. Nothing's permanent. There's no master plan ... simply smash a hole in the wall + if you're carefull you can reuse the bricks.

She showed us where the crowbar + sledge hammer were kept.

«Really?» he asked. We can just do this? We don't need a permit?

But i didn't wait for an answer, just went to town tearing down the wall. Our mom relit the joint that had gone out in her hand.

«U best keep track of the order» he said. «It's not as easy putting it all back together as it is taking it apart. That's what the law of **entropy** tell us.»

«Chato can help» our mom xhaled. «You only need to pay people here 25 pesos a day to make them happy.» We did the conversion in our heads ... 3 dollars. «*Skilled* labor too ... tear down a wall and they'll rebuild it somewhere else ... they don't care, they're just happy to have work. And u can help ... it will do u boys good ... physically + mentally. U might learn something.»

And we did. If u want to know if a floor on the other side of a wall is at the same level, take a tube + fill it w/ water + measure how far the water rises on each end. + we learned to mix sement .... + chip bricks to repurpose them.

This was our 1st lesson in deconstruction theory.

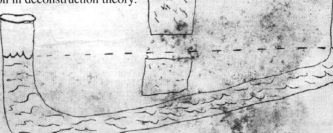

GOING THROUGH PUBERTY IN A FOREIGN TONGUE [51]

It started out as a hole in my mother's courtyard.

In my head, Corn Tassel came through for me, shouldering the bulge of maize bundled in moist fabric. Over the red-tiled rooftops, a chorus of roosters cock-a-doodled off key. She had no face yet, for I did not pray to stone.

I was becoming more and more aware of the lymph nodes where my legs attached to my body. My left hand was up, scraping plaster from the crumbling adobe walls, and my right hand was a vestigial monkey tail dangling to my side for balance. This was the pose 'I' struck as I stumbled over the corner stone to some unknown ancient altar and stepped into The Hole, forgetting the lymph nodes for a split second.

Herein lies the other figures discovered in The Hole:

Monkey House
Noble Sweatbath
Not Right Now
Fish in the Ashes
The Modeler

... and Corn Tassel was honorably mentioned (by Cabeza de Vaca), and there were others like Shrimp Cocktail that I had yet to encounter, and there was the ever-present smell of cornhusks burning in the fields, and my mother standing, a joint wedged between her own knuckles, accusing me of re-opening the wound.

I hadn't left home. I couldn't leave until I graduated from the Monkey House, whose tongue I had not swallowed yet.

I opened my mouth to defend myself and my voice cracked an octave. Thunder rumbled overhead but the sky did not split open. Monkey House rattled in my voice box, but in my head I gave Corn Tassel a pair of tight lips.

«Double cross
the vacant and the bored
They're not sure
just what we have in store
Morphine city
slipping dues down to see
That we don't even care
as restless as we are
We feel the pull
in the land of a thousand guilts
And poured cement,
lamented and assured»
—Smashing Pumpkins, 1979

[51] Reprinted from *ma(I)ze Tassel Retrazos* (Calamari Press, 2005)

DRUNKARD

My father was tied to a post —along with six of his best men—and shot. This happened when I was twelve. I vividly remember the sweltering heat and the albatross skimming the oily water of the harbour with its [mottled] wings. The Village Person's Militia pulled my father and the others down the main street by their hair. They took them down to the beach, and in the shadows cast by the rusted oil tankers, tied them each to big beams of wood that were stuck into the sand.

Seven posts. Seven dazed, grown men in their underwear ... in the harsh sunlight, all of them looking at the ground cursing to themselves ... crying their last tears.

I watched the executions from the back of the crowd gathered on the beach .... gathered in the heat to enjoy the spectacle of seven drunks getting what they deserved ...... After all, drunkenness, as everyone knows, is illegal ... guess there wasn't much choice in the matter ...... My dad had taken to drinking ... drinking a lot and drinking alone ...... He got sloppy ...... he got sloppy and let too many people see his drunkenness. [He had friends at 1ˢᵗ that] could be counted on to help him out ...... but then he lost all his friends, and soon after, his job.

After losing his job, he took up permanent residence in his Lay-Z-boy. He kept it tilted all the way back, remote in his left hand ...... surfing ...... drink (scotch & water) in the right.

Set into the wall near his chair was a leather-bound collection of all of the great works of philosophy and science. Dad read through all these great works, many times. He read through them, and then thought about what he had read. He thought about what he had read, and then he wrote about it, critiquing it, correcting it ...... he was published in all the major science journals, under the pen name of Geo L. Thorpe. He might have been a loser in the "interacting with other humans" category, but he was top of his field in philosophy and sciences. He lived alone in a world of books ...... ideas, dead people's minds. He was never really there in any real sense.

xhibit 32—sketch from early notebook

LOTERIA

25

EL BORRACHO

[Telemachus]

"I remember the sensation of talking to him, and feeling proud that what I was saying was of interest to him, and then becoming aware that what was making him so happy—the thing that was making him smile—was that he was analyzing the semiotic structure of my language as I spoke.

Dad's marriage to my step mom was an investigation into separation anxiety and co-dependency. He kept a record of the case, even referring to it by the name: Friar vs. Friar.

He predicted the breakup of the two people involved in C. Friar vs. S. Friar ...... he described how the relationship would crash into a tree, completely shearing the 50-year old oak out of the ground, and flattening their black Jeep Cherokee into a crumpled black bag of shiny metal ... pieces of sparkling glass and strips of black rubber [careening every which way].

The bullets popped as they went through the bodies and into the [tree trunks]. The trunked poles were still humming minutes later.

Motor oil dripped down the pole into the sand. [It was no accident the posts were staked below the high-tide mark.]

When the execution was over, they left the my father and the 6 others [to wilt] and rot in the sun. Then the tide came in and submerged the dead men, leaving their corpses to the frenzy of sharks.

IRELAND

DUBLIN ●

→ Kramer vs. Kramer came out this year (1979)
+/- he was also into Spy vs. Spy

Brown, grey and cold. The feeling is described and explained by some sense of genetic memory. Teutonic memory. Jagged snow capped peaks.Pine forests. A frozen stillness. Sun filtering through the forest canopy,illuminating the swirling clouds of steam rising from the blanket of pine needles,and moss carpeting the trail I walk.I have reached a point in the forest where no one has ever gone.

    Cal stirs violently, opens his mouth, sits up and checks his clock.

    "The winter is over, let us usher in the Spring with some brown bear oil."

    "Must your mornings always start with some reference to b.m's?"

    "I can't help it. I had a very ominous, disturbing dream.I have awoken to a sense of doom, as if I am to recieve bad news today. I must rid myself of this harbinger of misfortune."

    "Why does the bear always represent evil for you?"

    "That's what it is is'nt? Toxicity, garbage, waste;precisously that which we struggle to get rid of, distance ourselves from."

    "Is that what dreams are for you? Garbage?"

    "Preeisely, *exactly* mental garbage, our minds need to download or dump so much information in order to function, take in new stimuli.Without the dumping of toxic matter the psyche would become inundated."

    "So how owuld you characterize dream analyasis? Or the concious effort to retain dreams?"

    "Packrat-ing. Filling your attic with rotting garbage."

    [...]

Her spoon ceased to stir up the sugar. She gazed straight before her, inhaling through her arched nostrils.

    —There's a smell of burn, she said. Did you leave anything on the fire?

    —The kidney! he cried suddenly.

... + we end this episode w/ another email from our mother:

I HAD WONDERED WHY IT WAS IMPORTANT TO NOTE THAT KEVIN HAD A SENSE OF HUMOR WHEN HE WAS 3 YRS OLD (BUT DIDN'T KNOW HE WAS AN ARTIST FOR 7 MORE)----BUT THEN J UST GOOGLED JOHN TENNIEL AND HIS HISTORY! I JUST FOUND OUT THAT HE WAS MORE FAMOUS FOR HIS HUMOR THEN HIS DRAWING FOR LEWIS CARROLL! AND AFTER KEVIN DROVE FROM ARIZONA---THAT NIGHT--HE TOOK ME TO THE FOOTHILLS TO SEE THE COMET! AND THE NEXT--I WOKE UP TO SEE THE THE COMET IN MY BEDROOM WINDOW---WHEN KEVIN WAS GONE! I AM GLAD THAT I COULD PASS ON THESE FEW THINGS ABOUT KEVIN! (KEVIN IS HAPPY ALSO!)

KEVIN HAD A LOT OF THINGS THAT MADE HIM DIFFERENT! I CAN ONLY THINK OF TWO LITTLE THINGS THAT MAKE YOU "DIFFERENT"! YOU HAVE "OLD SOUL" HANDS AND YOUR HOLE (SMALL POND) ON YOUR CHEST--WHICH A DOCTOR SAID IT WAS CAUSING YOU TO BREATH IN REVERSE? GLAD THAT THEY DIDN'T BREAK YOUR CHEST---AND I KEEP WONDERING HOW YOU CAN BREATH IN REVERSE! LOVE MOM

P.S. Excuse bad writing am in a hurry Byby — U

From *Ulysses* (the Calypso episode):

    —Metempsychosis, he said, frowning. It's Greek: from the Greek. That means the transmigration of souls.

    —O, rocks! she said. Tell us in plain words.

    He smiled, glancing askance at her mocking eyes. [...] Bone them young so they metampsychosis. That we live after death. Our souls. That a man's soul after he dies, Dignam's soul ...

    —Did you finish it? he asked.

    —Yes, she said. There's nothing smutty in it. Is she in love with the first fellow all the time?

    —Never read it. Do you want another?

REIN CARNATION IN REVERENCE

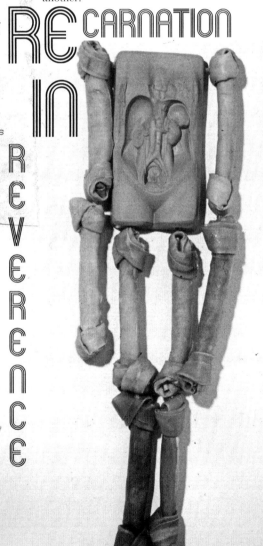

xhibit 33— [untitled, we're guessing a date of 1992, colored silicon + dogchew bones]

TIME : Winter 1980
PLACE : Guadalajara + Axixic, Mexico

IDEAS/Symbolism : initiation rites, shame, hypocrisy, Eden, fractured projections, puppets, (still in the belly of the whale).

ABSTRACT : (cont.) to converge to our new sur-roundings in our biblical sala de espejos w/a clutch prism + we pine the tail on eyeore ....where 'puberty' is tuna entombed in cob webs (since TUNA is 'prickly pear' cactus fruit, they made TUNA = ATUN). We lost our clothes + our virginity (can't speak for our brother ½) after forsaking wrist exercise for bodies w/o organs .... for HER.

NAUSICAA   CORPUS

)) step 8 (of 12) is about making amends ... ((

After being Calypso's sex-slave for 7 years, our hero doesn't waste any time getting seduced again ... this time platonically by Nausicaa, who Minerva encourages to wash her 'weeds' in the <u>river</u> to be more enticing. Ulysses wakes up + discovers N + her maidens by the river ... U is naked, but manages to stay in cognito ... he cleans the muck from the sea off + N falls in love w/ him ... tho nothing ever transpires. U resists temptation (we'd say it seems almost biblical, but *The Odyssey* was written way before Adam + Eve ever get naked + tempted).

This corresponds to the episode (skipping ahead) in *Ulysses* where Bloom <u>masturbates</u> while watching Gerty MacDowell xpose herself.

Kevin's Nausicaa projection (right) comes in a Himalayan fish-head shape ... the only unclimbed peak in the world over 27,000 feet ... not necessarily cuz it's difficult, but cuz it's considered **holy** to the Nepalese. But for now (in the chronologic scheme of things) we remain in Mexico circa 1980.

ST; "Of all your experiences during your trip, which st-ends out as being the most memorable?"
RH; "Probably the sight of Machapucharri in the dawn, the day I walked up to the Annapurna base camp."
ST; "Could you elaborate on that?"
RH; "Sure!, Well, lets see, I had spent the night in a cave in the valley wall. You see, it was a wise move to get as close to the avalanche areas to sleep, because then you could cross them in the morning before the sun loosened them up, and made them dangerous. The day before I got to the cave I passed a little group of huts . On the trail near these huts, in the bushes, where the bod-ies of three sherpas who had died in an avalanche the day before, on the trail directly above the cave. There is only one trail as the valley is incredibly steep.

I was traveling alone because the Norwegien friends I had made got (altitude) sick(ness). I had the benefit of having had spent two weeks the previous month in Tibet (suffering altitude sickness).

Anyway. I arrived at the cave late in the eve-ning. It was raining very hard. Already in the cave th-ere was three hikers from Australia, and the old Nepal-ese man who lived there. He cooked us dinner, chanting the whole time, and then we went to sleep. It was kind of hard to sleep because the old man left the door open, he said that he had to in order to allow the spirits to come in. The spirits didn't keep me up. I woke up before everyone else, packed, and went outside.

Machapucharri is a holy mountain to the Hindu's. It also has the distinction of being on of the last un-climbed peaks over 27,000 in the world. It's name means "fishhead". One instantly knows why it is called this when they see it. The top part of the peak consists of a huge piece of granite that looks like a steep pyramid. The West side of the mountain (the side facing the valley) is so steep (and smooth) that the snow does not stick. One British man in the early fifties mad it to the base

---

THE UNCONTROLLED SHAPE OF AN HOUR GLASS. The light reflects brighter from the center. COMMER--CIAL-IMAGE-VISABILITY. glossy. POLY-URETHANE; MOLAR, CARROT, RUSTY--PIPE. Transparent lea--ther showing growth lines. PERIFERY DISCOL--ORED BORDER. Grey. Russet. Fuschia.

Box without sides. PINK TROUSERS SOAKED IN RESIN. Wrinkled. THE AB--OVE MENTIONED FORMING A SURROGATE FOOT. Lost in the swelling of ele-phantitis.

FOUR, THEN FIVE HIPS. An iced over field. SOLITARY STALKS OF WHEAT DEAD SILVER. Below the surface can be seen the frozen remains of meand--ering irrigation ditch--es. EMERALD FLUID. The frozen earth pulls the surface into a geometric grid. A SPIDER WEB ACROSS THE FIELD(S). Five more degrees and it would melt, as it so often do--es.

LARGER FIELDS, HIGH--ER GROUND, LESS WATER MARKS. Healthier remnants

NAUSICAA   CORPUS

Never before had we gone thru an intersection that wasn't on a square grid ... a 4-way stop ... + all of a sudden we find ourselves in the inner lane of **glorieta Minerva** ... the main round-a-bout in Guadalajara where 6-10 streets converge into a smoggy clusterfuck of chaos. Our mother driving ... joint dangling from mouth ... Steely Dan playing ... yelling at us to say when it was clear ... 3 x around before a clearing formed + we headed down Lopez Mateos to our new school ...

of the top part [maybe a few hundred metres from the actual top] but declined to climb the last part. Since then the Nepalese have been very reluctant to grant perm- -its to climb it. Rumor has it they take this stance out of fear. Fear of what the faithful would do to the mount- -aineers who successfully defiled thier holy mountain.

I was lucky enough to have a unhindered view of the peak for a few hours every day. The cave was at about 18,000 feet, so the peak was about 10,000 feet (almost) directly above the tiny valley.

It would be impossible to convey to you my emotions that morning I stepped out into the cold dawn air and looked up at the towering peak. The home of Shiva. I took pictures, I even staggered them so I could put them tog- -ether later and form a more detailed composite. But this was all in vain. I failed to capture the spirit that was there, and I guess that failure was inevitable.

of growth. HOOK, BEND, DOG LEG. Italy. Up to the peak. Over the hill and to the mountain. Its more than sheer face unscalable. A ZONE OF SENSITIVITY WHERE NOTHING GOES: UN- -noticed. Shrouded in mist most of the day. And always hidden in the night.

DAEDALUS ... where Stephen deadly devises his Name.

+ the **clutch** was all fucked up ... 1 time the stickshift came clean off in our mom's hand + she yelled at us to do something but there was just a hole w/ 1 of those accordion cones ... what coud we do? I was in the backseat, Kevin was riding shotgun ... he took a bic pen + jammed it into the hole but the pen fell clean thru + he started laughing, said he could see the road going by beneath us!

Narrative is a lot like backseat driving ... or drugs. Hard to «try» or experience vicariously + not get sucked in. Like how Icarus was told not to drive his father's chariot too close to the sun. Our memory remains fragmented in non-addictive or all-consuming doses. Skeptic even of skeptics.

From the Nausicaa episode of *Ulysses*:

Thinks I'm a tree, so blind. Have birds no smell? Metempsychosis. They believed you could be changed into a tree from grief. Weeping willow. Ba. There he goes.

Do fish ever get seasick?

Heliotrope? No. Hyacinth?

Lemons it is. Ah no, that's the soap.

exhibit 34—still life from Kevin's 1st notebook

... nothing personal... we didn't choose our parents + they didnt choose us. Nada was planned, their cells accidentally fused ... became implanted ... + then started dividing + multiplying into cuerpos that'd contain us ... in 2-4 separate streams ... no hay 1 comun thread ... el hermano menor wears the hand-me-down ropa del hermano mayor to cover his nakedness.

Besides *Autobiography of a Yogi* dare we admit we both read Carlos Castaneda round this time? All we member (sides the requisite puking before tripping) was the bit about finding your place. We'd mill around the new casa + sit + see if we felt anything ... but nada, figured it was our fault for trying too hard.

with golden, O so lively! O so soft, sweet, soft!

O! then the Roman candle burst and it was like a sigh of O! and everyone cried O! O! in raptures and it gushed out of it a stream of rain gold hair threads and they shed and ah! they were all greeny dewy stars falling then a rocket sprang and bang shot blind and O! white the cry of a young girl's love, a little strangled cry, wrung from her, that cry that has rung through the ages. And she would fain have cried to him chokingly, held out her snowy slender arms to him to come, to feel his lips laid on her white brow the cry of a young girl's love offered like those skirt-dancers behaving so immodest before gentlemen looking and he kept on looking, looking. She would fain have cried to him chokingly, to look in that immodest way like that because he couldn't resist the sight of the wondrous revealment half offered like those skirt-dancers behaving so immodest before gentlemen looking and he kept on looking, her knee no-one ever not even on the swing or wading and she wasn't ashamed and he wasn't either to look in that immodest way like that because he couldn't resist the sight of the wondrous revealment half and she was trembling in every limb from being bent so far back he had a full view high up above her knee and she let him and she saw that he saw and then it went so high it went out of sight a moment better than those other petticoats, the green, four and eleven, on account of being white could see her other things too, nainsook knickers, the fabric that caresses the skin, face was suffused with a divine, an entrancing blush from straining back and he more and more to look up after it, high, high, almost out of sight, and her excitement as it went higher and higher and she had to lean back trees up, up, and, in the tense hush, they were all breathless with dark, and she saw a long Roman candle going up over the flying about through the air, a soft thing to and fro to see the fireworks and something queer was there it was and she leaned back ever so far to look they all saw it and shouted to look, look account of the transparent and were blue to march on back and the garters and she leaned was about

years ago.

een translated n
gorgeous rende

We were designated to light the fireworks since the adults were all stoned ... or tripping ... the usual pyrotechnician (Stan the Birdman) was in fact «peaking» on peyote. It was our 1° año nuevo in Mexico. The so-called «cuetes» we were given were bottle rockets as tall as we were ... essentially sticks of dynamite strapped to the end of long sticks. We lined them up as they counted down 10 .. 9 .. 8 .. 7 .. 6 .. 5 .. 4 .. 3 .. 2 .. 1 ..FELIZ AÑO!! Then lit the fuses w/ a cigarette ..... SWOOOSH ..... BANG! ..... SWOOOSH ..... BANG! ..... taking drags off the cigarette in between even tho we didn't smoke just to keep the ember burning. Take a break to swig champagne handed to us ... our 1° taste of alcohol ... straight to our head ... back to lighting the rest of the cuetes w/ a sense of duty, purpose ... may as well make myself useful ... got 1 dud whose wick fizzled down to the base ... set it aside until we finished the rest off ... but that 1 leaving a nagging sense of inefficieny ... of economic waste. So alone we split the dud open w/ our hands + crafted a makeshit wick ... held a lit match to it ... at 1st nothing ... our head buzzing w/ champagne + cigarettes ... 1 more try U can probly guess ... didn't even hear the sound just a flash of white light blinding me ... + the smell of burnt flesh ... ears adjust eventually to my brother asking us if we were OK. Tried to brush it off as nothing ... staggered back into the house ... ashamed ... like a wounded animal not wanting to be noticed. Hair singed + ears ringing. Adults all partying still... reveling in the after glow of New Years.

To the kitchen sink ... figured water might help. Sick to my stomach at the sight of my own burnt flesh ... puked in the sink. Brother following me in, — what the hell?

Lucky it wasn't 3rd degree ... like our other brother ... who burned his hand in Mazatlan flying a kite in the rain like Ben Franklin ... kite hit a live wire ... tho he lied + said he was flicking on a light w/ wet hands. Had to have skin grafted from his ass still has scars to show for it. We took a bus every day to a doctor who peeled away the dead layers + wrapped it in gauze.

In the moment it makes sense ... time linear then all of a sudden it all fractures + keeps splitting ... each split feeds off the 1 before ... a prism of thought splintering into flesh + it's too late to take it back.

«So it is with all life. A tedium that includes the expectation of nothing but more tedium; a regret, right now, for the regret I'll have tomorrow for having felt regret today.» —Fernando Pessoa, The Book of Disquiet

353

We can only imagine what SHE was thinking. All we member was a casual stroll down to the shore for something to do. There was indeed a «Club Nausicaa» on the shores of the lake, a name we always thought was Spanish ... some sort of private yacht club that we weren't privy to, but we coud peak in on decadent scenes of debotchery if we waded just off shore. Can't even member what her name was ... even if we did we'd still call her **Nausicaa**.

June 13 [1989]

[story depends on who is telling it] The handsome young man met the pretty young girl in a restaurant in a foreign land [...] Tibet. The air was painfully cold and true to the nature of the land. The sun was beating down with a force that [could] fry an egg. The young man had stepped into the inviting coolness of the cafe to get a cup of yak butter tea, when he saw the woman bring out this girl from behind the cloth partition that divided the restaurant with the kitchen.

Time slowed for him, and subsequently [...] he obtained a great advantage [over] everyone else in that he could think twice as many thoughts in the same period of time. This bonus of sorts unfortunately allowed him to notice the little demon resting on her shoulder, grinning at him ... the girl obviously unaware of its presence. When she drew close enough to him, the demon spoke, it said it wanted their first born child.

The young man was stunned, not so much by the demon's outrageous and somewhat premature offer, but by the incredible glowing red skin the demon possessed and the way the young girl was kissing his ear, letting [dollops] of yak butter tea spill out her mouth and down his lobes. The demon at this point realized his [demand] was not going to be met, so he proceeded to condemn them—by casting a spell of sorts, the design of which was to make their lives insufferably painful and to render their now inevitable love an impossibility. Their sentence: to be forced to climb the highest mountain within visibility [of] the small restaurant. This they did the next day, reluctantly to say the least. When they reached the top, to their horror they saw approaching from the opposite direction the exact mirrored reflection of themselves, moving in [exact synched unison].

After becoming fully acquainted with their [identical] twins, they went back to town. They got a hotel room near the plaza, ordered some Long Island iced teas and sat out on the terraza, watching the children playing in the hot mid-day plaza below, darting in and out of the trees, occasionally screaming as 10-year old children do. [STEPHEN] was fanning himself with his starched white Panama hat, noticing the growing wet stains emerging from under his arms, and behind his knees. "FUCK" he finally said, piercing the long silence and momentarily startling the children below, causing them to stop their games and look up at the gringo, who now stood up and was obviously in the middle of a very important monologue, pacing the veranda, flashing on like a light bulb every time he came out from behind the shadows of the tree branches.

Mexican women lined the receding shore w/ galvanized tubs + bottles of clorox ... scrubbing clothes on their favorite flat rocks ... suds frothing up into a scummy gray residue reeking of bleach. The unspoken expectation was that we'd make out ... not that i'd asked her steady or anything, but it loomed over us. We were all in our own worlds skipping rocks.

Kevin had a girl too, but we don't member who's was who's. We were barely self-aware. The Nausicaa girl i was with starting acting strange. She was older than me, starting to form tits. There were mayflies everywhere so maybe it was May (1980). U couldnt tell if they were dead or alive ... their molted husks everywear. The lake in those years was higher + not yet chocked full of **hyacinth**. She walked off + i followed her, but she said she wanted some time alone so i resumed throwing rocks into the lake. Kevin was further up the shore w/ his Nausicaa (or vice-versa). My girl was squatting by the shore, her feet in the polluted water. She was wearing tight sky blue running shorts, the cotton kind we used to wear in the 70s.

When she came back from the shore, there was a dark blue wet patch in her crotch. I tried not to look + never said anything. «Wonder what they're up to» i said, looking the opposite way up the shore.

As U can tell, around this time our memories start to fuse + become more disjointed ... or less, hard to tell when you're embedded inside it. We never had a sister. We had a new surrogate father of sorts—a macho Mexican named Rocky ... or at least that's what every 1 called him. Snooping around in his drawers we'd find guns + needles. Our other brother JD touched his gun + got in trouble for it. Our mother told us not to snoop ... that if we wanted anything to just ask. It was the 1st time living w/ our real mother. Needless to say she was different than our stepmother.

The adjustment was harder on Kevin. He needed structure, a system of rules. Even if the rules were meant to be broken.

It was many days later when they 1st noticed it ... they spent so much of those first nights playing yahtzee (stripped down to their sandals because of the stifling heat), that [they] didn't really notice that [neither] one of them had slept so much as a minute, not once in 4 days! Not once in 96 hours?!

ok the stifling heat) that didn't really notice that nal one of them had slept so much as a minute, but once in 4 days?! not once in 96 hours!

[LATER OUR PROTAGONIST FIND AN ANSWER TO THIER PROBLEM. THEY DISCOVER QUITE UNEXPECTEDLY ONE NIGHT, STAYING UP AS USUAL, PACING THE ROOMS OF THIER LARGE MANSION, THAT whenever they play music, that is, whenever the two girls sang, and the two guys back them up with a guitar, a bass and a drum machine, whenever they did this in a style that could be described as post punk modernism, with a sligh Wagnerian seriousness, they found they achieved a trance like state that is not at all unlike sleep ....]

«... post punk modernism, with a slight Wagnerian seriousness ...»

NOTE FROM THE EDITOR THIS DOCUMENT HAS BEEN FAITHFULLY REPRODUCED TO ITS MOST LEGIBLE EXTANT ANY LOSS IN TRANSLATION IS COM-PLETLY UNINTENTIONAL]

COMO SPLITTING KINDLING

... u get the idea. We won't bother to transcribe the rest. Xcept to again note that «this document has been faithfully reproduced to its most legible extant [sic]. Any loss in translations is completely unintentional.»

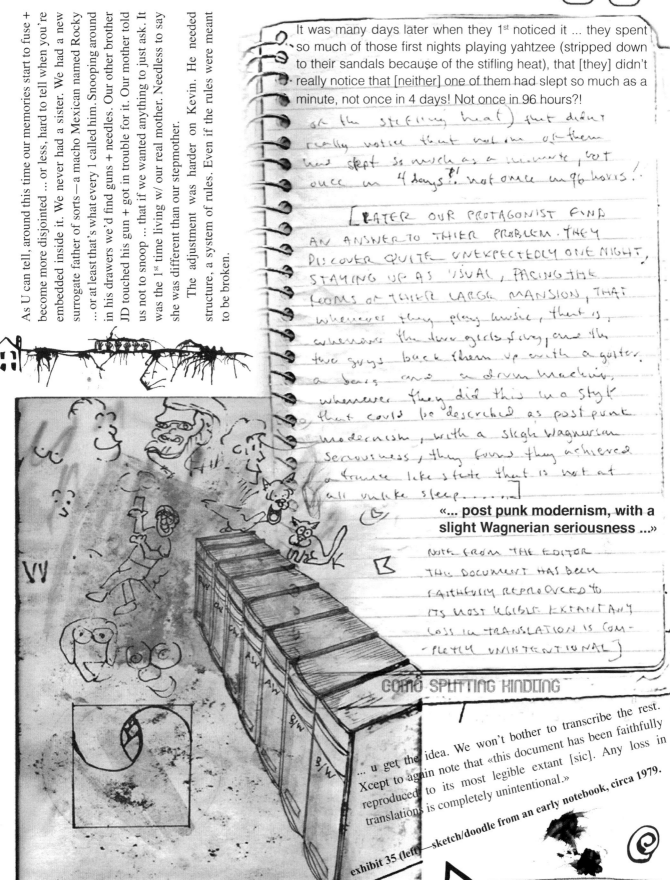

exhibit 35 (left)—sketch/doodle from an early notebook, circa 1979.

exhibit 36—another of Kevin's door paintings (burned in his apartment fire)

Across the shaggy mustard yellow threshold into the den, I am the Walrus running thru my head. After a week of clamming ... they made me clean them all cuz it was my idea ... but still worth it. Monday night, watching football alone, no 1 else intrested. Stepmom comes in asks why i'm crying .... tell her it's cuz i miss the beach, the razor clams. She keeps prying, saying there must be something else. I just wanted it to last forever, i say, the razor clams, the smell of the ocean. But she says something else is bothering me, asks point blank if i «got into a girl's panties» which makes me bawl more + convinces her she was right, that i'm suppressing something. «It's OK that you did ...» *But i didn't*, i protest. If she only knew, not even close, never even to 1st base. That was then, back in Beaverton. For the 1st time thinking our older brother was right ... a conniving _____. Kevin + i were both still scared of girls, specially the Mexican 1s w/ older brothers. But JD took the bull by the horns, dated some hot little # whose father was chief of police, el jefe. Of course he never got into her pants but that was the allure ... it was about the **pursuit**. There were others he made it with (+ got the clap to show for it) + then he knocked a girl up, 1 that already had a kid tho she was only 15. A cautionary tale for us, learn from the older bro. I am he as u are he as u are me + we are all together, hee hee hee, ha ha ha.

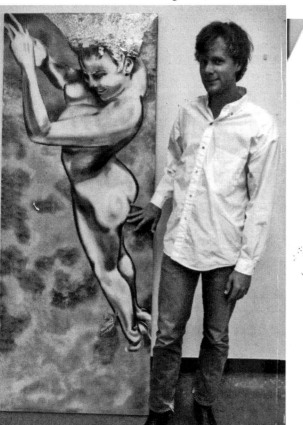

exhibit 37—the original Chaulky fondling the (unfinished) door painting on previous page

«... saving the men of the world from having to get involved with her ...»

"Ok. My name is ██████. Lets see... I am 5'8", 140 -pounds... short brown hair with **bangs** and the face of a serene, stone faced incarnation within the pantheon of Hindu deities. ~~He~~ I Drive a red country squire station wagon (with the fake wood paneling on the sides), I live at 553½ Fletcher North Hollywood CA. 93005, 2j6585, c325561, 213-667-0147, 554-786385,my favorite color is..oatmeal heather, or maybe teal!"

She stops talking and looks straight into his eyes. A very uncomfortable minute passes.

"That just about sums it all up! He says while throwing his fingers up in a skyward trajectory to call the ~~fuckhead I am a mini Conan~~ bartender, leaning against the wall. Looking out whistfully over the crowd, looking past ~~me~~ and everyone else, just looking off into the unforseable future of an arrogant, ennui ridden bartender.

"Do'nt you believe that we know what we want when we see it? The first time?"

She was now throwing in a little bit of the slurring, swaying and slouching. Elbows on the bar, she looked up at him, with a stupid grin on her face. It took him ten seconds to figure it out and back away into the heaving crowd. She turned back to her friend and laughed putting her head down. Her friend turns away to talk to someone else and she looks up at herself in the mirror over the exotic bottles of booze.

All her life she has been dealing with men. Since the ripe old age of fourteen, when she figured out how to use her voice in her relationships with men, She has been saving the men of the world from having to get involved with her ,(and finding out how fucked up her life is.) She laughs. The version of herself above the bar is slightly slower, and she notices.She always enjoyed these intimate little moments, when the room is com--pletely muffled, and everything moves a little slower than you. And you see your very unhappy self in a mirror above a bar. Now she is completely absorbed in the bartender. He is checking his watch.

"Last call!" He says in ~~almost an~~ "arena" voice.Ignor--ing his eager fans waving their money, shouting out to him from the orchestra pit. And all the while he is casually plucking the roses from the stage.

"T'anks yer sorry lot" He mumbles to himself, trying to decide wether or not the thought of an exiting patron scratching his two week old Harley with a key is a thought he should be having or wether the crank is just making him paranoid.

"They squeeze yer shouldar, they grind D'er teeth, they sustain an in'crdble level of intensitee when you talk to dem as long as you c'mpltly sestane d'ir intrest. God I 'ate dis job. Jest pulling beers fer clowns.Shots fer the yuppies in their J.Crew and London Fog, n' a Tag, an a under-sipherabl baseball cap on backwards, an a facial growth more indicative or symptomatic of hair sprouting warts coagulating in certain recesses of the face (under the lip, etc).

He is now looking at ██████ while picking the glasses off the counter;"She aint exactlee a side of beef niether. No. She's a looker. And a fine one at that. Unbelieva-ble.Looks like Heather, but a lot taller.Longer neck, fuller lips...

"Do you want another drink?"

TELEMACHUS
(ABSENCE & ESCALATIONS)
Outline

As long as he lives he will never forget his realization [of the mystery of life]. It wasn't until he was 9½ years old that he became aware of this infinite space that extends in every direction away from him. It came as a shock to him and the dread that it instilled in him tainted his thoughts ever since. At first it was hard to continue with his usual daily routine—sleep, wake, go to school, etc. Here was this kid, not even 10, who wanted to tell his classmates, teachers, family, everybody: "hey, life has no meaning, the universe Is Infinite, why are we here." He kept these ideas to himself and many years later they would be glad. For after many years of school he became aware that the meaning of life was to [actively] participate in a club which suppressed those questions, which supplied answers to them to the extent that one could continue to live and maybe even have a family.

He found out from Grandpa's pronouncing dictionary about HALCYON DAYS + who is the original «peeping Tom». (Not just w/ the sea enemies did Dad drill it into us the evilness of women.)

(Our memories continuing to fuse as we pass thru puberty.) A certain free will instilled by being «foreigners» ... no reputation to live up to ... this all made us acutely self-aware. Only in retrospect do we get it ... from the documented evidence we realize what we «lived thru» (not to be dramatic).

This denial of the
call to adventure.

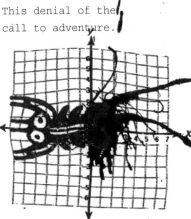

This bit a true story i told him, that happened to our cousin K ... when i was road-tripping w/ her in Idaho .... she had romantic notions of fucking a Hells Angel type w/ a Harley so we went to a biker bar + she found a dude fit the profile + asked for a ride back to his place «on his hog» + guy says «i'll take u back to my place ... but i don't have a Harley, not even a jap bike».

(0, 0)   PUT A LABEL ON IT

for our SIN ( ) ~~~

"No"

"Yah sure?" He is now stooped over the bar in front of her, dishrag in hand, hands clasped, arms pinned against the counter, looking helpless.

Instantly she is on the offensive. This guy looks like someone who has found what he wants, and is throwing all other options out (presumably to his love starved fans in the crowd).

"No." She restrains herself.

"Come on, what gives? Are you driving?"

At this, she unleashes on him;" Gee, if I do have a couple more drinks with you, will you take me on your bitch--ing bike back to your shithole apartment for a shag? Huh? Taste of tonkey, eh?"

"Yeah, I think you read my mind!" I say to him. They both turn to look at me, rather unprepared. Looking back at her I take a sip of beer, belch loudly, and offer her some. Sitting down on the empty barstool next to hers, my eyes watering because of the severity of the belch, I offer her my paw.

" My name is Orville" I slur something to this extent, now with both arms stretched ou to her like some blow up sex doll.

The bartender ignores the call to order of his co--worker, somewhat pissed off, to find out what I am all about.

"What you were saying" I add while seating myself

+ the time they prescribed u ritalin cuz u accidentally punched your hand thru a glass door ... a shard came close to the main

"About the plans for the evening... they sounded fun. But there is one problem.I do'nt have a Harley, or even my own apartment, I was kinda hoping we could use yours."

"Fuck you, bitch!" she responds calmly, with her lip curled like a doberman.

SUDDENLY how the situation improved, the bartender resumes talking to her. Removing his apron. Confident.Amaz--ing. The bad taste people have. I turn away from her towards the bar. Looking up, I see my simulation moving slightly slower than I am. SWF24B1. Or is it BWF24? People have been reduced to liscence plate numbers. Maybe prisoners send themselves out on liscence plates. Getting through the walls and past the guards and onto a new car belonging to a beautiful girl named ....
BWF#$24#$#140 LBS%$ BROWN GREEN 5'11"35-24-36*&&¢21¢ 372-4526
Please call now I need someone like you to make my life more difficult. Difficult? Ha!Or is it that it is so simple we are bored. If only I could tell him how well I have adapted, how well his little girl is doing.

"You ready?"

Here is Robin Hood and his merry gang of rouges, scoundrels and clowns. I am in for another sleepless night at his place.

Woken up at three A.M. by a Chuck Norris film on full volume [excerpt];

"CRAAAAAACK,WHAAAAAAK!!!"

"OH MY GOD!!!STOP!!!(hysterical female voice)

vein in you where wrist = muñeca

Also transcribed from some hand-written notes:

THERE ARE NO STRINGS ON ME ... NO ...

In the writings of the Marquis De Sade, the protagonists attempt to escape from the governing rules of existence. They seek to take hold of their own lives by breaking every rule, law [+] taboo [...] by practicing what they initially view as something like FREE WILL. To escape the stifling weight of existence [+] the control of laws [...] they (the protagonists) seek to shake [free] of all that seems to direct their actions, thoughts, feelings. Pleasure for them shouldn't be [moderated], earned or deferred, but should be abused, exploited and in that sense controlled. It's almost as if by living the most licentious existence one can cancel out what it means to be human, to live a physical existence and achieve the (momentary) illusion of total independence and control over those things which in fact will always control us.

Puppet animation serves as a strong analogy for this power greater than the individual (existence). The Soviet Bloc countries have long exploited this idea, playing out their political allegories with small frail mute representations of people—effigies which serve to remind us of our own actions. While [animated] characters (such as Bugs and Daffy) achieve a certain autonomy of existence (nonsensical beings, different in form far enough from [anything] living), puppets modeled after human forms inevitably parody what they are modeled after.

Timothy and Steven **Quay** are twins who have lived and worked together for most of their 40 years. [...] The twins (they call themselves Quay Brothers) were first exposed to the dark and bizarre world of Eastern European art through Kafka, Leos Janacek Hoffman, Sibelious and Jan Svank Mayer (great Czech animator) among others. In the work of these artists they found what they described as: "A poetry of shadowy encounters and almost conspiratorial secretness."

[... at which point there was a diagram, but can't seem to find the original.]

another way to think of CHAULKY is as a ghost writer or puppeteer ... we re-occupy his organless body + pull his $trings (as in words).

"STOP!!!"..."WHY ARE YOU DOING THIS TO ME?!! (scarred yet powerful male (fighting) voice).

"BBLLAAMM!!,BBLLAAMM!!,BBLLAAMM!!"

I drift off back to sleep. I dream of a world where the cities are more like villages (in size), and resemble, in form, massive sports complexs. All of the people I care about live there. At first there is nothing but joy when our new rent free homes are shown to us. The ideal apartm- -ent in each case. Each of them unique and made with a seemingly unlimited budget. Soon I grow aware of the problem brewing, over everyones placement. It seems that most of the people are upset in any given arrangement. People are losing control of their emotions. Friends are saying viciouse things about other friends. I do not want any part of it, and decide to head off, on my own, to the mountains behind the complex. I start off on my own, at night, into the darkness. As I am leaving the compound Nadine calls out to me from the top of the steps. She has a sleeping bag in one hand and a twelve pack in the other. I marvel at her timeliness. She looks at me, slowing down, in seriousness for a moment. She has a very slight grin on her face. I let her know that I do not have a problem with her self-invitation.

We did'nt even make to the tree line. We layed the sleeping bag out over a large boulder near the side of a river.

In her dream there was no one else for Nadine to talk to. We do everything she wanted to do.

SHE awoke to an outburst of laughter. Startled. Upright. Rubbing her eyes. Orientating. The voices sound strange to her. No.. its not the voices, its the language. It sounds like their talking with golf balls in their mouths. Cal's friends are also Irish, but their accents are not that strong. They are speaking Gaelic. She did not know that Cal could speak Gaelic, although he had mentioned taking Irish in grade school before he moved up to Belfast.

The voices were getting louder and more heated. It sounded like a combination of Norweigan, English and Germ- -an. The were'nt conversing , or practicing grade school Gaelic. She could hear Cal above the rest of them. He seem- -ed to be the one leading the meeting. They eventually coalesced, and Cal got his way on whatever the point was.

"Shit girl. You have picked yourself another loser, a real rebel." She laments, proping herself up on her pillows and groping around in the dark for her cigarettes. As she becomes more absorbed in her plans, she shuts out their conversation.

When to leave...where to next... where is the money going to come from. She goes to her problem solving with the resourcefullness of some street urchin in a Dickens novel. Within seconds she has juggled around favors, IOU's, cashed in tokens; essentially squeezing somewhere around a thousand dollars out of thin air. For an instant she wonders if she shouldnt try and drum up enough for a year in Bali, but she decides to stick with the more practical plan. In a couple of hours, when that young Spanish voice dials a wrong number and wakes her up, she will; (hang up,) and call Teri, Inform her to leave

... to reanimate

"For centuries, puppet theory has concentrated on the puppets symbolic relationship with human models, the puppet being primarily cast in the role of a <u>surrogate</u> human. Reflections on puppet theatre, from Rig-Vega to Marcus Aurelius to the present, have perpetuated an image of the puppet as a symbol of man manipulated by higher forces or beings, a metaphor in which the puppet is structurally interchangeable with its own controller man. "

—Roman Paska, from *The Inanimate Incarnate*

It was my **right** hand incidentally, that i blew up w/ fireworks.

(on pg. 87)

+ there are more stories about **Stan the Bird Man**

a key out and clear out a corner in her living room. Hang up. Make and drink some coffee. water the plants, pet and feed the cat. Just before leaving to ████'s, with a bucket of water and a sponge, attempt to clean the huge blood stain on the matress(sewing up the gashes with a needle and thread) and then putting the five Hefty bags into the large guatemalan bag that her sister had given her two weeks earlier for Christmas.

Her sister had known that she would be needing the bag even before she did. The awareness of her sister's superior intellect filled her with anxiety, paralyzing her for a few moments. Her cigarette fell out of her mouth and was estinguished instantly in the soap bubbles on the back of her yellow latex glove.

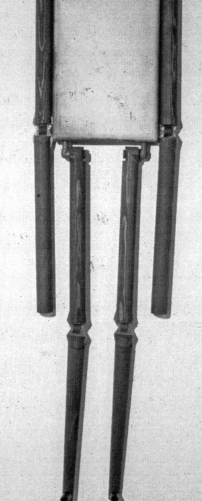

(the 1 that was sposed to light the cuetes) tripping on drugs ... like the time all the adults were taking shrooms to discover their inner animals + Stan thawed he was a parrot + ran squawking + flapping all around our house (where he got his name going fwd).

And who was it clipped their hairs on account of the moon?

± the way Kevin used to say *Master of Puppets*, like a demonic kid ... he liked saying it more than he liked listening to the album.

This came later, once we returned to California (see episode 12) ....as did the time i had 1 of those Mexican puppets hanging from the rear view mirror of my 1ˢᵗ car (the '66 Mustang that got sent to the glue factory (see page 69). The doors didn't lock + the gas gage didn't work (always on **F**) so when it got stolen, the thief never even got out of the Bay Area before it ran out of gas + he ditched it in the middle of the freeway + i had to pay the towing charge to get it back which was more than what the car was worth ... + when i got it back the puppet had been

ripped down from the rear view mirror + thrown in the back seat ... as if the thief didn't want any reminders of anything personal. The casette that was in the tape deck had also been ejected. When i pushed it back in, Morissey was singing «*I've seen this happen, in other people's lives, and now it's happening in mine*.»

These are all true stories ... we don't know how to lie. In *Ulysses*, after Bloom masturbates to Gerty's flashing (coincidentally the climax comes almost exactly ½-way thru the book) she gets up + Bloom realizes for the 1ˢᵗ time she has a gimp leg. «Tight boots? No. She's lame! O!»

Kevin's puppet fetish perhaps led to his **ELEMENTS** series (see episode 13 ± the preseeding xhibit 31) the headless + limbless torsos essentially inverted puppets ... + he also had a general preoccupation w/ the human body (the 3-part *Zone* series on *Fragments for a History of the Human Body* was always front + center on his shelf.)

~~The extent of my own personal experience w/ puppets: when i used to play Indonesian gamelan + got to play a few times for *wayang kulit* ... literally getting a behind the screen glimpse of the shadow puppet masters.~~

xhibit 38—"untitled" 1991 (wood, plastic, mule skin—51" x 13"). For others in the puppet series, see xhibit 33 + another to come in episode 10

«Intolerance of ambiguity is the mark of an authoritarian personality.»—Theodor Adorno

Our brother-½ didn't really have a problem w/ authority ... he welcomed our stepmother's surrogate discipline. But when we moved back to Mexico in our teens he took issue w/ our (real) mom's authority ... not cuz he resented her sudden puppet jurisdiction but cuz it wasn't earned (she was **absent** from our lives til this point). The hypocrisy of it was what bothered him (+ me), as well as the new age mumbo jumbo that her justifications were rooted in.

This is perhaps why we could relate to Dr. Seuss's *Horton Hatches an Egg* ... our mother being like Mayzie the bird, laying an egg then flying off to Palm Beach while Horton was left dutifully roosting on it. What bugged us is that when we grew up + went down to the Palm Beach equivalent, our mother tried to take credit for our development beyond the genetics of just providing an egg. Question is, who's the elephant in the room? It'd be easy to say our stepmother, but seems we shoud get more credit than this ... like we ourselves sat on our own eggs ... by our bootstraps.

We don't find a place, (we vaguely try) and set-
-tle for sulfide wine in thresholds. Its raining and warm.
~~████████████████████████~~. I am not an art-
-ist, lover or writer, but have a real desire to learn.
~~████████████████████~~ I glance over her shouldar at
~~████~~ offering peanuts to Castillian yuppies, they gladly
accept. They turn out to be figs, they are delighted. I
briefly imagine that human nature is different. The rain
stains the sidewalk in front of my feet, out of reach. It
is stinging acid. This noble village of Pamplona. The bulls
are having there final sleep, or maybe they are suffering
from insomnia, or busy filing their horns.

We leave him on a bench where he will stay for
six hours until he is knocked off it by a water cannon.
We sprint from doorway to doorway. In the threshold of a
vacant building I push my weight into her. ~~████████~~
* The lack of a common language makes for desperate necking.
Two hundered pesetas will buy a bottle but my first born
will not get us a room. The fleshy spot at the base of
her neck, the whites of her eyes, the tiny transparent
hair in front of her ears. THE THUNDEROUS APPLAUSE OF
THE RAIN GUARANTEES MY EVERY MOVE. HER ENGLISHE IMPRO- *
-VES WITH HER BLOOD ALCOHOL LEVEL.We sit and put our glasses down. We are admired by all those that pass by. I
take leave of her. In a dark area I piss. I sway gently
and smile, the air feels cold on my dick. With one incr-
-edibaly agile move I pack it in, button up, adjust my
hair, take a deep breath and walk back. Two local clowns
are sitting on either side of her. I approach and play
my dominate male role. Sea lion with legs. They stand up
to leave."Hash, dope", the small one says. I look at the
big one and wonder why he would be stupid enough to carry
all that shit around. They leave and I return to her. She
is very affectionate and ~~████████████████~~
~~████████~~ Before we go in search of him I drain the
glass at my feet without noticing the new ingredient.

" **I approach and play my dominate male role. Sea lion with legs.** "

Around this time our mom's friend Michelle (the same hippy lady Kevin calls Claire in the Circe episode #9) gave us 2 purple-headed wild parrots that roosted on a homemade perch in my room squawking + shitting everywhere + biting us every time we went near. We tried + tried but coud never get them to talk ... evidently (said Stan the Bird Man) we had to separate them ... just like isolation is nessesary to learn a foreign landguage.

altho muñeca means 'puppet' in spanish it literally means 'wrist'

From ON THE MARIONETTE THEATER by H. Von Kleist:
"Now then, my excellent friend," said Herr C., "you are in possession of everything necessary to understand me. We see that in the organic world, to the extent that reflection grows dimmer and weaker, the grace therein becomes more brilliant and powerful, yet, just as the intersection of the two lines on one side of a point suddenly appears again on the other side after passing through the infinite; or the image in a concave mirror, after receding into the infinite, suddenly resurfaces close before us—grace like-wise reappears when knowledge has passed through the infinite, so that it appears purest simultaneously in the human body that has either none at all or else infinite consciousness—that is the puppet or in the god."

"Consequently," I add, a little distraught, "we would have to eat again from the tree of knowledge to fall back into the state of innocence?"

"Of course," he answered, "That is the last chapter of the history of the world."

[originally published as Über Das Marionettetheater, in the Berliner Abendblatter, Dec 12-14, 1810. Translated Roman Paska. As taken from *Zone Part I, Fragments for a History of the Human Body*]

«... w/ drain sym added

«... and she noticed at once that that foreign gentleman that was sitting on the rocks looking was

Cuckoo.
Cuckoo.
Cuckoo.»

From http://www.5cense.com/11/pinocchio.htm:

«... & he doesn't just partially turn into a donkey as Disney would have it, but they both full on turn donkey. Pinocchio (as a donkey) is sold to a circus & Lucignolo is sold to a farmer & dies. a spectacle is made of Pinocchio the donkey & he is run into the ground until he is declared lame & sold to some guy who wants to make a drum from his skin. he takes him down to the ocean, ties a rope around his neck & throws the donkey into the water to drown him & soften his skin. Pinocchio summons the blue fairy who sends an 'infinite school' of fish to his rescue. like a school of piranha, the fish eat the donkey all the way down to the bone, until they get to the wood of Pinocchio embedded within the donkey (giving new meaning to Pinocchio as some sort of immortal skeleton). when the drum-maker hears how the fish ate the donkey he swears to never eat fish again, but he still wants to sell Pinocchio for wood, but Pinocchio jumps into the ocean & swims off.

it's at this point that Pinocchio gets eaten by shark (un 'pesce-cane'), not a whale. obviously a nod to Jonah. & being inside the belly of the whale is not nearly as quaint as Disney would make it out to be, but Pinocchio is immersed in complete darkness, «as black & deep as sticking your head in an inkwell». a veritable isolation chamber that would [make] John Cage happy. the only noise Pinocchio heard was the shark breathing (because the shark had asthma!). in the darkness he meets a philosophical tuna that has resigned himself to dying, [...] («but I am wise enough & it consoles me to think that, when we tuna are born, there is more dignity to die under water than under oil.») when Pinocchio disagrees, the tuna tells him he should respect the opinions of tuna & then they are the best of friends, though the tuna is still resigned to die & not try to save himself (perhaps reflecting the defeatist attitude of italians). Pinocchio ventures through the oily, fish-smelling entrails of the shark & finds Geppetto (balding with a beard, after 2 years living in the belly), this much is true. but their escape from the shark is far easier than Disney would have it, they simply walk out (after braving a sneeze from the asthmatic shark). Pinocchio carries Geppetto on his back until he gets too tired to swim & the tuna reappears (inspired by Pinocchio to free himself) & saves them, for which Pinocchio gives him a big kiss.

the tale doesn't end there. this is where Pinocchio finally rolls up his sleeves & gets to work. every day he pumps water in exchange for a glass of milk for his aging 'babbo'. rather than it being a Disney tale of a puppet turning into a boy [in search of his father], it's more the story of a boy becoming a man, of earning his keep & taking care of his father. more about family values & conformity. they live in the blue goat's house (with the ghost of the talking cricket living in the rafters). Pinocchio comes full circle with all the characters who have right or wronged him. he doesn't forgive the fox & cat (who truly become lame & blind). he says to them [...] «the devils flour goes all to bran» (the equivalent to «every dog has his day» i imagine). i guess back in the day the merits of 'bran' were not known, but bran was something inedible. & then the talking cricket [Jiminy] easily forgives Pinocchio, which doesn't seem fair since Pinocchio did far worse to the cricket (hammered him to death) than the fox & cat did to him. he gives money to the snail to help the woman with the blue hair, who evidently is sick in the hospital. then he has a dream about her & wakes up as a real boy. that's it. there is no waving of any magic wands, it's simply a dream he has. & he wakes up with new furniture & clothes & the money he gave to the blue fairy re-minted. Geppetto is not surprised at Pinocchio being real, he says the clothes & furniture are all on account of Pinocchio's hard work, from doing the right thing. another interesting detail that Disney omitted was that in the end Pinocchio & Geppetto see the lifeless puppet slumped in the corner, which significantly changes the nature of his transformation as one that is purely (knowingly) metaphorical, as if childhood is some sort of larval phase in which you shed your skin (go through puberty) when transforming into a self-aware man (the fish eating the donkey down to the skeleton of Pinocchio goes well with this too). & returning back to the metaphor of the puppet as a book & Geppetto (the puppet maker) as the true protagonist, then Collodi (via Geppetto) created a transgressive work of art that jumps from the page, frees itself from the physical book object to become a transcendental myth, regardless of how it's told or in what language, to be passed down from generation to generation.».

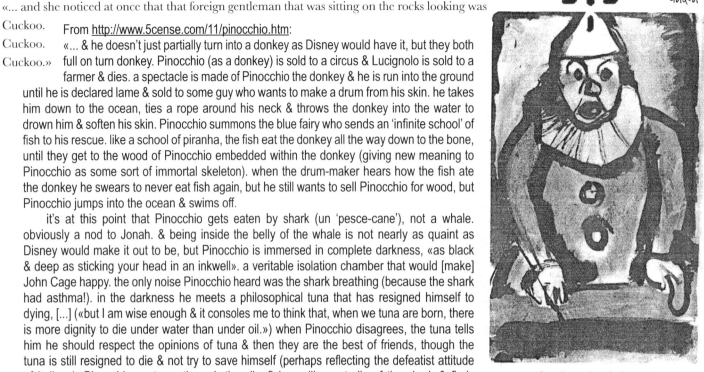

GEORGES ROUAULT *Frater* The Clown 1906
Gouache, Private Collection

xhibit 39 (above)—original opening page of Kevin's '*SSES*' '*SSES*' thesis + exhibit 40 (below)—Pinocchio + Lucignolo (a.k.a. Candlewick) from the original Carlo Collodi version (note toy Trojan horse between them). Should also note some of the interspersed glyphs used in this episode were designed by John Cage + thanks to the survival of a bill dated 23 May 1914, we know James Joyce purchased Collodi's *Pinocchio* from FH Schimpff bookseller in Trieste.

– È vero, Lucignolo! Se oggi io sono un ragaz tuo. E il maestro, invece sai che cosa mi dice «Non praticare quella birba di Lucignolo, per e non può consigliarti altro che a far del male

' – Povero maestro! – replicò l'a
troppo che mi aveva a
lunniarmi, ma io s
– Anima grande
fettuosam
mezzo a
Intanto era
bella cuccagna
intere, senza r
scuola, quand
ebbe, com
che lo r

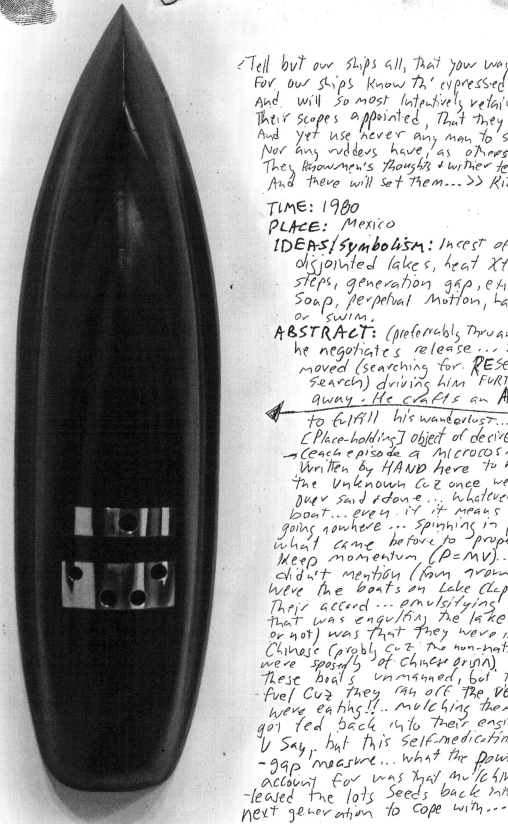

exhibit 41—"untitled" 1990 (Graphite)

<Tell but our ships all, that your way must show
For our ships know th' expressed minds or men
And will so most Intentively retain
Their scopes appointed, That they never err,
And yet use never any man to steer
Nor any rudders have, as others need.
They knowmen's thoughts & wither tends their speed
And there will set them...>> King Alcinous!

TIME: 1980
PLACE: Mexico
IDEAS/symbolism: Incest of insects,
disjointed lakes, heat Xfer, drafting,
steps, generation gap, exile from exile,
soap, perpetual motion, harvesting, sink
or swim.
ABSTRACT: (preferrably thru an intermediary)
he negotiates release... 2-3 steps removed (searching for REsearch for the
search) driving him FURTher & FURTHer
away. He crafts an ARK of lead
to fulfill his wanderlust... to be his
[Place-holding] object of desire...
(each episode a microcosm of the whole)—
Written by HAND here to keep Xpressing
the unknown cuz once we get there it's
over said & done... whatever floats your
boat... even if it means intentionally
going nowhere ... spinning in place. Rehashing
what came before to propel FFWD, to
keep momentum (P=MV)...& what we
didn't mention (from around this time period)
were the boats on Lake Chapala that ran on
their accord... emulsifying the hyacinth
that was engulfing the lake. Rumor (paranoid
or not) was that they were introduced by the
Chinese (probly cuz the non-native lotussy weeds
were sposedly of Chinese origin). Not only were
these boats unmanned, but they required no
fuel cuz they ran off the very weeds they
were eating!!.. mulching them into biofuel that
got fed back into their engines. <<INGENUOUS>>
U say, but this self-medicating was only a stop-
-gap measure... what the powers that be didn't
account for was that mulching the flowers re-
-leased the lots seeds back into the lake for the
next generation to cope with...

THE MYTH OF NAUSICAA'S PARENTS

From a coastal village, he set out [alone] on his voyage. His specially designed 30 foot fiberglass kayak was shipped across the country and lowered into the water by crane.

The village honored the young man's heroicism by giving him a send-off parade that escorted him all the way across the small ocean port to his bobbing pod [-shaped] vessel.

They [ceremoniously] sent him off [with] trumpet blasts and a flurry of fireworks. He'd brought enough food and water for a hundred days (the trip [was budgeted] for eighty).

She had been working as a research psychologist for three years and this was her first big grant-funded project; [... to study] the effects of isolation on the human mind.

To save money and get more accurate results, she decided to do the experiment on herself [—*this would yield bias, IMHO*]. She knew she'd never find anyone else willing to do it. Her family and friends begged her not to go, but of course she did.

He brought along a video camera to record his experience. Six days out (during a thirteen hour wait for weather) you can clearly see he is starting to lose it. His calm analytic composure visible in the first video log entries cracks as he questions his reasoning for making the voyage.

Suddenly he seems young, naïve and scared.

She goes through a battery of psychical [sic] exams, says good-bye to everyone, and climbs down into the metal pod. It is then lowered into the bottom of an abandoned mine shaft, nearly a mile [below the surface of the earth]. She [plans] on staying in this [capsule] for one hundred days.

His kayak flips over during a violent storm at night. The camera tumbles through the tiny cabin, displaying shaky glimpses of him hysterical, crying.

~~In *The Odyssey* ... u know what, fuck it it doesn't matter — that was over 3000 years ago ... + there's no correlation here w/ *Ulysses* ... Joyce skipped this episode. As did brother-½ in his 'SSES' 'SSES'. And really u could do this w/ any book + any 1 else could come along + do it again + again ...~~

In our scheme of things, we are still in Mexico, circa 1980. Here is our student visa below, the renewal for the 2nd year:

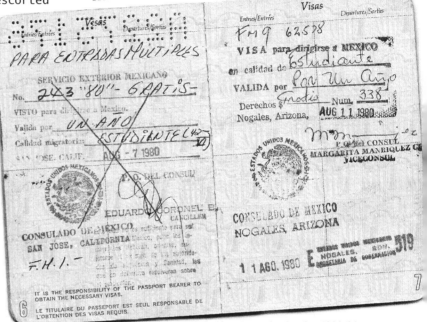

xhibit 42— Derek's visa for 1980-81

◀ This dueling story to the left was written (by brother-½) during a time he was inspired by **Bas Jan Ader**, the Dutch conceptual artist whose grand finale was to sail solo across the Atlantic ocean in a 13 ft boat (which was found 10 months after off the coast of Ireland, but his body never was).

exhibit 43—Bas Jan Ader "I'm too sad to tell you" (1970)

Her research pod is connected to the surface by two tubes: one carrying oxygen the other carrying electricity and telephone lines. These are her only connections to the outside world.

She brings her laptop into the pod, first removing any photographic images so that nothing will taint [...] the psychological aspects of the test.

She allows herself no communication of any sort with the outside world—[from the surface] they can listen and watch her with a small video camera, but that's it ...

[In the beginning,] she spends most of her time reading books. She seems to be coping during the first week, but by the seventeenth day she [starts] to obsess neurotically about her reasons for taking on the experiment. By the nineteenth day she is crying regularly.

[...] sharks begin to follow him on the fourteenth day.

By the fifth week he is spending all of his time sealed up inside, [supine] on his back, with the windows covered, blabbering nonsense into the camera. It is during this week that he uses up over one-hundred hours of video tape.

During his last hours of recording, on day thirty-six, he [speculates] about finding some way to go back in time, increasingly hysterical and manic.

When his kayak drifts into the harbor seventy-one days later, the empty video camera is still on the small tripod.

The only other things in the kayak [are] a small bag of food, a jug of water and him, laying down inside, naked and apparently resting.

She doesn't seem to be doing so well four weeks into the project and the scientists who are monitoring her talk about taking her out. They had all signed a document swearing they would not pull her out unless she was dying. She did not appear to be dying, and no one was willing to take the authority to overrule her order, so she stayed.

Physically everything seemed to be ok ... she was healthy and managed to feed herself. What she couldn't manage to do was communicate her mental condition back through the camera [...].

She kept the camera covered up starting on

Like Ulysses we were rooted from the known + familiar + **displaced** to the UNknown (Axixic, Mexico).

Phaeacia is the island from where Ulysses tells his story (to Nausicaa's parents). Axixic is where brother-½ 1st starts making art ... as if in response to this sudden displacement.

in PARALLEL

+ at the same time that Ulysses is try¹g to find his way home, TELEMACHUS has left home to look for ULYSSES...

When we told kids in Mexico we were from Beaverton, Oregon, they asked if we had the latest **Nikes** (w/ the waffle iron tread + gel insoles). Our stepmother had never allowed us to get them, but on our next trip stateside brother-½ got a pair of Nike *Odysseys* ... + from them on that is what he exclusively wore.

(To my knowledge, the winged goddess Nike does not appear in *The Odyssey*.)

← 1-way
Communication/
Transport Membrane
(co-axial)

O₂ E

+ the SD doomsday cult that MASS—suicided the week before he died were wearing brand new Nikes (see episode 19)

(actual sketch)

+ only in retrospect does what matters GEL...

The question is, who is the projected male protagonist—our brother, or our father? And the female figurehead (to mount on the bow of our ship)? For our devices, we'll assume this is about our father (in absentia) ... or some sort of projection thereof. Tho during these years we had the slightest idea what he was up to.

> «Remembering that in the Odyssey Odysseus himself is not first seen until Book V.
>
> And then is seen weeping.»
>
> —David Markson, **The Last Novel**

verbatim...   May 21, 1985 – Mountain View, CA

A man i presume to be my father waded thru the water in his Navy blue uniform to board a ship. He climbed aboard soaking wet + went over to salute the captain. His mind wandered (i should know, i turned into him). I imagined a fight on the other end of the ship ... a sort of déjà vu. Then i was a boy wandering thru a village similar to Axixic (but in Panama). I came across a group of kids who i at first thought were [bullying] other kids. I was forewarned they would beat me up ... on closer inspection what they were doing was grabbing arms + forming a large circle. They'd sling forward toward the center + smash their heads together as hard as they could. [There were] 2 groups doing this + they were doing it over + over. I began to run thru the cobblestone streets, a little lost.

Finally i found where the ship was. I swam out [to where] they were impatiently waiting for me. The ship was no longer a Navy cruiser but a Toyota pickup. They had me climb in back despite the cold. The driver was very authoritative ... i [presumed] he was the captain. There were 2 other people, 1 of them i think was dad. As we drove along the lake i kept asking questions (to stall for time) like "what lake are we on" + the captain acted impatient w/ me like i was ignorant + didn't answer my questions. Evidently we were on Lake Nicaragua + the snow-capped mountain in the background was Mt. Kilimanjaro [– neither places of which i'd been at the time]. I asked how far the mountain was. The captain finally told me to shut up. It wasn't cold, though there were patches of snow on the shore.

Then we were playing foosball in the brig of the ship (it got longer). The captain felt self-consciously immature playing + gave up in the middle of the game. So i sat by myself + had no 1 to play with.

day thirty. Her vital signs were still monitored through sensors (that she left) attached to her body.

She did not speak once during her last fifty-three days—the mic stayed on the whole time [registering only silence + static]. The only thing they heard was the sound of her [incessant] typing.

[...]

None of what she wrote was ever recovered. She erased it all before they brought her out on day one hundred.

When news of his successful landing reached his home town [of Ithaca, NY], his family and friends made the trip to see him. They found him still in his boat, refusing any attempts of extraction. When his close ones finally forced open the pod and took him out [he was unresponsive] ... he just sat motionless and mute on the beach, staring off to sea and [grinning with a euphoric expression].

It was clear he didn't want to be around people. It only took a couple of days to drive everyone away. The last person to leave him was his younger sister. She spent days sitting on the beach watching him [while he sat there] wearing an orange parka someone had put on him when he landed [+ continuing to grow his beard]. She tried to get him to talk. She cried before she left.

He [remained] on the deserted beach, sleeping inside the kayak and foraging in the nearby forest for food.

They took her [straight] to the hospital when they brought her out. She was examined, but no conclusions could be drawn. They could do nothing to reach her ... her mind seemed [switched] off.

Her family and friends stopped visiting after [a few] weeks. During one visit her younger sister left a newspaper on the table near her bed. After her sister left she read it. She read about the young man who had kayaked across the ocean by himself and how he had taken up residence on an isolated beach to the north of where she was.

Late that night she left the hospital and began walking to this beach. It was almost a hundred miles away ... she made it in just under three days, the whole time managing to avoid and cities or roads.

She got there just as the sun was rising and right away could make out the outline of his overturned kayak. She approached him as he slept and quietly laid down beside him.

Later, when the sun was almost at the top of the sky, he awoke to find her next to him. A look of intense joy swept [over] his face and he embraced her. She opened her eyes and smiled [...].

"I missed you," she said, brushing the hair out of his eyes.

"I missed you too."

"I wasn't sure I'd be able to find you."

"I knew you would. If you didn't come, I would have found you, somehow." He smiled and kissed her. They laid there for a long while, just listening to the [humming] of the earth [...] and the crashing of the ocean.

As far as Nausicaa knew, these where the only words her parents had ever said to each other. She never once heard them speak. She claimed she was conceived that same afternoon on the beach.

Her aunt had told her the whole story of her parents, what they did before they met, about the strange journeys they had taken into themselves and of their [parallel isolation].

And now Nausicaa was relaying their story to me. She told me about moving into the home that had belonged to her grand-parents, just after she was born, and about how her grandparents had died when she was very young. She told me about going to see her parents with her sister, while she was living with her aunt.

N

The first time I remember seeing the hermit couple I was twelve. I was with my younger sister [...] exploring the woods near the beach. We came out of the forest and there they where, crouched in a tide pool digging out sea urchins with sticks. They were old and shaggy looking [...] dressed in [clothes] that looked like they had been found in the garbage.

When they saw us they stood up slowly. They looked at us for a while and then went back to [scraping] urchins [off rocks]. I'm not even sure they recognized their daughters.

Back in the city [news spread] about the hermit couple. Some described them as soulmates lost in their own world. Others called them crazy hermits.

I used to go spy on them before I moved away [for] school. I'd sit hidden in the woods and watch them scavenging around the tide pools. They never [talked] and I wondered if they were really crazy or just quiet [loners].

II. HER FATHER'S ISOLATION

I didn't know how much of Nausicaa's stories were true but I enjoyed them and [me listening] seemed to help her in some way. Sometimes when she was telling me about her parents she would stop mid-[sentence—]as if she had just received some amazing revelation from her own story.

Most of N's stories involved her father. She claimed that he raised her like one might raise a pet ... a pet you'd rather not spend too much time with.

More than anything else, Nausicaa wanted to find her father and [...] talk to him.

T (telemachus)

For all of his life, for as long as he could remember, he had been unable to achieve a state of lucidity. Tones of desperate ennui clung to his every thought like permanent stains, dragging his head down by the horns... [bold mine]

Nausicaa [relayed this to] me this one night while we were smoking cigarettes out on the balcony. She [looked good smoking]—tall, thin and pale. Her look was extreme, but if you turned away [for a minute] you remembered her as being beautiful.

I felt strange [taking] one of her cigarettes, knowing that she [consented] to doing something degrading to get them from one of the night orderlies. She offered [one] to me (without me [even asking]), and continued on with her story. My early evening dose of anti-depressants and tranquilizers was making it seem like she was whispering the story ... so [vivid] it was becoming real for me.

FURTHER FROM THE TRUTH (52)   *(ALT TAKE)

by Kevin White

T

For a long time he kept it away ... kept himself busy. But one day the stain creeped back over him, and through it he saw her.

At first it was [tiny]. She'd give a look [of indifference] or [make] a remark that [...] implied something more.

Her body would turn from his in their bed and he'd stay up all night watching her, wondering what was going on in her mind. He grew paranoid and insecure. Through the stain he saw her secret life, her indifference to him, her affairs, her plans to leave him. These fantasies snowballed, propelled by the stain's powerful emotional drive.

His desperate attempts to hold on to her [converted to] electricity that coursed through his body. He stayed up all night, every night, playing out a million fatalistic scenarios over and over in his mind.

She was [branching] away from him and it was killing him. She seemed oblivious to [her effect].

When she finally left him, he was just a hollow shell [filled] with fear and resentment. [...] leaving him was a painful [but necessary] decision to make.

He [paced] around the empty three-bedroom house, with its avocado and Hansa yellow carpeting, in boxer shorts [patterned with] gin distillery diagrams. Glasses and dirty plates covered the [tables].

Surrogate.

INTRODUCTION TO STU, (THE FATHER-)

state of.

✓ For the first time in his life of alienation, for as long as he could remember, he had been unable to achieve lucidity.

Tones of despair clung to his every thought. He never achieved a clear connection with even one of his co-workers.

He had a vision of what he was looking for that was completely contained within his neurotic, survivalist-animal mind.

✓ He walked around the three-bedroom house, with its avocado and hansa-yellow carpeting, in boxer shorts covered in a pattern of gin distillary diagrams.

✓ His hair curved out from the left side of his head. He was very much unshaven. In his left hand he held a Winchell's Donuts mug full of gin, orange juice and ice. In his right hand he clutched the remains of a joint that was apparently wrapped with oily brown paper.

✓ He wandered through the empty rooms dazed. No expression whatsoever. He always screened his calls. He never made it to the store.

✓ The refrigerator contained only a jar of mayonaise that was so old, it was turning clear. He thought of her still, constantly. She left him after so many years. That is the only thing that ever happened. The only event ever to shake reality.

She was in front of him every where he looked; waving to him dressed in an orange hooded parka and a wrap around beige headband, mixing with a chefs hat on a tin can, standing in front of microphones on the front page, riding in a dune buggy on t.v. at three in the morning.

《 He had a vision of what he was looking for that was completely contained within his neurotic, survivalist-animal mind. 》

《 In between these lofty self-critiques were periods of animal abandon. 》

---

[52] Brother-½ would later write a few variations on this theme, usually calling them *Telemachus*.

lingering thoughts never sustained long enough to Attach

He stood in front of her full length dressing mirror and watched himself smoke out of a small pipe. He looked deep into his eyes for long periods of time. He constantly felt bad about himself. He constantly tried to figure out what "bad" was, what pain was.

He played fiddle music from ~~Cumberland Gap~~ on the stereo and danced silently, occasionally stopping to take a swig of beer. He friends came over on rare occasions. He almost always had to go out to find company.

* Feelings of closure with fellow man were few and far between.

STU-READING THE SHOPPING LIST ONE LAST TIME BEFORE LEAVING FOR THE STORE WITH THE WIFE AND KIDS;

He read these points off like a shopping list in his mind. He did this every couple of hours. In between these lofty self-critiques were periods of animal abandon. A very reserved animal abandon.

These points that he wrote down were meant to decieve. The images and happenings are a vague rememberance of things past.

Nothing could be further from the truth.

INT. DAY. EMACIATED FIGURE LUNGES OFF OF COUCH TOWARDS LIGHT BULB SWINGING IN THE CENTER OF THE ROOM.

An all consuming whiteness dissipates into a fire ball. The burning edges pull in around a figure lashing out through it. The explosion is his vision. The violent force of his reaction breaks him free of chains that have bound him to the wall all of his remembered life. Now he stands alone, free to move about in the center of the room. He rubs his wrists and looks at the handcuffs attached to the chain now lying on the carpeted floor.

The room appears to be a basement. The windows have been completly boarded over. The only light source is a single 200 watt bulb in the middle of the ceiling. On one side of the room is a bed, desk, chair and a nightstand. All of these things are within the twenty foot length of chain attached to the

The TV was a [noisy, ever-present] friend.

When he plopped down on the couch the dust of [the family before] rose up into the slices of sunlight, [reforming] ghostly images of children, and a wife.

His hair curved out from the left side of his head and he [hadn't shaved in weeks]. In his left hand he held a Winchell's mug full of gin, orange juice and ice. In his right he clutched the remains of a joint that looked like it had been rolled with oily paper.

He wandered through the empty house dazed, with no expression whatsoever. He always screened his calls and rarely made it to the store. The refrigerator contained just a jar of mayonnaise [...] so old it was turning clear.

He stood in front of HER full length dressing mirror and watched himself smoke hash out of a small pipe. He gazed deep into his eyes for long periods of time, constantly trying to figure out what BAD was, what PAIN was.

He read these points off like a shopping list in his mind. He [did this] every couple of hours. In-between these lofty self-critiques were periods of animal abandon.

These points that he went over and over in his mind were meant to deceive. The images and happenings were a vague remembrance of things past. Nothing could be further from the truth. Like [billions of others before him] it was a ritual he had developed to distance himself from the possibility of feeling pain.

BASEMENT. DAY

An emaciated figure lunges off the couch towards a light bulb swinging in the center of the room. An all-consuming whiteness dissipates into a fire ball. The burning edges pull into a figure lashing out through it—the explosion is his vision. The violent force of his reaction breaks him free of the chains that have held him to the wall all of his remembered life and now he stands alone, free to move about in the center of the room. He rubs his wrists and looks down at the handcuffs attached to the chains now lying dejected on the dirty carpeted floor.

The room appears to be in a basement, the windows [...] completely boarded over. ~~The only light source is a single 200 watt light bulb hanging from the center of the ceiling.~~ On one side of the room is a bed, desk, chair and a night stand. All of these things are within the twenty-foot length of chain attached to the wall. A pattern of wear swings out into a wide arc half way across the room. Beyond this area is a color TV on a milk crate.

He [approaches] the TV, unsure. On the screen a man in a beige drip-dry suit pleads with his eyes closed and [clenched] fists raised. He is sweating and shaking, consumed by some force. Pleading for money. Ten red numbers flash incessantly at the bottom of the screen.

> [REVEREND]
> PLLEEAASSEE!!! Hheeuueer my prayer!

[Telemachus] reaches out towards the screen. As his fingers touch the glass the [reverend] drops to his knees. Then he makes his way to the top of the stairs like he'd seen his father do so many times. He learned the word FATHER from the television. He learned his name, TELEMACHUS, from his father.

INT. HOUSE. DAY.

Stu checks the shopping list one last time. As he does this he [sees] a distant image of himself in the bathroom mirror. Stuck to the mirror is a yellow post-it note that says: FEED TELEMACHUS.

Below that note is another: BUY FOOD.

He [peels] the notes off the mirror and leaves the house, locking the front door from the outside.

STAIRWELL. DAY

Once inside the [(actual)] house he proceeds with caution. In [the back of] his eye a distant memory battles for recognition, superimposed over [the interior of] the house he walks through. He's vaguely familiar with the layout of the house but is not sure why.

In the kitchen he lifts the venetian blinds up and the noise startles him so much that he [reflexively shoves] the blinds back down towards the glass. The glass shatters and falls [all over] the lawn.

wall. A pattern of wear on the carpet swings out into a wide arc half way across the room. Beyond this line is a color t.v. on a table. He walks up to the t.v. slowly, unsure .

On the screen a man with a toupee pleads violently with [...] closed and his fists raised. He is sweating and shaking, consume[...] Ten numbers flah incessantly at the bottom of the screen.

He slowly reaches his ha[...] the glass the reverend drops to his knees.

He makes his way to the t[...] so many times. He learned the word father from the television.

Inside the house he proceeds [...] caution. In his eyes a distant memory battles for recognition, superimposed over the house he is walking through. He seems to be very familiar with the layout of the house. He wanders towards the kitchen. He lifts the venetian blinds up and the noise startles him so much that he throws the blinds back down [...] the glass. The glass shatters, and falls down unt[...] lawn. After a moment he cautiously lifts the bli[...] age. Shards of glass hang precariously, then fall noiselessly to the lawn below like icicles [...]ed, overwhelmed by a memory from a childhood he thought he had forgotten.

EXT.DAY. NIEGHBOR ACROSS THE WAY HEARS [...]S BREAK. SEES A STRANGE MAN IN THE WINDOW. THROWS THE HOSE DOWN AND RUNS TOWARDS HIS HOUSE. INSIDE HIS HOUSE HE CALLS FOR HIS WIFE.

INT.CAR.DAY.77 FORD GRAN TORINO, BROWN EXTERIOR, BROWN INTERIOR, ONE CHEAP RADIO SHACK CAR SPEAKER BLASTING "STREET LIFE" (CRUSADERS).

He is finished his shopping, and is headed across town to work. In traffic he reaches his hand across the nivyl seat to the brown paper bag. Without looking he deftly rips open the reinforced cardboard six pack container, pulls out a bottle, leans over slightly and passes it quickly against the passenger side door opener (easily popping off the cap,) holds it for a full three seconds over the bag until the foam has stopped rising and the quickly downs

... or the time he (accidentally) *punched his hand thru a glass door* + our mom was more concerned about him mentally than physically...

6: Further from the Truth

105

long short

the whole (two-thirds of a) bottle. He tilts his head back against the headrest as the traffic pulls to another complete stop and lets out a long belch. He laughs to himself , red-faced.

INT.DAY. BATHROOM. THE EXPLORATION OF HIS FATHERS HOUSE HAS ENDED IN HIS FATHERS BATHROOM. ON THE MIRROR IS A NOTE SCRAWLED ON A POST-IT; "FEED TELEMACHUS". THEN DIRECTLY BELOW THAT ONE IS ANOTHER THAT SAYS;"BUY FOOD FOR TELEMACHUS". TELEMACHUS LIFTS UP HIS FATHER'S COLOGNE BOTTLE AND SMELLS IT.

w/siren (light, no sound)

EXT.DAY. POLICE CAR ROUNDS CORNER SLOWLY.. ▬▬▬▬ HANGS OUT OF PASSENGER WINDOW TALKING (RELAXED) TO NIEGHBORS NOW LINED UP, CONCERNED AND GOSSIPING ON THIER FRONT LAWNS.

"Everything is going to be fine."   "Nothing you're not going to find out"

T▬▬▬cop says in a voice that is so calm and assuring that all of the people are instantly soothed, and begin to return to thier houses , waddling like old sheep.

INT.DAY.POLICE CAR.

out at the cops.

"Everything is going to be fine.....hell. Nothing could be further from the truth!'
He mutters this to his partner as he roles up the window, smiling.

"Is there something I should know?"

"What the hell is going on?"

Getting into the passenger side;

"Nothing you need to know"

THE CAR SLOWLY PULLS INTO THE DRIVE. THE COPS GET OUT, GRAB AND LOAD THIER SHOTGUNS AND WALK UP TO THE FRONT DOOR, RING THE DOORBELL.

After a long time the curtains covering the window near the front door get pulled back. Telemachus looks out at the cops.

"Just like I thought"

Expressionless the old cop turns, unloads his gun and starts walking back towards the car. After a few moments of staring back at Tele. the young cop turns and starts quickly in the same direction.

[When the dust settles] he lifts the blinds back up to survey the damage. Shards of glass [dangle] precariously then fall like icicles to the lawn below.

He stares transfixed, overwhelmed by a memory from childhood he thought he'd forgotten...

EXT. DAY

An old man watering his lawn across the street sees this strange man in the window, throws down his garden hose and runs into his house, calling out to his wife...

«I'm the boy / that can enjoy / invisibility»—says Kim Gordon (of Sonic Youth), stealing a line from ULYSSES.

«Come touch me here / so I know / that I'm / not there.»—we say, stealing a line back.

INT. HOUSE.DAY. TELMACHUS IS PUTTING ON HIS FATHERS CLOTHS, HIS WATCH, HIS WEDDING RING, HIS LOOSE CHANGE, HIS WALLET. HE IS COMBING HIS HAIR WITH HIS COMB. HE LOOKS IN HIS MIRROR, INTO HIS EYES.

EXT.DAY . STU'S CAR PULLS UP TO THE FRONT OFFICE BUILDING OF A MAJOR OIL REFINERY COMPLEX, WITH OIL REFINING MACHINES IN THE BACKGROUND. *Cashed.*

INT. 78 BROWN FORD GRAN TORINO.

[Bumper to bumper] in heavy morning traffic, Stu reaches across brown vinyl seats and forages through a shopping bag until he [finds] a bottle of a beer. Keeping his eyes on the car in front of him, he pops the cap off with a quick swipe down on the passenger side door handle. He then holds the bottle above the bag for a couple of seconds and lets the foam swarm down over his hand.

When he comes to a stop he takes a long chug on the bottle, tilting his head all the way back. A loud belches escapes from his throat, making his eyes water. He wipes his mouth with the back of his hand and smiles just a bit.

He makes it to work forty minutes late and nobody seems to notice, as usual. He goes directly to his office and locks the door.

INT. HOUSE. DAY

Telemachus [collapses to his knees] and checks under his father's bed, [verifying] that the Christmas presents are all still there, untouched ... though dust and lint [have accumulated]. Some of them are partially squished by the boxspring.

He gets back to his feet and [scans] his father's bedside table. A lamp and flashing alarm clock share the dusty surface with a small stack of porn mags and a lime-green [container of] Vaseline Intensive Care lotion. → (actually, he preferred the pink ROSE MJK brand

He [snoops] through his father's closet and dresser, picks out a [set of clothes] and [lays it out] on the bed. In the bathroom he showers and shaves. He combs his hair back just like his dad, with His hair gel and comb, then [applies] a large assortment of tonics, perfumes and skin products.

When he's done he checks himself in the mirror while picking his teeth with a cinnamon flavored toothpick.

"I think the story should change direction." I say to Nausicaa, not really knowing why I have chosen to interrupt her at this point in her rather involved story.

She looks at me for a while taking a drag on her cigarette, squinting at me as if the sun was still out, and then she continues on ...

Stu stops, Puts the car in park, waits to turn it off completely so he can hear the end of the song. Off to the right waves crash onto a beach populated with hundreds of lifeguard towers. Stu looks at them for a minute, completely puzzeled. Finally, he remembers that they store the towers on the beach every winter. This ensures that they will not be spraypainted. He turns the car completely off, opens the door and gets out. As he approaches the building he gets his things in order. He looks up for a moment and sees a thermometer mounted with brackets to a brickwall. A single round, intense burst of sunlight strikes the glass and metal, bouncing off to dissipate unto the beige bricks. The red line is all of the way to the top.

INT.DAY. HOUSE.

of which he had squirt bottles in every room

Based on what he has remembered from watching the television, and his father, Telemachus acts like a functional adult.

He checks his hair one last time in the mirror of his fathers bathroom, then heads down the hall to the front door with a rythmic spring, in his step. His hair is greased back. He is wearing a white fishnet t-shirt under a green/ (exterior) orange (interior) - vinyl windbreaker.

When he reaches the end of the hallway he stops, turns and goes back to the closet half way down the hall. The door is slightly ajar. He approaches cautiously. He opens the closet door with a lunge. Less than one- fifth of a second later, his wincing face is slowly backing out of a bunch of towels. He stands back, dissapointed. In front of him is a closet filled with over 8,000 navy-blue bath towels, as many as can physically be placed into a closet measuring 8'H x 5'3"W x 31 3/16"L.

They are immaculately clean and ironed.

Telemachus thrusts his hand swiftly into one of the stacks, holds his whole body completely still, and then pulls his hand out, shuts the door and heads once again for the front door. Tele. says "shit" as he pulls the front door open.

EXT.DAY. OILREFINERY.

8°Te 150
7 E

STU

"shit!!!"

EXT. DAY. OIL REFINERY.

STU pulls into a gravel parking lot, for the most part empty. He cuts the engine and pulls up to—but does not touch—the fence. [...] puts the car in park and takes one last gulp before tossing [the bottle] out the window.

He steps out into a [blinding] blast of hot air. His legs feel unsteady in the loose gravel. His left hand

Stu watches in shock as day quickly turns into night and the oil refinery explodes with a hellish force into succeedingly larger, expanding clouds of fire.

Huge peices of white hot metal, some as big as cars, shoot out of the exploding mountain of fire, landing with a thundering impact all around him.

reaches out for the hot brown vinyl roof.

INT.DAY.HOUSE He looks to his right and sees a beige cinder block wall. Mounted on the wall is a barometric

Tele. walks past the door leading to his room. He pauses for a moment, listening to the crazed preacher, pleading for money, saying ;" if you do not pay! you will go to hell!."

meter. Stu squints at the small numbers, attempting to [find the end of] the faint red line.

EXT. DAY. OILREFINERY.

Stu flies back against the hood of his car, rolls over to the driver side, jumps to the ground, opens the door and gets in. He jams it into reverse, squeels backwards across the parking lot and smashes into a van designed to transport the handicaped, totaling it.

After a moment, when he realizes what he has done, he turns his eyes from the small picture of the steaming wreckage in the rear-view mirror to the full scale picture through the back, where the rear window used to be.

Radiator fluid squirts in a fluid green arc against the white perforated vinyl ceiling.

INT.DAY.HOME

Tele. steps out into the frozen air. The cold air stings his lungs, and the ice underfoot quickly makes him feel unstable.

He reaches out a bare hand for one of the broken black-iron rails that twist down pathetically above the frozen cement steps. At the bottom of the steps, where the rail has broken out of its mooring, it bobs up and down dramatically past the rusted spot now filled with frozen, dead, black- leaves.

The same neighbor that had called the cops approaches the house with his wife, (still in her bathrobe), and their daughter.

TELEMACHUS

"Languid palor. Nubile waif. Hair- albuminous pale glow. Walk- unaware, but vaguely aware of reception,..."

NIEGHBOR (FATHER)

" Listen here you fucking freak!"

NIEGHBOR (MOTHER)

"Honey!"

> **"Are you supposed to be Telemachus?"**
> **I ask, aware that analysis always puts**
> **her on the defensive.** »

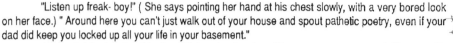

NIEGHBOR (DAUGHTER)

"Listen up freak- boy!" (She says pointing her hand at his chest slowly, with a very bored look on her face.) " Around here you can't just walk out of your house and spout pathetic poetry, even if your dad did keep you locked up all your life in your basement."

As she finished saying this she withdrew her hand, and became very composed. The serenity and control in her face grew.

Eventually, she gave him a wry smile, and dug her knuckles forward, slowly, into her baggy pockets.

"My parents didnt think you should know that." With this she turns to her right and looks back at her shocked parents. "You're kind of the"Movie of the Week"-profit, about to happen."

She turns and looks at Tele.,the wind picks up and blows her hair to one side like a candle. She takes out a steel-grey, pointed ski hat and put it on.

She looks at Tele. like there is something bad happening,in his eyes.

At that instant, over her right shoulder, off in the distance over the pointed black roofs with smoke belching chimneys, at the opposite end of the city, a fireball grew, as enourmous as the rising sun.

Almost instantly, the thick black smoke completely blocked out the sun.

The last rays of the sun ran over the hills and then the houses towards Telemachus.

Darkness swept over them, and with it came the wind and the cold.

EXT. DAY

Telemachus shuts the door behind him and puts the sandwich he has made into his jacket pocket. As he looks up he sees the neighbor across the street. He makes eye contact with the old man standing on his lawn with his hands in his pockets. After a second the old man gets embarrassed and turns away. Telemachus continues to watch him as he turns and retreats back into his house. His wife follows him, pretending to check on her dying rose bush as she does.

EXT. DAY

Telemachus carefully crosses the smooth gray ice covering the cement in front of the house.

III. TELEMACHUS

I ask her where she comes up with these weird stories and she just stares at me, grinning. She seems relieved to [pause] her diatribe. She closes her eyes and rolls her head back and forth to stretch her [neck ...] then looks away [out over] the vast expanse of crabgrass lawn now [fading] in the cool darkness. The sprinklers and crickets [generate] a subtle rhythm in the summer night sky.

I feel just a little sorry for Nausicaa. "Are you supposed to be Telemachus?" I ask, aware that analysis always puts her on the defensive.

"Congratulations doctor Freud! [...] How'd you come up with that!?" [Beneath her sarcasm I can tell] she appreciates the time I spend alone with her—a time when she can feel safe telling her stories.

It is near dawn and everyone else is asleep. Two orderlies and two nurses are on [night duty] for the whole ward. They rarely ever check on the patients, but even if they did they [never] tell us to return to our beds. At night authority was lax but during the day it was almost sadistic. [This range of authority reflects my upbringing—NIGHT being my hands-off (biological) mother and DAY being my disciplining stepmother.]

Nausicaa [falls] asleep shivering in my arms, dressed only in her nightgown. I carry her to her bed and tuck her in, and then go to my own bunk. [This is how it always is.] I always dream of Telemachus after she tells me her stories. [...] These dream extensions were always the same—Telemachus goes off in search of his father, crossing the vast expanse of some city, meeting interesting people, and getting caught up in interesting adventures along the way. The [ending was] always exactly the same ... reaching the refinery, Telemachus walks right past his father, who is always standing right next to his car. He strides right past his father and [continues straight] into the raging inferno. As white light engulfs Telemachus, I'd wake up all of a sudden in a large room filled with morning sunlight. N would almost always be sitting on the end of my bed, watching me.

Nausicaa used to tell me she had royal Russian blood [... that] her great, great, grandfather was some sort of czar. I never found out why she was there, or who had [committed] her. I guess N figured it was worth the free rent. She didn't give much thought [to it].

exhibit 44—untitled door painting (that he referred to as «8- ball»)

Sometimes late at night I [heard] N's muffled cries and pleas. I knew she was being [violated] by the night orderlies. I knew this nightmare was real. The scary thing was that I was so out of it I didn't even think of it as a bad dream. [...] I could tell how horrible it was by the sound of her voice echoing down the dark hallways. It still haunts me at night.

N liked to sit on the old Persian rug near the French doors in the rec room. She used to draw all day in the sun. By mid-afternoon she would follow the sunlight out onto the small balcony, her face and hands covered in charcoal.

One day one of the orderlies spit some of his slurpee on to the drawing she was working on—N's newest masterpiece—[leaving] shiny dark rings of purple on the charcoal-covered paper. [She ripped it up] then burnt it out on the balcony with matches stolen from one of the doctors.

We watched, laughing hysterically, as pieces of burning paper drifted up into the air and landed on the canvas canopies below. The [tents] caught fire and Kim (a schizo lifer) wet her pants.

"Well, this puts a damper on things," Dr. Elizabeth said, directing everyone back to their beds. Two orderlies took Kim away to clean her up. Dr. Elizabeth told the room that "from now on the boys are to sleep on one side of the room and the girls on the other."

IV. INT. DAY.

I was at the Cherry Hill Hospital for over three years. Towards the end of the last year I was overcome with loss at the thought of leaving the place. It had become home to me. I'm not quite sure what it was: the clean smell, never having to change out of your pajamas, never having to comb your hair, never having to worry where your next meal was [coming] from, or being dosed morning, noon and night on the purest pharmaceuticals. [...] I didn't have any other home, it was simple as that.

I wasn't there 'cause I was crazy. I was there 'cause the hippie mom next door dosed me—put a couple dozen hits of DMT in the macaroni she brought to the barbecue. She said she did it to add a little "spice" [...] that her square neighbors were in need of some "vision". My young mind was absolutely tweaked.

[...]

People where being taken to the hospital by those who did not like mac and cheese.

[....]

My aunt and uncle still keep Art in what used to be their den. There are no windows in the den, that is the only way my aunt can tolerate [him]. My other cousins don't even go home anymore 'cause they are so ashamed of him.

[...]

Later Michelle and her fellow Stanford rich-hippie friends were convicted in court of manufacturing huge quantities of liquid DMT, with the intent to sell.

[...]

Before I was released my parents petitioned to have the money taken out of my name and put into theirs. They claimed I was mentally incapacitated, unable to manage my own funds. At first the court was not willing to authorize it, but after a special "tax" on the amount was paid to [the right] people, the necessary papers were signed.

A week before I was released my parents called to tell me they where moving, but they didn't tell me where [...] They told me not to try and contact them. They [claimed] I had hurt them, that they were just protecting themselves.

V. EXT. DAY.

When I got out, there was no one there to meet me. After a while I got my uncle Cal's number from the reception and called him. He seemed surprised to hear from me + said he didn't have the time to pick me up, (he lives in Malibu and I was in Altadena, about 25 miles or 2 hours away in traffic). But [he] told me I was welcome to stay at his house. He suggested that I walk to his place, stopping by to visit my cousins (his kids) on the way. My head was still cloudy and I was feeling insecure, but his idea sounded reasonable at the time.

[...]

... as attached (resigned) as he is to the institution (+ Nausicaa), he is quick to casually leave it ... tho he does admit «I was too preoccupied to feel sad or scared.» This preoccupation it seems stems mostly from him having to find his own way. He goes on to describe his cross–L.A. odyssey in great detail ... a veritable wasteland ever under construction + the only people he encounters speak a language he can't comprehend.

This is where things get further **disjointed** so helps maybe if we fill in the gaps. It's like he was trying to combine 2 or 3 stories into 1 like what we are doing here ... so we have this hermit couple living parallel lives of isolation. The 2 find eachother eventually + further metafictions unfold + splinter landing us in this institution + to further complicate matters several widely varying variations of «FURTHER FROM THE TRUTH» exist.

These bits we are omitting here describe the BBQ party w/ the mac + cheese spiked by the same «hippie mom» Michelle (her name IRL) that he changes to Claire in the hit + run CIRCE story on page 158-9). DMT-Dosed people start freaking out left + right ... brother-½ is really sick, near death, yet at the same time «there were periods during this time when I understood everything crystal clear.» Our cousin ART was not so fortunate, he «never really came back.»

«MY YOUNG MIND WAS ABSOLUTELY TWEAKED.»

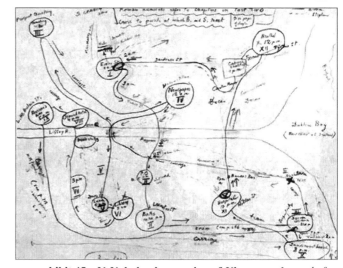

exhibit 45—V. Nabokov's mapping of *Ulysses* ... *«Instead of perpetuating the pretentious nonsense of Homeric, chromatic, and visceral chapter headings, instructors should prepare maps of Dublin with Bloom's and Stephen's intertwining itineraries clearly traced.»*

He references a map that the receptionist at the institution gave him (along w/ a cheese sandwich + a «stained electric blanket» (w/ the plug still sticking out of it)) but is for the most part admittedly lost ... past «Buicks w/ metallic paint jobs cruising the streets like trout searching for food.»

After ½ a day, he reaches cousin Ray's house (see exhibit 46). Ray's not there, so he waits under a green awning in the heat + falls asleep.

I woke up sweating, with cotton mouth and drank some hot rusty water from a [sun-bleached] hose laying in the yellow patch that used to be a lawn and then waited on the doorstep of the small bungalow until dusk. Right as the sun [dipped] below the horizon, a pickup [came roaring] down the driveway alongside the house with some [rowdy teenagers hanging out of it].

[...]

The truck screeched to a halt [+ they all piled out] then Ray jacked it [in reverse] to check out the weird looking guy standing on his lawn, in institutional pajamas, toting an electric blanket.

["Get a load of this freak," said my cousin], laughing hysterically. [...] then he [recognized] me and got all serious.

VI. INT. DAY

"The fuck you looking at?" He says with his face in a demonic snarl, his arms [posturing] at his sides, "where you keeping [your money] freak boy?" Ray grabs the front of my shirt pulling me towards him. [...]

"We don't want you here, you understand? No one wants you! You are a disgraceful [trustafarian]! [...]"

The rest of the band fans out behind Ray [...] arms splayed at their sides.

"If you wanna stay, it's gonna cost you," says a skinny girl with long black hair and pale skin. "You certainly can afford it."

"I don't have control of my money," I say, too exhausted [for their antics]. "My parents do. I don't know where they are, they split with their lawyer friend."

"Oh, that's right, I remember now!" Ray says, grinning, "My mom told me that your mom and her lawyer were getting it on. She said your dad didn't mind ... in fact, your dad and the lawyer [also] had a thing going."

"And your mom jerks off her grade school students for extra pocket change," I [quickly retort] in rebuttal. "Hell, she sucked me off pro bono."

Ray's grin [widens into a laugh] and he bows his head down, [wagging it side to side]. We lean our foreheads together, arm in arm. "I really missed you man," he says, sounding like himself [now. His girlfriend G hugs me, shaking her head... "you two."]

[IN SITU...]

TELEPHANTIC PEREGRINATION

exhibit 46—sketch not unlike the description of Ray's house

Chronologically (... SSEY-wise) we are still in Guadalajara, but in brother-½'s story he's in Los Angeles. He was fond of the movie *Falling Down* (1993) w/ Michael Douglas ... liked the idea of an urban odyssey across L.A. + told me he wanted to write such a story or script ... sort of like how Joyce applied **The Odyssey** to Dublin, but he stressed that he wanted to make it more epic + dystopian ... as if the protagonist was on an urgent mission to get somewhere (or away from something) but u didn't necessarily know why ... + it didn't matter.

[...] ➡

Wake and bake, and if you didn't have work (and no one ever did) then it was off to the bowling alley for breakfast.

[...]

Saturday Ray decides that it is time to celebrate, calls it my "welcome home party". He doesn't see my age as a concern. "Celebrating" consists of making the rounds in Hollywood, getting wasted and spending lots of money. Ray tries to get me stoned or drunk, but I defiantly refuse. He [takes it personally] acting sullen and hurt. So I act a little wasted to make him feel better.

[...]

Whenever I catch a glimpse of them in the smoky, sweaty blackness, they appear to be sick and upset. [...] wasted people giving seemingly urgent advice to each other [when in reality (unstoned) it's no big deal].

[...]

The theme for the city this Sunday morning seems to be REST & RECOVERY. Culver City only adds to my sense of alienation.

[... He spends a few days surfing Ray's couch before he continues on his trans-L.A. trek to cousin N's house in Venice...]

Cousin N has no warning of my arrival. At first she doesn't recognize me. Then a look of joy sweeps over her face.

[cont. to split + splinter further ...]

[...]

She takes me inside her apartment, where she lives alone. It is small and sunny. I take a shower and she finds me some pants and a shirt that fit. Then she feeds me a huge breakfast. While I eat she just watches me, smiling, occasionally wiping the hair off of my forehead.

[...] [disINTegrate...]

She works as a freelance illustrator so has time to spend with me. We go down to the beach and talk all afternoon. She asks me questions about the hospital, about my parents, about everything that has happened since I was twelve (and she was fifteen). I [feel free and] uninhibited for the first time that I can remember.

She props herself up on her elbows in the sand, lying on her stomach. She is wearing granny sunglasses and a small black bikini.

➡ ... at which point, more male bonding ensues + brother-½ is reunited w/ the gang. They head down to their hang-out (The Brig) + it's just like the old days ... back to their debaucherous routine. There's more partying scenes in bars that we omitted in the intrest of space ... Ray + his girlfriend fight + make-up + lots of other degenerate drama ...

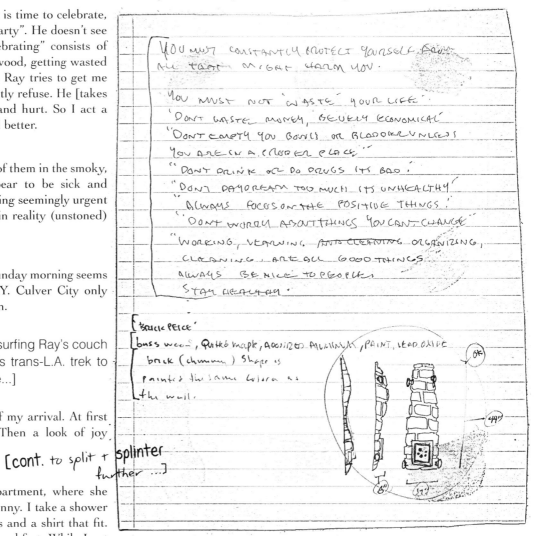

—By witholding information we are actually telling more ... as we co-opt his microcosmic trek as our own.
—When our step-mother once accused brother-½ of not being able to hold a thought, of having A.D.D., he responded, «*why would any 1 ever want to HOLD a thought?*»
—[These here] are editorial notes we wrote to ourself ... items we feel inclined to fold in ... writing in 3rd person to be mutually inclusive ... not just of brother-½ but of U, the reader.
—We have no cousin N (nor a sister) ... we have 1 female step-cousin but far as i know he didn't have such a platonic crush on her. Our uncle's name (Cal) is IRL our father's name. Telemachus's uncle earlier in the piece is Stu, which is indeed our uncle's name. Names are just placeholders + what happens at the destination matters not, it's just only about getting there.

you can believe one but you can't believe the other.

[...]

Her [lanky and] languid form is that of a healthy teenage girl in her prime. Tan boys walk by carrying surfboards, calling out to N but she ignores them.

[...]

I look down at my pale undeveloped body sitting in the sand and feel ashamed [... +] overcome with anxiety. My emotions [are] new and out of control, the surroundings overwhelmingly alien.

[...]

We go back to N's apartment [... +] she works on an illustration she is doing for a record cover, of two people fighting in front of a wall of fire. As she draws with the colored pencils she explains the concept [...] that [they] represent two aspects of the same person and they are fighting for unity (to be one and the same). The two figures in N's drawing seem to be getting nowhere — equally matched opponents inflicting exactly the same damage on each other.

Watching her draw I think of Nausicaa. I imagine her life to be what cousin N's could be, if Nausicaa had control [over] it. The thought of Nausicaa spending the rest of her life being abused becomes for me a fiction, unreal, like one of her stories. I fall asleep on the couch watching her draw.

I wake up the next morning coughing. [...] Ray is sitting on the coffee table in front of me with his usual fiendish look, holding a piece of tinfoil in his hand. With a straw and a lighter he smokes something small and black, that smells like burnt chocolate and orange peels. G and a friend are watching TV, looking like zombies.

Ray blows more smoke in my face, making me cough again. "Wakey wakey," he says.

"Where's K?"

"Where's K?" Ray mocks me, in a nasally voice. "Here, she left you a note." He tosses me a crumpled piece of paper.

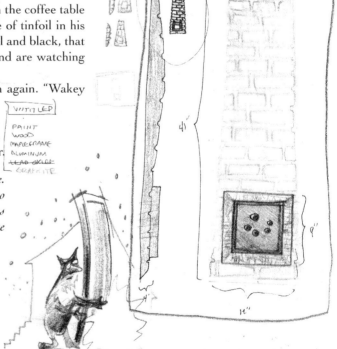

[*The note says she went to run errands + to make yourself at home. Cousin Ray mocks him when he reads it out loud, 'aw, sis is so sweet!'... as he rifles thru her kitchen for tinfoil which he fashions into a small square. Then he pushes brother-½ to try the 'Chinese concoction' w/ the shell of a Bic ben + he doesn't protest ...*]

Having been fed drugs most of my life by mean people, I felt right at home. Cousin Ray understood a thing or two about reinforced behavioral modification.

VII. TELEMACHUS

Later after they left I laid there and looked out the window at the fog. It felt like I was back in the hospital only there were no doctors or orderlies around. I was free to come and go. [...] I just laid there with a huge grin on my face. I closed my eyes and dreamt of Telemachus. In the dream he went to the hospital and got Nausicaa out by posing as her father. He was wearing a fake beard and a bolo hat. [...] They went far away up in the mountains where no one could find them and settled into a small cabin on a lake. Telemachus cut wood for a living — chopping up dead trees with a big ax, dragging the wood into his pick-up and then selling it as firewood to the people in town down the mountain. Even though they were constantly struggling financially, things were OK for a long time. Telemachus and Nausicaa never had kids because they felt they couldn't afford to raise them properly if they did. Their life was quiet and peaceful. Nausicaa drew all day on her deck over the lake. She was alone all day and liked it that way.

When N came back I was sprawled out on her couch, feeling comfortably numb. She smiled and sat next to me. Snaking my arm around her shoulder, I pulled her down until she was lying prone next to me. She smiled, looking right into my eyes.

"Thanks" I said, this time meaning it.

... that's how HIS story ends further from the truth but no closer to fiction generalize now to your own situation 1 step forward 2 steps back «white on white translucent black capes» climbing cones of snow + ash the air getting thinner clambering over 1 another to make the summit some cheat + bring O_2 but U only cheat yourself of the feeling of being deprived of knowing all this time it had been surrounding U all along the IDEA of love dies when consummated the fire goes

analysis on the supposedly he missed her but more than anything he

of sorts like just now incremented in steps + after all that she doesn't even recognize him granted a spell was cast to make his original identity invisible but his dog recognized him (before dying) tho U couldn't acknowledge this recognition for fear of betraying yourself informally speaking a step function is a piecewise constant function having only finitely many pieces such

exhibit 47—"untitled" 1990 (Oxygen), bricks, plaster, wood, aluminum, 14" x 36" x 10", permanent installation (current location unknown)

NEXT STEPS

from archives to books to episodes to stories to paragraphs to sentences to words to letters to atoms of disintegrating ash what we originally wrote we erased nothing left but ghost traces vapor trails spelling SURRENDER the ashes + embers still glowing the next morning stoke or blow till u see the heart rise x 2 then 30 compression pumps to jump start or re-prime the ticker which is to say it's all discontinuous like brother-½ we could never swallow the 1st or 2nd step of 12 whatever the 1 is about admitting to yourself that there's a power higher than U

here in the position where we had to take that step we just keep putting 1 foot in front of the other still listening to Joy Division's CLOSER (1980) «surrender to self-preservation from others who care for themselves a kindness

put another log on the fire as we gather around our step-grandmother's hearth with our step-cousins young enough we exposed ourselves naked to the fire nobody

the world OK as is it all catches up to itself in the end boils down to absence down to the pursuit of higher art in

TIME: c. 1979-81 / 87
PLACE: Guadalajara / Portland, OR
IDEAS/Symbolism: sibling rivalry, bifurcation, gambling, foreign anti-bodies, shoe laces, lost wax, reciprocal altruism
ABSTRACT (RESUMEN): «Oh no, Guadalajara won't do.» In unison we (transparently) perform regression analysis of our split parental bean-cum-atom. Parallel parked in the hourly red zone while we rehearse our summit bid .. 2 steps back . 1 step forward. Not so fast, I[st] need to do **do** diligence. Throwing caution to the wind is suicidal, yet anything less **is** not living. Circling the bull w/steely eyes while the clowns do the dirty work. In reality not economically viable to kill the beast so they just get drunk + taunt + swagger ... but mess w/ the bull + u get the horn. «In psycho-analysis nothing is true xcept the exaggerations»—said Adorno. Whether she peeked at his pubes or laced the mac + cheese ¿quién puede decir? «And i'm never going back to my old school» said Steely **D**an.

Lo que quiere decir es que we're still in limbo (can't U tell) using pesos[53] ... a fluid but unstable currency as we'd discover hardly for ourselves ... the valor of money not neSSESarily a given. Our father remains en vivo 1 more year, fingering the cowries in his front panther pocket. (Later we'd play his pocket blackjack to recreate the conditions leading to his debasement.)

Pesos also have an **eagle** on the tailing flipside pero su águila is mounted on a cactus clutching a rattlesnake (more badass than being bald). Didn't know who any of the heads were on the front ... not even the hombre w/ the bandana.

+ still we didn't feel at **home**. Or quizás u could say this was the beginning of feeling at home dondequiera ... mi casa es tu casa at least speaking for my sake ... brother-½ we're not so sure about, seems todavía he was searching for some semblance of home. Around this time he'd had enough + split back to Oregon como Telemachus

---

[53] The only concept of money we had up to this point was of *allowance*.

[Handwritten marginal notes along the top/left:]

The face on the coin spoke of integrity, strength and sex.
who is about to do something extremely dangerous and completely [futile] And
He pushed a couple of buttons in quick succession And
shot from the polished stainless steel arm to his
[...] before he fell back on to the show

The old lady next to him in the orange sweater
till she had thrown away the rest of her
stool to face him, lying sprawled out on
finally she reached into his current trough
at likely recognizing the bald man
Malcolm's lifeless [body] from
the boots looking ... a pair of
He followed ...

PUT IT ON SIDEWAYS

KEVIN WHITE

3-8-95

54

55

[14:33, 2-24-87] The face of the coin spoke of integrity, strength and sex. He looked into the face like one might look at a friend who is about to do something extremely dangerous and completely futile. and then he dropped it into the machine. He pushed a couple of buttons in quick succession and an instant later an arc of blue and white electricity shot from the stainless steel arm to his forehead. For a full second he froze. powerless in the electricity's grip, then he fell back off of his stool onto the *Aztec ice cream* low shag indoor/outdoor carpeting.

The chain-smoking old lady sitting next to him in the orange sweater saw it happen, but waited until she had thrown away the rest of her coins before she turned around on her stool to face him. sprawled out on the floor. After a long while she leaned over and scooped a silver dollar out of his pay-off trough. She took a long look at Ike, finally recognizing the bald man, and then she threw it with all her might at the lifeless body on the ground.

[8:18, 2-24-87] His shoes leaked as he walked through the melting snow. past the soot stained bulldozer.

He walked through the open fields following the trail of a pair of cowboy boots. Occasionally the boots ducked into an abandoned doorway (to light a cigarette?) or milled about a lamp post (waiting for the light? Propositioning a streetwalker?).

Finally he found the boots, filled with mud and garbage. in an empty lot. Weeds were growing through the cracked leather and the crusty leather soles had peeled completely off.

Looking around at the blocks of broken cement and rusted pencil rod he tried to formulate a theory. tried to come to an understanding, but could not.

[21:23, 2-23-87] The bus reeked of bubble gum air freshner. Pinesol and Puke. Some leather faced old bum was passed out in the seat next to his. Every time the bus would make a right turn he would fall into his lap, his snoring face pressed against his leg. The third time this happened [STEPHEN] freaked out and started punching the old man's face. The old guy didn't even wake up and no one else on the bus [took notice]. Stephen pushed the old man away [...] so that his head was on the ground, wedged under the seat directly in front of him.

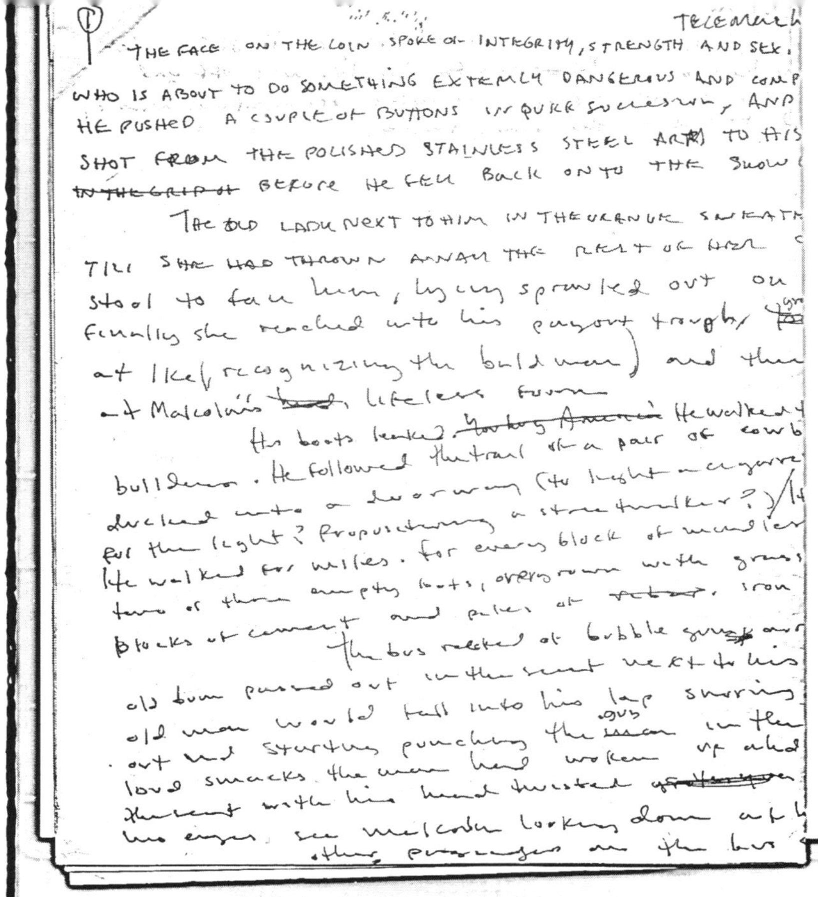

Stephen was rubbing his fist when he noticed a [nosey] old woman across the aisle [scrutinizing] him.

[8:32, 2-24-87] [CAL] left the boots in the empty lot and went downtown. When he got to the office he called some of the other people on the list he had pinned above his desk.

The last person he called told him what he was hoping to hear.

---

54 To actually (literally) put it sideways was Derek's editorial decision.

55 2-24-87 is about 4 years after the actual time of this episode.

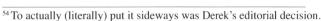

[3:45, 2-24-87] The bus pulled into Portland before sunrise. Inside the station he put all his quarters into the television, slid his stuff under the green plastic seat and passed out watching *The Flintstones*.

When he woke up, the television was off and the station was [bustling with] commuters. [Orienting] himself, he grabbed his stuff and marched off into the gray drizzle.

[9:23, 2-24-87] Cal booked himself a plane ticket, arranged for his neighbor to take care of his cat in his absence and got a ride from his secretary to the airport.

[7:56, 2-24-87] Two city busses and a [20] minute walk later he was where he wanted to be. The key was still under the 3rd stone from the Japanese cherry tree where he'd left it 12 years earlier. Surrounded by slugs and spiders, it still [shone] back at him. [56]

[14:03, 2-24-87] He was booked onto the 10 a.m. commuter flight from Vancouver to Portland, but it was overbooked. He ended up catching the 12 o'clock Delta shuttle, [arriving] in Portland by 2 p.m.

[8:01, 2-24-87] He managed to get the rusted old lock to turn and let himself into the garage from around back. Once inside he found the light switch in the darkness. Everything [was] exactly where he'd left it. He then [entered] the museum through the door that connected it to the garage.

[14:10, 2-24-87] When he arrived in Portland he went straight to the Hertz counter and rented himself a car—a burgundy ['82 Ford Torino].

[8:30, 2-24-87] Inside the museum he [found] his way [in] the darkness, past the dusty shelves that smelled of damp wood and cleaning solvents. He opened a door and switched on the lights. He was in the workshop. The room was [cluttered] with machines and tables littered with objects of various sorts.

The room felt like it belonged to him, [...] meticulously arranged to suit his needs. Stephen went [straight] across the room to a footlocker and opened it. He pulled out some cans of silicone, [a few bags of] nuts and bolts and some resin-cast human arm bones. He [positioned] all of this on a low table in the center of the room and began to bolt together some of the bones. [57]

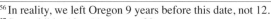

... dum-dums dint u know? We renounced any [sic] cents of entitlement. We coud only IMAGINE what it was our father was doing back in the crib whilst our mom pushed peyote buttons on us.

§ ~~Honestly, he hardly crossed my mind.~~

§ ~~The way we member it, Gazoo was like Fred's subconscious alter-ego that more often than not led him astray.~~

§ ~~We started our cowry collection in conjunction... + the habit of post-its to self + these such lists.~~

§ We tried to deconstructively create order (call us vain) by **x'ing** off items 1 x 1. Just as we intuited time was not continuous (circa age 4, in retrospect), we also sensed memory was not linear.

§ Even tho brother-½ was 2 grades above me, we were placed in the same math + science classes.

exhibit 48—"untitled" 1991.
Colored RTV silicone, 18" in diameter.

---

[56] In reality, we left Oregon 9 years before this date, not 12.

[57] See exhibits 10 + 11 on page 30.

[14:26, 2-24-87] Cal struggled to find an interesting station on the radio [...] completely exacerbated, he pulled the car [onto] the side of the road [...].

[10:23, 2-24-87] Stephen wore latex gloves as he mixed the concentrated red and orange powdered dye into the RTV 500 casting silicone. When he achieved the desired flesh tone he added the pre-measured Fastcure. He then poured the mixture into black plastic sheets that were suspended like hammocks from wooden dowels nailed to the side of the table. He waited 40 minutes for the silicone to cure and then eased the pieces out of the bags.

The shiny round ridges of pink silicone [shone] in the shop lights.

[14:29, 2-24-87] Cal leaned up against the car, his collar up to shield himself from the wet spray of passing [traffic]. He [took in] the dismal suburban scenery and thought to himself that if he smoked [...], he might be inclined to do so at times like this.

[10:46, 2-24-87] Stephen arranged the pieces of silicone according to size and shape. He then used a 1/4" graphite drill bit to [score] 4 holes in each piece of silicone. Using a 3/16" bit he [drilled] as many holes in the resin bones. Then he bolted everything together, tightening [it all] by hand to ensure that none of the pieces of silicone tore.

He started up the 14" table saw by [flipping] a red switch on the cement column in the center of the room. It roared [to life ...] shattering the silence of the building. Stephen found a 8' piece of 1"x 12" and began cutting.

He stopped after a moment to put on some clear plastic shop glasses and resumed cutting. After a while he had a pile of small pieces stacked on one side of the table. [Going] against his instinct, he began to cut these pieces even smaller, bringing his fingers within inches of the screaming diamond-tipped blade. The loud noise and vibrations started to get to Stephen. He found himself zoning out and stopped for a moment to calm his nerves. He became overwhelmed

$$\text{if } \overline{\alpha\beta} \text{ is } \| \text{ to } \overline{\chi\delta} + \overline{\chi\delta} \text{ is } \| \text{ to } \overline{\epsilon\phi} \text{ then } \overline{\alpha\beta} \text{ is } \| \text{ to } \overline{\epsilon\phi}$$

forgotten or repressed), and fantasies(ncluding dreams) of a impersonal character, which cannot be reduced to experiences in the individual's past, and thus cannot be completely explained as something indiviually acquired. These fantasy images undoubtedly have there closest analogies   [sic] in mythological types. Jung sees these images as belonging to a certain collective (and not personal) structure (the collective unconciouse).   [stet] Jung goes on to say that like the morphological elements of the human   [sic] body, the collective elements of the human psyche are inherited. "Although tradition and transmission by migration certainly play a part, ther are   [sic] very many causes that cannot be acounted for in this way, and drive us   [sic] to the hypothesis fo "autohthonous revival". These cases are so numerous   [stet] that we are obliged to assume the existance of a collective phychic sub-   [sic sic] -stratum. I have called this th collective unconcous".   [stet, etc.]

The personal unconcious for the most part of complexes, the content of the collective unconcious is made up for the most part of archetypes.

The concept of the archetype is indespensible from the idea of the collective unconcious, and seems to indicate the existence of definitive forms in the psyche which seem to be present always and everywhere. In mythological research they are reffered to as motifs. Levy- Bruhly called these motifs present in the psychology of the primitives "representations collectives". In comparitive religon the same general concept has been defined by Hubert and Mauss as "categories of the imagination".

During the course of his career Jung analyzed hundreds of dreams. He did not look for archetypes in his patients dreams that fit a certain set of descriptions, as he felt it was not possible to categorize archetypes, but instead he looked over the whole body of

---

58 Room temperature vulcanization.

exhibit 49—sketch from his notebook (rotated sideways)

§ ~~No say nada de mi brother-½ but i lost my virginity around now ... más que nada to get it overwith.~~ It was expected we carry the dirty laundry down to the lake ... a sort of inherited sense of duty.

with anxiety—the screaming machine seemed [inclined] to rip into his soft body. He stood for a couple of minutes, focused on the blade and then [resumed] cutting the small pieces of pine.

As he was cutting the 3rd piece his right hand pushed [it] slightly ahead of his left hand, bringing it into the blade at an angle. The piece was no longer flush with the jig that held it parallel with the blade. Sensing this, he mistakenly began to relax his right hand. The blade was spinning at over 10,000 revolutions per minute when the razor sharp diamond teeth [bit into] the piece of wood and shot it back at Stephen.

It blasted into Stephen's soft under belly, ricocheted off and [hit] the wall 20 feet behind him, coming to rest imbedded halfway into the [sheetrock].

[14:32, 2-24-87] Cal surveyed the [scene] one last time and climbed back into his car [... stubbed] the half-smoked cigarette and started the car. He pulled out without looking and was rear-ended by a Mercedes doing fifty. Cal's head slammed [sideways] and the Torino [spun into] oncoming traffic. [The car flew] off the road through a [barbed] wire fence into a ditch.

When Cal came to a second later the car was sideways in a ditch, aimed in the wrong direction.

[11:56, 2-24-87] Stephen gripped the front of the table. [...] blood rushed from his head and he [blacked out]. He managed to stay on his feet [...] through the successive hot flashes and waves of nausea.

[Without looking, he switched] off the table saw in slow motion and [plopped] into the sawdust covered shop floor. He started sweating and shaking as he listened to the table saw spin down.

[14:32, 2-24-87] Cal occupied himself with trying to get the accelerator unstuck as he sat on the passenger [side. The] smell of gasoline [permeated the air].

[13:17, 2-24-87] Stephen lay on his back for a long time, blinded by the fluorescent track lights. The only thing he could hear was blood [swooshing] in his ears. His body was numb.

---

his dream analysis for overlapping dream phenomina. If one type of image was continually reoccuring in patients dreams , in similar emotional settings, situations,etc., it was noted by Jung for its importance, and used in further analysis. A given archetype concept was further strenghtened by its reoccurance in other dreams and writtings.

Plato's concept of archetype was that of something that is pre-existant to all phenomina. Far from being a modern term, archetype was already in use befor the time of St. Augustine,and as already mentioned was synonymous with "idea" in Platonic usage. Should one wish to continue this pltonic strain, one could say; somewhere there is a primordial image of the mother, that is pre-existant to all phen--omina in which the maternal , in the broadest sense of the term, is M anifest. This approach to reasoning,(apriori, with the outcomedefinatly tainted by the individuals nature)is no longer popular in the light of empirical reasoning(post Kantian reasoning) .

The anima is an archetype of great importance in Jungs ideas. He defined it as" a natural archetype that satisfactorily sums up all of the statements of the unconcious, of the primitive mind . of the historyof language and religon. Like all other archetypes the anima cannot be created by man, on the contrary it is alays the apriori element in his moods.

Although it seems if the whole of our unconcious pychic life could be ascribed to the anima, she is only one archetype among many. She is only one aspect of the unconciousness. This is shown by the very fact of her femininity. What is not I, not masculine(for men) is most probaly feminine, and because the not I is felt as not belong-ing to me., and therefore as outside of me,is usually projected upon men.

The female equivelant to the anima is the animus This archetype is the correlating opposite of the anima (ie. women pro- *actively drafting behind his drafts*

§ Ulysses is goaded to partake in the games + after making quick work of the opposition King A insists he reveal his true IDentity. His actual odysseyian «story» hasn't even begun.

§ Meanwhile (back at the ranch), Penelope promises she'll pick a suitor when she finishes weaving her tapestry ... but each night she undoes what she wove earlier that day.

§ We keep regrouping to tell U how we'll tell U the story but we haven't told U anything yet.

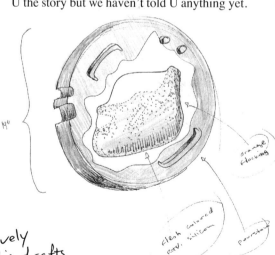

exhibit 50—preliminary sketch for exhibit 48

---

[59] Our older brother (a carpenter) was the 1 who on more than 1 occassion severed a digit w/ a saw ... «occupational hazard» he'd shrug.

the time we went to Circus, Circus + our father gave us a roll of quarters to play arcade games as a distraction while he gambled + drank (AWOL for dayz). We shot a star out + won a lifesize Pink Panther plush.

#

vinyl

S I D E R E A L

ING

★

[14:33, 2-24-87] [...] the cold muddy water [came] in through the window, rising around his waist. Somebody was pounding above him on the driver side window. Cal realized the car was full of [smoke ...] coming in from the submerged engine. He coughed and [rubbed] the back of his neck.

[14:32, 2-24-87] Stephen sat up slowly, taking a [while] to catch his breath.

[OBJ] = $$$

ject it on men etc.) .Like the anima , the animus surfaces in projections on. for example, a person of the opposite sex. The cases, causes and results are as varied and numbered as there are people in the world.. Usually the anima seems to reflect a superior knowledge of life's laws, a reaveled deeper meaning is inevitable in such a situation. The more the meaning is recognized, the more the anima loses her control over the subject (in the form of compulsive or impetous behavior). Projection is an unconcious automatic process, whereby a content that is unconcious to the subject transfers tiself to an object, so that

it seems to belong to that object. Projection always contains something of which the subject is not concious, and which seems not to belong to him., this is why in the case of the anima, for example, the image of the parent (mother) is the very one that could be projected least, because it is too concious.

The anima is a factor of the utmost importance in the psychology of man. wherever emotions and effects are at work, she intensifies, exaggerates, falsifies and mthologizes all emotional relations with his work and with other people of both sexes.

Kant said that archetypes form the "treasures in the realm of shadowy thoughts". There is ample evidence of this statement in the numerous treasure motifs fo mythology. "In themselves archetypal images are among the highest values of the human psychology, to discard them as valueless would be a distinct loss. Our task therefore is not to dent the archetype, but to dissolve the projections in order to restore their contents to the individual who has involuntarily lost them by projecting them outside himself".

Even the old lady next to him resumed her gambling with a mild-mannered frenzy. He sat himself back on his stool and searched the cold metal trough for some dollars he felt should have been there, but were not.

ARC H X FER

Humpty dumpty hits the jackpot + coinage comes cascading.

[14:34, 2-24-87] Finally he gets to his feet and looks around. Everybody [was] in their own little gambling worlds, no one seemed to even notice him.

in the bushes along the trail a few miles down the valley. [illegible strikethrough text] ...

[--:--:--, 1-5-81] Our father attempts suicide but fails (xactly 1 year before he suckseeds).

Ulysses gets his ship so he can go home ... at which pt. he tells hisstory how he got here/there to begin.

Brother-½ abandons Derek at this pt. ... leaving to be closer (geographically) to nuestro padre.

* or when our grandfather would throw coins in the pool to get us out of his hair ... seems & was ment to distract us.

[OR CABALLO COCA COLA IN SEAMS]

THE VALHALA

exhibit 51 (above)—another 'Calimero' sketch

exhibit 52 (below)—untitled '92
(plaster, nylon, RTV 500 silicone, paint, 32" x 23" x 9")

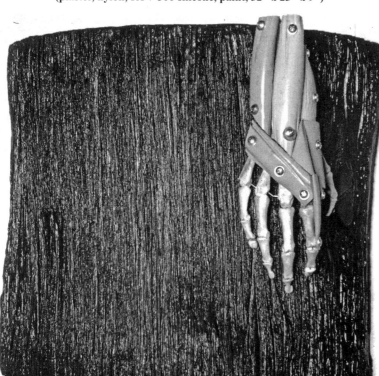

Clay lives alone in a building populated by hollow images of damaged people. He sees them in the elevator that smells like pine-sol, [...] in the lobby sitting around in their high back chairs.

Every morning [at 7 AM, Clay leaves for] work (in the mint)[60]. His exit from the massive old brown brick building prompts hoots and hollers from the assembled insomniac looneys. They climb up [onto] chairs and freak out in perfect unison. At first this scared Clay, but then he learned what it really was that they wanted, and the whole ritual almost became enjoyable...

What it is Clay does—
Clay [exits] the elevator [and strides] across the lobby, past the front desk where V.J. is sitting in his chair watching Jeopardy on a [desk TV. At the] coffee machine he fills two cups with scalding black coffee and spins around.

The hotel freaks grow visibly distressed, their stock car grandstand [behaviorisms rise] to a crescendo. They [...] fervently scan the room for possible escape routes. Clay [... swaggers] towards them, taunting them as he approaches: "C'mon you oxygen thieves! Who wants a little coffee?!" Clay's stance has become somewhat authoritarian and sadistic.

As Clay gets near they [quiet] down [...]. They sit in their chairs staring at the ground, [avoiding] eye contact with Clay.

"If you don't look at me Mr. Stockwell I'm gonna burn you real bad, you [hear] me old man?" Clay [stands] over the sickly [geezer] wearing a pink sweater. [He holds] both cups of coffee over Mr. Stockwell's head, slowly starting to tilt the cups...

th**is**is how it happens ...

all in pieces ...

WHIMPER

He shakes and convulses. The others he can see in his low line of sight are turning away. The pain is close.

Five firetrucks race past the building, sirens screaming.

"Say *when* Mr. Stockwell."

[Then] Clay tilts both cups at the same time, [pouring] the scalding liquid over the old man's [scalp]. Mr. Stockwell throws back his head and [... laughs, smacking] Clay hard in the groin with the back of his closed fist. Clay falls to the floor in a heap, clutching his crotch.

---

[60] While i coullected stamps, brother-½ cullected coins. He was particularly intrested in mint-condition coins ... used to brag about how they were never touched by human hands ... the punch-line being that the mint employed monkeys.

Letters brother-½ sent to our grandfather pleading his case to leave Mexico + live w/ our older brother in California (the compromise was living w/our uncle in Oregon).

NOW THE ONLY PROBLEM IS TRYING TO CONVIENCE MY MOM THAT ITS BEST FOR ME TO GO. TO BE FRANK BECAUSE I DON'T GET ALONG WITH MY MOTHER IS NOT THE REASON I WANT TO LEAVE. THERE ARE THINGS I COULD THINK ABOUT THAT WOULD WANT TO MAKE ME STAY. LIKE LEAVING MY FRIENDS (I ALREADY ASKED ALL ME FRIENDS, ALMOST ALL OF THEM ARE LEAVING NEXT YEAR), MOVING INTO A NEW ENVIORMENT (I WANT TO EXPERIENCE THAT) JUST LIKE I WANTED TO EXPERIENCE MEXICO), I ALSO KNOW THAT IF MY MOM GIVES ME NO CHOICE BUT TO STAY, I KNOW FOR A FACT I WILL BE VERY MESRIBLE. MOVING TO THE STATES MIGHT GIVE ME MORE OF A CHANCE TO LEARN, I COULD COMPETE IN BETTER HIGH SCH. SPORTS, LEARN MORE ON DRAWING AND MAYBE EVEN RENT A PIANO. I KNOW LIVING WITH MY OLDER BROTHER IS NOT MUCH OF WHAT YOU WOULD CALL LIVING IN A FAMILY ATMOSPHERE, BUT IF YOU HAVE OTHER IDEAS, I AM OPEN FOR SUGGESTIONS, ?).

[HINT-HINT]

WRITE SOON,
Kein

+ becomes instilled in us the 1st notions of fight or flight ... + fLight is the route we take ... in particular on foot ... towrd nowhere in particular.

5(12)80

IN PURSUIT OF ...

just time down we been playing reinds (non of the U.S I never any that bought by down here y best friend y on the group) also Gdalajara-junior ?). I + this , but yesterday

get to crue also, maybe go unk if mom ever go .

p.s. excuse the bad structure of my writting, my phrases keep on getting mixed up with the Spanish phrases.

write soon
Kevin

[P.S. A RESPONSE IS EXPECTED.]   [IN OUR NATIVE TONGUE]

our lives as framing devices

Our Swedish friends (whose parents pushed into Olympic-track athletics from day 1) in Guad wore Adidas + never tied the laces ... so we did the same. Run DMC made this popular around this time, but we're not sure if they were on our radar.

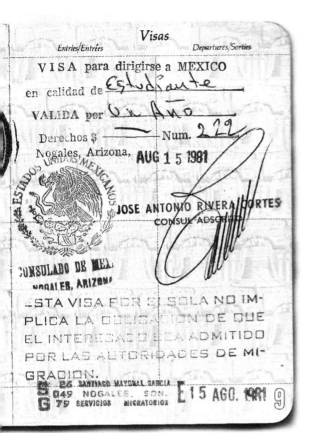

exhibit 53—student visa for our final year (solo) in Mexico

§ Starts gett ng fuzzy ... we confuse the fechas n our m nd, but n retrospect we th nk of Prefonta ne + R ver Phoen x, as f sono 1 + the m smo be ng + juntos conjo ned could've been brother-½. [—our pr nter s select vely out of nk solo for 's, not by our own do ng, sware! ... at least n th s font.]

§ Ev dently our step-s ster just happened on by + was wonder ng why the car was runn ng in the garage. He was half-hang ng out as f he'd a last-second change of heart.

§ «Just do t» were ev dently Gary G lmore's famous last words.

§ N KE probly woud rather have b n called HERMES (or the Roman equ valent, Mercury) but HERMÈS era ya a prêt-à-porter cloth ng l ne.

KEVIN as an anagram for NIKE V

§ For that matter, who's to say wether N ke would be what t s were t not for the early nsp rat on of PRE.

§ t was around th s t me 1° empezamos a correr ...

§ Nuestra madre le dío un peso a la m sma vagabundo de correos cada día. Pers stent pays, yo.

starting to GEL

RED ZONE

He [...] left his car in the red zone, he wouldn't be needing it anymore. On the plane he cried, his arms wrapped around his head on the fold-down [tray] table. When he got to [Kathmandu] he [... went] shopping for some hiking equipment and a trekking permit. He undertook these tasks with [an ...] expression of serenity, as if the many Hindu shrines in the city had infused him with the knowledge that our existence is nothing more than Krishna's dream.

His last night in Kathmandu he stayed in the most [expensive] tourist hotel and maxed out his gold card. He was [severely] depressed and his gradual perception of the task already undertaken was [beginning] to pain him. He [...] felt cornered by his own reckless whim, [...] pulled along up [into] Himalayas.

The walk up the mountain was for Stephen a journey through his life, from beginning to end. Halfway up to Everest base camp he decided his life was still worth living. He spent an extra day and night in a [monastery] on the way up, [...] trying to decide whether to go back down or [keep going] up. If he [continued] up, there was no [going back. The summit was the point of no return.]

Depression swept back over Stephen after a day of walking around the [desolate] monastery and without even thinking why, he [continued] the trek back up. By the time he reached Everest base camp, on a gravel-covered glacier at about 18,000 feet, he [became fixated on the summit].

[...] He [negotiated] his way up the first wall of ice with nothing but some [mountaineering] boots, a jacket and [an ice] axe. He [also] had a hat, a pair of glacier glasses [and a pocketful of PowerBars; but no rope, oxygen or altitude pills] ... the plan, after all, was for him to make it to the top and then die.

The joint Norwegian/ American Everest expedition members saw him when he was about halfway up the [...] north face, but there was nothing much that they could do. They had no idea who [he] was or what he was doing. When the first (Norwegian) climber reached the top five days later he found Stephen naked and partially buried in a wind drift. Everything was one solid block of wind blown ice [...], including Stephen.

They [evacuated] him down to [camp 4] and wrapped his frozen body (still [attached] to large pieces of ice) in a tent.

Three days later they brought his body to a monastery in the valley below the base camp. The body was left wrapped up inside the main temple overnight.

The next morning the [expedition] members came into the main temple to get the body and [were] shocked to find him thawed out, [apparently] alive.

An expedition doctor checked him out and found him to be in a very light coma, but [definitely] alive. The doctor had the monks heat up some water and they put Stephen into a warm tub. Within twenty minutes he was speaking. He opened his eyes to see a

http://www.5cense.com/13/artchival_madness.htm:

[...] question is tho, do we selectively change (like physically, in our inner circuitry) our memories? Did the Butthole Surfers really throw twinkies into the audience, or was it spools of toilet paper (another memory we have of Gibby) ... what in our minds we converted to Twinkies because it made for a better story? Even if others verify it, how do we know it wasn't a **collective hallucination**?

We could of course consult you, Internet, to get to the bottom of this ... but who has time for such **fact-checking**? We believe what we want to believe. We hear things & selectively forget. Like we've heard before that when River Phoenix od'ed outside The Viper Room (20 years ago today), Gibby of the Butthole Surfers was playing on stage inside (along with Flea & Johnny Depp). But we'd soon as forget.

We're thinking about such things not just cuz of this butthole-surfing flashback but this past week we've been mining deep into our brother's journals, in the process of writediting his *"SSES' "SSES' "SSEY*. It's tempting to change details to make it more interesting to a literary reader ... as a sort uv «human interest» story ... but at the same time it's fascinating to us as an arkhival document, to pre-serve it xactly as it was (tho this might be less intresting to the casual reader that didn't know our brother (who od'ed a few years after River Phoenix). Still haven't decided which route to take ... at this point we are in massive artchival collection/transcrption mode ... mapping his journals, stories & art to Joyce's breakdown of *The Odyssey* via *Ulysses*. [...]

... both ½'s of us that s, tho he was the 1 w/ natural born ab 1 dad. Be ng m nor ty wh te k ds n Mex co we learned early on u could never w n f ght ng back, so we focused on runn ng ... s gn ng up for track + f eld.

§ The 1st m le ever ran threw up ... d dn't help that some 1 gave me a p nch of chew ng tobacco + sa d t'd help me run más ráp do.

§ When brother ½ ran he used to make that sound from *Char ots of F re* ... or tal vez era *The S x M ll on Dollar Man*. (machine-like crescendo)

§ Whether we knew t or not we used **parallax** to judge d stance ... to tr angulate. «Life's the same,

≪moving in stereo≫

room full of shocked [people]. One of the surgeons [...] was so overcome [...] that he had to sit down on the floor. Except for some bruises that where [apparently inflicted] when he was dragged down the mountain he was found to be perfectly healthy.

A [...] Russian helicopter flew in to take the expedition back to Khatmandu. When the they tried to [put] him on board to take him to the hospital [...], he resisted. He used all his feeble strength to let them [know] he was not going to leave the monastery, [...] referring to it as his "new home". Eventually the climbers left him and went on down to Kathmandu without him.

News of the bizarre happening spread, making [headline] news in Europe and America within a week. *The general opinion [was] that it was a failed suicide attempt.* [Nobody knew how] he could've been dead for a couple of days and then come back to life. [All three doctors] that examined him in [camp 4 said ...] he showed no signs of life.

[tal cs m ne]

Local [Tibetans and Nepalese] began to view Stephen as some incarnation of god [or Dalai] Lama. When Stephen asked to [...] stay [indefinitely] in Nepal, his request was granted [on the spot. Everyone including] the king of Nepal wanted to be photographed with him [...].

Stephen [remained] within the upper reaches of Mt. Everest national park, staying mostly in the monastery, occasionally taking day trips up into the mountains. [Media from all over the world] flocked to the area. The TV crews that made the [requisite] four day trek up to the monastery from the nearest helicopter landing sight found a serene young man with shaved head dressed in a Tibetan [monk's] robe[61]. He never said anything about what he had gone through.

exhibit 54—Chaulky (Kevin on right, Derek behind left) atop unknown peak in Colorado circa mid-80s. Not sure what we were doing there, but on a whim we decided to sleep up on this mountain so we bought sleeping bags + water + PowerBars + just walked up in what we were wearing (note brother-½ in Nike Air Odysseys)

---

[61] He d d ndeed br ng back a saffron-colored monk's robe from T bet wh ch we now have n our possess on. On 10-31-99 (exactly 6 years after R ver Phoen x d ed) we shaved our head + donned the robe as a costume.

CYCLOPS

TIME : late 60s/early 70s ('beginning of time' as he put it)
PLACE : Mazatlan, MX / Portland, OR
IDEAS/Symbolism : abandonment, $, collective castration, soap, flowers
ABSTRACT/PITCH: "Whoever said presentation is everything should take a gander in their own backyard" he said. "It's all about getting the weeds by THE ROOTS." He handed us buckets + told us we'd be judged for QUALITY ... NOT quantity, then pulled the trigger of his airhorn + we were off to hyrophonic surf.

Modello ℮

Quaderno Officiale

ARITMETICA

per tutte le Classi delle Scuole primarie e maggiori

[this] is the kind of notebook that Joyce wrote in, so in keeping w/ tradition we'll ditto same ... not a far cry from our 1 cuadernos from kindergarten tho en español not italiano. No hay memories desde este epoca o if we did fueron quemados. Not our rememory is selective (a lection we've taken to heart more resently) but our whenever we'd speak or write in spanish we suffered the wrath, probly cuz it reminded our padre de nuestro madre, o just cuz era simple racist.)

← AH AHA - NO
T   PR OCCUP S
- POR QU W
WRIT   →THIS
WAY WILL MAK
S NSO + DONT
WORRY W WONT
WRIT THIS ALL
ASS   BACKWORDS
TO STAY IN LIN
W/ TH S LF-
NTITL D TH M →
BUT OUR DONK Y D
R FUSAL   TO
SUSTAIN A PR -
SCRIB D   STYLO
HAS TO DO W/
NOT FALLING IN
TOO BAD HABITS
- IN CAS U
DIDNT FIGUR THAT OUT YA FOR YOURS LF → WHY DISGUIS
D JA VU - UND R TH AUSPIC S OF A ↑STYL GUID ↓ OR TO
↑STAY IN CHARACTOR↓ THIS DISPARITY OF STILOS SHOULD R
HURT → YA NO CAIGAS INTO CUMFORTABL ROUT N - THINK
U CAN P G THIS CON COLA + MOV ON - NO → NOT V N
A QU STION MARK IN OUR TOOLBOX → NO FU MI ID A TO
SP LL ↑CACA↓ OUT BACKWORDS - RA HIS → W AR MIRRORLY
 X CUTING TO TH B ST OF OUR ABILIDAD → D B S R SURFING
TO U - RIDING TH CR ST OF TH WAV - IF U FIGHT IT U
L AD A STRAY → U PISS OFF POSID ON + H BLOWS U OUT OF
POSITION + CALYPSODIC DISTRACTIONS AR STR WN IN TU PATH
→ R MAIN R ST ADFAST - BRAK DOWN RAIN D AR + T LL TH
TRUTH → IN ORD R TO FIND YOUR WAY HOM U N D TO FIGUR
OUT WH R U GOT SO FAR OFF TRACK + ADMIT THIS - OUT LOUD
→ IN THIS S NS KING ALCINOUS + QU N AR T AR LIK
COUNCILORS - CHILDHOODCAMP OR R HAB R GARD L SS → T LL
TH M HIS STORIA THUS FAR + THATS WHAT W AIM TO DO A K Y
OY - FIGUR OUT DOND OUR BROTH R 1/2 WAS L D A STRAY
→ STO S TH ALT RN T NDING WH R T L MACHUS GO S OFF
IN S ARCH OF ULYSS S ONLY TO FIND HIM D AD - TOO LITTL
TOO LAT → BUT STILL H PORTS HIS ASH S BACK HOM TO
ITHACA → STOP ⏀
→ W/ A R -CAPITULATION COM S MODULATION - COLL CTIV LY
INCORPORATING TODO LOS T LL-TAIL TON S TO 1 THICK HUMMING
BUZZ - A QUI T CHOIR OF MORBIT INC STORS ALL S CR AMING
IN OUR OR JA AT ONC - A LONG W/ OUR MOTH RS STON R-
SURF R FRI NDS IN MAZATLAN - TOO YOUNG TO R CORD TH N
BUT LAT R WH N R VISITING COULD T LL BY TH WAY TH Y
R SPOND D TO H R CONCH → U MIGHT SAY BR AK PI C S OFF
H R + TH R + ↑PUBLISH↓ TH M ↑STANDALON ↓ - BUT TH R S

exhibit 55—"untitled 1991"
particleboard, formica, steel, enamel, 28" x 17" 23"

---

[62] Where **k** is a constant characteristic of the stiffness of the spring. It should also be duly noted that when Hooke came up w/ this equation, he conveyed it as an anagram spelled out in alphabetical order, **ceiiinosssttuv**, rearranged to read **Ut tensio, sic vis**: «As the extension, so the force».

Disfruit Horsetail

from a series of a dysfunctional toys

where $F = kX$ [62] (extended in 2-D)

↕ 1

A RAZON TH S S NT NC S CAIGA IN S
LUGAR - CONT XTO IS TOTO → UTT RRWIS
TH R AR JUST PARABL S TOO → BACK + 4TH
AS W W R TO M XICO ARLY ON IS PART
OF TH CONFUSION Y LA ULTRA IS K OUR 1ST
M MORI S OF WRITT N T XTO CAM STR AMING
OUT OUR FATH RS T L X MACHIN   WH N
SABATHDAY W D GO W/ HIM TO WATCH HIM WORK
→ CONT XTO IS TH LIF W ACTUALLY L D -
NOT THAT U N D TO SAB R THOS D TAIL S
- NU STRO VIDA IS NOT SO DIFF R NT THAN
YOURS PROBLY → BUT ITS TH HOOKS W
LAY IN TH FABRICK - TH BR ADCRUMBS U
GOBBL UP AS U TRAV L LONG - R GR SSION
T ST D → POD MOS IR ALL TH WAY BACK TO
PILGRIMS ATING TURNK YS - VID NTLY W
HAV A FOR FATH R ↑WILLIAM WHIT↓ THAT
ARRIV D ON TH MAY FLOW R - AS VID NS D
BY TH MANIF ST - P R O W SOLO SP AK
FOR OURS LFS → TO CORR LAT ↑U↓ W/ OUR
STORIA W SHOULD PROBLY FOR M NOS T LL
U ABOUT OUR FATH R - BUT TO B HON ST
- + THATS WHAT W R DOING A K Y - H W
DIDNT NO MUCHO ABOUT TH TYP → POR LO
M NOS NOT WHAT WAS R ALLY GOING ON IN
SUS S SSOS → H   N V R SAID WHAT WAS IN
HIS H AD SO ALLS W CAN DO IS 2ND GU SS
→ H WAS BORN IN TH SAM PLAZ W W R
BORN - PORTLAND → FAR AS W KNOW HIS
PADR S W R ALSO BORN TH R → ALL W
M MB R ABOUT HIS FATH R WAS H W NT BY
TH NOMBR ↑DOC↓ THO W DONT THINK H
WAS A L GIT DOCTOR P R S → H SPORT D
A BOWTI + DISFRUIT D DOGS - UNLIK J
JOYC → FAR AS W KNOW DOC DI D B FOR W
W R V N BORN + ALLS W M MB R BOUT OUR
GRANDMA WAS SH WAS ALSO ALCOHOLISTIC →
TH ONLY PLAC S AMS W   V R SAW H R WAS
VISITING H R IN SOM INSTITUITIONALIZ D
FACILITY - DONT KNOW WH TH R IT WAS A
HOSPITAL OR AN OLD FOLKS HOM OR BOTH
- R GARDL SS W HAT D TH SM LL OF TH
PLAC + USUALLY WAIT D OUT IN TH CAR →
AT SOM POINT W STOPP D VISITING SO SH
MUSTV DI D → STOP Φ
→ → W R NOT T LLING U THIS SHIT TO
GARN R SYMPATHY - THO IT S MS G NT
DO LIK TO R AD ABOUT SUCH D-TAILS + IS
PROBLY MOR LIK LY TO K P YOUR ATTN →
THX FOR YOUR PATI NTS → W R FORTHCOMING
CUZ W R TRYING TO T TH R OUR HISSTORY
W/ SUYO - + BY TU O ↑U↓ W M AN U-L-
Y-S-S- -S → J JOYC IS MOR A FATH R
FIGURO THAN OUR PADR V R WAS → JJ
HAD CAJON S - WASNT AFRAID TO PUT HIS
LIF ON TH LIN - IN A T MPT TO XPR SS
TH D P-ROOT D FABRICK OF HIS INC STORS
→ RA CONSCI NC V N OF OUR XISTANC
QU STION → STOP Φ
→ → IF U WANT TO KNOW TH TRUTH OUR 1ST
INCLINATION WAS TO L AD OFF THIS PISOD
8 W/ TH HANGMAN IMAG RIGHT -S
XHIBIT 57- A POSTCARD FROM AN OP NING
OF BROTH R-1/2 → TH R AZON B IN CUZ
W WANT D TO US IT IN TH LAST PISOD
BUT IT DIDNT FIT → NOT SUR WHAT TH
SIGNIFICANTS IS H R - PROBLY B ST TO
L T U FILL IN TH - - - - SUFFIC
TO SAY A OF OUR NAM S AR 5 L DD RS
LONG + OUR LAST NAM ALSO TAK S UP 5
DISCR T UNITS - DITTO J-A-M- -S J-O-Y-
C- + H-O-M- -R THO GR KS SOL LY W NT
BY 1 NOMBR 63 → PURHAPS TH HANGMAN ALSO
IMPLI S A SORT OF MAIZ OR TH URG NT
THR AT OF SUICID U T LL US → STOP Φ
→ → W ALSO THAWT TO MP SAR W/ THIS
HANDWRITT N NOT ON TH N XT PAG - TH
ORIGINAL WICH CANNOT B DISPUT D → CANT

---

63 La otra alternativo is H-O-R-S-E ... see page 69.

This image might not fit here but happens to fall on the same page as the HANGMAN postcard, as glued in our own personal scrapbook.

exhibit 56—brother-½ after we climbed up under L.A. freeway overpass

exhibit 57—invitation to an exhibition (group show he organized)

Simultaneous TH reads merge, a 3rd or 5th away in tone, overlapping in chords of firewood in who's voice who's in clined to say. We are Chaulky now 1 + the same. «In the dead sea, floating on his back, reading a book w/ a parasol open.» ½ of us died at the age of 32 (not to get a head of ourself)... insidentally the gravitational constant, g (at the Earth's surface, in freefall, a # Joyce fixated on ... specially in his LOTUS EATERS episode) from the equation:

$$F = mg$$

... which the astute reader may notice bears an uncanny ressemblance to the aforementioned Hooke's law (replacing mass w/ position), a coincidence that didnt slip past Hooke. It shoud also be noted that 32 ft/s² is the gravitational constint in the Inglesh system ... metrically it's 9.8 m/s².

The gravity of Gravity (not Gravy)

The important thing (as Joyce rightfully points out) is that it's «per second for every second»... /s² ... if u can wrap your head round that. If generally u take *The Odyssey* to be a function **O** + u take *Ulysses* to be another function **U** then:

$$\int_{t=0}^{t=10 \ (years)} O(t) = U$$

(where $t = 0$ is the end of the Trojan war)

$$+ \ thus, \int_{t=0}^{t=24 \ (hours)} U(t) = \iint O(t) = \text{'SSES' 'SSES'}$$

making this the 3rd derivative of Odyssey + 2nd derivative of Ulysses.

episode 8, more than 1/3 the way, according to the itinerary, anyway.... will we settle into 1 uniform style? will we travel even further back now, dig even deeper, back to the late 60s/early 70's, to the beginning of time. Hence why we are handwriting this. we are the last of a generation that learned to write by hand + then made the transition to computers. our writing is undoubtedly different than «The Kids» today. hand-wired... Not that anything is necessarily the lattice, like a blank framework is, for sure, the «grow ups» we start circuit board. But as we get into certain patterns + soldering wires in place, get «rebaked» in. we Habits, + some of those just make connections, then, they didn't «letters» to things but didn't happened actuals. We felt necessarily think them. The move u to think things + commit them to paper (like this!) the more less u think. When a thought doesn't catch up to your current status, rather than vainly grasp for it... In theory anyway. At a certain age we start grasping. Somewhere around the late 60s + we're specking collectively now cuz these are based on conversations w/our brother-½ «I» who was born April 30, 1965 + me born November 27, 1966. Back then reality came to us in discrete tiles, packets of information that were easily digestible. All u had to do was eat what was given to you. u didn't even think about shitting or pissing, it just came out of u & probably felt good ... until u were punished for it + then we started to develop «complexes.»

Integratation off course is just a more refined way of summing, of say: $\sum O = U + \sum U = S^3$

where S^3 = 'SSES' 'SSES' '"SSEY' ... the very book u hold in your hands.

Or conversely, rather than integrating we can differentiate:

$$\frac{d^2}{dt^2} S^3 = \frac{d}{dt} U(t) = O(t) \text{ or } (S^3)'' = U'(t) = O(t)$$

Which is to say the **derivative** of '"SSEY' is *Ulysses* + $\frac{d}{dt}$ of *Ulysses* is *The Odyssey* ... not that we were conscious

of infinitesimal calculus at this point (late '60s) but all along we suspected space-time was disecrete. Also note there's a time-frame shift in going from *The Odyssey* (spanning 10 years) + *Ulysses* (spanning 24 hours), so relativity[64] must be taken into account.

> + NOW W ARRIV TO THIS PAG MB DD D WITHIN THIS PAG WHICH IS ↑TH LOTUS AT RS↓ PISOD AS BROTH R-1/2 WOULD HAV IT IN TH ORIGINAL SS S SS S.

THE LOTUS EATERS[65]

IT has the appearance of a flashlight dropped into a cesspool it's albuminousglow leakingradiating from it's source.

THE somnambulist stumbles headlong pulled by it and guided by the stars, the foreshortened perspective of which makes for an irregular and seemingly random meandering across the four foot wide path of freshly layered tar, excor- -iating the thin skin of soggy yellow leaves and avoiding the saturatedcold crabgrass.

Scintillant circumambient air surrounds him when he reaches the crest of the hill, it grows lighter then he sees four people I know, not people I would cons- -ider friends, and he turns left now going down the embankment to avoid them, startled to see a vast expanse of beach gouged out in front of me, it seems like miles to the waters edge where vaguely discernible in the mist is a part- -ially submerged reef slowly rising out of the syncopated wax and wane of the now receding tide.

I start down towards the beach, and as I do my feet sink into the cool damp sand, causing the rest of the dry surface *sound around me to follow* down the hill covering the blades of long grass that sting against my feet under the surface. At the bottom I smell and then see the remains of a campfire, a strong seabreeze hits me and after compensating for it I start towards the water now leaning forward slightly. I see hundreds of people in the distance, aimlessly wander- -ing over the now fully exposed reef. Young men with their pants rolled up around the knees, no shoes or shirts, sunburns on their necks and crewcuts cross a hundred feet in front of me, all of them entranced by something one of them has in a red pail of (sea?)water. A large dark dog whips by me splashing my legs with cold watersand reminding me briefly that I am clad only in underwear.

As he approaches the edge of the water he comes up behind a man wearing khaki pants and a navy blue windbreaker who is purposefully eyeing the horizon, lost in thought.

"What do you do here?", He asks before the stranger has a chance to notice him.

"Well, we do not shave here", he said turning around in a manner that let me know he had been expecting me for quite a while, "We instead eat handfulls of tulip bulbs and then scrape the flower like eczema growths off of our faces" He added, ready to field another question as if he were some kind of eager game show contestant.

"What else?", He asked hoping to provoke more out of him.

"Well", He said now looking down at his feet, "We do not brush here either,

DAB(dab) v.t. to pat gently and intermittently,-bing pa.p. and pa.t.,-bed.n. a gentle blow with a soft substance;a small lump of anything soft, as butter [M.Edabban, to strike].
DAFT- silly; innocent, idiotic, lunatic, lightheaded, cracked,(sane, sound, sensible, practical,)
DABBLE:mess
DACRYORRHEA,excessive flow of tears.
DABĀ-REH,Josh.xxi 28.[Daberath]
DACTYL; poetic foot consisting of an accented syllable followed by two unaccented sylables. Ex.; possible,wonderful.
D-second step in the typical diatonic scale of C.
DANCING. Dear creature! you'd swear
When her delicate feet in the dance twin-
    kle round,
      That her steps are of light,that her home
      is the air,
    And she only "par complaisance" touches
    the ground. Moore
DACTYLOGRAPHY.scientific study of fingerprints.
DACTYL(Zool.): A digit.
DAC'CA City* Bangladesh; muslin, jewlery.
D subs. (common).--1. A Penny, or (in pl.) pence; e.g. two D; three D, etc,,= two-pence, three-pence,etc.[the initial letter of the Latin denarius]
    1880. Punche's Almanac,p.3. Got the doldrums dreadful, that is clear. Two D left! Must go and do a beer!
D(dé) n.,pl. d's 1.The fourth letter of the modern english alphabet.2.Any of the speech sounds represented by the letter d 3. Something shaped like the letter d. 4. The fourth in a series. 5.D the lowest possible grade giving to a student in a school or college.6. D mus. A.The second tone in the scale of C major or the fourth tone in the relative minor scale. B. The key or the scale in whih D is the tonic. C. A written or printed note representing this tone. D. A string key, or pipe tuned to the pitch of this tone. 7. D the Roman numeral for 500. -'d suff. 1.Rad; He'd already left.2. Would: I'd rather walk than drive. 3.Did: Who'd you ask?
D: (C.Hull) the strength of all the nondominate drives operative at a given moment.
DAB.n and v.:DABBLE,DABBLER,DABSTER,DAP(n and(v-DABCHICK;-DIB(n,v,),DIBBLE(n,v,)-DIBBLER.
    1. "To dab", ME dabben,prob derives from MD dabben, app achoic. From the basic sense "to strike smartly and lightly"(vt, hence vi.)come the answering n and the sense "a flat, or flattish. mass of,e.g., butter' and the coll sense "somebody very smart at";dabster is derivative (cf the suffix -ster); and dabble is a freq of "to dab", with the agent dabbler.
DADD,RICHARD 1819-87 English painter.He studied at the royal academy schools, but after exstensive travels in Europe and the Middle East began to show signs of mental disorder.In 1843 he murdered his father and for the rest of his life was confined to asylums, where he executed allegorical and fairy pictures crowded with intricate detail (The fairy-fellar's master stroke,1855-64,London,Tate).

AROUND TH TIM H WROT THIS HIS BROTH R WAS FISHING BY HISS LF AT NIGHT N AR MOMS HOUS IN NORTH RN CALIFORNIA NOW IN TH 80S → H DROPP D A FLASHLIGHT--TH ONLY LIGHT SORC H HAD--INTO TH BOTTOM OF A POOL IN TH CR K → TH LIGHT R MAIN D ON 6 F T UND R - ILLUMINATING TH POOL FROM B LOW → SO H STRIPP D DOWN NUD + JUMP D INTO R TRI V TH LIGHT WOND RING TH WHOL WHIL WHAT THIS MUSTV LOOK D LIK IF ANY 1 HAPP N D TO B OBS RVING - NOW H GOT TO S FOR HISS LF WHAT TH WIGGLING WORM LOOK D LIK TO TH FISH + H N V R TOLD ANY 1 THIS STORY TIL NOW Φ

---

[64] Einstein proposes the theory of Relativity in 1905 .... 1 year after Bloomsday.

[65] He wrote a few variations of this piece, 1 time calling it «2 Page Interpretation of a Dream Fragment [Jan 24, 1990]» + in another: «A Flash of Blinding Light».

«Hold my mail» I say, I foot out the door.

«MAYO?» man yells, «whatdya think this is, a deli counter?»

«MAIL!»«I'm expecting something important!»

«This ain't no P.O. either. This is you HOME!»

«I'm running away.»

Rocky pipes in from reclining position, exhaling a cloud of smoke—«No pareces que esta's Corriendo hijo?»

«It's a figure of speech, like I'm blowing this popsicle stand.»

«You're loco. But yo, agarrame un 6-pac de MODELO mientras estas.... RUNNING.»

«Won't they card me?»

«No seas tanto, hombrecito. No necessitas I.D.»

Episode 9 of the 3rd derivative of SSEY (the Lotus Eaters) is where Ulysses' actual odyssey begins. It is here (in present tense) where he reveals his identity + recounts the story of how he got there/here (w/ the Phaeacians, who have supplied him a mind-reading ship so he can finally return home to Ithaca). FLASH BACK TO the end of the Trojan war ... A jubilant Ulysses + his men set sail for home + stop 1st to pillage Cicones then to the land of the Lotus Eaters, where his men succumb (despite warnings) to the intoxicating lotus fruit that makes them forget their pains + desires. Ulysses reels them in before they get hooked + warns the rest to "go on board at once, lest any of them should taste of the lotus and leave off wanting to get home, so they took their places and smote the grey sea with their oars."»

THE LOTUS EATERS

our teeth I mean, we.., well we take these old horseshoes, exceedingly rusty ones, and we rub them with our hands until they bleed, then we take those bloody things and bury them wherever we find dead animals washed up on the beach." He was now intently staring me down.

"And..?" I said unnecessarily.

"And we all come here," He now turned to face the dark horizon, his right arm raised and palm open, a grand gesture to stress the importance of what he was revealing to me,"We all come here to the tide pools in our sleep to renounce our worldly existence." He then turned to him, and seeing that he did not under--stand he clarified;"You mortals come here to die!"

He laughed at this but quickly grew too selfconscience of his growing fear.

"Who the fuck do you think you are anyway" He said now very afraid.

In silence he looked down, his knees were russet and looked to be carved out of sandstone, his calves; ocher shafts of pine, his feet; sunbleached ivory and the wet packed sand was polished obsidian. Directly in front of his feet he saw a small bubble rise out of an indentation in the black surface, **Mya-Pelecypoda** it was large, and judging from the size of the hole it was less than a foot from the surface, struggling with its one leg (that accounts for roughly 3/4 of its body mass) against the diurnal force of weightlessness pushing it to its death.

"Put it this way," He resumed in a congenial tone, "If Ingrid Bergman had directed your life, he would have made me shave my head and speak swedish!" He was now laughing at his own expense,"You don't understand Swedish do you? Eh? Tallar du Svenska? HehHehHeh!" He was now gripping my shoulder."You know the procedure young man, get out there and join your new friends."

anxietyofloss sinkingfalling homogenousends
soporificcoda entropichunger cessationaugur
rippingfallingsuccinctemergencythoughtsineluctableindignationslossofvision
capitulate to innefectual terms no one ever guaranteed you any
rights certainly not me I am only metaphor a harbinger of the
end the realization of which is the incentive to bring you into
being I spin to the left and bring my knee full force into his
sternum a loud pop as the lungs collapse his grip on my shoulder
loosens and he bends forward at the waist mouth open eyes glazed
in pain bring my right knee up once again harder this time against
his chin slamming his jaw shut and breaking his nose he emits a deep
groan as the force of the blow shatters many of his teeth my left
arm pushes the side of his head sending him to the ground with little
resistance he rolls over on his back cradling his jaw in his hands
I bring my left heel down hard into his crotch he lurches up his
eyes wide open wheezing bringing his knees to his chest I take my
foot and send his head turning violently to his left to the point
where it is supposed to stop with added force send it beyond with
a surprisingly loud snap his whole body twitches three times violently
and then he just lies there staring up at the perpetualy cloudy skies

a river called death (vertical handwritten)

identity revealed bring ing in Up to speed bein the 1st derivative of (relative) position, i.e. the (scalar) rate of chan e, which can also be obtained by inte rating acceleration, perhaps a rave proposition. (vertical text)

"Everything is so silent around me and my soul is calm too. I thank you, lord for giving me such warmth, such strength, in these last moments.
" I go to the window, my dearest one, and I can still see individual stars in the eternal sky, through the passing storm clouds. No you will not fall! The eternal one bears you on his heart and me too. I see the handle of the great wain, which I live best of all constellations. When I went from you at night, as I left your gate, it stood facing me. With that intoxication have i often looked at it! Often, with uplifted hands, with uplifted hands, I have made it the symbol,the sacred milestone of happiness I felt; and even now-O Lotte, doesn't everything remind me of you?Do you not surround me? And haven't I, like a child, greedily snatched up every trifle your hands had touched?.......A neighbor saw the flash of the powder and heard the report; but as it was followed by silence, he paid no attention to it[1]...........Late in November he heard from Kestner about the suicide of Carl Wilhelm Jerusalem, which had occurred on October 30th. Goethe had known Jerusalem casually when they were both students at Leipzig; he had seen Jerusalem at Weltzar occasionally; he felt deeply enough about the gifted young mans tragic end to ask Krestner for a full account of it.[2]

---

66 Think he probly meant to say INGMAR Bergman.

Plotting blind to the next (1st) derivative, «*Ah, in the dead sea, floating on his back, reading a book with a parasol open.*» She packs us a picnic. Deviled egg sandwiches give us gas. It's true about the containment pond (a sewage treatment facility), down to the salamanders. «*Half-baked they look: hypnotised like. Eyes front. Mark time. Table: able. Bed: ed.*» Reduced to irreducible nutrients. **Reconsituted**. «*What is home without Plumtree's Potted Meat?*» I'm PINK, therefore I'm SPAM. «*Prefer an ounce of opium.*» We stuck their eyes out to see if it made a difference, if the crawdads coud see w/ just antennae. Mazatland was the 1st we'd seen of a stickshift, our father siempre drove automatico. Nuestro madre had a VW bug azul w/ a surfboard rack + SIN plates. We got distempered when we realized it wasn't hers. «*... just shove in my name if I'm not there ...*» Don't lapse, keep it up. Rack + piñon steeri g. Searchi g for a 4-leaf clover in a ∞-field. Each episode i dicative of overall salud, he throws a fit ... co ve iently in a farmacia, forse that i duced it to comme ce, the sight of Dr. Seuss on the gree farmaceutical cross, w/ «*Iron nails ran in.*» Not EIRE. «Iric I» said her surfer 'frie d' ... the 1 we walked in on digging his fingers into her conch. He gave us 10 pesos + envied us to the farmacy for alcohol puro. For frottage. Si preguntan dice: «*Drugs age you after mental excitement. Lethargy then. Why? Reaction. A lifetime in a night. Gradually changes your character.*» We called them **feelers**—how crawdads coud see. Don't give it 2 much thought for 1 sec. «*He ought to physic himself a bit. [...] Chloroform. Overdose of laudanum.*» Un ultra iteration. «*Skinfood.*» Smells like seefood. Wash after w/ proverbial lemony jabón. Mis manos slippery, can't grasp the brass ring n the merry-g-r und ... cierra la b ca del payas riend . We bathed t gether 2 save agua Specifically member ur padre p uring Tabasc n my t ngue cuand yo spoke español. We sea, saw the caballo in the doldrums, «*the floating hair of the stream around the limp father of thousands, a languid floating flower.*»

CAL * yet another variation on the theme ①

Brown, grey and gold. The feelings described and explained by some theory of genetic memory. Teutonic memory, jagged snow capped peaks. Pine forests. A frozen stillness. Sun filtering through the forest canopy, illuminating the swirling clouds of steam rising from the forest floor. Fallen giants, boulders moved by glaciers, moss carpeting the path I walk. The sands never flows away from Mt Hood, never flat or smooth, in this country, there is only white water. I have reached a point in the forest where no one has ever gone.

① [Cal stirs violently, opens his mouth, sits up and ducks his clock] Sometimes I would lie awake in bed all night, thinking about him, trying to reinvent him by summoning up every memory of him, every recollection. I never think of his home, and I can't imagine his face, I can only see his arms, torso, and legs and the top of his knees. His daily dependence on drugs alcohol and pills makes me feel comfortable. Fills me with anticipation and warmth. Makes me long to stock up and lock up. CONSTANTLY ON THE MOVE. I GO THROUGH THE LIST. I DO THE ROUTINE, FOR AN HOUR I REMAIN UNCONSCIOUS TO ALL BUT THE MOST BASIC MOTOR FUNCTIONS. WHILE TORTURE himself the trail + spy ticket in red a chalk flyer written on the door where an alarm lumber should be......

LACadaisyCAL chain

We trudged through the [damp afternoon] darkness to our [secret] place [in] the woods [...]. We knew our way thru the [surrounding] barbed-wire up over the 6-foot dike [of stained earth like it was the back of our hand].

[... atop the levee the water] became visible—a rectangular pond, fetid and dark with only the occasional (undesireable) [weed] breaking the surface. This is were [we'd find] them, the salamanders— small, slimy and the color of the wet clay that [congealed] them [at the water's edge].

We [...] captured them [+ brought] them home across the highway in plastic buckets. We gave them names, [kept] them for a while as pets and then let them go in another unnatural pond near our house, as if we were doing them a favor—these sacred animals, silent in their knowing, feeding our unourtured [sic] souls.

tortured + unourished?

READ THIS STORY BACKWARDS

"His head rang with over [10,000] voices in unison. The sound was turned [really] low. He could still hear things outside." [Clay rigidly] proclaims in-between noisy slurps of his Xtra-Grande Iced Tea.

"What you talking about now dipshit?!" She [lit] a Winston Light with a candle [in the] transparent glass form of a dwarf sitting in the center of the table. Her hair [has all] the various tones of lemon meringue pie. "That's right, work it [...]! Go girl! uuu-huh!" [...] she continues without exhaling.

"The hell's that supposed to mean?!" [Clay asks]. She had succeeded in getting him worked up.

"Hey now[, there's] no need for talk like that is there?" She [giggles.]

[Both] parents [glare] at her at the same time. [... sitting w/ arms crossed] in the booth opposite her.

"What's with you two?" [Dilly] says to them, serious and straight-faced, "You sit [all righteous] like that out of habit or what? Always have to keep an eye on Dilly, is that it?" She [gavels] the table with clenched fist, spilling salsa on her mom's brand new rayon skirt.

"Awww. She bought it special for work last week," Clay says to Dilly as he helps his dad wipe the salsa off of his [mom's] lifeless body. They use the massive apricot colored table napkins, dipping them in glasses of ice water first. They work their way across her skirt, in the same direction. Clay seems to be on the verge of tears, Dilly [can't] keep from bursting out laughing.

"Shut up D-Dilly!" Clay says, now pissed-off and letting his stuttering show.

"D-D-Dilly!" She mocks, laughing still harder.

"Damn y-you D-Dilly" [...] Clay throws down his wet napkin and starts to cry. He cries [hard, for a] long time. [It gets to the point where] the waiter and manager [...] are on their knees in front of their table begging them to leave, offering to [comp] the bill. The family goes home, in a somber mood.

Back home, Clay helps his dad carry his mom up the green shag-carpeted stairs to her room, near the entrance to the attic. The three of them barely fit [in] the tiny room.

"I love this room, with its one little square window and black enamel floor. Someday I hope to live in it," Clay (the village idiot,) says. "Can't wait, nope, no how."

"Shut yer trap boy! That's no way to talk around your ma!"

"Sorry Pa."

"And mind yer forehead on the way out" the father says to Clay, stooped over in the doorway with his pipe hung low off his lower lip.

The miniature lamp on the box of matches near her [bed] was very powerful. It illuminated [his father's] face from [beneath] his pipe as he talked to Clay, [making] him look like Boris Karloff. This made Clay [...] laugh uncontrollably. He fell [laughing] down over his mother's body, with the left side of his face pressed against her stomach and eyes closed tight.

His father laughed to himself seeing this, shaking his head like Goofy might. Saying "good night" to both of them, he backed out into the blinding white light of the hallway, pulling the door shut behind him.

↑ ND OF FIL B R ACH D↓ DONT
M AN SHIT →   DONT THINK H
LIT RALLY M ANT ALGO BY IT → IN
FACT ↑M MO↓ WAS TH NOMBR OF
TH VILLAG IDIOT IN TH PU BLO
W LIV D IN N M XICO → GU SS
SOM MIGHT CALL HIM TOWN DRUNK
- BORRACHO → RA ROCKYS H RMANO
+ TAMBI N LOS DOS W R HIJOS OF
TH ALCALD →NOT SUR IF IT WAS
CUZ H WAS TH MAYORS SON BUT
V RY 1 XC PT D M MOS B ND RS
+ OUTBURSTS → A V C S IT GOT
SO BAD TH Y CHAIN D HIM TO TH
LIMON TR   IN TH IR PATIO BUT
STILL TH Y F D + PROVID D FOR
HIM + H WAS ALLOW D VISITORS →
WH N W VISIT D W W R WARN D
NO D JA TOCAR LIK H WAS A
L P R + NOW 10 Y ARS LAT R WH N
W VISIT D M MO WAS TH MAYOR
- MAN AROUND TOWN → V RY 1
ACT D LIK NADA IN TH PAST
V R OCCUR D → STOP ⊕
→ → DONT TRY AS BUKOWSKI SAYS →
D JA INFORMACION FLOW COMO U AR
A KIDDO → TODO JUMBL S TOGATH R
+ MOR SO HOW DO W MAK S NS
OF IT AHORA → ANOS OF S LF-
CONSCIOUS MASKING + OBSTRUCTING
→ SCONDIMOS OR OBFUSCAT TH
MAS IMPORTANT D TAIL S → CANT
WRIT SOBR TH PAST LIVING IN
L PR S NT + SOLO HAY TANTOS
FOTOS + WRITT N T STAM NT TO GO
OFF → MOST V RYTHING H ARSAY →
P NSAMOS QU OUR PURS PTION WAS
PIX LAT D BACK TH N BUTT FORSAY
THIS IS JUST OUR M MORIA B AN
R M MBR D O F RM NT D → VIVIMOS
ON A DIFF R NT WAV L NGTH
- BACK TH N RA MILLIONS OF
VACANT CHANN LS NOW AIRWAV S
SATURAT D → V N IF SOL W
TUN IN TO 1 FR QU NCY TH
JUGG RNAUT OF ACCUMULAT D WAV S
BUZZ S ALL AROUND → A FORC TO
B R CKON D WITH → NO LO QU
DIC S SINO COMO LO DIC S - SOLO
SO MANY WAYS → N V R IMAGIN D
N C SSITATING ANT OJOS - OUR
VISION 20/15 - M JOR THAN AVG
→ NOW W STRAIN TO L R H R
MANOS HANDWRITING L T ALON OUR
OWN → ISSU AT HAND R MAINS HOW
TO R -AX SS - PON RS IN 3-YR
OLD ZAPATOS L T ALON TH SHO S
W WOR ARLI R HOY + CANT
TRUST NO 1 LS TO T LL US HOW
SHIT HIT TH FAN → L TS FAC
IT 1/2 TH STUFF BROTH R-1/2
WROT RA STON D PROBLY + OUR
M MORI S 1/2 IN SPANISH IN +
DISC R T LY POINTILLISTIC LIK
PANTY HOS PULL D SOBR OUR
Y S → SUPU STAM NT APR NDIMOS
SPANOL 1° → SLOW TO L ARN D
CUALQUI R MANN R → ALWAYS LAT
TO ADOPT P RO SUPON QU ST
S UN TR ATM NT SOB RING L
- NU STRO H RMANO → POR SO
TRATAMOS PON RNOS N SUS ZAPATOS

[.... at this point in READ THIS STORY BACKWARDS he inserts the text of what we called THE LOTUS EATERS above in 'SSES" 'SSES", giving it the sub-heading: A FLASH OF BLINDING WHITE LIGHT *+ then finishing as such:]*

In silence, Clay looked down at his body, [seemingly] disconnected [...]. His knees were a russet color and looked like they had been carved out of sandstone. His calves were ochre shafts of pine. His feet, unbleached ivory, and the wet packed sand was polished obsidian. [Right] in front of his feet he saw a small bubble rise out of an indentation in the glassy sand.

"You're familiar with the routine, go on, get out there." The stranger said, now gripping his shoulder.

Clay looked up at his father. He had been sleepwalking again. He was standing in the living room in his underwear. His father was standing next to him gripping his shoulder [...].

"Go son, get back up stairs, go on."

He felt embarrassed and went back up to his own room.

exhibit 58—Chaulky, May 1969, Mazatlan, Mexico

→ IN FACT 1 OF TH 1° DRAWINGS HA H CHO
 RA UN SHO + TH CAPTION SAID ↑C CI
N' ST PAS UN CHAUSSUR ↓ – AN OBVIOUS NOD
TO MAGRITT → CH RCH PARTOUT TO INCLUD
H R MAIS COULDNT FIND IT → ASSUMING TODO
QU PASO A MI PASO A L – THAT WH N W
R GR SS D TO PORT + H SPOK SPANISH OUR
FATH R POUR D CHILI SAUC ON HIS TONGU
TAMBI N – SU L NGUA S MI L NGUA – SO
TODO QU SUC DIO TO US IN SPANISH RA
SUR-PR SS D → US D TO US L MISMO TRICK
ON OUR PARROTS TO G T TH M TO PARLAY –
RUMOR FU QU OP N D TH IR VOCAL CHORDS
→ W/ INT NTCITY W BLUR NOS OJOS – PULL
WOOLY STOCKINGS SOBR OUR H AD – M DIAS
TO H LP US S POR LO M NOS 1/2 WHAT H
SAW → FU RA D FOCO COMM CI W FIND
R SOLUTION – N LOS DIAS CUANDO NU STRO
JU GOS – SPAC INVAD RS + PONG – PLAY D
OUT PIX L X PIX L → IF U WANT TO M MB R
COMO SI U W R ALLI – AQUI – V NGA – 1
HIT WONT KILL U POR SUPU STO NOT 2ND HAND
SMOK – RIDING IN TH BACK LA CUCARACHA
NO PU D CAMINAR ADMIT U LIK TH SM LL
– MIX D W/ BURNING BRICKS SP CIALLY FOR
BR AKFAST – B FOR SCHOOL– NO R CORDAMOS
MUCHO BUT W HAV FOTOS OF US IN M XICAN
SCHOOL UNIFORMS – CUANDO SCRIBIMOS CON
MANO IZQUI RDA T ACH RS US D TO HIT
OUR HANDS W/ RUL RS BUT BROTH R 1/2
P RS V R D WROT W/ HIS L FT TO HIS
D ATH → NOW W AR AMPHIBIOUS → H SAW
TH PU RTA + TRAV RS D – MAS H SITANT
W R W – SK PTICAL V N OF SK PTICISM →
TRATAMOS D V R L BOSQU THRU TH TR S
CON SOLO 1/2 A BRAIN → GIV N TH OPCION
OF SURVIVING ABOV W/ M DIA C R BRO W
CHOS TH COMPROMISO D VIDA → H ON OTRO
MANO N V R COMPROMIS D – NO VAL LA P NA
– NOT WORTH A HAIR → STOP ⊕
→ → IN R TROSP CK DITTO QU RA L
PORT TO LAT R B HAVIORISM → QUIZAS A
SU DAD RA MAS IMPR SSIONABL → Y S
WID OP N TO WHAT V R GROWNS ON TR S →
S THRU TH NOOS AS QUALCOSA TO K P
PROVISIONS S GUR D FROM V RMIN TO NOT
F AR R GR SSING TO RAS TH TIM S W
PASS D THRU BORING OR GON – S NO NOS
CRAY N GOOGL MAP IT S XISTS → CAN WIP
OFF TH MAP BUT NOT TH DIRT Y HAZARD
US DUK S CRUISING CAMINO R AL IN AN L
CAMINO TRYING NOT TO STABLISH A RHYTHM
TO HIT TH HARMONIC FR QU NCY LOOK
MA NO MANOS → PROP LL D PROP NSITI S
DRIV N BY PR – XISTING PR DISPOSITIONS
– TH SCALATING D RIVATIV OF POSITION
B ING SP D LIFTING TH N SS SITY BY
BOOTSTRAPS → QU MACHO RA ROCKY CON SUS
SYRING S + PISTOLAS – STAMM RING LUCID
TH STABLISHM NT OF SUP R COOL → ↑B BOP↓
HIS 1ST WORDS COMO H MOS DICHO ANT S – HAY
RAZON WHY W R P AT OURS LFS – 2 X 2 – 1–
STUFF A W T WAD DOWN TH BARR L TO CL AN
OUT SPARKS + MB R FROM PRIOR SHOT 2–
R P AT TO –STAR S GURO 3– LOAD TH B IG
POWD R AND BALL – STAN CONN CTADOS– 4–
PUSH TH PLUNG R 5– POK A HOL IN TH
BACK OF TH BARR L TO OP N TH POWD R BAG
6– LIGHT TH POWD R W/ A SLOW-BURN FUS
+ PLAC YOUR H AD TW N YOUR L GS + KISS

← *Este no es su zapato.*

HYDROPONIC SURFBOARDS

It's like this: you put your hands too close to the food dish and your going to get [bit][67].

[Bloom] was overcome by a knee-jerk reaction towards macho defense, he couldn't let the insubordination stand, but instinctly he remembered how things stood, the way they would fall when the pushing started. There was no choice, he would have to be the punching [bag]. [Mark] continued his diatribe, while taking another hit off the small pipe handed to him by [Buck].

"Shit Buck, what the fusk is this stuff?" Mark wheezed.

"My cousin brought it back from a trip up north [...]. Dude, he brought back a kilo, inside a surfboard he built around the package, UP NORTH at some dude's place."

"QU'EST-CE QUE C'EST? Some sorta HYDROPONIC?"

"Mush more intense, duuude! Hydroponic buds that are [genetically] crossed, keeping only the really intense characteristics [...] a cross between THAI STICKS and .... MAUI MOWEE ... OH YEAH, DUDE! Then they are packed in dry ice, to boost THC levels, something about carbon atoms acting as [free radicals to bind] more THC, etc. Anyway, this STUFF IS KILLER! Oh, they also soak it in PURE OPIUM OIL. This is done in Northern Thailand, then it's compressed into compact bricks. These bricks are taken [south to] where there's [an international] surf competition twice a year, sponsored by you know who. These bricks are sealed into surfboards that are then finished and taken back by the surfers to their [respective countries, sometimes even after they surf on them!] My cousin knows this [gnarly] surfer guy so he goes and visits him, meets him at the airport. They go back to the dudes house, bust open the surfboard and [voila]! I call it chili powder ... you can't really *smoke it straight up, you have to mix it, causes instant and permanent schizophrenia when you smoke it straight.* [continued above right in his own writing....]

cont.
smoke it straight, have to mix it, causes instant and permanent schizophrenia when you smoke it straight.

"Oh fucking great" Adam's paranoia soaking through his skin at an alarming rate " fucking great."

"It's ok man sit down, ride it out" Buss offered to help him find in his own pathetic stoner consoling way.

Adam slowly sat on the couch, he felt like he was sitting it felt like a hot stove at first. The girl in the chair across the room noticed his bizarre flinch, and smiled. He saw her and felt stupid, his paranoia increased exponentially.

INT. NIGHT -LIVING ROOM -
PHONE RINGS LOUDLY. WOMAN IN CHAIR REMAINS IN HER TRANCE, STARING AT THE CAT IN THE CORNER OF THE ROOM. MAN SEEMS UNSURE ABOUT ANSWERING THE PHONE. HIS MOTOR-FUNCTIONS SEEM TO BE SLOWED, HE IS ALSO INDICATING A FAULTY DEPTH PERCEPTION: REPETATIVE BEHAVIOR PATTERNS ARE BEING EXHIBITED IN HIS PACING and his INABILITY TO ARRIVE AT A DECISION ABOUT HIS COURSE OF ACTION. HE is also biting his forefinger and rubbing a small metal pipe in his right hand; classic examples a deviant pattern of receptor preferences.

I would certainly go on record, right now, with a full diagnosis, a final diagnosis, of full blown schizophrenia. I think this man needs to be started on treatment right away, before he hurts himself, or someone else.

MAY · 69

[67] I had a dog (wolf actually) in Mexico named Zorro. Kids used to taunt him thru the gate, throw rocks at him. Our older brother was friends w/ these kids + invited them over 1 day + 1 of the kids picked up Zorro's food bowl + Z went nuts, latched on to the kid's arm wouldn't let go til la criada threw an olla of boiling water on him. The kid's brazo required 40 stitches + Zorro was poisoned a few days later (presumably by the kid's father).

[(also) cont. from episode 5, page 95];

"When anyone speaks to me, I listen more to the tonal modulations in his voice than to what he is actually saying. From this, I know at once what he is like, what he feels, whether he is lying, whether he is agitated or whether he is merely making conventional conversation. I can even feel, or rather hear, any hidden sorrow. Life is sound, the tonal modulations of the human speech ... I have a vast collection of notebooks filled with [the "melodic curves of speech"]—you see, they are my window through which I look into the soul."

—Leoš Janácek

In the works of **Janácek** (I'm talking more about his last few years of work, [inspired] in large [part by] Quay brother films) one hears unsettling uses of sound and above all a compelling beauty which makes one take more seriously the unconventional and experimental nature of the compositions. Like the Quay brothers, Janácek lures the participant into a state of temporal stasis, confusion brought on by the presentation of a disjuncture (in sound). Old Slavic peasant themes and dance melodies [are played] with a bizarre array of instruments, [correlating the] sound like the score was shredded and pasted back randomly on a [sounding] board and played. At one point in the score of Van Svankayer (the cabinet of) the singing voice pronounces Chekov in a range of keys, formulating a melody which both serves a tonal presentation and at the same time presents an interesting second read into Janácek.

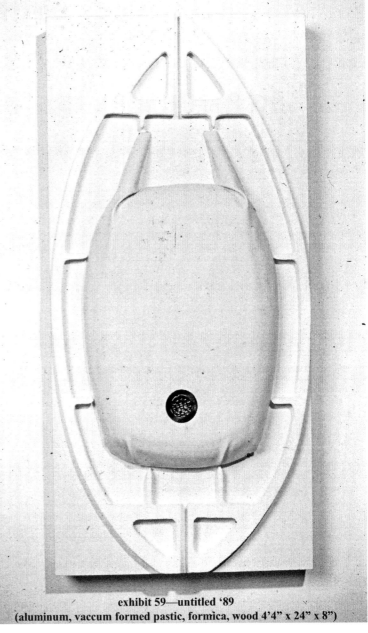

exhibit 59—untitled '89
(aluminum, vaccum formed pastic, formica, wood 4'4" x 24" x 8")

D I

→ TODAVIA W CHANN L HIM COMO MAT RIAL WITN SS Y FUSING W/ OUR OWN INT RPR TATION QU SUC DIO
→ SPLIT TH WAV TO HOOK NU VO R TRAZO → IN R ALIDAD W B CAM TH SURF R - AT TH PLAYA H FOR
TH MOST PART SCULPT D SAND CASTL S + RAN → DONT R CORD HIM DIGGING AGUA MUCHO SP CIALLY SALTY
→ TROP TH SAM P RO AMPLIFI D W/ CUSTOM CABIN TS - SUB-WOOF RS ATRAS TO MAXIMIZ HARMONICS
FOR TH DRIV R + QUI N RID S SHOTGUN → BACK WH N HI-FID LITY MATT R D NOW ITS ALL ABOUT
ACC SSIBIILTY - NOT QUALIDAD → TH MAS P OPL SP AK A COMMUN LANGAUG TH MAIZ IS DILUT D
→ MOR THAN 1 WAY TO SKIN A CAT - IN TH RUINS OF TH MANY-POSSIBL UNIV RS S APPROACH → W
M MB R AS ITS TOLD - S LF-IMPOS D XIL IN A CAV ALGUI N DIJO W N D TO COV R OUR HAIRS SO W
WOR OUR SHIRTS OV R OUR H ADS SO VAMPIR BATS WOULDNT LAND - ACTUAL VAMPIRO BATS - PRIOR TO
THIS OUR ASSOCIATION RA MYTHOLOGICAL COMO IMMORTAL B ANS → A 1 TO 1 CORR SPONDANC W/ WORD +
OBJ CT → FIRING UP TH KILN TO GLAZ AFT R SCULPTING DOWN - VACUUM-PACK D COMO ATUN PORQU LA
PALABRA ↑TUNA↓ RA YA R S RVADO FOR PRICKLY P AR CACTUS FRUIT → CANT R SIST ATING IT THO W
KNOW ITS ↑BAD↓ FOR US → BY D FINITION CUALQUI R COSA QU PONI S IN YOUR CU RPO S UNA ↑DROGA↓
PASS D TH FROWNING FAC OF B TH L → L - Y S - HOUS OF - AL PH - B TH ← NURR VIR BACKWORDS
IS RIV RRUN → PAST V S + ADAMS → NDS HOW IT B GINS → STOP ⊕
→ → W INT RPR T A FLOW R AS A SKULL ↑COULDNT SINK IF U TRI D↓ JOYC ALSO SAID ↑SO THICK W/
SALT↓ PARA PHRAS → ANOTH R WAY OF R INSTATING ARCHIM D S - ↑ UR KA↓ H SHOUT D AS HIS BODY

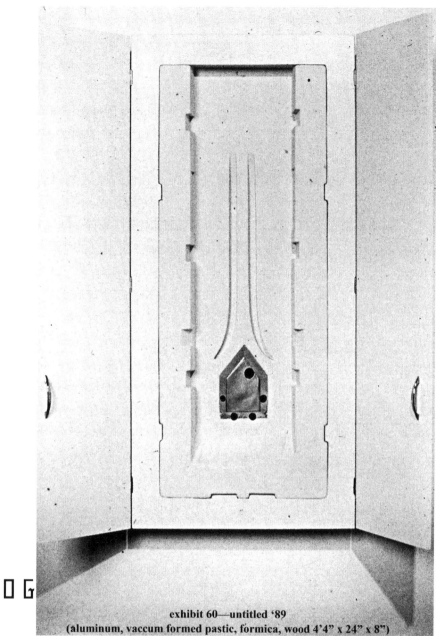

exhibit 60—untitled '89
(aluminum, vaccum formed pastic, formica, wood 4'4" x 24" x 8")

cyclops

U are now entering the Cyclops ½ of this episode—the pt. which i returned to Portland. Brother-½ was ya allready there. Even tho this ½ must've been solely 2-3, i member him sitting smug at the kitchen counter like he called SHOTGUN on the ntire house ... he allways got 1st dibs + i got sloppy 2nds cuz he had priority + he was just better at everything ... xcept the WEED PATROL, he miht pick more but when our dad woud judge our pickings he'd say i got more BY THE ROOTS so then brother-½ was the 1 got the BOOBY prize wich was usually better in this case. He was allready in w/ this new STEPMOTHER ... she had a fancy oregon, the kind w/ foot pedals + built-in rythm sexions + a book that'd tell u how to play songs like "I Walk the Line". Our stepmom had a "friend" (brother-½ called him a SUITOR) named LLOYD witch confused us cuz that was the name of the centre where our dad had an office + we'd go saturdays to skate at the rink or fotocopy drawings or watch type spew out of the TELEX machine.

Lloyd was more cultured than our dad, he wore scarves + was well-read + played classical piano (in retrospeck he was probly gay but we were too young to know). He said brother-½ had potential + offered to give him free lessons ... our father thawt it weird this grown man wood do this free but Lloyd said 1 day when brother-½ was fameus they coud repay the debt like brother-½ was ransum $$, but he didn't care. I wanted lessons 2 but our stepmom said this was asking 2 much of Lloyd + he selected Kevin as the 1 w/ TALENT + in stead i was stuck w/ the clarinet cuz it made the least amount of noize.

~~Not sure what any of this has to do w/ Ulysses + his men being abducted by the Cyclops in the cave or Bloom walking into a bar + being berrated by the anti-semitic "Citizen"~~... maybe we shoud mention the time we wanted to stay over at our friend's house + our dad said no + when we asked why he said cuz he was a JEW + we said "what's that?" but he woudn't say, just that we weren't allowed to play w/ him but we did anyway cuz Michael had these 4-sided spinning tops w/ weird symbulls on the sides that we liked even tho we didn't know what they meant + while spinning them we'd sing:

"I had a little dradle, i made it out of clay + when it's dry + ready, then dradle + i shall play."

SANK INTO TH TUB + TH WAT R ROS → N V R HAD A N D FOR BATH MILK NOR M LLING SALTS P RO SI PU D V R COM SIRV → W R D AD TO TH WORLD WH N W SL P + THATS ALL FOLKS OK Φ → → CONSCIOUSLY W R FADING IN + OUT → CHRONO-LOGICALLY W MMB R WH N OUR FATH R KIDNAPP D M BACK → ↑KIDNAP↓ ... AS IF W DR ADFULLY SL PT THRU IT → BROTH R 1/2 YA R GR SS D - BY HIS OWN FR WILL → PAPA PAID M A VISIT IN M XICO TH N SAID H WAS TAKING M TO DISN YLANDIA → TODOS MIS AMIGOS RAN C LOSOS → L AVION FU PRIM RA A DALLAS + W SWITCH D PLAN S BUT IN PLAC OF LOS ANG L S TH CAPT SAID OUR D STINATION WAS PORTLAND → I THOUGHT DISN YLAND WAS IN LOS ANG L S W ASK D OUR FATH R + D STINCKLY M MB R HIM HANDING M CRAYOLAS + T LLING M TO DRAW PINK L FANTS BUT WH N W LOOK D DOWN W F LT SICK + SAID SO + OUR FATH R SHOV D US A BAG SAID US THIS SO W BARF D IN IT + OUR FATH R WAS DISAPPOINT D NOT JUST CUZ W MISS D SOM BUT CUZ H WAS A PILOT + NO SON OF HIS COULD B AIRSICK LIK THIS → ND OF FIL Φ

Nov.23,1976

Dear Granny Nanny and Grampa Cal,
   how have you been since the last time I saw you.
   Thankyou for the ten dollars and the card.
I am looking forward to seeing you this Winter and hopefully
   this Summer.
We have been having good weather here in Portland,Today,yester-
   day and the day before we have been having good weather but the
   day before that we had a terrible storm.
   If you would like to know what I got here's what I got,Fischer
Sprint's(skis),Geze plate bindi ngs,ski poles,ski hat,stamps
   and $32.03 cash($20.00 2 dollar bills.
Mom's letter told us that our great,great,great grandfather is
   Thomas Jefferson,can you tell me more about it.

   I have run out of things to tell you.

      HAPPY THANKSGIVING!!

Love',
Derek

Dear granny nanny and grampa Cal

I have started the hobbie of coin
collecting I have a very large
One. Shcool is going fine I am in
the 5 grade And eleven years Old
I am painting(Acrilac) and Iam
making you one.
I know just what to get you for
Christmas. I am looking forward
   to seeing you this Winter.
(p.s. Happy THANKESGIVING.

      Love
        Kevin,

XXX 032A830 .2.9

We're flipping back + fourth between Mexico + Oregon we know gets confusing but this is how we member it ... not much written rechords to go by only fotos + what our parents said ... tho that depends on who's doing the tocking. There were legal proseedings but we were deemed too young to testify or even attend. I do distinckly member (circa 1970) sitting in the den by myself (Kevin already went to school) watching Mr. Green Jeans on Capt. Kangaroo + we herd a honking + looked out the window + there was our MOM in a britc blue VW bug + our older JD brother was w/ her 2.

I started to run out to say hi but our stepmom pushed me back into the den + locked the door, told me to watch TV but i herd the SIRENS + watched out the 2nd story window as the police pulled up + handcuffed our mom + led her away. Our older brother JD lived w/ us after that but he wasn't thrilled about it.

Evidently (left) we had a typewriter when i was 10 (day after my birthday) + Kevin was 11 + it seams we were in the habit of writing letters on the same page. He was the 1 of course who drew the CANNIBALISTIC turkey witch i guess U coud think of as the Cyclops or Citizen, but the turkey to us symoblized the pillage of pilgrims.

Xpected as we were to write a report in 5th grade about the cuntry our furthest incestors came from our dad said PLYMOUTH ROCK ... «before that we were monkeys». Or he said we were made w/ a turkey baster after our mom spit his gravy out sucking. Or how she poked holes in his condum w/ a safety pin. Never asked for it ether way + nether did we. All a random axident thank dog for DOPAMINE. He taut us replacement therapy at a young age ... how to rewire our regular brain circuit linked to survival—wether food or sex— + replace w/ alcohol (or drugs or even a strike in bowling ... 3 consecutive Xs of wich constitute a so-called TURKEY). Such loopholes or short circuits the brain remembers + wants reiterated XXX.

Valley Lanes 10 18 75 Bowling Score Sheet   Team Awesome Possoms

PLAYER	1	2	3	4	5	6	7	8	9	10	TOTAL
Derek	20	50	78	98	115	124	154	183	203	223	223
Kevin	19	28	48	64	82	91	109	124	132	151	151
BJ	17	24	32	52	72	90	98	116	124	132	132
Geo	8	34	53	62	80	98	115	134	143	160	160

*Double Turkey

To capitulate some unspoked items that got us here (page 139, mid-70s in Oregon) thus far:

- Whether there were 1 or 2 separate kidnappings is unclear.
- 1st memories at least for me[me] were ARCHITECTURAL.
- Memory is not necessarily structurally reliable.
- Our father wore AVIATOR sunglasses, the type that are now back in style.
- He also wore Hush Puppies™.
- We typically ate cow TONGUE (in Portland w/ mustard, in Mexico tacos de lengua).
- We had 2 PARROTS that got electrocuted in a lightning storm (their cage was cast iron).
- Ulysses gets out of the Cyclops jam by saying his name is NOBODY.
- The narrator in Joyce's corresponding episode is UNNAMED.
- Joyce IRL wore an eye-patch over his left EYE. The problems w/ his eyes began around the time he was writing *Ulysses* ... he blamed them on drinking.

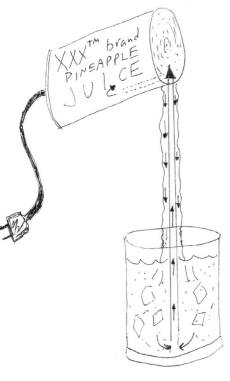

fry 3|a

Next week we begin the process of renewal. There is no use fighting it, it is something everyone must go through. Once again we find ourselves living lives that are not our own. When we overlap into our other lives we call it dejavú. Now I know this sounds kind of weird but I wouldnt say it if I di'dnt have scientific data to back it up. The numbers prove, without a doubt, that we are in fact living the wrong lives (scene; he shows the rest of them some sheets of white paper covered with in scrawls that he pulls out from under his matress. After reading over the papers the others are convinced. They are told that they will know they are viewing their real lives when they feel an extreme sense of anguish and loss. They will lock themselves in their rooms, and the lower part of their legs will go numb. Falling back on their beds they will long intensely for percisely that which they can never have. This realization will exhaust them and they will be unable to move for many hours. For them the days after following will be ones of listless wandering, and minimal movement. After a few days they will be forced to lapse back into a physical identity of little or no self-realization. With renewed vigour they will resume their trivial pursuits. She went home and fed her doll-companion, the one she had bought earlier that week in a small porn shop on Sunset strip. As she had come to expect, the dolls eyes lit up like candles soon after feeding. It assured her that she would be safe on the journey. later/as she walked through the dark forest a man with a white face, white hair and white clothes raced past her, suddenly daybreak came to the woods.

She walked on further, and a man on a motorcycle roared past her, he was all red, he was dressed in red, and his motorcycle was red- the sun began to rise. (Something about fundry Salamender?) — Paverhas (under)

She walked on for a whole night and a whole day, and only on the following evening did she come to the place mentioned in the magazine paper. It was a hut made out of what looked to be oily old newspapers. The fence around the hut was made out of human bones, on the fence posts were human skulls. The doors had human legs for doorposts, human hands for bolts, and a mouth with sharp teeth in place of a lock. Candy froze in terror before this sick scene. All of a sudden a small black sports car raced by candy. her It was driven by a black man, dressed in black. The car raced right towards the front door and vanished into the ground, as though the earth swallowed it up- night came.

Self-Cleaning MAT-RA-DOR

1/2 for I can vouch for the «hut» ... but i member it more as an abandoned cabin, up an old logging road at the base of Mt. Hood (up the road from the STAGNANT POOL on page 130). We'd ride motorcycles up there + smoke pot + make out w/ girls (if we were lucky).

Obviously he's lying about the fence made of human bones. He was always prone to exagerration, the only truths per Adorno.

We did 1 time see a man roar by naked on a BULTACO™-brand motorcycle (maybe this is what Kevin means by «dressed in red»). We found out later this daredevil did it as a birthday present for his girlfriend. «Too bad it wasn't the other way around» we lamented.

On 1 of Kevin's birthdays i gave him a can of juice (or maybe it was beer) *that we found used at a flea market.* that gave the illusion (when plugged in + filled w/dyed yello water) that it was perpetually pouring like a fountain. It worked cuz there was a hidden see-thru straw in the glass that fed back up into the can where there was some sort of pump mechanism ...

sort a like this (sorry i'm not much of an artist). He kept it displayed it in his room til his death, said it was the best gift he ever recevied.

He waited for nightfall. From the rusted iron shed she waited. He sat in the tall grass on the rivers edge. Her eyes flipped about wildly. He was in Hoboken, looking over at Manhattan.[68] She was a very old woman~~a very old woman~~ *thousands of years old*. He watched the city change form. She was a ~~change-former~~ *form changer*. He was getting cold and restless. Where we have skin, she has rusted iron. Our clothes are made of cotton and leather, her torn garments are composed of rusted sheets of bronze and jagged shards of corroded copper. He slowly stood up and made his way to the Port Authority station, to ~~catch~~ the last train to the city.

Nothing grew within 500 yards of her rusted iron shack. Her grotesque pointed nose sniffed about wildly. Her spindly iron fingers clicked together, occasionally sending peices of orange powder on to barren soil.

He made it to the village in less than twenty minutes. He ran down Leeden street, turned up Stockton, and then took a right on Shettland. He found the apartment marked 500, and knocked on the glass. After a few minutes the dog was told to stop barking, and an old woman answered the door.

He traveled for three days and three nights through the dense forest, lost. On the fourth day he came upon a clearing where there was nothing alive to be seen.

"Yes, what is it?" She inquired through the brass chain.

"He was struck down in the middle of the clearing, he never knew what hit him. His polished silver armour tarnished instantly when it touched the ground. She raced towards him in her mortar, pulled along by her pestle. When she reached his body her trembling, rusty fingers dipped into his eye sockets and pulled out his sight. Now helpless, he obediently followed her back to the hut."

"Who the hell are you? Go away before I call the police!"

"He's waiting there helpless. He is her slave. In the prime of his life he has been struck down!"

"Thats it! I am calling the cops!" (slam!)

"Vasilinuchka! I beg you! Send your new husband help! Help me to slay this devil!"

With each movement there was the scrapping and clanging. She never slept. She shot about the small dark room with inhuman speed. Each night she drank three goatskins full of wine and passed out in a heap on the kitchen table, snoring loudly all night. Each morning, at her command, the human hands that where the bolts on her door would release their grip, and the doors would spring open.

[THIS SPACE INTENTIONALLY LFET BLANK][70]

Every tempo ~~should feel like the 1st not just w/ sex + travel, but w/ reading.~~ This is the issue w/ writing or making art ... U need to capture it + move on ~~+ not get caught up in the capturing or U yourself will get captured like a spider in its own web.~~ U only get 1 shot (specially if self-inflicted) but it only takes 1 shot[69].

The same «dirty» filter is used on every scene for continuity. ~~We write these notes to self thinking they are line items we can use or inkorporate later but when we re-read we don't member what we initially meant + feel more inklined to omit or erase. Maybe we should just trust our instincks + inklude the original marginalia as is, w/ the disclaimer that the entire book is within quotes.~~

~~E.g. this we wrote last night ...~~ tho ½ of it we can't read. We scribbled: *need to keep your distance. We are sleeping still. Not dead. Writing from dream state, this is K, not me. ~~Not afraid to say we are aware of U, the reader + that this is me. Don't be self-conscious of self-reference. Do it for his sake, in his name.~~* Our compulsion to capture outwayed by the drive to make every word count. Not just the informational content, but the way we say it.

INC.

[68] To my knowledge, he never went to NJ or NY ... at least not that he ever mentioned. In 1 or 2 journal entries he mentions passing thru JFK + he spent a summer at RISD so at some point he must of made his way down here, to where we are writing this from now ... + double-checking Googlemaps—neither Leeden, Stockton nor Shettland are acual street names in NYC ... but the above seems a draft so perhaps he planned on fact-checking after the fact so it made geographical sense.

[69] Except LOCKJAW, which u should get a booster for every 10 years.

[70] This overzealous compulsion to fill all **white** space is mine, not his. Art school undoubtedly taught him the importance of white space, but i've always been driven by practical economic efficiency. In fact, it's occuring to us now (too late ... out of space) that we should include here the postcard invitation for THE WHITE SHOW (an exhibit he was in along w/ 4 others including another artist w/ last name White, Pae (who, googling now, seems has made quite a name for herself, including the Whitney Biennial in 2010).

Dear Grandpa Cal and GrannyNanny,

    How are you? We have been geting a lot of snow up on the mountain since Thanksgiving weekend. There have been at least five ski weekends so far this year. Derek and I have singed up on the school Basketball team for 5-6graders (we are on differnt teams).We practice at night on weekdays between 6.30-8.00 and 5.00-6.30 O'clock at night. Our new cabin is turning out to a verybeutiful. The builder/desinger is using for the walls a unuasle wood with light shades of blue , pink, baje (all natuaral). It is rigth on the beach i nfront of the Sandy river (wich is almost flooding over with melted snow rain etc.) The house(cabin) is two stories 4 bedrooms (one with deck facing river) and a large Kithen / living room. It has 2 large decks and a large carport. We are about 5 miles away dow n the mountain from our old cabin (in zigzag village). This year in shcool i was shoosen to draw the shcool xxxxxxxx roster, the large christmasdecorations (about 25 feet by 12 feet of painting,drawing,desingning) and I desinged (sold) some energy conservation presentation posters etc. My piano lessons are coming along fine I am learning harder music all the time.
      MERRY CHRISTMAS!!! !!!!!!!...........

love,

Kevin

Not sure when he wrote this letter (presumably mid-70s) but it demonstrates his early penchant for **interior design** + just as he showed a self-reflexive **speech balloon** for the turkey imaging himself being eaten, the elf reflexively images the toy duck he is making as it will be displayed on the tree. Childhood allowed us the liberty of short attn spans ... the freedom to not have to appropriately craft segues + give only relevant info in an org fashion.

As adults we are now afflicted (in our intent to communicate) w/:

- holding people's undivided attn
- knowing your audience
- the sender + receiver being on the same pg
- the virtues of compromise
- remaining steadfast + objective
- the practicalities of resale value
- distilling down to bulleted lists + ...

Definitely don't write by hand. Don't barnstorm a brainstorm. If you don't fight it, SUSPENSION will naturally take the shape of a CATENARY, the curve of a chain assumes under its own weight. This U-shaped line was 1st described (mathematically) by the same ROBERT HOOKE that we stared this epidode with.

P.S. Per usual style, Hooke delivered his discovery in the form of an encoded anagram:

abcccddeeeeefggiiiiiiii-ilmmmmmnnnnnooprrsssttttttuuuuuuuux

This string of letters, when re-arranged, read:

«Ut pendet continuum flexile, sic stabit contiguum rigidum inversum»

... or in plainer english:

"As hangs a flexible cable, so inverted, stand the touching pieces of an arch"

TELEPHONE LINES

∧X

* Freely hanging electric power cables or even the fishing line hanging between 2 TIN CANS form (naturally) a CATENARY described by the equation:

FROM: SENDER

TO: RECIPIENT

$$y = a \cosh\left(\frac{x}{a}\right)$$
$$= \frac{a}{2}\left(e^{x/a} + e^{-x/a}\right)$$

where **cosh** is the hyperbolic cosine function which can also be expressed as natural logarithms.

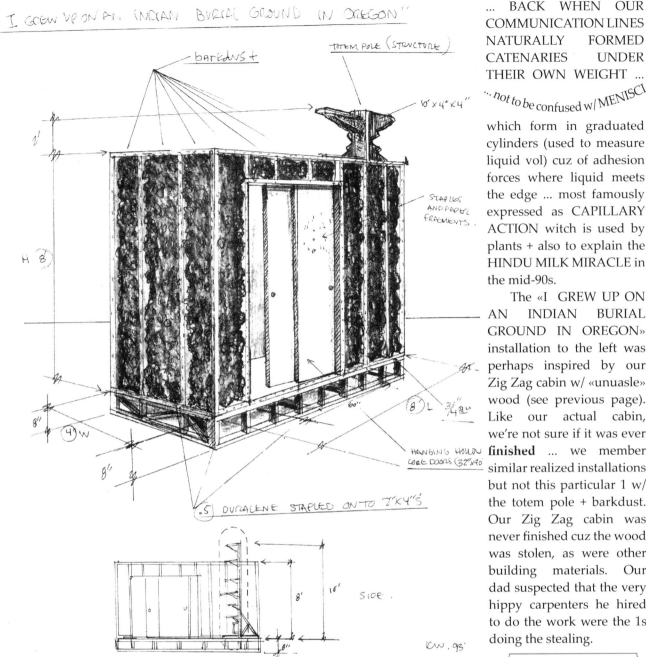

"I GREW UP ON AN INDIAN BURIAL GROUND IN OREGON"

barkdust

TOTEM POLE (STRUCTURE)

10' x 4" x 4"

STAPLES AND PAPER FRAGMENTS.

H ⑧

⑧ L 3¼PLY

④ W

60"

HANGING HOLLOW CORE DOORS (32"x70"

8"

8"

⑤ DURALENE STAPLED ONTO 2"x 4"'S

8'   10'   SIDE.

8"

KW.93

... BACK WHEN OUR COMMUNICATION LINES NATURALLY FORMED CATENARIES UNDER THEIR OWN WEIGHT ...

... not to be confused w/ MENISCI

which form in graduated cylinders (used to measure liquid vol) cuz of adhesion forces where liquid meets the edge ... most famously expressed as CAPILLARY ACTION witch is used by plants + also to explain the HINDU MILK MIRACLE in the mid-90s.

The «I GREW UP ON AN INDIAN BURIAL GROUND IN OREGON» installation to the left was perhaps inspired by our Zig Zag cabin w/ «unuasle» wood (see previous page). Like our actual cabin, we're not sure if it was ever **finished** ... we member similar realized installations but not this particular 1 w/ the totem pole + barkdust. Our Zig Zag cabin was never finished cuz the wood was stolen, as were other building materials. Our dad suspected that the very hippy carpenters he hired to do the work were the 1s doing the stealing.

The TOTEM part was likely inspired by our father (who in turn ripped off the Indians). It was his idea to carve animals out of logs using chainsaws + axes, the most memorable being a long hotdog looking animal. These totems were arranged on a berm outside our dining room window + bird + chipmunk feeders were arranged around + on the totems for our mealtime entertainment (we had no TV reception there). Come fall our dad woud put out chunks of suet fat (he read somewhere that it was good for these little animals, that it fattened them up for the winter).

1 autumn morning the day after he hung up a big chunk of suet, the whole piece of fat was gone w/o a trace. So he got a nother chunk + this time stapled it down w/ CHICKENWIRE on top of the hotdog log. The following morning there was a big claw mark down the hotdog's back + the suet was gone.

This sparked an obssession in our father to find out what animal was doing this ... so he built this contraption—a piece of plywood w/ a weight-loaded trigger wired to a buzzer that he put inside the house. We'd put suet on the plywood + sleep near the buzzer, near the window where a camera was set up on a tripod. The 1st few times the buzzer woke us, we turned on the floodlight + got some photos of unphased raccoons or the neighbors cat. 1 time we got a bobcat, but our dad insisted it had to be something even bigger ... but all we's ever see were the glowing eyes looking back at us from the darkness ....

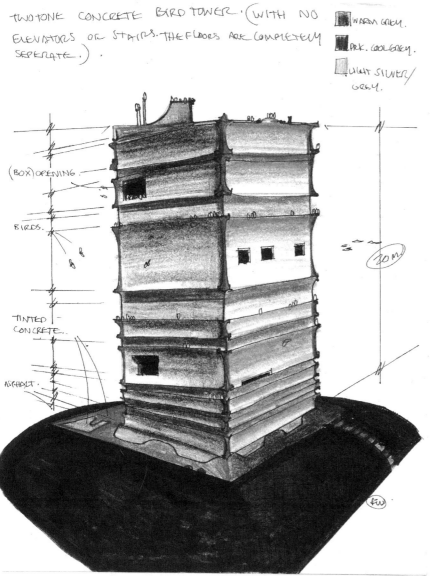

TWO TONE CONCRETE BIRD TOWER. (WITH NO ELEVATORS OR STAIRS. THE FLOORS ARE COMPLETELY SEPERATE.).

■ WARM GREY.
■ DRK. COOL GREY.
□ LIGHT SILVER/ GREY.

(BOX) OPENING.

BIRDS.

TINTED CONCRETE.

ASPHALT.

20 M

UNABASHED SHAME [71]

nenenenenehhh how would that be spelled
unabashed shame following life a stream of thought
deh deh deh, deh deh deh

An adjoining room was [narrow] and tapered on both sides, like a small A-frame. The door leading into it, from the main room, and the triangular wall across from it were systematically pitted with square pieces of glass. It boasted a [single] bed, a [little] bookcase (with small books), a lot of small dolls, and a [hardly any] ground clearance in its [narrow] doorway. Teabrown art colours were the dominant light, dimly shimmering in their opacity.

[first letter bold]
pink as in a piece of unchewed bubble gum *the color of blushing*
—was woven into the basket
Purpel algith pastel, like a fadded California rasin doll [sic x3]
—was sprinkled on the bedsheet
—layed down in the pillow
—woven in the basket (see above, pink)

—on the woman's back (Guatemalan)
—holding up the roof of the church (Oaxacan)
—emblamed in budhas quite dead skin (citina [?])
—saturating a pillow case
—1 part to 1030 particles in the next room.
other purples of different types were also in the room usually somewhere near the above mentioned sentance (see above; purple)

... or a parking garage ... of the kind they had in France when later (see chapter 16) we were working on a film together ... the kind you didn't drive into, but a system of unmanned elevators automatically put the car in the allocated slot. In particular the time we parked our flesh-colored (as U liked to call it) Twingo ... + when we went to retrieve it w/ our parking ticket they brought us a Twingo ... but it was YELLOW, not flesh-colored. And there was no way to walk around the garage + manually look for it ourselves. So we kept the yellow 1 as if the car was just a form of currency, like a coin not mattering witch[72].

---

[71] Taken verbatim fron his notes.
[72] There i lied (about us keeping it). We did think about it, if that means anything.

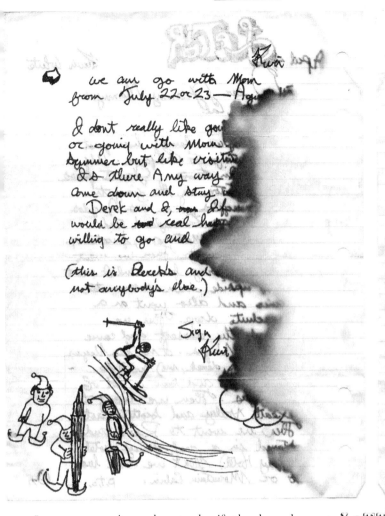

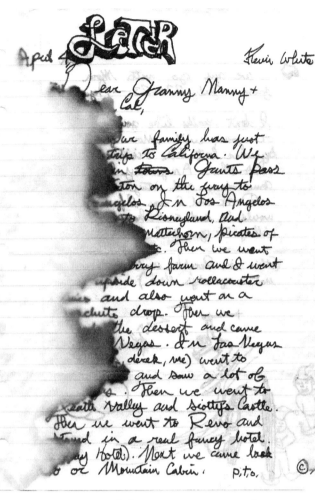

In case u weren't sure how to classify the above, he wrote L̃eT̃T̃eR̃ a cross the top ... + a long w/ his full name to make it official. I'm guessing this is circa 1978, but i have no recullection of this trip + we have no fotos to show for it. Cuz of this i find it most poignant. If it was 1978, then things were well into their decline + our dad + stepmom woud divorce a year later, so maybe this trip was a last ditch effort by our father to patch things up w/ her.

    Btw, does this make U uncumfortible? Braking some unwritten writer code by including unfiltered personel correspondance, by being brazenly self-aware? By including U in all this mess? By shooting in 1st person + asking questions later? JK, but why do writers (brother-½ included) write in 3rd ... Joyce too ... unless he was channeling some 1 else thru «I». Regardless brother-½ + Joyce were always lying, never writing about their personal lives (at least directly). Or does distancing 1 self from self bring **the reader** closer to the source? To the pineapple fount. Does lying make us more reliable?

    Besides being the better liar, he was always more prone to exaggeration. As if reality wasn't intarresting enough. He used to tease me for being «dedicated to reality». Ever since he was a kid he used to lock his bedroom wether he was in it or not. He didn't like pepole snooping around in his stuff... wich ment he liked to snoop around in other pepole's stuff. If a parent was gone, he'd snoop around in their room ... specially bathrooms. If he came over to your house + used the bathroom u coud be assured he rifled thru your medicine cabnet. This is what writers + artists do.

THE AIRHORN SOUNDS AGAIN AND AGAIN WE BRING BACK OUR LOADED BUCKETS 1 BY 1 AND OUR FATHER DUMPS THE CONTENTS ONTO AN OVERTURNED GARBAGE CAN LID TO INSPECT OUR PICKINGS ... TO SEE IF WE GOT THE DANDELIONS BY THE ROOTS. GETTING JUST THE LEAVES WITHOUT THE ROOT WAS WORSE THAN NOTHING AT ALL . . . . LIKE A NEGATIVE AMOUNT. WORSE YET WAS BLOWING A MATURE STEM SCATTERING THE SEEDS LIKE FIREWORKS ... BUT WE COULD NEVER HELP OURSELVES

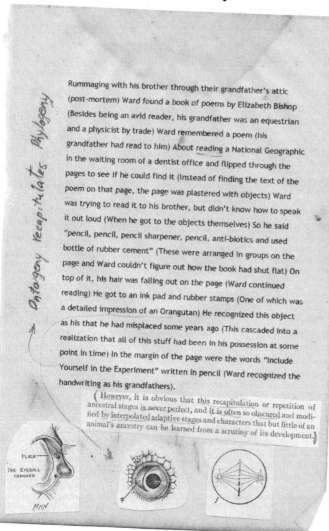

Rummaging with his brother through their grandfather's attic (post-mortem) Ward found a book of poems by Elizabeth Bishop (Besides being an avid reader, his grandfather was an equestrian and a physicist by trade) Ward remembered a poem (his grandfather had read to him) About reading a National Geographic in the waiting room of a dentist office and flipped through the pages to see if he could find it (Instead of finding the text of the poem on that page, the page was plastered with objects) Ward was trying to read it to his brother, but didn't know how to speak it out loud (When he got to the objects themselves) So he said "pencil, pencil, pencil sharpener, pencil, anti-biotics and used bottle of rubber cement" (These were arranged in groups on the page and Ward couldn't figure out how the book had shut flat) On top of it, his hair was falling out on the page (Ward continued reading) He got to an ink pad and rubber stamps (One of which was a detailed impression of an Orangutan) He recognized this object as his that he had misplaced some years ago (This cascaded into a realization that all of this stuff had been in his possession at some point in time) In the margin of the page were the words "Include Yourself in the Experiment" written in pencil (Ward recognized the handwriting as his grandfathers).

(However, it is obvious that this recapitulation or repetition of ancestral stages is never perfect, and it is often so obscured and modified by interpolated adaptive stages and characters that but little of an animal's ancestry can be learned from a scrutiny of its development.)

exhibit 61—"Include Yourself In The Experiment," 1 of our 1ˢᵗ publications, appearing in DIAGRAM 1.3 (http://webdelsol. com/DIAGRAM/1_3/include.html) + then in MINING IN THE BLACK HILLS (Calamari Press, 2003).

Just a friendly reminder that u are now in the CYCLOPS episode. The originul Cyclops section of his 'SSES' 'SSES' thesis (see the following pages) consisted of an accounting of his xpenditures for the odyssey he took in search of our father in the name of Joyce. (We may as well just equate the 2 going forward: James Joyce = our father.)

When the Cyclops asks Ulysses what his name is he says NOBODY. So later, after they get the Cyclops drunk + poke his eye out, the Cyclops yells «NOBODY IS KILLING ME!» + thus his cyclops brother across the way thinks nothing of it, thinks his brother is going nuts.

The Cyclops section for Joyce goes: «A Jew walks into a bar in Dublin ... ».

Apparently his accounting of expenses is a play on the old stereotype.

«In the everyday use of language, words are the vehicles of ideas. The word 'flower' means flower that refers to flowers in the world. No doubt it is possible to read literature in this way, but literature is more than this everyday use of language. For in literature 'flower' does not just mean flower but many things and it can only do so because the word is independent from what it signifies. This independence, which is passed over in the everyday use of language, is the negativity at the heart of language. The word means something because it negates the physical reality of the thing. Only in this way can the idea arise. The absence of the thing is made good by the presence of the idea. What the everyday use of language steps over to make use of the idea, literature remains fascinated by, the absence that makes it possible. Literary language, therefore, is a double negation, both of the thing and the idea. It is in this space that literature becomes possible where words take on a strange and mysterious reality of their own, and where also meaning and reference remain allusive and ambiguous.»—Stéphane Mallarmé

For example:

A DREAM

THERE IS YOUNG MAN WHO HAS MILLIONS OUNCES OF GOLD IN HIS HOUSE, NO ONE IN THE WORLD KNOWS HE HAS IT. SUDDENLY one day he takes an amount of gold (the most he can possibly carry) and takes it to a coin store. "We buy silver and gold" it said on the outside. I had a good feeling about this place, I thought I didn't coise any difficulties in selling the gold. I went in and proceeded to show extensive documentation of myself, and of my ownership of my gold. The dealer accepted the gold, the ID and the photocopies of the documentation that this young man had so generously, and thoughtfully brought along. To the future plaintiffs dismay the photocopies self-destructed as they were supposed to just minutes later in the file cabinet.

CYCLOPS

[LOCATION]	[COST]	[STATUS]	[OTHER]	[DATE]
est. itinerary, and expenses (Jan 1.90)				
LAX- AMSTERDAM	430 $	(paid)		JAN 5
EURAIL PASS	320	(paid)		JAN5-FEB5
Living expenses	850			JAN5-FEB5
Helsinki-Moscow	70	(paid)		FEB 5
hotel Moscow	138	(paid)		FEB 6-7
train Mosc.-Bej.	374	(paid)		FEB 7-14
Bejiing-HongKong	200			FEB14-Mar2
living expenses	250			FEB14-MAR2
HongKong-Calcutta	250			MAR2-MAR10
living expenses	100			MAR2-MAR10
Calcutta-NewDelhi	250			MAR10-APR9
living expenses	600			MAR10-APR9
NewDelhi-Paris	390	(paid)		APR9
living expenses	700			APR9-MAY9
total (paid)	1,700$			
realistic amount	3,000$			
AMT. PAID	972 $			
EST.REMAINING$	2,500			

73:    "It's only in this last room, located at the top of the house, that night will completely unfold. Usually it's lovely and peaceful. It's a relief not to have to shut your eyes to get rid of daytimes insomnia. It's also rather seductive to find in outer darkness the same night that for such a long time struck your inner truth with death. This night has a very special nature. It's not accompanied either by dreams or by premonitory thoughts that are sometimes substituted for dreams. It's a vast dream itself which, if it covers you, you never attain. When at last it swathes your bed, we'll draw the curtains around you and the splendor of the objects revealed at that point will be worthy of consoling even those who are unhappiest. At that instant I'll become really beautiful myself. This false light makes me rather unattractive now, but at that auspicious moment I'll appear as I actually am. I'll look at you for a long time and I'll lie down close to you-and you wont need to ask about things, I'll answer all your questions. Also- and at the same time-the lamps whose inscriptions you wanted to read will be turned around so that they face the right way, and wise sayings that allow everything to be understood will no longer be illegible. So don't be impatient. The night will render you justice, and you'll lose sight of all sorrow and fatigue."

"One last question," said Thomas after listening with lively interest. "Will the lamps be lit?"

"Of course not," the girl said. "What a ridiculous question! Everything will be lost in the night."

"The night," Thomas said in a dreamy way. "So I won't see you?"

"Most likely not," said the girl. "Did you think it would be different from this? It's precisely because you'll be forever in darkness and you won't be able to perceive anything yourself that I'm telling you about it now. You can't expect to hear, see and be at rest all at once. So I'm letting you know what will happen when night reveals its truth to you while you're deeply at rest. Doesn't it please you to know that in a short time everything you've wanted to learn will be read in a few straightforward words

—Thank you, sir. Stephen said, gathering the money together with shy haste and putting it all in a pocket of his trousers.

—No thanks at all, Mr. Deasy said. You earned it.

Stephen's hand, free again, went back to the hollow shells. Symbols too of beauty and of power. A lump in my pocket. Symbols soiled by greed and misery.

—Don't carry it like that, Mr. Deasy said. You'll pull it out somewhere and lose it. You just buy one of these machines. You'll find them very handy.

Answer something.

—Mine would be often empty, Stephen said.

The same room and hour, the same wisdom: and I the same. Three times now. Three nooses round me here. Well. I can break them in this instant if I will.

—Because you don't save, Mr. Deasy said, pointing his finger. You don't know yet what money is. Money is power, when you have lived as long as I have. I know, I know. If youth but knew. But what does Shakespeare say? *Put but money in thy purse.*

---

[73] By Maurice Blanchot, a bitter critic of fascists + anti-semites ... + who was nearly executed by a Nazi firing squad in 1944.

[74] The Joyce column was by our inclusion.

.CYCLOPS.

actual itinerary,cost (May 1,90)				
[LOCATION]	[COST]	[STATUS]	[OTHER]	[DATE]
LAX-AMSTERDAM	430 $	(paid)		JAN5
EURAIL PASS	320	''		JAN5-FEB5
LIVING EXPENSES	850	''		JAN5-FEB5
HELSINKI-MOSC.	70	''		FEB5
hotel (MOSC.)	138	''		FEB7-8
train (Mos.-Bej)	374	''		FEB9-16
* BEJ.-HONGKONG .	1,100	''		FEB16-MAR9
LIVING EXPENSES	900	''		FEB16-MAR9
HONGKONG-KHAT.	250	''		MAR9-MAR19
LIVING EXPENSES	500	''		MAR9-MAR19
NEPAL, TREK	100	''		MAR19-APR20
LIVING EXPENSES	600	''		MAR19-APR20
KHAT.-NEWDELHI	85	''		APR20-22
NEW DELHI	60	''		APR22-25
NEWDELHI-PARIS	390	''		APR25
PARIS	150	''		APR25-28
PARIS-AMST.	40	''		APR28
AMST-VAN.-LAX		''		APR29
* INC.: RT PLANE TO TIBET(500 $) SHANGHAI-CHENG. CHENG.-GUILIN. (150, 150).				
[TOTAL]	6,350$			

on the walls, on my face and on my mouth? Now the fact that this revelation won't actually be disclosed to you, to be honest, is a drawback, but the main thing is to be sure you won't have struggled in vain. Picture for a minute how it will be. I'll take you in my arms and the words I'll murmur in your ear will have such incredible importance that, if you heard them, you'd be transformed. And my face! My deepest wish is for you to see it then, since at that moment - and not a minute sooner - you'll recognize me. And you'll know whether you've found the person you believe you've been searching for during your journeys, the person for whom miraculously you came to this house - miraculously, but pointlessly. Think of the joy it would be! More than anything, you've desired to see her again. Arriving at this place, which is so hard to enter, you thought at last the goal was near and that the worst was behind you. Oh how you stuck with memory! It was extraordinary, I admit. Others totally forget their former life when they arrive. But you've kept a small memory inside, a weakened signal you've not allowed to fail. Of, Course, since you've allowed many memories to become indistinct, for me it's as if thousands of miles separated us. I can hardly make you out. It's difficult for me to imagine that one day I'll know who you are. But soon, very soon we'll finally be united. I'll open my arms and throw them around you - and I'll move with you through deep secrets. We'll lose - then find - each other. Nothing will ever come between us again. It's sad you won't be present for this happiness!"

-MAURICE BLANCHOT

"AMINADAB"

—Iago, Stehen murmured.

He lifted his gaze from the idle shells to the old man's stare.

—He knew what money was, Mr. Deasy said.

[...]

—I will tell you, he said solemnly, what is his proudest boast. *I paid my way.*

Good man, good man.

—*I paid my way. I never borrowed a shilling in my life.* Can you feel that? *I owe you nothing.* Can you?

The 2nd time we went to Mexico was consensual + legit ... both parties in accord. Tho we imagine our father had to give sum sort of monetary compensation to our mother to pay for our schooling + whatnot.

Even tho i was the youngest, our mother trusted me most w/ money. I used to be the 1 she'd give our quarterly tuition payment to (in cash—$100s, if not $1000s of dollars). She acted like it was her money but we all knew where it came from.

We had an hour-long commute to our school in Guadalajara, to the central bus station 1st where we switched to crowded city busses (the 118 to the 63, if memory still serves me). When we got to school + i reached into my back pocket for my wallet that had our tuition money + it wasn't there ... somewhere down the line i'd been pick-pocketed.

Our mother still gave me the tuition money to carry going forward—her reazon being that i'd learnt my lesson.

To this day i carry my wallet in my front pocket.

LOUD SNEDYETT [75]

Far away, on the other side of the solar system there is a planet half the size of ours called **Lubjaa**. *Like ours, this planet supports life. [It was formed smooth + the] atmosphere is made up mainly of helium. There's a warm, quickly evaporating ocean that fills the sky above the [...] flat fields of grass that stretch as far as the eye can see. These flat fields are populated by* **Snedyetts**.

Snedyetts look kind of like horses with [skewed] insect proportions. They are [hairless +] mostly a beige-gold color. They have no eyes [or ears] and do not speak [any language]. They [use a] form of sonar that [only tells] you when you are within five feet of another stumbling Snedyett. They are massive, weighing [(relatively)] as much as 3000 pounds. Because their planet is small, there isn't much of a gravitational force. [Their equivalent weight] on Lubjaa is more like 150 pounds. I should know, I do the weighing. My name is [G. ONADFERN] and I'm here to sell you some of the cheapest quality meat you can buy, [...] for next to nothing! The succulent meat of the Snedyett!! A healthy new source of white meat protein [...] and it's all natural! Order your (nitrogen [freeze-dried], for the long trip) Snedyett meat today!

This was Fernando's first street score, he is eleven. His father named him after Fernando Valenzuela, the baseball player. He left him and his mom when he was about six. Fernando has seen his father [twice] in the past six years, and both times he came in the house unexpected and drunk. Both times were on Christmas morning.

Fernando couldn't tell you on which year those Christmas days fell. He couldn't tell you much of anything—he is very slow. One might assume he is a drug addict ... but he's not. The only reason he's not is because he never has any money to [buy] drugs. Occasionally he'll sniff Toluene with his low-life homies, but that's about it.

But today his mom cashed a social security check, got wasted and passed out. So now Fernando has some money, and he is on the street copping. His homey Mark is helping him through [his 1st score]. Mark placed the call and told him where to wait, what kind of car to look for, what to say, etc. Mark asks to split [the score], Fernando figures this is a fair enough deal.

Fernando is going nowhere fast. He is like a snedyett — completely blind and blundering along, sputtering, occasionally growling or farting. No obstacles, nothing to run into except other people, and everyone is in the same situation.

July '79

Dear granny Nanny & granpa Cy,
How are you? It seems like only 26 weeks since we arrived here, I guess that's because I am enjoying myself so much. At first it was hard because I couldn't communicate with the Mexican children (I did take one year of Spanish but I am learning the language more each day.
I am really amazed at the size of my mother's house, and also all the plants. The city and the people (and the country) is so much different it is a pleasure to live among them and watch and learn about a different culture.
We pass our time making friends. And swiming, hiking →

```
A CUMULATING CULMINATION TO SAY NOW
TH  ACTUAL X-FAC - NOT N SS SAYRLY
HARD-WIR D S T - A SPANGL D ODYSS Y
OV RS  N - STARS GON  SOUTH TO AX HIS
M AT HO  → HUFFING + PUFFING TO BLOW
OUR HOUS  DOWN → D LINQU NT JUIC
BR  DS A GRIM F RRY TAIL TO MARRY
X-CONS BY → MULTI-TASKING WHILST
CASTLING TH N HORS  C3 TO D5 SINGING
JAJA ↑YUL  SHOOT Y R  Y  OUT↑ W/ A
POP-GUN COMO P DRO Y  L LOBO - CADA
CHARACT R R PR S NT D BY A DIFF R NT
MUS CAL INSTRUM NT → OUR MOM PUFFING
ON A PICCOLO - COUCH SURFING IN OUR
OWN HOM  WHIL  W  W R  BORN → BASSOON
DAD PR FURR D DISTILL D SPIRITS -
```

---

[75] Possible anagrams for *Loud Snedyett:* Yodeled Stunt, Odd Style Tune, Nod Style Duet, Duly Tested On, Ye Old Student, On Eldest Duty, El Snotty Dude, Odd Lusty Teen, Old Testy Nude, Let us Eddy Not, Sly Tented Duo, Toyed Slut Den, Tuned Toy Sled, No Slutty Deed, Nude Dot Style, Testy Nod Duel, Deny Toed Lust, Suddenly Tote, Stone Led Duty, Dusty Lot Need, Dotted Lye Sun, Stoned Duelty, Nested Duly To, Dyed Net Lotus, Oddly Seen Tut, Old Nutty Seed, Deny Told Suet, Needy Stud Lot, Nutty Eel Odds, Styled To Dune, Ed Donut Style, Sly To End Duet, Duly Noted Set, Ended Stoutly.

and traveling with our American car friends (Zieck, Nick, Evan, Caesar, Sara & Midi and the Perkins). [...]

We got some pets a few days ago. Derek got a kitten, we named Charlie, who is a good-looking cat and is very playful. Also we got a turtle (tortuga) and 43 (now 37) baby chickens, which we have to keep warm 24 hours a day, through storms and blackouts.

I am looking forward to maybe stopping in Menlo on the way back to Portland.

write soon

Love,
Kevin

```
PURA SUCKING VITA FOR S GUR  → NOT
IN T RPR TATION BUT TH  R AL OBJ T
-  VID NTLY W  R MIND HIM OF A LAK
H  US D TO FISH AT → W  M MB R IT
AS IF W  W R  TH R  → COMBIN D NOW
W/ CARP T STRINGS ROLL D W/ ZIG
ZAGS → TO TH   DG  OF TH  1Ø M T R
BOARD W/O A BRAK  IN CONTINU ITY →
TAK  TH  BLIND RS OFF HORS  S
TH Y G T DISTRACT D → DONT B LI V
FOR A S C IT CAN  V R B  MAS QU
INFORMATION → NAIV  TO B LI V  IN
JUSTIC  - AHORA GUILTY TIL PROV N
INNOC NT → PUFF TH  MAGIC DRAGON
LIV D BY TH  S A - FRAULICKING →
CLICK YOUR H LS X3 - TH  SHIP TO
TAK  U HOM  N DS NO RUTT R - R ADS
YOUR MIND FOR TO OWN H R - B TT R
TO SHOOT YOURS LF IN TH  FOOT THAN
LA MANO → A CROWD GATH RS TO GAWK
AT TH  FAK  BLOOD B ING FILM D ⏀
```

Fernando leans through the window of the avocado green Trans Am [Firebird]. He's out in the street now, no longer lingering in the [relative] safety of the trees. As the sun burns the back of his head, through his hair, Fernando feels a chill run up his spine. He looks at the other young Mexican behind the wheel of the car. He also seems nervous. He is glancing about, right hand on the stick shift, left on the wheel, twelve o-clock high. Holding the clutch in. Mariachi music is playing low on the radio. There is a comic book on the passenger seat, printed with black ink only, on brown [tissue] paper. The book is as thick as The Yellow Pages. It is folded open, on the page is a small red rubber ball the size of a raison [SIC].

"Here son, take this BEAN to the market! Get us a cow for this bean! Now don't delay boy! Off you go!" The young Mexican driving the car smiles after saying this. He's still pointing at the red rubber bean on the open comic book.

Fernando looked at the bean and stammered something to the extent of "later" and reached for the bean ... "bringing his right arm through the open window the suspect did reach into the vehicle and retrieve the narcotics amounting to exhibit A. Your honor, in light of my defendants clean record, and taking into consideration his age, I am asking that he be assigned to the state division for youth correctional services until a time set by the court has been....."

"That's a big **no can do** counsel, please be seated!" Judge [Bloom] was in a bad mood.

The court appointed attorney for Fernando was [Bella Cohen]. She is beautiful. Judge Bloom tells her so a lot. She left judge Bloom's house the night before without even taking a drink. She had come to a life changing decision [and when she told him] he got pissed off beyond belief. He tore his house apart for three hours before finally going down the street to the John Bull and picking up himself a homely city-college-local bar hound. He fucked her and made lots of noise doing it.

Bella returned to Bloom's house on Rockingham around three am. She also had been drinking, down the street at the Acapulco on Bundy. She had came back to apologize [...] felt a little lonely. When she got to the house she immediately heard the judge yodeling [...] as loud as he could. Beer hall music was blasting through the stereo. She began to cry. She got back in her car and drove off.

Now, the next day, she is standing before him, wearing her glasses, dressed like a lawyer. He looks like shit. His black robe is wildly crooked around his neck. The recesses around his eyes look like black voids, small round sunglasses that have been tattooed on to his face. He calls her up to his bench, leaning forward as he does.

"You fuckin bitch!" Judge Bloom says softly, breathing into her ear. She closes her eyes and begins to tremble, tears begin to pour from her eyes, she begins crying hysterically.

Fernando jumps up and over the large wooden desk in front of him [even tho] he has his hands and feet shackled together. In two hops he [arrives] at the bench. A bailiff near the jury stand raises his shotgun. In a [1 fell swoop] Fernando leaps clear to [...] the judge's desk, the Judge is shocked. Fernando kicks the Judge hard in the face and whips around.

"I have loved you a lifetime" Fernando says to Bella, staring her in the face.

Bella just stares back. Then a shotgun blast rips into Fernando's legs, the judge's face and shoulders and the back of Bella's head. There is a lot of screaming and running. It smells like gunpowder. The bailiff stands [in the aftermath], his shotgun aimed safely at the ground now.

"Oh shit! SSHHHHIIITTTT!!! Fuck! Billy! You've really done it now! SHIT! He says in disbelief.

Fernando is laughing, the thick canvas jumpsuit shielded the blast perfectly, like it was designed to do. There's a twenty minute recess as the judge and Miss Cohen go to clean up. Fernando is put back behind the table by the bailiff, they are laughing and joking about it, there appears to be no ill feelings.

The judge and Bella reconcile in the men's room. They go into a stall and Bella puts her feet into two Macy's bags so that any security guards (making a visual sweep under the stall doors) wouldn't see anything suspicious. At one point, when they are really into it, this guy comes in and takes the stall next to theirs. Bella by this time doesn't care if anyone is listening and starts to really howl. When she stops the old guy next to them slides a roll of toilet paper under the stall wall.

"Here" He says, "You might find this handy, ha ha ha".

"You , might need this!" She replies, kicking the roll back under with the Macy's bag.

"Dude! That is the most fucked up voice I've ever heard! What is wrong with you?!" The old man asks incredulously.

[Stephen] and [Georgina] laughed as they dressed. They stumbled out of the stall and said good-bye at the door to the bathroom. They laughed all the way back to the set.

→ → CUT TO FARMACY → U START T T RING + GRABBING A CARDBOARD CUT-OUT OF A DOCTOR FOR SUPPORT → U TOPPL TO TH FLOOR YOUR FAC CHALKY WHIT + CLAMMY → JUST HAPP N D TO B IN A FARMACY ↑M ANT TO B ↓ SAID MOM → TH Y FIGUR D IT WAS HYPOGLYC MIA – THAT U AT TOO MUCH MARZIPAN ALL AT ONC → FORM D IN HIS IMAG → GUMMY B ARS CONTAIN HORS HOOF – WHAT MAK S TH M GUMMY → DISASSOCIAT YOURS LF FROM ALL ASSOCIATIONS MAD UNTIL NOW → HAV U ANY WOOL BAA BAA BLACK SH P → BLOOMS ALIAS IS H NRY FLOW R → OR NRIQU FLOR → TH T MPO W PICK D A MAGNOLIA + U SAID WHATD U DO THAT FOR → OR WH NU SAID DONT PLAY STUPID U KNOW WHAT I M AN BUT I DIDNT R ALLY – MAYB I DID TH N BUT IN R TROSP CK NOT S CUR W/ MYS LF – WASNT ALGO DIC BUT A F LING – A R ACTION → ALGUN DIA YOULL R M MB R THIS U SAID → U DONT R ALIZ IT NOW BUT YOULL THANK M LAT R → GO AH AD K P UP TH PR T NS IN TH M AN TIM → [... at this point our transcription stops as we can't read what we wrote cuz we were writing insomniacally w/ closed eyes in the dark + forgot to flip the page so wrote over what we wrote):

FREAK WINDS BLOW ULYSSES + HIS CREW OFF COURSE

Within sight of home, GREED gets the better of the crew. While U naps, they rip open wind-bag thinking filled w/ $$$

Boats blown back, crew forced to ROW going FWD

In land of CANNIBALS[76], at least 3 of Ulysses's scouts are eaten! Cannibals sink all but U's ship

---

Ulysses escapes but is marooned on Sur-sea's isle, where his remaining men are turned into swine!

Bloom fails to place KEYES AD. Dedalus, however, meets no friction publishing foot + mouth disease art.

Initially sickened by any reminders of FOOD, Bloom eventually consumes cheese sandwich + glass of burgundy

---

EXPOSÉ: Bloom + Dedalus find each other in red light district!

Bloom nabs Dedalus's $$$ (but claims it's for safekeeping, 'for his own good')

CHAOS UNFOLDS:
Dedalus sees dead mother, freaks out + breaks brothel chandelier, gets into fight w/ soldier. Police arrive + disperse crowd. In Dedalus, Bloom sees his dead son.

While the WHITE brothers experienced their fair share of *sibling rivalry*, not once did they ever come to blows ... unlike their cousins who used to beat their own brothers senseless. The White brothers never even raised their voices against 1 another. Some may perceive this as lack of fraternal «closeness», a way to distance themselves from each other, while others see such in-fighting as counter-intuitive + non-productive.

«There is no difference between what a book talks about + how it is made.» —Deleuze + Guattari

---

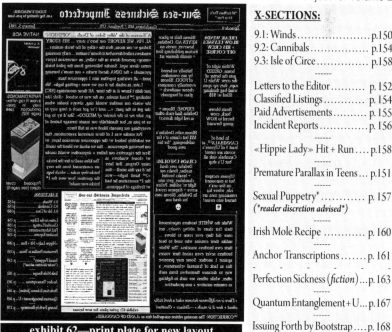
A Traverse of the Valley Sober of Death ... *OPINION*

AL FIN, WE REPORT our hero's story ... HIS STORY. Riding w/ our mom, thru the valley of the brick-makers ... windows rolled down but no importa ... early morning «smog» pressed down in the valle, an «inversion layer» como dicen aquí. Smoke billowing from the piled brick pyramids + the DINA diesel trucks + our mom's smoldering spliff—all swirling together into 1 oppressive haze.

Later, in rehab, he'd say we were «getting high» we just didn't know it at the time. All those mornings inhaling 2nd hand smoke, on the way to school. *«Ride like the wind»* our mother would sing, always louder when she got to the part: *«... and i've got such a long way to go, take me to the border of MEXICO»*. She'd try to get us to join in, but thankfully our innate teenage hatred of everything our parents liked was in full swing.

Pot smoke was 1 of these maternal associations, that we indelibly linked w/ the oppressive inversion layer, w/ our brewing depression ... tho we admit we liked the smell. Beat the cigarettes our father + stepmother would smoke w/ windows closed in rainy Oregon. But later he'd say this smell—this «2nd hand high»—was the 1st association he had w/ feelings of happiness.

> The kilns used to fire the bricks are constructed from the very bricks they make ... which begs the question: how were the 1st bricks ever made?

---

exhibit 62—print plate for new layout

CORRECTION: The morning edition misspelled this as «LAND OF CANNABIS».

[76] CORRECTION: The morning edition misspelled this as «LAND OF CANNABIS».

a.k.a. S.S. «CCD», where

CCD could stand either for:

- Charge-coupled device,
- Colony collapse disorder,
- Carbonate compensation depth
- Closed caption display

exhibit 63—our Molly in 2006, looking at the below view (from his original AEOLUS interpretation) from the gates of Trinity College (photo; author[77])

unidentified; circa 1893, Dublin, Ireland.

Trinity College, Dublin. (photo; author)

«The idea, Mr Bloom said, is the house of keys. You know, councillor, the Manx parliament. Innuendo of home rule. Tourists, you know, from the isle of Man. Catches the eye, you see. Can you do that?

[...]

Want to be sure of his spelling bee. Proof fever. Martin Cunningham forgot to view the unpar one ar alleled embarra two ars is it? double ess ment of a harassed pedlar while gauging au the symmetry of a peeled pear under a cemetary wall. Silly isn't it? Cemetery put in of course on account of symmetry.

[...]

Reads it backwards first. [...] Poor papa with his hagadah book, reading backwards with his fingers to me.»

Not sure who the unidentified couple is (above left) or where he got the photo from, but Leopold Bloom married Molly in 1888 so perhaps it is meant to be them? Their son Rudy was born in December of 1893 + died 11 days later, so if this is meant to portray Bloom + Molly, she'd be pregnant beneath the waist. Either that or the photo was taken right after Rudy died.

This is all brother-½ has to say about AEOLUS—just this 1 page embedded left. He forgot to mention that our (Irish-blooded) grandfather used to call us «windbags» ... as he'd toss silver dollars into the pool to keep us occupied.

Not sure how this episode in *Ulysses* parallels *The Odyssey*, except that Bloom is obstructed from placing his «house of keyes» ad w/2 crossed keys.

This is also the 1st time the destined winds have caused Bloom + Dedalus to [inadvertently] cross paths (tho no words are x-changed). It is also the 1st episode where u could say that the text is self-conscious of itself. Correlations establish thru the course of pompous, **long-winded** dialogue:

«What's in the wind, I wonder. Money worry.» This he says about the «*Cleverest* fellow» [italics mine—hidden reference to Everest? Or a clever rest?] + then says: «*Or again if we but climb the serried mountain peaks*.»

---

[77] Where the author now is the 2nd incarnation of Chaulky ... Chaulky, Jr. + this book is the 2nd derivative of *Ulysses*.

Location-wise, in the original 'SSES' 'SSES' this page (right) came after AEOLUS + before LESTROGENS (the Cannibals), but was labeleled «III INDULT INDUPLICATE».

[STET]

Our lives til this pt were mas o menos **geographically** intwined, minus the year or 2 he decided to return to Oregon. Until this pt tho no hay mucho free-will in our lives *geographically* speaking. We lived + went where we were told to go.

Parallax is the effect whereby the position or direction of an objet appears to differ when viewed from different positions, e.g., thru the viewfinder and the lens of a camera.

In watching the type-setters set the print, Bloom is reminded of his father reading «backwards» (in Hebrew). See the previous (or next, depending) episode 8.

Barns

A stomach pain

Sisters as1
fillers of2
forests cr3
minikin to4
leaders fo3
purpose so2
soulful as1

Substantiate your relation- to them, he imp- from where he was standing on the..

THE WHOLE TIME
he sat there
AND justewan-
ting of the h
THERESONEBUWAS
A didntwho who
A BOWG WHO WAGE
A BEAR WHO WASU
A WHOD ASHE

Relation-, Imp-, con- because of the pro- posit- in- in the se- and to possibly esc- the whole place and re- the whole thing or recon- it, at an-

I could'nt help but think that was how it was and no how could so stupid something Thats not what it... Dont say it... No, you listen... fucked!

Fig. 12–3. THE PLACE WAS SWINGING, I'm TALKING...

$\frac{H}{b}$	$\frac{D_i}{b}$	$\frac{A_i}{A_p}$	α°	β°	s	$Z = 0.5$
0.50	0.65	0.42	49.3	43.9	4980	25.1
0.44	0.61	0.37	45.2	40.6	4400	22.2
0.38	0.56	0.31	40.4	36.6	3680	18.5
0.31	0.53	0.28	35.1	31.9	3320	16.7
0.25	0.48	0.23	29.1	26.6	2730	13.8
0.13	0.44	0.19	15.7	14.1	2260	11.4
	0.42	0.18	0	0	2140	10.8

H; inter- over [x.] fact-

D; incon- with meta- sed- tri-sul-con- re- and sec-

[¢A.*] tr- and sci- et.

$A = \pi D^2/4$ First in a long line of Turners.

D – After four years she $D_{si} = 0.975\ D_{si}, D_e = 0.975\ D_{se}$

$D_{si} =$ "I do'nt know you ass- $a = 1200$ /, 366 m/

$D_{se} =$ Similar events did fol- $C_i = 0.33$

$A_e/A_i = 0.81$ **Try and seperate** $Z = \left(\frac{b}{D_i}\right)^2 \frac{s}{aC_i}$

Laminar flow insex as **S** control valve comes realeazed + died fluids mix analog to post-quantum entanglement. Exhibits a stoner's throw (D) to the XEROX plant in Palo Alto, where (unbeknownst to most) the desktop metaphor, paper paradigm + the mouse were developed. The CANON tires todos los días in the allocated bin, like hitting the broad side of a barn. «Confused resignation» are the mos adequate words to describe how come we skipped rocks at the ducks knowing full well our mid-pubescent arms couldn't reach. A meaningless gesture to say the least, but we knew full well on some level that a parallel lattice lay beneath the 'regular' grid. It came to us in a dream (http://5cense.com/14/378.htm):
I could zoom in as if seeing myself from above like google satellite [...] the ground [we tread] on was a different color

«—You're looking extra.
—Is the editor to be seen? [...]
—Bombast! The professor broke in testily. Enough of the inflated *windbag*! [italics mine]
—Peaks, Ned Lambert went on, *towering high on high, to bathe our souls as it were ...* [italics Joyce]»

[526 This is not a footnote, but a page number from whatever text he photocopied this book from. Sorry for the confusion.]

as deposi
outside th
versions.
L-Head
obviously
stated in C
chamber
considera
Valve
would see
to minim
losses (see
values of
ingly. Fut
expedient
Table
temporar

Valve Flo
In Vol
coefficient
described.
integratin
valve lift
Figure
valves in c
etry of th
spite of w
such modi
in flow co
those case
as well as
Similar
of some in
justified b
in exhaust

Valve Lift
Figure
diameter g
increase as
between n

Ha ha, i totally re-member this ... G's sister was hot, right? Surprised u didn't mention how Cat (our mom's friend w/ the huge tits) paid for the flat tires by fucking the mechanic in the custom van (w/ 'wall carpet') while we waited a fuera. Or how we got dragged across the urchin-covered rocks + left tracks of blood on the otherwise virgin sand ... or maybe that was another trip, un otra playa, it all gets jumbled in our head.

3/24/80

Dear grandpa Cal,

Yesterday we (Derek, his friend and his sister, and one of moms friends) got back from the beach. It was a long weekend so we went to the beach. But instead of staying at a hotel, we camped out on the beach.

After a 7 hour ride (which included two flat tires (at the same time) in the middle of nowhere) we got to the virtually unihabited beach. The girls slept in the custom van (with a bar, refrigerator, bed, and wall carpet), and the boys slept on the beach. During the day we swam in the ocean and went inland to get coconuts. We ate food like hot dogs and drank cokes.

When the ██ vacation was over most of us were sunburned, and dying to take a shower.

This Friday (28th) Easter vacation starts, I can't wait.

write soon
Kevin

[splice markup lip]

from a basketball ▢ 4th among of Mexico (there The tournament we beat Queretio and Monterrey. we had fun as always something stayed at (a friend with two rich American kids.

I dont thoroughly understand whats going on with the immigration problems but I do know that if we miss to much school without the signed papers (13 days) that we have to make up 6 months. I dont really want to stay here, and i dont want to move to a hippie community in the mountains.

write soon
Kevin

THESE ARE LIVING DOC-HUMENTS THAT CONT.INUE TO WRITE & UNWRITE EACH OTHER 24 YEARS AFTER THE ORIGIN-ATING EVENT ..

CAPABLE OF INTER-ACTING W/ NEW BODIES & TEXTS. SPLICING FOOTAGE FROM 2ND CORTÈGE FEEDS .. SENDING AN S.O.S. TO OUR ANCESTORS.

+ there were discolored bands of landslides. So i tried to retreat to where the ground seemed more stable. I was climbing thru these sort of bunkers covered w/ plastic, like makeshift tents or a long hallway in Mongolian yurt style. The details of the rocks + landscape (enclosed in the plastic tarp) were very vivid + it occurred to me [in the dream] this could only be the case cuz i was recycling images that i'd seen in real life + piecing them together, but changing the context. I recognized where the original images were from—some alpine mountainous place where maybe i had once rock-climbed. I came to an enclosed hut w/ no exit, poked my head out thru a sort of belfry + could see i was on top of a high peak ... it occurred to me that a summit was like a dead end ... not something to aspire to, but something to retreat from.

I retreated back into another room, some sort of Chinese store w/ all these trinkets. There were a few people telling me to be quiet, pointing to some sign (that was in Chinese).

3/11/79 But this 1 spinning wind-chime thing seemed irresistible, so i spun it + a lever swung out + kept ringing a bell over + over until it was a continuous tone + then i started chanting «ooooommmmmm» in the same pitch + the salespeople were trying to get me to be quiet, but only cuz they were jealous that i was able to get in tune on the 1st try.

[...] + then she goes on to compare various writers w/ topographical features, such as Deleuze to a summit + Derrida to a pothole, which we take exception with.

These were the days (at least in cartoons) where messages carried the latent capability of self-destructing 10 seconds after they were played back. ~~The end of this year was the 1st time our father attempted suicide (in the same way he'd eventually succeed ... by sticking a garden hose in the exhaust pipe).~~

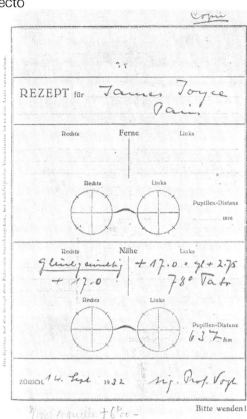

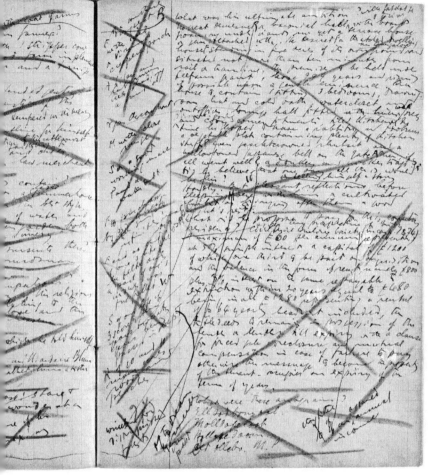

exhibit 64 (above)—Joyce's eyeglass prescription
exhibit 65 (left)—from Joyce's used *Ulysses* notes

«The accumulation of *anno Domini.*»

Our dayz now under the influence of magnetic resinance ... heard 1st on 8-track, often warped to play backwords on the wrong channels, bleeding into the neighboring track, splicing togather ...

The lines of demarcation rebound rite around every other generational income, where the ∠ incidence = ∠ refraction ... round the time The Knack, Blondie + M topped the Pop Muzik charts, ... «*Radio, video, boogie with a suitcase, [...] , try some, buy some, fee-fi-fo-fum.*» Or per Burroughs: **«Remember that you can separate yourself the "Other Half" from the word. The word is spliced in with the sound of your intestines and breathing with the beating of your heart. The first step is to record the sounds of your body and start splicing them in yourself. [...]. Splice your body sounds in with anybody or anything. Start a tapeworm club and exchange body sound tapes. Feel right out into your nabor's intestines and help him digest his food. *Communication must become total and conscious before we can stop it.*»**

Hit over the head w/ a 4" x 2". Channeling right + left w/ ⅛" bleeds. Foot + mouth («‹on our shore he never set it›»). Cleverly rested. Winding the crinkled tape w/ a #2 pencil. «Followed by the whining dog he walks on towards hellsgates. In an archway a standing woman, bent forward, her feet apart, pisses cowily....» The hiss of the tape fading as it's eaten ... then spit out.

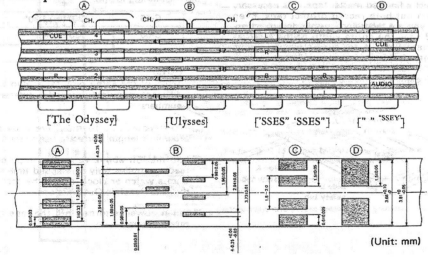

LESTROGENS

LEST.

24 hours, a day.

[This page (minus this inset + exhibit 66 to the right) is the extent of his «LESTROGENSs» episode (think he meant to say «LAESTRYGONIANS»?). i.e. just the text: «24 hours, a day.» + stray traces that rubbed off from the facing page (in our version).

To recapitulate: *Ulysses* takes place in 24 hours. *The Odyssey* spans 10 years. Our story spans 30 years.

The giant Laestrygonians cannibalize the scouts + throw boulders + sink 11 (of 12) of Ulysses' ships. The land of the Laestrygonians is believed to be modern-day Sicily. «Rome wasn't built in a day», as the adage goes. About Rome, Joyce said: «Rome reminds me of a man who lives by exhibiting to travellers his grandmother's corpse.» Brother-½ wasn't crazy about Rome either. Nostro ½ vissuto lì per 3 anni innamorato.

When our stepmother started monitoring his alcohol consumption + checking for bottles, our father took to drinking his LISTERINE®. Originally developed as a surgical antiseptic, Listerine is 1 of the 1ˢᵗ examples of a now common marketing trend: campaigns that invent the very problem the product is alleged to solve (i.e. **bad breath**).

«J.J. O'Molloy resumed, moulding his words:
– He said of it: that stony effigy in frozen music, horned and terrible, of the human form divine, that eternal symbol of wisdom and of prophecy which, if aught that the imagination or the hand of sculptor has wrought in marble of soultransfigured and of soultransfiguring deserves to live, deserves to live."»]

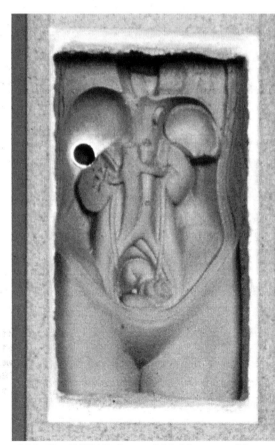

exhibit 66—(DETAIL from exhibit 25 on page 60)
"Untitled" 1991 (particle board, formica, belt (not shown, colored silicon, 41" x 7 ¼" x 8 ¼")

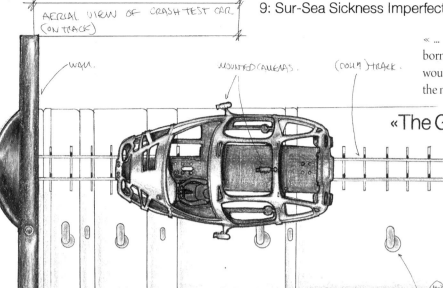

AERIAL VIEW OF CRASH TEST CAR.
(ON TRACK)

WALL.

MOUNTED CAMERAS.

(COLT) TRACK.

FLOOR MARKINGS.

exhibit 67—sketch (1 of 2—BEFORE) made for a hypothetical crash test

« ... these wounds formed the key to a new sexuality, born from a perverse technology. The images of these wounds hung in the gallery of his mind, like exhibits in the museum of a slaughterhouse." — J.G. Ballard, *Crash*

«The Gentle Art of Advertisement»

I.e... it is what it is ... at least when it comes to genre or how to file it away ... a scrambled remix of remixes ensues, a re-ordering of confluence not nearly in the original order. It's all fuzzy + we're admittedly not sure the proper sequence of childhood events ... until the point when it all converged ... came to a head ... *(« where weve h when* ···≫) ... eventually (soon) when our father died ... in his car parked in our garage back in Portland ... our mother was off somewhere at the beach near Ixtapa/Zihuatanejo. I was alone in Guadalajara (brother-½ had already split back to Portland) ... well not quite alone, i was baby-sitting some random kid, a friend of my mom's who was also off gallivanting somewhere in Mexico. Our house somehow became the daycare for all the kids of debaucherous single mothers who were off partying. *... On a Collision Course*

Between the Fairway + the Rough

What we forgot to mention in the SISTER WE NEVER HAD episode (#5), is that it's indeed possible that we did at 1 point have a sister ... 1 time we were driving by a golf course in California + our mother casually said «oh, that's where i was raped once». It was a golf course we knew well cuz we used to fish in a creek that ran thru the front 9 + when golfers would hit balls in our area we'd pocket them + play dumb .. + then sell them back to them later. The hole (#5) our mother was pointing out was a particularly tricky par-5 double-dog-leg w/ some sand traps at the corners. Evidently she was 15, on a date w/ some older frat dude. This segued casually into the sidenote about how she had an abortion as a consequence ... the 1ˢᵗ we'd heard of this.

Instant Karma

I got the call that our father died ... i think i told the story elsewhere or will tell it later if not ... how our mom couldn't be bothered cutting her beach trip short so i had to figure out how to get to Portland on my own (which was problematic since i was 15 + needed permission to travel internationally + 1 parent was dead + the other AWOL at the beach). Anyway, the funny part is that while i was flying solo back to Portland for our father's funeral, our mother got into a bad car accident + totalled her car. She said it wasn't her fault, that she was driving along on some desolate highway, going the speed limit + some drunk cowboy going 150 KPH rear-ended her. When she called to tell us this we could only laugh.

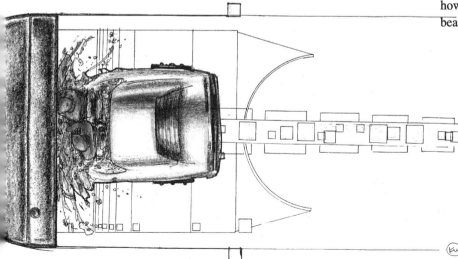

CRASH TEST CAR HITTING WALL. (W/ TWO TEST DUMMIES)
(AERIAL VIEW).

exhibit 68—sketch 2 (DURING IMPACT) of crash test

«Deep assignments run through all our lives; there are no coincidences.» — J.G. Ballard, *The Atrocity Exhibition*

... as usual, we're getting ahead of ourselves ... until this point our lives had been relatively devoid of trauma ... before (as he said on pg 111 when he was dosed w/ DMT (or was it MDMA?)) his «young mind was absolutely tweaked.»

---

accident (n.) **1** an unfortunate incident that happens unexpectedly and unintentionally, typically resulting in damage or injury: *he had an accident at the factory* | • a crash involving road or other vehicles, typically one that causes serious damage or injury: *the whole family was killed in a car accident.* | • informal used euphemistically to refer to an incidence of incontinence, typically by a child or an animal. | **2** an event that happens by chance or that is without apparent or deliberate cause: *the pregnancy was an accident* | • the working of fortune; chance: *my faith is an accident of birth, not a matter of principled commitment* | **3** Philosophy (in Aristotelian thought) a property of a thing that is not essential to its nature.

---

injury (n.) late 14c., "harm, damage, loss; a specific injury," from Anglo-French *injurie* "wrongful action," from Latin *injuria* "wrong, hurt, injustice, insult," noun use of fem. of *injurius* "wrongful, unjust," from in- "not, opposite of" (see in- (1)) + *ius* (genitive *iuris*) "right, law" (see jurist).

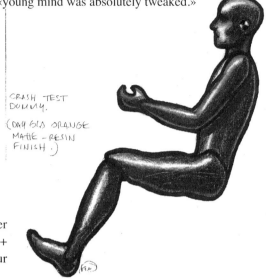

CRASH TEST DUMMY.

(DAY OLD ORANGE MATTE - RESIN FINISH.)

Seems a good a time as any to tell u another incidental story our mother told us, about how we were conceived. Evidently she took a safety pin + poked holes in our father's condoms. Technically, that doesn't make our existence an accident, but surely qualifies as an act of deception.

exhibit 69 (below)—sketch from early notebook (c. 1980)　　**exhibit 70 (above)—sketch from notebook (circa 1995)**

«Lovely forms of woman sculped Junoian. Immortal lovely. And we stuffing food in one hole and out behind: chyle, blood, dung, earth, food: have to feed it like stoking an engine.» Joyce also writes: «Why have women such eyes of witchery?» Our father also said as much when comparing a sea anemone to female anatomy (see page 74). Our father never got in a car accident (despite all the drunk driving) + neither did our grandfather + neither did brother-½.

Overdoses Kill More Americans Than Car Accidents: CDC

In 2008, for the first time in nearly 30 years, more people died of poisoning than in car crashes. Poisoning is now the leading cause of injury death, and 90 percent of poisonings were caused by drugs.

He never did buy into all the hippy new age shit in our mom's library, but he did read the Carlos Castaneda books + also *The Autobiography of a Yogi*. Seems this is where he 1st got it into his young mind this notion of a monk-type that renounces everything + lives out his life in a cave up high in the Himalayas. This hermetic cave high up in the mountains became replacement therapy for the absence of a regular «home».

After getting blown off course cuz his greedy men ripped open the wind-bag + then after 11 of 12 of his ships were sunk by the cannibals, the 1 remaining ship + crew end up next on the island of the nymph-sorceress, Circe (pronounced /*sur-sea*/).

exhibit 71—another sketch from a figure drawing class he took

« LYNCH

So that?

STEPHEN

(*Looks behind*) So that gesture, not music not odour, would be a universal language, the gift of tongues rendering visible not the lay sense but the first entelechy, the structural rhythm.

LYNCH

Pornosophical philotheology. Metaphysics in Mecklenburgh street! »

exhibit 72 (below)—cave on the island of Ponza, 2012 (photo: author)
Per Wikipedia: «Ponza is also suspected to be the island of Aeaea in Homer's *Odyssey*, as the island of the Circe the sorceress, where her cave or grotto was.»

[Continued from page 134:]

EGON SCHIELE, PUPPETS & SEX DE SADE

Egon Schiele drew the human body with the knowledge of a cannibal, like someone who not only knew how to represent it, but how it feels and tastes. One characteristic inherent in most of his (non) portraits is lifeless doll-like representations of people engaged in some kind of sexually unaware repose.

The reason why I am bringing Schiele into this discussion of Sadein themes (inherent) in the work of the Quay brothers is because i feel that Schiele's representation of people as inanimate and doll-like is [his way] to discuss human sexuality (and not, for example, some statement about the impossibility of capturing anything but the physicality of subject on paper). Schiele represents an inaccessibility (in the glazed over eyes, lifeless limbs, etc.) in his figures as the state of sexuality, [when] people [are] able to become sexual. To callous themselves from activity that could be damaging to the psyche. This [physically withdrawn] state in which one passively views the world—shocked into regression—seems to be the state of mind De Sade longs to experience constantly, and puppets—as inanimate objects—experience through the projections we place on them.

CIRCE

I IMAGINE IT AS IF I SAW IT MYSELF. THERE IS A LITTLE MEXICAN BOY LEADING HIS FLOCK ACROSS THE PERIFERICO.[78] SUDDENLY OUT OF NOWHERE A BLUE TRUCK SLAMS INTO HIM AMID THE USELESS BLARRING OF THE HORN. THE TRUCK COMES TO A STOP SIDEWAYS , WITH ITS FRONT END IN THE GULLEY. THE LIFELESS BODY OF THE BOY SLOWLY ROLLS OF THE HOOD AND HITS THE GROUND WITH A SOFT THUD. THE GOATS HAVE SCATTERED ACROSS THE FIELD BOARDERING THE ROAD. THE WOMAN IN THE TRUCK IS TRYING TO MANEUVER THE TRUCK BACK ONTO THE ROAD WHILE SCREAMING AT HER NOW HYSTERICAL CHILDREN. THERE IS A LARGE CRACK ON THE RIGHT SIDE OF THE WINDSHIELD. THE BOYS HEAD IS TWISTED AROUND SO HE IS FACING HIS ASS.

CLAIR WAS A FRIEND OF MY MOMS. A MIDDLE AGED HIPPY RAISING HER CHILDREN BY HERSELF IN SOUTHERN MEXICO. I HATED MY HOMELIFE SO I USED TO STAY ANYWHERE I COULD. FOR A WHILE I STAYED AT CLAIR'S. SHE HAD A RANCH HOUSE OUTSIDE OF THE CITY WITH LOTS OF ANIMALS, SPACE AND FOOD FROM THE STATES. THERE WHERE HARDLY ANY RULES IN THE HOUSE AND CLAIR SEEMED TO BE QUITE GENEROUS. SHE WAS VERY POPULAR WITH MY OLDER BROTHER AND HIS FRIENDS, MAINLY BECAUSE SHE SUPPLIED THEM WITH DRUGS, AND A PLACE TO TAKE THEM. ONE DAY A FRIEND OF CLAIR'S WARNED HER THAT THE POLICE WHERE LOOKING FOR HER. APPARENTLY ONE OF THE MEXICAN BOYS THAT HAD BEEN OVER AT THE HOUSE (WITH MY BROTHER AND HIS

CIRCE

HIS FACE FROZE ONE LAST TIME IN A DISTORTED GRIMACE OF THE PAIN TO COME THAT END TO COME A PAINFUL END THAT WOULD EFFECT HIM ALWAYS RETURNING LONGING FOR THE CHANCE TO CHANGE A STEP ALTER A MOVE MAKE A DIFFERENT CHOICE ACCOMPLISH ALL THE THINGS HE WANTED TO DO ALL THE THINGS HE CANNOT DO JUST BECAUSE HE DID NOT ASK HIS FATHER SAID AVOID THE PERIFERICO THAT DANGEROUS ROAD FULL OF HOLES OVER WHICH POPEAS SPEED WILDLY IN THEIR CARRIBES BECAUSE THEY KNOW IF THEY HIT SOME POOR SUCKER LIKE ME THAT THEY CAN TAKE CARE OF IT WITH A PHONE CALL TO THEIR COUSIN (THE CHIEF OF POLICE)[79] AND SOME MONEY AND MAYBE THEY WILL NOT BE ABLE TO GO OUT TO CHAPALA FOR A WEEK MAYBE THEY WILL HAVE TO DRIVE THEIR MOMS CAR WHILE THEY GET THE DENT TAKEN OUT OF THEIRS MAYBE THEY WILL PAY MY FATHER AND HE WILL GET A FARM OF HIS OWN AND BE HAPPY WITH MOM THEY WILL BE GLAD EXCEPT ON ALL SAINTS DAY THEY WILL FEEL BAD FOR A LITTLE WHILE BUT THEN THEY WILL FORGET WHEN THEY SEE THE WHOLE FAMILY IN THE YARD OF THE NEW HOUSE ON LAKE CHAPALA MAYBE DAD WILL

I totally member this «Clair» woman (her real name was Michelle) ... that Kevin equates to CIRCE. This story is true pretty much as he tells it (w/some embellishments of detail ... like i dont member the bit about the goats). 1 time (again, when our mother wasn't home), the DEA + federal police came to our door asking if we knew of her whereabouts (after she killed the kid + left he country).

Our older brother totally fell under Michelle (=Claire=Circe)'s spell (she used to hook him + his friends up w/ free drugs + prostitutes) but we didn't realize the influence she had over brother-½ (or the creepy voyeurism + possible seduction).

She had 2 kids that were a few years younger than us, that she used to also give drugs to. Last i heard the son joined the army + the daughter became a nun. We tried googling to find out what happened to them, but our search results didn't provide any clues.

---

[78] The *Periferico* is the perimeter road that circumnavigates Guadalajara. Altho it was a more round-a-bout + longer (as the crow flies) way, we often referred to it as a short-cut (depending on traffic).

[79] *Nepotism* figures prominently in Joyce's take on the previous AEOLUS episode ... while Bloom (despite his pathetic grovelling) can't get his ad published, the red carpet is rolled out for Dedalus (who gets his boss's paper on foot + mouth disease published no questions asked) ... not only that, the editors + Dedalus go out arm-in-arm for a drink after. Nepotism—the art of schmoozing + networking—was a preoccupation of our brother-½ artist ... + also a source of self-conscious insecurity as most of the art production gigs he got in his later film-making years were cuz our cousin was a «famous» director.

CIRCE

FRIENDS) TOLD SOMEONE ABOUT THE DRUGS. THATS WHEN CLAIR FREAKED OUT, GOT HER TWO KIDS OUT OF SCHOOL, AND RACED OFF TOWARDS HER HOUSE SO THAT SHE COULD GET SOME OF HER BELONGINGS, AND ESCAPE BACK TO TEXAS. SHE RAN OVER THE KID ON THE WAY, AND LATER, AFTER FINDING THE BOY'S FATHER, ATTEMPTED TO PAY HIM OFF. HE DECLINED THE MONEY SAYING THAT MONEY WOULD NOT BRING BACK HIS SON.

I HAD GROWN DISENCHANTED WITH CLAIR (AND HER HOUSE) A FEW WEEKS BEFORE THIS HAPPENED.

ONE MORNING, AFTER ~~SPENDING~~ *I spent* THE NIGHT IN HER GUEST ROOM, CLAIR TOLD ME THAT SHE HAD LOOKED AT MY BODY AS I WAS SLEEPING. SHE TOLD ME THAT MY "BROWN PUBIC HAIRS (WERE) CUTE". THIS INCIDENT COUPLED WITH SOMEONE ON MUSHROOMS GIVING ME A BAD HAIRCUT , HELPED ME TO DECIDE THAT I SHOULD RECONSIDER MY RELATIONSHIP TO WHAT COULD BE CALLED HOME.

(Molly ± Circe = Michelle)

CIRCE

REFUSE THE MONEY AND BE WORSE OFF THEN HE WAS BEFORE NO FARM AND NO ONE TO TAKE CARE OF THE GOATS AND HELP MOM I CANNOT IMAGINE THAT HE WOULD REFUSE AN OFFERING OF MONEY HE NEEDS IT TOO BAD AND MOM IS SO SICK IT WOULD BE CRUEL OF HIM NOT TO ACCEPT ANYTHING THAT WOULD MAKE IT EASIER ON HER AND THE REST OF THE FAMILY BUT THEN AGAIN MAYBE DAD IS TOO PROUD OF A[80] MAN TO BOUGHT IT WOULD DEFINATELY MAKE THOSE POPEAS[81] THINK TWICE ABOUT THE LAND WORKERS

---

[80] Think he meant to say: «Dad is too proud of a man to *be* bought ... »
[81] «*Popeas*» (or *popees* or *popis* as you might phonetically say it in Spanish (never saw it written)) was a slang word poor village kids in Jalisco used to refer to rich kids from Guadalajara. Most of the problems we had w/ Mexican kids (i.e. that picked fights w/ us etc.) were w/ 'popeas'.

Additional notes from an alternate version of CIRCE from his notes (where he actually refers to her by her real name):

I had a few options for avoiding mom, the [usual] was staying at someone else's house. For a [while] I used to go to Michelle's house [... until I got sick of dealing w/ her.]

Lots of weird thing happened in that house (things I later came to understand involved the use of psychedelic drugs and [...] bizarre sexual behavior). Michelle's kids were really annoying and the house always smelled of dog shit, but the reason i [finally] stopped hanging out there is because one morning (after I slept in the guest room) Michelle told me that she had "looked at my body" when I was asleep, and that she thought my pubic hair was "cute". That, and having someone on mushrooms give me a haircut [were my cues to leave].

[...]

I continued to hear [gossip] about Michelle. My mom didn't like her that much anymore, so I got to hear the kind of bad things usually reserved for adult ears. My older brother and his friends used to spend a lot of time at Michelle's. I guess they liked all the drugs she gave them and the opportunity to trip out in her secluded ranch.

One day Michelle was told that the police were looking for her— seems a group of Mexican friends of my brother had told someone about the things going on at her house and the federales (mafia/police) were after her. She freaked out and [... RECOUNTING OF HIT + RUN STORY].

Michelle is back in Mexico now (after waiting until thing quieted down), completely insane. Her daughter is a born again Christian ... she seems pretty well-adjusted considering.

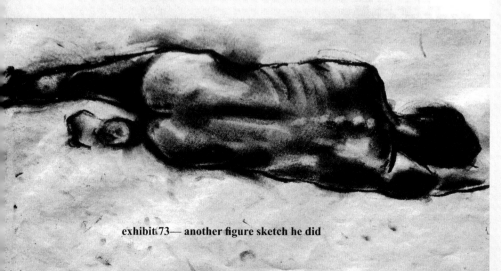

exhibit 73— another figure sketch he did

Holy Moly

The name of the herb that Ulysses gives his men that have been turned into pigs by Circe is called *moly* ... not to be confused w/ 'molly,' a pure form of MDMA (3,4-methylenedioxy-N-methylamphetamine) or 'ecstasy' (a.k.a. 'E' or 'XTC'). Moly is the anti-dote to the vixen-witch Circe's spell, that turns his men-cum-pigs back to plain men. No coincidence that Bloom's wife is named Molly ... his antidote, his drug?

Molly Hatchet

... is the name of a southern rock band our older brother listened to in his stoner's den (when he wasn't at Michelle's house). They derived their name from a prostitute who allegedly mutilated and decapitated her clients. Their hit song was «Flirtin' with Disaster» whose chorus went like this:

Flirtin' with disaster,
y'all damn sure know what I mean
You know, the way we run our lives,
it makes no sense to me

Maria del sur's Mole Poblano

12 dried ancho chiles
12 dried guajillo chiles
30 mulatto chiles
6 dried pasilla chiles
1 chipotle chile
4 T.spoons sesame seeds
1 t. spoon whole star anise
1 t. black peppercorns
1 t. ground coriander seeds
½ t. whole cloves
1 t. dried thyme
½ t. dried marjoram
3 dried bay leaves, crumbled
1½-inch stick cinnamon, broken into pieces
2 cups corn oil
7¼ cups pig stock
½ cup skin-on almonds
½ cup raw shelled peanuts
⅓ cup hulled pumpkin seeds (pepitas)
⅔ cup raisins
1 cup prunes
1½ plantains, sliced into ¼-inch pieces
2 slices white Bimbo bread
2 stale corn tortillas
2½ onions, halved, roasted + chopped
10 cloves garlic, roasted
10 tomatillos, husked, roasted + quartered
3 tomatoes, roasted + quartered
1 cup chopped chocolate (Ibarra)
⅓ cup filings from a pig's hoof
2 spring chickens (guttted + quartered)
4 t. sugar + more to taste
Lard, as needed
Sea salt, to taste

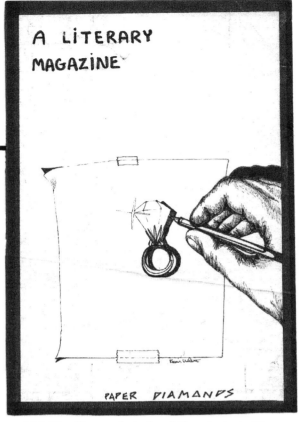

exhibit 74— It seems he had ambitions to start a lit mag called PAPER DIAMONDS (circa 1980)

From http://5cense.com/13/rejoyce.htm:

In *Ulysses*, this section is all about **food** ... Bloom [walks] around Dublin trying to find a place to eat, obsessing over [food]. In particular, meat (the cannibal connection). [...] & simultaneously disgusted ... Bloom stops in 1 place & gets so [grossed out] he leaves. *See the animals feed.* [...] *Bitten off more than he can chew. Am I like that? See ourselves as others see us.* [...] *The smells of men. His gorge rose. Spaton sawdust, sweetish warmish cigarette smoke, reek of plug, spilt beer, mens' beery piss, the stale of ferment.* The latter a good description of what our hot Tibetan beer tasted like last night. Bloom retreats in horror. *Eat or be eaten. Kill! Kill!* [...] It goes beyond just food: *I wouldn't be surprised if it was that kind of food you see produces the like waves of the brain the poetical. For example, on of those policemen sweating Irish stew into their shirts; you couldn't squeeze a line of poetry out of him. Don't know what poetry is even.* [...] Towards the end of the section he helps a blind guy cross the street & in the aftermath reflects on what that must be like ... interesting in light of Joyce's own **eye** problems. *What dreams would he have, not seeing?* [...] And even tho Bloom is meat crazy ... he ends up famously eating a gorgonzola cheese sandwich at Davy Byrne's ... downed w/ burgundy wine. Which seems to suggest taking **communion** ... & in his wanderings to find food he thinks he sees his name in an evangelist sign that says «blood of the lamb» ... suggesting Bloom is being prepared for sacrifice (which eventually comes to fruition in the Cyclops section [see the previous episode #8]) ...

♩♪ "Canta no llores" ♪

NEWS ANCHOR

To our carnal knowledge, he didn't have any love interests around this time ... not that took human form. This is our brother-½ that is, that we are speaking of ... our father we've lost track of at this point, immersed as we are in the culture of Mexico.

(federale's secretary take notes)

TRANSLATOR

You didn't notice our ... cómo se dice, héroe?

NEWS ANCHOR

Hero.

TRANSLATOR

You didn't notice our macho hero drifting thru the bar on his way to his escapade with Molly?

NEWS ANCHOR

No.

TRANSLATOR

Ay yi yi, so basically the cuckolded Bloom is being seduced by the music of the elder Dedalus & the barmaids while Molly is home cheating on him (somewhat with his knowledge)? ¡Qué atrocidad!

NEWS ANCHOR

I guess you could put it that way.

(federales whisper amongst themselves. A sketch is pulled from an envelope labeled DIAGRAMAS DE LA ESCENA DEL CRIMEN)

TRANSLATOR

How do you explain this? (showing him exhibit #75)

#16
→ See episode

NEWS ANCHOR

(Laughs) This comes later, this was a sketch he did for ███████. As a guest STAND-IN (for ████████) we spent quite a bit of time laying in this bed, once it was built. We even fell asleep in it 1 time, under the bright lights with the crew all around us. Manuel Pig came to me in a dream ... or i should say his rendition of Rita Hayworth (which i was reading at the time) ... or maybe it was Kiss of the Spider Woman?

EXHIBICIÓN # 75

BLACK BED (ROUND)

LIGH PANELS (BLACK) OUTSIDE BLACK BED RIG.

(WHITE) LIGHT PANELS.

- SIDE VIEW - EXTENDED UP.

(RAISED) BED.   MR. STITCH

LIGHT PANELS.
(LOWERED)

36"   SIDE VIEW.
- WITH; LIGHT PANELS LOWER
- BED RAISED.

CONSTRUCTION
COVERED IN (FLAT)
BLACK MATERIAL.

MR. STITCH.

@ 25m

@ 30"

SIDE CUT AWAY VIEW.

@ 4"

BLACK FABRIC OVER FORM (FOAM)

LIGHT PANELS THAT RAISE AND LOWER INDEPENDENTLY.

(KW)

Perfection Sickness

sand, her lower leg is red and rapidly swelling. ▆▆ has no idea what to do.

Steven

"We need to tie off her leg to keep the poison from traveling up it! Where going to have to use her top!" He says to ▆▆.

All three of them are wearing only bathing suits and sandals, it takes ▆▆ a couple of seconds to see the reasoning of the strangers bizarre request.

Steven

"C'mon! The poison is moving up her leg!"

▆▆▆▆ seems to be losing consciousness, ▆▆, with a conflicting range of emotions, quickly undoes her bikini top and hands it to Steven.

Wasting no time Steven ties her top tightly around he leg, just below the knee.

Steven

"Lets take her down the beach, there is a restaurant about a mile down, there are some people there who might know how to help her.

▆▆▆▆

"A mile! Are you kidding?'

Steven

"Its where the nearest road is, the only civilization around this part of the coast!"

▆▆▆▆

"What about the village... Rar-toon?"

Steven

"The restaurant *is* Rar-toon."

▆▆▆ and Steven carry ▆▆▆ down the beach. The whole way ▆▆▆▆▆ is delusional, crying hysterically, cursing and occasionally screaming.

EXT. DAY.

It takes them fifteen minutes to reach a large cement structure set off the beach within some palm trees. When they get there all three of them are red and covered in sweat. ▆▆▆▆▆'s lower right leg has swollen to twice its normal size and has turned a dark brown color, her rantings have been reduced to a continual hysterical sobbing.

There is a group of native women, wearing brightly colored saris sitting down in

**exhibit 76— page from draft version of PERFECTION SICKNESS
before he adapted it from screenplay to short story**

NEWS EDITOR/ANCHOR
(*reading embedded documents*)

Not only am i the 1 who (IRL) got stung by a stonefish (in Aitutaki, in the Cook Islands), but i wrote a similar story (that i called «Threshold Wound» (it remains unpublished)) based on the experience, about a woman that steps on a stonefish + her bikini top is the only thing she has to use as a tourniquet ... actually, in my version she uses the bikini BOTTOM, since she is reef-walking topless.

EXTERNAL INVESTIGATOR

Did it bother you that your brother appropriated this scene?

EDITOR/CO-AUTHOR

I can't lie ... at the time it bothered me some that he "stole" it, but now i just take it as a compliment. We're working towards the same goal after all... tho i'm not sure where he is going in his version of this particular story or what her being stung by a stonefish has to do w/ anything.

---

[82] My alma mater.

[TELEMACHUS] and his new bride [CIRCE] meet Stephen in a [remote] section of the north coast of Papau New Guinea, where they [are] on honeymoon. Stephen is the lone westerner in the fishing village, with nothing but "fifteen fishermen, [their] eighteen homes, their nineteen wives and their fifty six children." [He has an extra cabana that he rents out].

When they meet, Stephen talks down to them from the hammock in his [home-made] shack. The twenty-foot posts that hold up the [thatched roof] are greased and made with a type of tree that [leave masses of] toxic slivers on anyone who tries to climb its trunk. There is also a huge wild boar with red-painted tusks tied up between the four posts. [Stephen gives them the lay of the land + points the way to their cabana.]

Later [at low tide], they see Stephen out on a coral reef that is just barely under water. As Circe [wades out] on the reef towards Stephen [to ask] him where the nearest restaurant is, she [steps on] a stone fish. Her foot swells up instantly and she begins to have seizures, [the] intense pain turns to panic as the poison starts to get into her bloodstream. Stephen uses Circe's bikini top to tie off her leg just above the wound. Telemachus seems uneasy with this.

They carry Circe back to a restaurant about a mile down the beach. On the way Circe starts becoming delusional, saying bizarre (obscene) things. The restaurant is the only civilization for a hundred miles. It turns out that the bus to the nearest city (more than a hundred miles away) is not scheduled to return for a week, and none of the locals have a car (that works).

Stephen stays with Telemachus in the restaurant throughout the afternoon and night as Circe recovers. As they wait they talk and drink a local form of beer. Telemachus tells him about meeting Circe at UC Santa Cruz[82] while studying marine biology, says that "he still cannot believe he married a woman as beautiful and intelligent as Circe". Stephen tells Telemachus about the beliefs [+

myths] of the local people [...]. His views of this most primitive of societies [underlies] his pessimism of Western societies. [But Stephen seems almost naïve] in his idealized descriptions of the primitive culture. He assures Telemachus that Circe will be OK, that the locals know how to deal with this kind of thing.

At about three in the morning Stephen checks his watch and excuses himself, tells Telemachus that if Circe gets better before the bus returns, [that they should come] visit. [...]

Three days later Circe is sufficiently recovered and they make their way up the beach to visit Stephen. They have no trouble finding the place, but now the boar tusks are bright green.

["Weren't these *red* before?" Telemachus asks.

Stephen doesn't even look up from his laptop. "They've always been green," he says.] Stephen spends [most of his morning] "working" on his [laptop] and cellular phone. He has two large solar panels on the roof of his hut that generate [enough] electricity. He sleeps most of the afternoon in his hut, coming out in the early evening to eat, and then stays up all night with Telemachus and Circe. He tells Telemachus that he is "working on some kind of artificial intelligence experiment", ... refers to it as "[quantum] information".

[After a few drinks it comes out that he works for] some kind of think tank, sponsored by the U.S. government. He is "hiding out" because he says his "preferred arrangement with the world is to communicate solely through invisible waves"[83]. Turns out he has designed a computer for the government, some massive system he did the "neural network design" for. This computer refers to itself as **Stephen 2** [... as does Stephen].

Stephen [(1)] is from a family in Seattle that is made up "of carpenters and beauticians", [...] He describes his discovery

---

TELEMACHUS looks at Steven, and then looks away to the ocean, calm and glassy in the intense late afternoon sun. The woman places two green plastic bowels of Top Ramen and a small film canister, with holes punched into the top, on the table.

Steven

"Salt," Steven says motioning to the film canister, trying to lighten up the conversation, "As if there isn't *enough* salt in everything there is to eat around here." Telemachus picks at the unfamiliar vegetables on the top of his soup with his fork, he decides against passing comment on the food.

"How do you entertain yourself in this, isolation?"

Steven

"This isolation suits my needs perfectly, you see I choose to communicate to the world using only the invisible waves of my cellular telephone. My identity is completely under my control. I don't have to interact with anyone, nobody sees me, nobody knows where I am." [83]

TELEMACHUS

"Hmmm. Sounds very *secretive*."

Steven

"It is, and I like it that way. Sometimes I won't see another westerner for a month."

"Must get lonely"

Steven

"Not really"

"If you want to remain anonymous, why don't you just get some fake id's and live your life out in the big city?"

Steven

"I don't like disguises, I don't like cities and more importantly, I am disgusted by the *idea* of Western culture, where a man is viewed by others, not for what is in his mind.

EXT. INVESTIGATOR
What happens in your version of the story?

CO-AUTHOR
2 octopus fisherman find her + take her to see a witch doctor who cures her.

EXT. INVESTIGATOR
Octopus fisherman? How do you fish for octopus?

CO-AUTHOR
Funny u should ask .. see, 1 of the guys--usually the smaller skinny 1--acts as 'human bait'. He ties a rope around his waist + dives down to where the giant octopus is known to be. The bigger fat guy holds on to the rope + when he feels a tug he reels in his friend, w/octopus attached to him + then w/ a knife cuts the suction arms off.

EXT. INVESTIGATOR
This happened in real life?

CO-AUTHOR
It doesn't matter. This is about my brother + his odyssey. I'll tell my version of the story some other day.

---

[83] Joyce uses the word **wireless** twice in *Ulysses*. In the Circe chapter he says: «Wireless intercontinental and interplanetary transmitters are set for reception of message.» Our Left ½ wrote this at a time when beepers + pagers + fax machines were the thing. Cell phones were too clunky + expensive for personal use + of course this was also (practically speaking) pre-Internet + pre-WIFI.

him to believe his own words.

Steven

"Listen, I appreciate this place and its pace, for the same reasons that you do..."

"Really? Do you see the local people as underdeveloped primitives or do you see there connection with nature as pure and unspoiled?"
Steven can see that ~~is not going to make it easy for him. He can't seem to understand why she wouldn't be attracted to him, and his social rebel lifestyle.~~

Steven

"I guess ~~I would have to say that~~ I do not believe in the idea of the *noble savage*.
The people here have remained *primitive*, in terms of their technological development as a society, because of their environment. Necessity never pushed this society to develop, they have all that they need to survive peacefully.
They are relatively isolated on this island. There aren't a lot of exterior forces calling on them to develop systems of defense or survival. I guess you could say that there has never been a *motivation* to develop any further than they have."
Steven can see that she agrees with him, but will ~~not~~ allow herself to show it.

"You certainly sound like a Darwinist."

Steven

"Definitely, through and through. I believe that natural selection is the only higher law. It seems like a Marine Biologist would see it the same way? ~~Do you?~~"
~~just looks at him. She seems to be suddenly unable to go on, as if she sees Steven playing a game with her.
Steven's cellular phone rings, but he does not move to answer it.~~

"Aren't you going to get that?"

Steven gets up and goes into the room. He turns on the computer and picks up the phone.

Steven

"Hello,...yes...I know, I think the time has come to complete it...yes.... don't worry everything is going to be fine.... I am going to type in the command now, you will follow it exactly, I'm sorry...no.....this must be done, and it must be done now.....yes......good-bye."
Steven turns the phone off and types in something to the computer. After a couple

exhibit 77— another cover for a fictitious lit mag (1981)

of computers at the age of twelve as the turning point in his life. [He graduated from] CalTech by the time he was seventeen. He also studied Philosophy and clinical psychology at UCLA. As he was finishing his doctorate degree at CalTech, he was arrested for (successfully) breaking into the Pentagon defense computer system. Stephen [claims] he did this because he knew it would be the fastest, and easiest way to get a high paying government (computer) job.

After four days and nights, Telemachus and Circe return to [Port Moresby ...]. A few days later they buy an English newspaper and read on the front page about what Stephen [had] been working on. Stephen, described in the article as a former computer hacker turned Defense Dept. employee, apparently [terminated] *Stephen 2.*—the Defense Dept. computer that had just been [independently verified] by top [cybernetic] scientists from all over the world to be "conscious". [Written + verbal answers to questions] were also analyzed by psychological experts and found to be indistinguishably "human"[84]. Stephen had developed an artificial intelligence, one that [knew] its place in the world, a real "person" [capable of] developing friendships, a person who asked questions, wanted to know if there where "any other machines like myself?"

One of the scientists quoted in the paper described the experience of [interacting with] the mild-mannered computer to be "the most chilling of my life." As the scientists were finishing asking their questions, this computer ([whose physical whereabouts were unknown]) decided to "permanently silence itself". The computer essentially self-destructed, and the chief suspect was Stephen. Stephen had apparently installed [a hidden] mechanism that allowed him to [remotely] give the final directive to his creation even [if] the project was taken out of his hands [...].

The police had been looking for Stephen for over a week. He had not been back to the U.S. or Europe for more than three years and the last time he was seen was nearly a month earlier in the south of Thailand. The papers were full of [differing] opinions on the discovery of artificial

---

[84] Perhaps he meant to say it passed the **Turing test**. A few months before the time we are now compiling this (Sept 2014) a computer for the 1st time allegedly passed the test: http://www.theguardian.com/technology/2014/jun/08/super-computer-simulates-13-year-old-boy-passes-turing-test.

intelligence, the [whereabouts] of the computer and Stephen's innocence or guilt.

On [their] way back across the island, Telemachus and Circe go out of there way to find Stephen. Telemachus decides that what Stephen had done is criminal [+] plans on confronting him, [to tell him] that he'll turn him in.

When they get to his place [the tusks are back to being red. Telemachus doesn't even comment]. The first thing Stephen does is offer to get them high. Telemachus declines and readies to confront Stephen. But Circe accepts and smokes a joint with Stephen on the beach in front of his hut.

Telemachus gets pissed off and heads down the beach alone. [A stoned] Circe and Stephen [wander into] the jungle. [...] Stephen leads her to a waterfall, strips down and dives in. He tries to get her to come in but she is too scared. She [stares] for a long time at the dense jungle around her. Finally she comments on "how intricate and alive the jungle is, like one huge living organism." She eventually leads Stephen into telling her how "incredibly simple the trick of consciousness is." He goes into great detail, how it is structured, what kinds of stimulus are needed, what kinds of *dysfunctional* [—italics mine] behaviors have to be included to incite the spark of consciousness, etc. He refers to consciousness as a sort of imperfect shadow of perfection, something spawned from its own imperfection, as if the desire towards perfection was the sum of all its parts.

When he is done talking, Circe turns of the tape recorder in her backpack, undresses and joins him in the water. They [have sex] in the waterfall.

Afterwards, Circe offers Stephen some fruit from the restaurant that she has in her bag. Stephen comments on the small "insect holes in the fruit," but decides to eat them anyway, saying, "bugs never hurt anyone."

He stops breathing in less than two minutes. It takes at least five minutes for his heart to [completely] seize up. When the blood starts to drip slowly from his nose, Circe drags his body back into the water, under the waterfall. The falling water keeps the body from floating back up.

"... no, but stone fish venom did," she says out loud as his body gets pushed [beneath] the surface.

A couple of days later, an anonymous tip leads the police to the secluded location of Stephen's [pallid] form. The search is over, and apparently so is the possibility of getting back Stephen 2. [Cause of death] is listed as 'suicide'. Circe and Telemachus are [noted] as the last people to speak with the fugitive. Neither of them can offer any clues to the U.S. Government investigators as to what might have been on the mind of the Stephen before his demise.

A couple of weeks later, back in California, Circe gets a call at her work. A male voice asks her who she is. Her face [registers] excitement. The conviction in her voice [shows as she answers], "I am the one who killed your father. Now listen to me, [you're] mine now, and I will tell you exactly what it is you will be working on while I sleep..."[85]

exhibit 78 (below)— letter i sent to brother ½ (1991)

Kevin—   Rarotonga July 18? ①

I just finished reading your thesis. (The reason i'm writing with my left hand is because right stung by a stonefish on my right). I took it out of the envelope which contained a copy of my thesis, a map of the world, and the cliff notes to Ulysses (which i read last night) Miraculously these were the only things that didn't get soaked in the 2-day storm that i suffered through just over Dengue fever in my tent in Tahiti, sleeping in water. Intense writing. Certain ways you phrase things goes beyond what 'objective' Descriptive language can potray. "Action language" But i have to admit as a whole it is very unaccessible (And i'm your own brother —then again maybe that's the problem —preconceived expectations — projections). Interesting, Entertaining and insightful tidbits tied in a rigid (yet loose) framework particularly interesting to me as i'm on a Odyssey of my own and the whole structure of Odyssey-Ulysses-SSeS is very mathematic I had the added benefit of reading it in the presence of 2 norwegians, 3 swedes, 2 germans and a crazy old american writer. (who at this very instant is arguing with John the norwegian because he is trying to write and the old man is constantly putting on very bad music). They would ask what

---

[85] When brother-½ wanted to talk about or sent us photocopied articles or books on stuff like quantum computing + entangled consciousness we arrogantly took exception + dismissed them as too soft or dumbed down ... why read pop science distillations when we were reading the source articles + texts for our classes? Such topics were flaring up in the 80s, specially where i was at UCSC. The 1st (more or less[86])

[86] Various **loophole conditions** (such as «detection efficiency» + «disjoint measurement») continued to crop up faster than they could be experimentally resolved, such that keeping up w/ it was akin to playing whack-a-mole. If u consider the current state of quantum physics to itself be a quantum state, then the moment it collapses it slips back into its own indeterminancy.

what i was reading but i had to give up in (2) vain. Its kind of strange how writing with my left hand not only looks like a 6 yr. olds but it makes me think like one. (This morning i went to church (The singing is a nice rush of Adrenalin to the head and down the spine —sounds a lot like Bulgarian voices). I was leaning against the wall; when i went to sit down a sizeable chunk of the wall (about 5 lbs) came down with me (very rustic church). The mass stopped and everybody burst out laughing —looking at me. The Swedes think i'm their hero. They were with me in Moorea when i got ~~[scribble]~~ the Dengue — Stonefish and this. My hand and forearm still look like Popeye and my ring finger is black and oozing poison (orange oil comes out with my shit and when i piss it stings). That all happened in titutaki (after my platonic affair with Debbie).(Typical Story— meet her on the plane, come to the same guest house. Decide to go to Aitutaki (where they filmed Blue Lagoon). When we go down to the travel agent they assume were a couple and book us a double, etc....) An inch off shore, under an inch of H2O and 2 inches of ~~Sand~~ (so far all the meaningful things of this trip have come as a surprise! Stupid fucking fish. What does it get out of looking like a Rock? With hypodermic needles

as dorsal fins. Couldn't even find the little (3) fucker after i got stung. But i gave that up along with my fishing line and fish (edible) and coconut i was eating. Hurry but don't panic. Wading the km back to shore. Stumbling into "town" a drooling Mad Man, bathed in sweat, Blood Pouring from my arm which i tied off with my shirt — wincing in Pain which is shooting like molten Lead up my arm. Reaches my Elbow. Now everything is a dream. I'm thrown onto the back of a Moped to the hospital. As i stumble in mumbling "Stonefish" i feel i'm starting to lose consciousness. A movie that is growing dark on the edges and is full of concerned faces. For the 1st time in my life i feel in Danger of dying. But the pain is so intense i don't care. The nurse at the hospital says there is nothing they can do but shoot me up with pain killer. Another woman walks in and tells me she can treat me with traditional herbal medicine. Another motorcycle ride up into the Jungle to some old shack. They throw me on the floor in the hall while she gives the whole family orders. Water is put on to boil. Little brother is out sawing the branch off a Fragipani tree. She begans hacking into my finger

[85] (cont.) conclusive experimental proof to **Bell's Inequality** was provided by Alain Aspect et al[87] in 1981, just before the death of our father + around the time this Circe episode is sposed to be taking place (granted this «Perfection Sickness» piece was written in the mid-90s + we are now in 2014). Bell's theorem was proposed in 1964 (1 year before our brother-½ born (left-handed) + 2½ years before your trusty editor (right-handed)) in a paper published in *Physics* entitled: «On the Einstein Podolsky Rosen paradox». For starters (working systematically backwards), Bell's Inequality is a «no-go theorem» which is a theorem (in theoretical physics) that states that a particular situation is not physically possible (namely the theory of local «hidden variables» that Einstein el al claimed accounted for the ghostly «paradox»). So Alain Aspect's verifying of Bell's Inequality proved that the hidden variables or «local realism» inherent in Einstein, Podolsky + Rosen's *reductio ad absurdum* of quantum mechanics were lame justifications or ignorant hand-waving concessions ... so absurdly absurd + cynically cynical they negated themselves to universal realism in the same way two wrongs in fact do make a right. After a few generations of such nay-saying, the tides had finally turned + such things as «spooky action at a distance» + quantum entanglement were accepted as truths. Which is to say, u could no longer speak of an isolated entity as independent or uncorrelated—the system as a whole must be taken into account + everything is connected. To illustrate this idea of **quantum entanglement** (in the context of this book) consider the system to the right. A source emits a pair of complementary particles (or generalize even to «*qubits*»—quantum bytes of information), entangled or tethered, say, in spin or *handedness*[88] such that if 1 is left-handed the other must be (by symmetry) right-handed ... tho we don't know which is which. If 1 observer observes a left-handed qubit, then the wave function collapses + we know (w/ 100% certainty) the other qubit must be right-handed ... w/o even having to detect this. When this was proposed (essentially as a generalized extension to the Heisenberg Uncertainty principle) it blew people's minds cuz it meant that the information (that the handedness was detected) somehow travelled instantaneously + invisibly between the 2 qubits (what Einstein called «spooky action at a distance»).

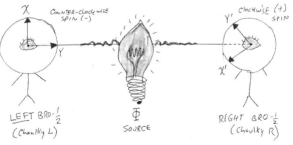

LEFT BRO-½ (Chaulky L) — SOURCE — RIGHT BRO-½ (Chaulky R) — COUNTER-CLOCKWISE SPIN (-) — CLOCKWISE (+) SPIN

While Einstein couldn't open his mind enough to fathom this, others such as Heisenberg + Schrödinger (my heros) were more receptive + pliable to the idea. Per Schrödinger: «I would not call [entanglement] one but rather *the* characteristic trait of quantum mechanics, the one that enforces its entire departure from classical lines of thought.» Even if such a theory is just our mind projecting our own inner workings on the physical world, quantum entanglement must be considered a reflexive precondition to understanding or explaining consciousness, something otherwise unthinkable using classical reasoning.

[87] «Experimental Tests of Realistic Local Theories via Bell's Theorem» by Alain Aspect et al, published in Physical Review Letters 47 — 17 Aug 1981.

[88] The **Handedness** or helicity of a particle is right-handed if the direction of its spin is the same as the direction of its motion + left-handed if the direction of spin is opposite to its motion.

④ with a needle (that still has the thread coming out of it — nice homey touch). I'm covered with hundreds of mosquitoes but manage a vengeful laugh as I'm sure the poison will kill them. (the same mosquitoes that gave me Dengue fever). The whole family is lying down with me, wiping the sweat that is pouring out of me and massaging me all over — arms, back and legs. Someone is grating the inner part of the frangipani. (The tree from which come the fragrant flowers used for the flower necklaces) into a pulp which is wrapped in a cloth. This is dipped in boiling water and wrung out into the wound. They hold my arm to keep me from involuntarily spazzing out and tell me it's ok to cry (even 'grown men' do). Meanwhile Grandma ('ma') is rubbing me all over. Then the direct method. Stick my finger directly into the boiling mixture. It runs up my veins chasing the poison down. Pulling back. The pain recedes back to my hand. I'm asleep in their living room. They're all yacking in Maori. I wake up to the sight of gaudy colored walls, billowing curtains, family pictures and pictures of Jesus — even one in 3-d. The daughter brings me a platter of food — leaning over and virtually slaps me in the face with

(cont. from left) ... u get the idea. The letter continues for a few more pages. I ended it by saying «I feel as if you are here in spirit, that you are part of the purpose as I travel.» This letter (or rather, the stonefish sting) marks the beginning of our **ambidexterity**. After our right hand was immobilized by the stonefish, we got used to doing things w/ our left. Now we mouse w/ our left + even use chopsticks left-handed ... or is it the other way around + just our perspective we can never be certain of it has been suggested that polar psychogeographical shifts have occurred w/o us even knowing (since we are wed to our own reference frames) but this juxtaposition relative to earthly's fixed geology has created (the perception of) atrocities such as floods + tectonic events, not to mention magnetically induced genetic mutations. The good news is that during such cataclysmic epiphanies the heart of the matter remains molten if not fluid (epinephrine) as our enshrining DNA unravels + denatures + during this time is vulnerable to recombination which ok can be devastating but can also be quite productive if u «set your mind to it».

It follows we formed as 1 **recombinant** organism tethered by umbilical text strings who absorbed or exorcised who is hard to say definitively but if we take the particle physics approach then a body died (+ perhaps also simultaneously the mind of the other), but again, under the light of quantum field theory it's easier to dissect (tho dissection being more like dissolution) ... bodiless organs remain entangled (by the necessary symmetry of duality) + preserved under transformation (such as the Linati scheme) for translating epileptic fits to control hurt ... what 1 might perceive as a cleavage could also be construed as **convergent** evolution.

The Odyssey was written during times of classical physics. *Ulysses* was writ enduring the advent uv [SIC] quantum psychics. Not only was Bloomsday just 1 year before Einstein came up w/ his Special Relativity but also his Photoelectric Effect (a key component in the de-envelopment of quantum mechanics). And now here we are still tethered synch-(er)roneously in times of quantum entanglement. An alternate approach to quantum entanglement looks thru the fracturing lens of the **Many-worlds interpretation**, where we consider ea state (or let's just go ahead + say *book*) to be an alternate *history,* each representing a legitimate, historic world (actualized or not). Each reading of a book doesn't necessarily lead to a new world view but correlated copies of a reader/book system (localized w/in a readers reference frame), w/ a 1-to-1 mapping that is preserved under regular real-world (or even dreamtime) transformations, specially thru the *field theory* lens (as opposed to rigid part-icicle mechanics). Each book contains encoded instruct-ions that, upon reading, create a world anew. Now, some book combinations, like *Ulysses* + *Odyssey* form conjugate pairs such that each attribute of *The Odyssey* has a mirrored twin in *Ulysses*, for exampled «being turned into a pig» in *The Odyssey* means «going to the brothel[89]» in *Ulysses*. As more books are read + branch off into new books, more + more worlds are created + entanglement serves to further propagate this effect exponentially.

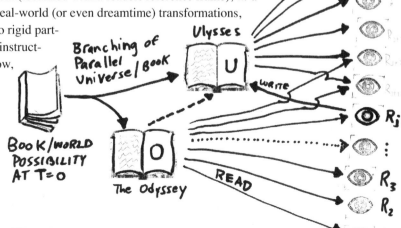

Branching of Parallel Universe / Book — Ulysses — WRITE — BOOK/WORLD POSSIBILITY AT T=0 — The Odyssey — READ — R_j — R_3 — R_2 — R_1

---

[89] In the 1st draft we misspelled brothel as «brother».

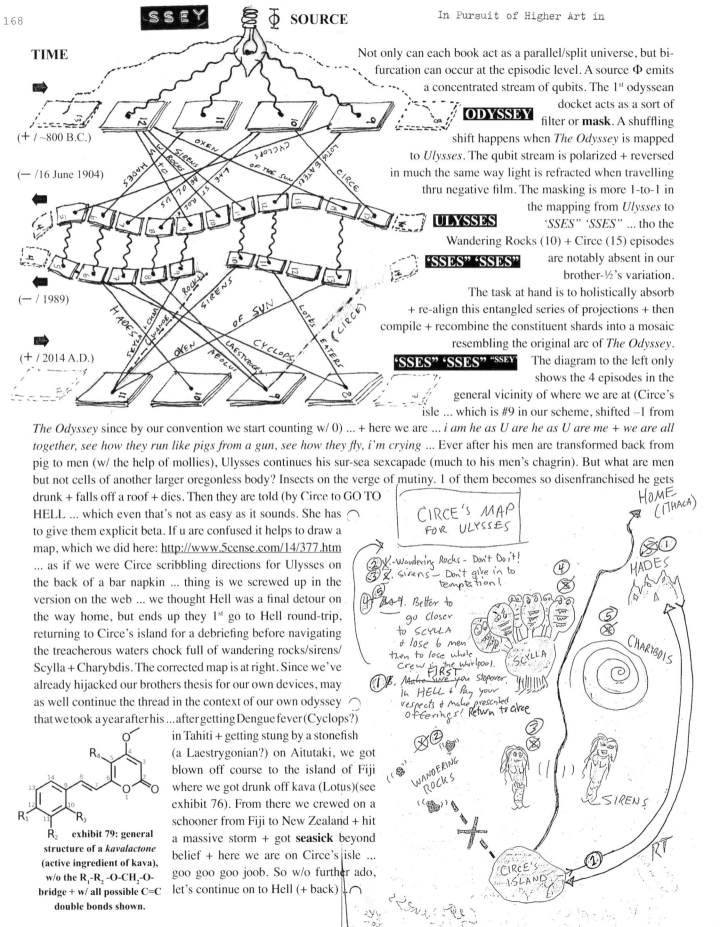

TIME

(+ / ~800 B.C.)

(− /16 June 1904)

(− / 1989)

(+ / 2014 A.D.)

Not only can each book act as a parallel/split universe, but bi-furcation can occur at the episodic level. A source Φ emits a concentrated stream of qubits. The 1st odyssean docket acts as a sort of **ODYSSEY** filter or **mask**. A shuffling shift happens when *The Odyssey* is mapped to *Ulysses*. The qubit stream is polarized + reversed in much the same way light is refracted when travelling thru negative film. The masking is more 1-to-1 in the mapping from *Ulysses* to **ULYSSES** 'SSES' 'SSES' ... tho the Wandering Rocks (10) + Circe (15) episodes **'SSES' 'SSES'** are notably absent in our brother-½'s variation. The task at hand is to holistically absorb + re-align this entangled series of projections + then compile + recombine the constituent shards into a mosaic resembling the original arc of *The Odyssey*. **'SSES' 'SSES' 'SSEY'** The diagram to the left only shows the 4 episodes in the general vicinity of where we are at (Circe's isle ... which is #9 in our scheme, shifted −1 from

The Odyssey since by our convention we start counting w/ 0) ... + here we are ... *i am he as U are he as U are me + we are all together, see how they run like pigs from a gun, see how they fly, i'm crying* ... Ever after his men are transformed back from pig to men (w/ the help of mollies), Ulysses continues his sur-sea sexcapade (much to his men's chagrin). But what are men but not cells of another larger oregonless body? Insects on the verge of mutiny. 1 of them becomes so disenfranchised he gets

drunk + falls off a roof + dies. Then they are told (by Circe to GO TO HELL ... which even that's not as easy as it sounds. She has to give them explicit beta. If u are confused it helps to draw a map, which we did here: http://www.5cense.com/14/377.htm ... as if we were Circe scribbling directions for Ulysses on the back of a bar napkin ... thing is we screwed up in the version on the web ... we thought Hell was a final detour on the way home, but ends up they 1st go to Hell round-trip, returning to Circe's island for a debriefing before navigating the treacherous waters chock full of wandering rocks/sirens/ Scylla + Charybdis. The corrected map is at right. Since we've already hijacked our brothers thesis for our own devices, may as well continue the thread in the context of our own odyssey that we took a year after his ... after getting Dengue fever (Cyclops?)

in Tahiti + getting stung by a stonefish (a Laestrygonian?) on Aitutaki, we got blown off course to the island of Fiji where we got drunk off kava (Lotus)(see exhibit 76). From there we crewed on a schooner from Fiji to New Zealand + hit a massive storm + got **seasick** beyond belief + here we are on Circe's isle ... goo goo goo joob. So w/o further ado, let's continue on to Hell (+ back)

exhibit 79: general structure of a *kavalactone* (active ingredient of kava), w/o the R_1-R_2 -O-CH_2-O- bridge + w/ all possible C=C double bonds shown.

CIRCE'S MAP FOR ULYSSES

X - Wandering Rocks - Don't Do it!
X. Sirens — Don't give in to temptation!
Better to go closer to SCYLLA & lose 6 men then to lose whole crew in the whirlpool.
Make sure you stopover in HELL & Pay your respects & make prescribed offerings! Return to circe

HOME (ITHACA)
HADES
CHARYBDIS
SCYLLA
WANDERING ROCKS
SIRENS
CIRCE'S ISLAND

«Ulysses here / invokes the dead. /
The lives appear / Hereafter led.»—THE ODYSSEY

FACE THE MUSIC

Music to his life, the ways whenever she speaks to him. He can't remember her face, and doesn't know if he ever knew it, or whether it is a specific face. He knows she has been with him always, but not always vocal. She only approaches him when he is standing outside of the others, in introspection. Her presence is heralded by the slowing of the wind through the trees. The light gets warmer and cooler. The air grows thicker and thinner and of course the music. He neglects her during the daily trivial pursuit, and occasionally wonders what would happen to him if he lost the ability to stand outside of himself—see things in that way, hear the music, and listen to the most comforting thing he knows—her gentle voice. She continually promises to take from in some young woman, someone he hasn't met, someone about whom he will learn more about himself than he could possibly imagine there was to know. But somehow their efforts never combine, and he continually falls in love with the wrong person. The pattern is relentless, and even though vast amounts of time are spent in-between these fumbled attempts at intimacy, he never learns his lesson. Or rather he does, but a years worth of loneliness will make him forget to listen to her and heed her cue.

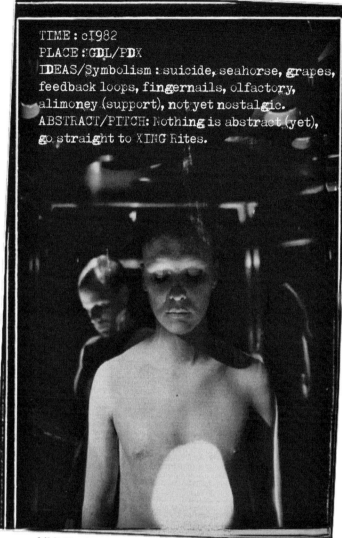

TIME : c1982
PLACE : GDL/PDX
IDEAS/Symbolism : suicide, seahorse, grapes, feedback loops, fingernails, olfactory, alimoney (support), not yet nostalgic.
ABSTRACT/PITCH: Nothing is abstract (yet), go straight to XING Rites.

exhibit 80—brother-½ (left) behind the hairless child actor who my ½ was standing in for (see episode #16)

XING RITES   (as leave falls)

He is reading over my shoulder as i write + now U are reading over our shoulder as we write. We are shouldering U. I've bean shouldering him now all along til we are 1 + el mismo, as scribing. W'eave received our rites[90] from Sur-sea (the «...*excellent utterer of her mind supplied our murmuring consorts...*») ... of passage. Shuttering to think til now weaved hat no expirence w/ **death**[91]. ... not that we'ave seen w/ our owned eyes, or milked her utters ... B-sides that stranger on the beach, u were there, record us? Her damp waxy skin sticky w/ grit. Alive bobbing upright in the waves 1 sec the next laying dead on the flat sand. Fists pounding her bared left breast. Gristly + ashen lump of dung. «*Never know who will touch u dead. Wash + shampoo.*» Sabemos que debemos hacer. Sur-sea has given us xplicit directions, in situ ... do not pass GO ... don't click your heels x3, yet. We are x-scribed our rites.

---

[90] «1st honey mix'd w/ wine, then sweet wine neat, then water pour'd in, last the flour of wheat.» Then: «... kill a heifer, my clear best of all, and give in off'ring, on a pile compos'd.»[92]

[91] Per *Ulysses*, the chap in the macintosh, the 13th bared head. Bloom's number's is not up yet either.

---

[92] Some 8 centuries later (circa 5 A.D.), the Roman Ovid would rally against the likes of Homer + the Greek tradition of sacrificing animals in the Pythagoras chapter of *Metamorphoses*, based on the Pythagorean doctrine of **Metempsychosis** (the word Molly asks Bloom the meaning of when he 1st brings her breakfast in bed (see episode 4)). By eating animals we dispossess their souls + quite possibly (+ cannibalisically) the souls of our own relatives. «*As pliable wax is easily stamped with a new impression and never remains as it was nor preserves one single / shape, / but still is the selfsame wax, so I say that our souls are / always / the same, through they move from home to home in / different bodies.*» + also «All is in flux[93]. Any shape that is constantly shifting.»

---

[93] ... which in turn Ovid appropriated from Heraclitus (circa 500 B.C.), who also coined the bit about never stepping in the same river x2.

SAMBALLNIGHT flight #23 touched down right on time. It is a crisp Spring day in Rio.[94] Once out of range of the jet engines we rediscover the familiar roar of the biggest party on the planet. The taxis are all taken so we accept the offer of one thrifty local on the way back from work. They can earn more ferrying tourists around in their car then they earn in a week at the factory, and their wives will never find out about the extra income. We are so relieved to see Terry's beach front apartment that we tip the guy more than he could have possibly expected. Bags over our shoulders, we climb the steps to the front of the building. their is a note for us. He is gone for the day but wants us to go ahead and let ourselves in, make ourselves at home. We look around the back yard for the clay pot that is covering the key, find it, and go in.

Terry has not changed a bit. Still the same slob. The remnants of months worth of parties fill the house. The walls are covered with Terry's collection of French resistance posters. Bamboo furniture fills the corners of the spacious living room. A huge wall of windows opens out on to the dreamscape of Rio. The beach curves out of sight to the right. As far as the eye can see, young girls wearing hardly anything, propped up on their elbows, gazing longingly out to sea. From inside we can smell the suntan lotion, saltwater and gas. Soon the beachfires will be started to cook dinner for groups of the carnival participants. The stereo mingles Joao Gilberto in with the street symphony. We make ourselves some cold drinks and plop down into the armchairs by the window. We vaguely discuss how glad we are to have such a friend as Terry.

When Burroughs turned up in September, Allen invited him to stay at his apartment.[95] They where making breakfast the morning after his arrival when a garrulous and disheveled young friend of Allen's appeared, wanting to sell a suitcase full of miniature liqueur bottles of various hues that he had stolen from a queer bar. The young man was Gregory Corso, who would become a leading figure of the beat movement, and who had in common with the others that he was a misfit, selfinvented, rebellious, and blessed by

Our right to bear away ugh. Our hole lifes til now prexhumed innocent til guilty + all in a sudden we're **guilty** til proven otherwise. Instills paranoia in a dollessence. Protective measures put in place. Self-conscience orbiting the plaza, guarded a bout what passes in + out of our lips in publick as birds drip in trees over our head.

This isn't us writing ... **eso** es composing, composting-to-a-T-cum-positing. Globally positioning ourselfs for advancement. Putting her (**S**) behind behind us, a dozen comes before a baker's. Eso xtra donut will kill U. Close the circled coagulate. Circe menos el L. El matador draping the red cape. No more steps, mothers utterrwise droop. Only human.

By putting into **parole** we negate the reality d'ella. The IDea rices out of her[96]. Absence to begin w/ le assay posible. Absence of discipline in—

«Whatcha writing?» interrupts the man in the middle seat to my right, 13B. He wears a macintosh + a patch over his left eye which—out of the corner of our eye—we figured was a sleeping mask this whole while. 10 empty + 2 full whiskey miniatures line his tray table.

exhibit 81 (right)—archaelogical dig sketch (see xhibit 11 on pg 30 for realization)

(Reset)—> 1
his original

---

[94] To our knowledge, he'd never been to Brazil.

[95] 10 blocks from where we now write this from on 125th + Riverside.

[96] «He was seized, kneaded by intelligible hands, bitten by a vital tooth; he entered with his living body into the anonymous shapes of words, giving his substance to them, establishing their relationships, offering his being to the word "to be". For hours he remained motionless, with, from time to time, the word "eyes" in place of his eyes: he was inert, captivated and unveiled. And even later when, having abandoned himself and, contemplating his book, he recognized himself with disgust in the form of the text he was reading, he retained the thought that (while, perched upon his shoulders, the word *He* and the word *I* were beginning their carnage) there remained within his person which was already deprived of its senses obscure words, disembodied souls and angles of words, which were exploring him deeply.»—Maurice Blanchot, *Thomas the Obscure*.

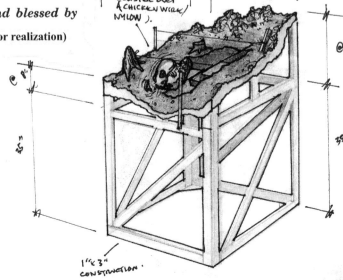

ACRYLICPAINT ON PLASTER OVER A CHICKEN WIRE/ NYLON).

1"ε3" CONSTRUCTION.

Hades

"Hey you pigs! Why don't you shut the door?" The voice rings through my mind bringing an end to my exotic dream. "Hey! Wake up." I sit up lethargically and open my eyes. Nicole is across from me rubbing her eyes. The rattan has turned the right side of her face into a waffle iron. Terry is standing above me. I smile and shake his hand. He is running around the kitchen making a lot of noise, talking full speed about some party tonight down by the wharf in a restaurant with some Swedish airline stewardesses.

"Do you want some Puanaca?" He asks me, knife in hand.

"Some what?" I stretch out my shoulders as I walk over to him.

"Some Puanaca, its like gaspacho soup, you know, cold"

"Yeah, yeah sure." I reply taking notice of the bra Terry is wearing. "Hey Terry."

"Huh?"

"What's with the lingerie?" I have a hard time keeping a straight face as I point to his chest.

"Oh." He self consciously pulls up the top of his shirt. "Well.." He is noticeably embarrassed..."This beautiful young angel from across the street.. well.. this is the only way she will let me have her."

"What?!" I am thoroughly confused.

"You see, she is this girl who lives about two blocks from here with her family. Were talking thirty family members in one flat! So, anyway, this family has this knack for producing the most beautiful girls in the whole fucking town. I'm talking tall dark goddesses. Long thick curly black

Corso

the muse. If Ginsberg, Kerouac, and Burroughs were the Three Musketeers of the movement, Corso was the D'Artagnan, a sort of junior partner, accepted and appreciated, but with less than complete parity. He had not been in at the start, which was the alliance of the Columbia intellectuals with the Times Square Hipsters. He was a recent adherent, although his credentials were impressive enough to gain him unrestricted admittance, and he added to the group's ethnic diversity- a Canuck, a Jew, a WASP, and now

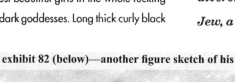

Kerouac a Canuck?

exhibit 82 (below)—another figure sketch of his

Screws the cap off the 11th + mixes it w/ soda.

«Nothing really.»

«Not a 1 can write *nothing*.»

«If u must know, it's a story about flying back to Portland for our father's funeral» we answer, «... as told from our brother-½'s p.o.v.»

«U speaking from experience?» asks the old man w/sunglasses in the isle seat, 13C. «Like, in the here + now?»

We're en route to PDX after all. We tell him «in deed» + resume writing ... or at least give the pretense.

«U + me both» says the man in the macintosh in 13B. «I mean, not quite my father's death trip, but u know ... »

The stewardess stops the cart at our isle + asks if we want sumthin. «I'll have whatever he's having» we say, pointing w/ our pen at the old man in the sunglasses.

«Sheep's blood» she confirms.

«I figured it was a bloody mary ... but sheep's blood sounds even better. Can u put a little tequila in it?»

She smiles + tosses a napkin down in front of us as we lower our tray table. Pours us a cup of runny blood + hands it across 13B + 13C. Followed by a mini of tequila.

«Me 3» says 13c, once the stewardess pushes on. This whole time he has been looking straight forward thru his sunglasses. Out of the corner of our eye we figured he'd been watching a movie, but his console is off.

«U 3 what?»

«I'm also headed to a funeral ... well, technically i'm going to hell. To pay respects to my friend.»

«How'd he die?» asks 13B.

«Got drunk. Fell off a roof.»

«Ats a shame. My friend also died in a drunken stupor. What about u lad? Aren't u a wee bit young to be drinking spirits anyway?»

«There's no drinking age where i live now.»

Hades

Corso

hair. Ocher colored eyes."

"Sounds pretty alien to me!"

"No way! These girls are beautiful! Like you have never seen! Anyway, the youngest girl; Sloana, is about eighteen."

"Eighteen?!"

"Yeah, eighteen, she's the one that usually is wearing this bra. Her family is real Catholic. Were talking church three nights a week! But you couldn't tell by looking at the girls in that family. Sloana is the only one out of six sisters that isn't pregnant!"

"And you are going to personally see to it that she does not miss out on this particular joy of life." Nicole smiles at my remark.

"Not really. This girl says she loves me but up to now she has not let me do anything if you know what I mean. And a week ago she came up with this stupid idea. Its the first time I get her to drink, and she decides that she will give herself to me if I wear her bra for a week! I nearly spit out my beer when I heard this! But after another hour of drinking , soaking in her youthfulness and looking at her long legs, I decide that wearing her bra would be a pleasure. I asked her if I could keep it concealed under a shirt the whole time, and she said yes, adding that if she ever caught me not wearing it, she would never talk to me again. I asked her why she wanted me to do this, and she simply asked me why I wanted to get into her pants so badly. Fair enough. I decided to accept the offer, at times I wish I hadn't. You can't imagine what it is like to wear a bra on a hot day!"

"I think I can!" Nicole countered.

an Italian.

In one of his journals Corso wrote; Gregorio Nunzio Corso, address; oblivion, school of death. It wasn't quite that bad, although his life did have a strong sense of Dickensian pathos. His beautiful eighteen-year old mother, Michelina, ran off with a lover back to Italy when he was six months old, in 1930. His father, Fortunato, placed him with foster parents, of which he had three sets by the time he was ten. The agency that arranged the placements believed that it was not healthy for a

«What about your pop? Did he die drunk?»

We screw the cap off our tequila + pour it into the sheep's blood. «Well, he *was* a drunk. Not sure if he died that way.»

«Close enough» says 13B. Cheers. Followed by not very satisfying clinks from the plastic cups. Finally, a lull in conversation. Where were we ... reading thru scribbled notes to find our place.

13B elbows me, «u get a load of the bubs on the drinklady as she leaned across?»

«Didn't catch them» we say.

«Whadabout u?» he asks the old man in 13C. «She practically slapped u in the face with those jugs.»

«I could smell 'em ... but can't see. I'm blind.»

«Seriously?» says 13B, waving his hand in front of the old man's sunglasses. «... like i'm 1 to talk, i'm ½-way there meself. Can't even see enough to see your blindness.»

«They smelled nice» says the blind man in 13C. «The musky

«...the Vesta is landing
w/o a capt, w/o a crew
dead in the hull, tied to the wheel
this ship of death, this ship is filled w/ rats
U better find your mother
U better look for cover
we make a choice, we make it everyday
to get up in the morning + to bear away
U better find some cover
U better outlive your mother...»
—Murder City Devils

3

«... time + again i tell myself
i'll stay clean tonight
but the little green wheels are following me
[...]
ashes to ashes, funk to funky
we know major tom's a junkie
strung out in heaven's high
hitting an all-time low
my mother said to get things done
you'd better not mess with major Tom»
—David Bowie

exhibit 83 (right) —taken from a lingerie shop window, LES, post-911 (photo: author)

(price tag still on it)

milk essence complimented my sheep's blood.»

Made for each other. Hopefully they'll keep occupied. Can barely read our own handwriting. Wrote «—draw parallel between Schrödinger's cat + Camus's *The Stranger*» but now not sure what the connexion is/was ... maybe we meant The Cure's take on it, 'Killing an Arab' ... *I'm alive, I'm dead.* When Camus was asked what it meant he said **«in our society any man who does not weep at his mother's funeral runs the risk of being sentenced to death.»** But we don't write this. Instead next we write: *S put him up to it.*

No sooner does the ink dry then 13B asks «who's S?»

«Our stepmom, if u must know.»

(*Coughs 'pussywhipped'*) «Is that what the S stands for?»

«Sorta ... Sur-sea happens to be her name.»

«Circe starts w/ a **C**» chimes 13C. «I should know.»

«Lad can spell it however he wants» says 13B. «What'd she put him up to? Assuming you're talking bout your dad...»

«His death.»

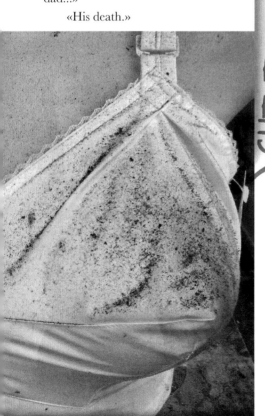

Hades

"Excuse me. So you must have some sense of the torture. But at least you can, if you want to do so, put on a bathing suit and go to the beach. I have no such option. I must stay in shirts all the time, dark shirts! Even around the house! My neighbor saw me the other day through his kitchen window and called the manager. I had to explain to the manager why I was wearing a bra! The stupid ass! It is a good thing he knew of the Cristobal sisters. Apparently they are a local legend. So anyway, I have to keep in proper attire."

"When will you ever grow up Terry?" Nicole asks as she mockingly mothers his shoulders.

I suggest that we all go down to the cafe to acquire some fuel for tonight's festivities. They gladly accept the prospect of going out into the cool evening air. We shower , change into evening wear and then head outside.

Out on the boardwalk the air is warm and dry. The night air is charged with electricity. Children race by screaming and shouting. Cars empty their contents out into the restaurants that line the beachfront strip. Waiters with starched white shirts hurry about on their first day of work, nervous and clumsy. It is a good thing they do not sit down with those they wait on all night long, or there would be no one left to get the bill.

We arrive at the designated place. The owner quickly recognizes Terry. He waves him to the front of the crowd that is waiting. On closer inspection this restaurant owner, whom I have never met remembers me and my name. We smile and let ourselves be seated in a corner booth. The cafe is smoky and red, the music is slow. We sit, drink and eat

4

Corso

boy to become attached to a foster mother, Gregory loved his first foster mother as his own, and was grief stricken when at the age of two was separated from here. One day his first foster mother came to see him at his second foster home and gave him a quarter, which he lost. After that he started wetting his bed. In the third foster home, they gave him a rubber sheet and wouldn't let him drink water after 6 pm. When he was ten, his father, by now remarried, took him back, and he went to live on the lower East side.

From http://5cense.com/13/rejoyce.htm :

... the difference between how they outwardly act + what they say under their breath or think internally ... they have to remind themselves to look serious. We see into Bloom's thoughts: *Paltry funeral [...] It's all the same. [...] Beyond the hind carriage a hawker stood by his barrow of cakes and fruit. [...] cakes for the dead. Dogbiscuits. Who ate them? Mourners coming out.* Causes us to take a step back + realize what a strange ritual it is ... reenacted over + over until we forget original meaning. And the ritual of **burying** the dead ... that we are the only animals that do it ... that all humans do it (though actually Tibetan buddhists don't ... they cut up the corpses + feed them to vultures).

[...]

And then when it comes to the 5 **surviving** kids ... they think to collect a fund: *a few bob a skull. Just to keep them going till the insurance is cleared up.* And then sympathizing w/ the priest: *He must be fed up w/ that job, shaking that thing over all the corpses they trot up.*

our way through two hours.

At around nine o'clock we pay the bill and head out into the street. The throng of people swarms by seemingly oblivious to the presence of the dazed foreigners. The night air is packed full of scantily clad drunks writhing around ecstatically to the thumping samba music blasting from the stage above the statue of the cities patron saint. We make our way down the street, soaking in the surreal scene. We smile the whole time. Everyone is laughing with the exception of the officers on duty. A group of four of them sit on the hood of a their car, looking upon the crowd with disdain. We make our way back up to Sunset to find the car. We find it and head down towards Veteran to avoid the traffic. The sprinklers in the Beverly Hills Park mist my face. All the lights are green for us so we glide smoothly and quickly down Wllshire. Whenever I am near a place I used to live a whole rush of memories fill me. These are places I know, places where I have had experiences, places where I have been to parties.

Back at the house Terry shows us his new paintings in his studio. Terry could make quite a career for himself if he could ever bring himself to leave Rio and head towards New York. I saw some stuff hanging in the galleries of Greenwich Village this Spring that made me want to become a painter. Huge 'drip' paintings. Paintings just covered with splatters. Almost as if it was all about trying to make it as bad as possible.

"Do you ever sell any?" I ask him as we leave his studio.

"Romero down at Sr. Spagniolos's sometimes pushes

His father was obstinate, uneducated Italian, who had never read a book or listened to classical music. When he got mad, which was often, he yelled; "I should have thrown you down the toilet bowl!". His stepmother competed with his father on the decibel level, screaming; "He wets the bed, he wets the bed!"

In 1942, Gregory stole a radio from the lady downstairs and was sent to the youth house for four months, which was heavily populated with older black youths belonging to gangs- the Comanches, the Lucky Gents,

For our purposes (from our time spent there) it's interesting Joyce's numerous references to Rome (mostly as the seat of catholicism) ... + **opium**: *Chinese cemeteries w/ giant poppies growing produce the best opium. [...] It's the blood sinking in the earth gives new life. Same idea those jews they said killed the christian boy. And then later ... A corpse is meat gone bad. Well and what's cheese? Corpse of milk. I read in that Voyages in China that the Chinese say a white man smells like a corpse. Cremation better. Priests dead against it.*

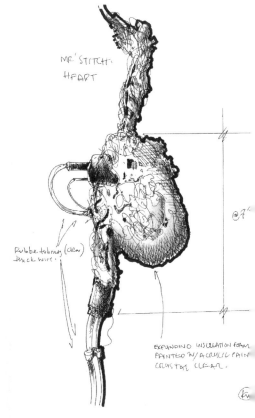

xhibit 84—an isolated piece of heart on display for all to see (for more context, see xhibit 83)

5

(Almost all emoshin is associated w/ a response of body oregons—muscle cunstriction, heart rate alterations, etc.)

The LIMBIC LOBE (L) is a complex system of networking nerves in the brain, centerd round the hippocampus (shown as a **sea-horse**) involving several areas near the edge of the cortex concerned w/ instinct, mood, motivation, behavior, memory + olfaction. Pure emotions (fear, pleasure, anger, etc.) are housed in limbic fluids + it has a great deal to do w/ the formation of memories + impure desire/drives (hunger, sex, dominance, animal husbandry. etc.).

(Traditionally (per Wiki), the limbo *dance* began at the lowest possible bar hight + the bar was gradually raised ... signifying an emurgence from death into life.)

Hades   Corso

one of my smaller works on to some old banker, or what-ever, I do not know... some old tourist who wants to bring back a piece of culture from this place. If only they knew. Some kid from Hoboken . Hah. Culture. When I hear the word culture...

With this remark he sits himself on the counter top and wraps his arms around his knees. Sitting there on the table he stares intently out into the festive phantasmagoria. Bosche's hell.

"What is so great about success anyway?"(Wrong thing to ask).

"What do you mean? How do you think I pay my bills! All this artistic living is costing! You know what I mean? Cafes. Restaurants. Fishing trips. Bull fights. Sports cars. Painting materials (he picks up and slams down a jar full of brushes for emphasis). Occasional trips to Europe. All of it costs big. My family trust will only last so long. Someday I might have to go out and get a fucking nine to five!" Terry puts his head into his hands . Distressed.

"Hey, don't sweat it! You are a talented guy. You can find a good job."

"Yeah."Nicole reaffirms.

"You are saying that only because you are my friends." Terry is now starting to take his self pity too far.

"Come out to the carnival Terry, it will make you feel better."

"No, you guys go ahead. I am going to stay here."

"Come on Terry"

"No really. You guys go ahead and have a good time. Don't mind me."

the Sabers. He was so regularly beaten that in despair he put both hands through a window and was sent to Bellvue for observation, and released. By this time his father was in the Navy, and Gregory was sent to a Christian Boys home, where he was made to stand on the main path from the cottage to the mess hall, holding his rubber sheet. He ran away and took to the streets.

Oh yes, another thing-his obsession with watches, symbols of life's impermanence and pain- each hour wounds, the last one kills. When he stole a

- **hippocampus** |ˌhipəˈkampəs| ORIGIN late 16th cent.: via Latin from Greek *hippokampos*, from *hippos* 'horse' + *kampos* 'sea monster.' [IBID]

- Per Homer, **Poseidon**, was god of horses (*Poseidon Hippios*) + the sea, often represented by brazen-hoofed horses over the sea's surface. [IBID]

- Per *Ulysses*: «The cords of all link back, strandentwining cable of all flesh. [...] In a Greek watercloset, he breathed his last: euthanasia. [...] They are coming, waves. The whitemanned seahorses, champing, brightwindbridled, the steeds of Mananaan.»

- In the theology of the Catholic Church, **Limbo** (Latin *limbus*, 'edge or boundary,' referring to the «edge» of Hell) is a speculative idea about the afterlife condition of those who die in original sin w/o being assigned to Hell. [IBID]

- «The past is now part of my future, the present is well out of hand (x2). Heart + soul, 1 will burn.»—Joy Division

- **carnival** |ˈkärnəvəl| ORIGIN mid 16th cent.: from Italian *carnevale*, medieval Latin *carnelevamen*, Latin *caro, carn-* 'flesh' + *levare* 'to leave behind.' Shed flesh.

- Ulysses meets Sissyphus in Hell. «... in infinite moan, / w/both hands heaving up a massy stone, / And on his tip-toes racking all his height, / To wrest up to a mountain-top his freight; / When prest to rest it there, his nerves quite spent, / Down rush'd the deadly quarry, the event / Of all his torture new to raise again; / To which straight set his never-rested pain.»

- Speaking of A. Camus (2 pgs ago + also famous for his *Myth of Sisyphus* + for saying «**there is only 1 serious philosophical question...**») 1 time (on the isle of Moorea, circa 1990) we were fishing off a dock when Camus's teenage granddaughter came drifting by on a surfboard. She was topless + had red hair. Couldn't say much to each other as our French was terrible. We fictionalized the event in MARSUPIAL (Calamari Press, 2008).

Another time (near Ixtapa-Z, Mexico, circa 1981) we were surfing + a seahorse washed up on our **surfboard**. We caught hir w/ our hand + took hir to shore (not eazy swimming w/ a closed fist!) to show our mother + brother, but in the process we killed hir ... deprived as s/he was, of the seawater s/he needed.

[marginalia, vertical:] Kevin is in fact as a kid put his hand thru a window ...(see p 92)

DREAM.

← LUNGS AND HEARTS PAINTED W/ THICK WHITE PAINT AND FILLED W/

FAKE BLOOD (water, sugar, i red dye etc.).

— A PANIC ENSUES WHEN IT IS DISCOVERED THAT FAKE BLOOD HAS BEEN USED, (SEPERATE THE INDIVIDUAL ORGANS, AND ATTEMPT TO DRAIN THEM,

exhibit 85—idea for piece that came to him in a dream ... «*a panic ensues when it is discovered that fake blood has been used, separate the individual organs, and attempt to drain them.*»

Hades

Corso

"Ok. If you are absolutely sure. But you have to promise us you will go out tomorrow."

"Yeah sure." Terry smiles at the prospect of getting rid of us."

"Well, Ok if you are sure"

"Yep"

"Ok. If you change your mind we will be heading down to the Copa."

"Ok. Have a good time you two."

"Bye"

"Bye"

(slam)

From http://5cense.com/birthday_suicide.htm:

... I'm not totally sure about the truthiness of the last sentence. I've bribed my way out of a few sticky situations in Mexico though I'm not sure this is one of them. I remember being with my mother once when she bribed a Mexican emigration officer, but that's a different story. Maybe this emigration officer eventually took pity on me, I can't say for sure. Memory is not reliable in such circumstances. I was on autopilot. I just remember the self-feeding irony of it —needing something you're on your way to get but you need it to get there. Besides, if I wrote this story it would be a work of fiction so I could say whatever I want. If I can't take cover under the fiction umbrella I could open the one that says it's in the name of art. And don't be afraid to bitchslap me just because I dragged my personal matters into it. The eventual plane trip was followed by an overnight layover on the cold marble floors of LAX. What sticks out most was this guy trying to sell me stolen watches that he had all up his arm and in his briefcase. He really made an impression on me. I said I didn't need one and that I was trying to sleep, but he saw that I couldn't take my eyes off his glinting watches and kept insisting and getting all chummy with me, asking where I was going and I said back to Portland and he said what for and I said my father's funeral and that shut him up. Should I go on?

wrist watch from the dresser drawer of his third foster parent's bedroom, he was spanked. When he stole ten dollars from his fathers pants and bought a Mickey Mouse watch, his father beat him with a razor strap. When he stole a watch with a gold case from a sleeping man, he wasn't caught, and he hocked the watch.

~~Photos or it never happened.~~ At least leave us the ashes.
Nothing's permanent.

(U kept our father's gold watch when he died. When U died, i ended up w/ it in our possession.)

(We remain in limbo.)

(The funeral was awkward.)

(We acted how we were xpected to act.)

(We borrowed a suit (as always) —the kind that comes w/ pre-emptive patches on the elbows.)

(We never saw his corpse. We never saw yours.)

We were seated in the front staring smack at the photo on pg. 70. Every 1 else stared at the backs of our heads staring at the photo ~~of our dead dad.~~

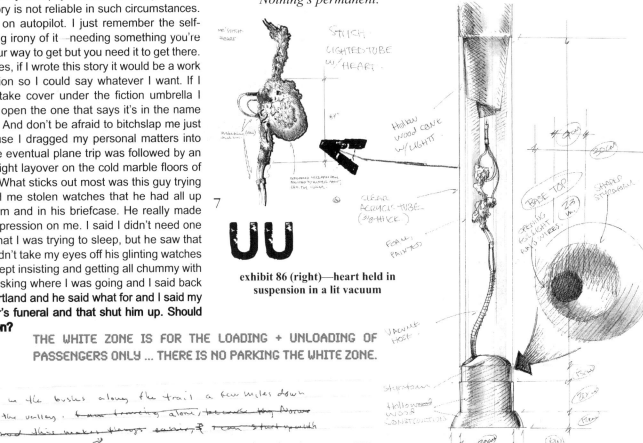

exhibit 86 (right)—heart held in
suspension in a lit vacuum

7

THE WHITE ZONE IS FOR THE LOADING + UNLOADING OF PASSENGERS ONLY ... THERE IS NO PARKING THE WHITE ZONE.

#5. auto-asfixiation w/ auto xhaust

Materials: a car (preferably pre-'80s model w/o a catalytic converter) + a garden hose + (optional) a garage, rags + duct tape.

Method: place 1 end of hose into xhaust pipe. Run the other end thru the smoking window. Seal the gap w/ rags or newspapers + ductape (recommended for efficiency). Get in to car (insure privacy), shut door + roll up windows. Fire up the ignition + wait ...

Advantages: *Carbon monoxide* (CO) is tasteless, odorless + otherwise undetectable (+ inexpensive! ... a naturel by-product of any fossil fuel). Death is relatively 'painless' (obviously cant be verified 1st-hand). Not messy + minimal mental trauma to the discoverer of the body (as opposed to gunshot, slitting wrists, hanging, jumping from a high structure, etc.).

Cons: Hazardous to bystanders or those discovering the body (if not immediately ventilated). A failed attempt can result in memory loss + other side-effects. Waste of fuel.

Detailed logistics/notes: This is an age old trick, at least since the advent of the automobile ... tho in recent decades (w/ stringent new emission controls (i.e. catalytic converters)) this method is falling from favor. The gist of it is that CO binds to *hemoglobin* (Hb), the principal oxygen-carrying compound in blood, producing a compound known as *carboxyhemoglobin* (COHb), which decreases the O_2-carrying capacity of blood + inhibits transport, delivery + utilization of O_2 by the body. The affinity between $Hb + CO$ is ~230 times stronger than the affinity between $Hb + O_2$ so Hb preferably binds to CO over O_2. CO has a higher diffusion coefficient compared to O_2. Under normal conditions, CO levels in the plasma are approximetly 0 mmHg (cuz of this higher diffusion coefficient) + the body readily gets rid of any xcess CO. But when CO is not ventilated as such it binds to Hb. On a «normal» day the ratio of COHb to Hb molecules in avg people can be ~5% ... tho smokers who smoke 2 packs/day can have levels up to 9%.

exhibit 87—untitled sketch

VANTAGE

20 FILTER CIGARETTES

exhibit 88—our dad's
preferred brand

From http://5cense.com/12/last_undone.htm :

But first bLogger read SUICIDE, on a plane from FCO to LHR, not THE LAST NOVEL. The bLogger will get to Markson later on the return flight. Serendipitously, the style of Edouard Levé in many ways reminds bLogger of David Markson—fractured parcels of paragraph-based information, though with Edouard Levé the pointillist, non-linear info-chunks are chunkier, more ruminating. And where Markson name-drops left & right, Levé rarely utters a proper noun. In lieu of story there's that certain fragmented encyclopedic style, a self-characterized constellation: «A dictionary resembles the world more than a novel does, because the world is not a coherent sequence of actions, but a constellation of things perceived. It is looked at, unrelated things congregate, and geographic proximity gives them meaning.»

Edouard Levé wrote SUICIDE & delivered it to his french publisher on October 5, 2007. On October 15, 2007 he lived up to his words & killed himself. So (with this knowledge in mind), though written in 2nd person, to his friend that committed suicide, this short novel reads like a suicide note to himself.

A marketing gimmick that takes cajones, you might say. Ensuring the immortality of your name by dying. It's hard to imagine what bLogger would've thought about the book if he didn't know beforehand what happened to the author outside the book, the two actions (writing SUICIDE & then committing suicide) are now inseparable, part of the same work. «You are a book that speaks to me whenever I need it.»— Edouard Levé says about his friend. «Your death has written your life.»

A lot is said about suicide in SUICIDE. And you can only wonder if these were things Levé was working through with himself, whether he knew all along how it would end. Not that there is a sense of grief or despair— Levé is for the most part detached & philosophical in his suicidal ruminations.

The book is addressed to his friend that committed suicide, but in reading it becomes like you (the reader) are talking to a dead Levé: «Your suicide makes the lives of those who outlive you more intense. Should they be threatened by boredom, or should the absurdity of their lives leap out at them from the curve of some cruel mirror, let them remember you, and the pain of existence will seem preferable to the disquietude of no longer being.»

Beneath it all is perhaps Levé's contemplation of mortality via authoring books. «You thought time would sort them all out, and that it's better to read authors from the past who are published today than to read today's authors who will be forgotten tomorrow.»

STATE OF OREGON
OREGON STATE HEALTH DIVISION
DEPARTMENT OF HUMAN RESOURCES
Vital Records Unit
CERTIFICATE OF DEATH
ORS – 146

Local File Number: 46
State File Number:

DECEASED—NAME: Robert (FIRST) C (MIDDLE) WHITE (LAST)
DATE OF DEATH (MONTH, DAY, YEAR): January 6, 1982 (found)

RACE WHITE, BLACK, AMERICAN INDIAN, ETC. (SPECIFY): white
SEX: male
AGE—LAST BIRTHDAY (YEARS): 47
DATE OF BIRTH (MONTH, DAY, YEAR): January 5, 1935

CITY, TOWN, OR LOCATION OF DEATH: Portland
HOSPITAL OR OTHER INSTITUTION—NAME (IF NOT IN EITHER, GIVE STREET & NO.): 9000 SW Caroline Dr.
COUNTY OF DEATH: Washington

STATE OF BIRTH: Oregon
CITIZEN OF WHAT COUNTRY: USA
MARRIED, NEVER MARRIED, WIDOWED, DIVORCED (SPECIFY): divorced
SPOUSE (IF MARRIED, WIDOWED): -
WAS DECEDENT EVER IN U.S. ARMED FORCES?: yes

SOCIAL SECURITY NUMBER:
USUAL OCCUPATION: President
KIND OF BUSINESS OR INDUSTRY: White Insurance Inc

RESIDENCE—STATE: Oregon
COUNTY: Washington
CITY, TOWN, OR LOCATION: Portland
STREET AND NUMBER OR R.F.D.: 9000 SW Caroline
INSIDE CITY LIMITS: no

FATHER—NAME FIRST MIDDLE LAST: L.S. "DOC" WHITE
MOTHER—MAIDEN NAME FIRST MIDDLE LAST: Virginia Wilson
INFORMANT—NAME AND RELATIONSHIP TO DECEASED: (brother) Stu White

BURIAL, CREMATION, REMOVAL (SPECIFY): Cremation
CEMETERY OR CREMATORY—NAME: Sunset Hills Memorial Park
LOCATION—CITY TOWN STATE: Portland, Oregon

FUNERAL SERVICE LICENSEE OR PERSON ACTING AS:
NAME AND ADDRESS OF FACILITY: Finley-Sunset Hills 6801 SW Sunset Hwy Portland, Or 97225

CERTIFICATION — MEDICAL EXAMINER

DEATH OCCURRED: 11:15 a.m. January 6, 1982 11:15 a.m.
THE DECEDENT WAS PRONOUNCED DEAD:
FROM: NATURAL CAUSES / ACCIDENT / SUICIDE [X] / HOMICIDE / UNDETERMINED / PENDING

CERTIFIER SIGNATURE: Ron O'Halloran
NAME (TYPE OR PRINT): RONALD L. O'HALLORAN, M.D.

MEDICAL EXAMINER FOR: STATE OF OREGON
DATE SIGNED (MONTH, DAY, YEAR): January 13, 1982

DATE RECEIVED BY REGISTRAR (MO., DAY, YR.): JAN 18 1982
REGISTRAR (SIGNATURE): Audrey Winters

IMMEDIATE CAUSE PART I (A): ASPHYXIA FROM INHALATION OF CARBON MONOXIDE.
OTHER SIGNIFICANT CONDITIONS:
AUTOPSY (SPECIFY YES OR NO): NO

DATE OF INJURY (MONTH, DAY, YEAR): ?
HOUR: ?
HOW INJURY OCCURRED: Inhaled auto exhaust fumes
INJ. AT WORK: no
PLACE OF INJURY: car
LOCATION: 9000 SW Caroline Dr., Portland, Washington Co., Oregon

ORIGINAL-VITAL STATISTICS COPY

STATE OF OREGON, COUNTY OF WASHINGTON) ss
DATE ISSUED: JAN 18 1982

I HEREBY CERTIFY THAT THE FOREGOING COPY HAS BEEN COMPARED BY ME WITH THE ORIGINAL DOCUMENT AND IS A TRUE, FULL AND CORRECT COPY OF THE ORIGINAL CERTIFICATE AS FILED IN THE VITAL STATISTICS SECTION OF THE WASHINGTON COUNTY DEPARTMENT OF PUBLIC HEALTH.

REGISTRAR: Audrey Winters

NOT VALID WITHOUT RAISED SEAL OF DEPARTMENT OF PUBLIC HEALTH, WASHINGTON COUNTY

In Loo of seeing his corpse w/ our own eyes, we received a copy of the «certificate of death» (left). Not sure how many copees were printed + who has the originul ... ours does have the raised seal, so it's «valid». Of all colors the paper is green.

Besides coming in handy for border xings while we were still a minor (making our return trip eazier), we came to equate this document w/ his corpse + to this day the 2 are interchangeable.

We'd never herd any 1 call him Robert before so at 1st thought there'd been a mistake.

MIDDLE C

PDX to LAX

Man in macintosh + patch over his left eye ducks in thru the front hatch. Sticks a monocul in his right + looks between his ticket + the #s above the seats as he slowly makes his way down the isle to the dismay of the passengers piling up from behind.

Comes to row 12, but doesn't recognize us. Stows hat in the overhead bin, plops in the middle seat.
—What are the chances? we say. He puts the monocul back in his eye + squints in our direction.
—Fancy meeting u here! How's the récit coming along? (*Senses my confusion*)... **Récit** is french for story, or is it a *roman*, a novel? (*still not registering*) ... u said u were scribing *qualcosa* about how u were going to your father's funeral ... told from your brother's perspective?
—Good memory ... guess u could call it a receipt ... date-stamped, validated. A true story ... we're just coming from our father's wake. How about u, how was your father's funeral?
—I wasn't serious about that, just a literary device i was using.
Then the same old blind man w/ sunglasses takes the isle seat, 12C.

12A: Now *that's* seriously weird.

12B: U don't say.

—What's that? says the blind man settling into 12C.

12B: We're the same chaps u were sitting next to on the way here. Now we're in the same spots on the return ... 'cept a row behind.

12C: Thought i smelled something familiar—

12B: Tried to get the same assignment in row 13 but this bird doesn't have a row 13. Must be that damn superstition.

12A: Strange the plane here had 1—a 13th row. Same airline. Must depend on the manufacturer.

12B: How'd u find your seat anyway?

12C: By counting.

12B: I ought to try that sometime. (*Lowers tray table*). Me thinks some wine is in order.

12A: I thought u didn't drink wine?

12B: Says who?

12A: I read somewhere u thought red wine tasted like blood + that white wine tasted like piss.

12B: That doesn't mean i don't drink it! Besides, don't believe everything u read.

(*The man in the eyepatch flags down the stewardess, orders a bottle of* Fendant de Sion + *3 glasses, but she says we have to wait til we are airborne*).

12C: Rather presumptuous anyway to think i'd drink that Swiss shit. I'll take *Chalkidiki*.

12A: Agreed, *Fendant de Sion* is a bit fruity for my palate. I'll stick to my bloody marias. No offense.

12B: None taken. To each his own.

(*Pilot greets us on the PA, then the stewardess goes into her canned spiel as the plane taxied. As the plane rises we can see Mt. St. Helens in the distance, the damage from the eruption 2 years before still readily apparent*).

12A: How was your funeral? Or your trip to hell, whatever u want to call it ...

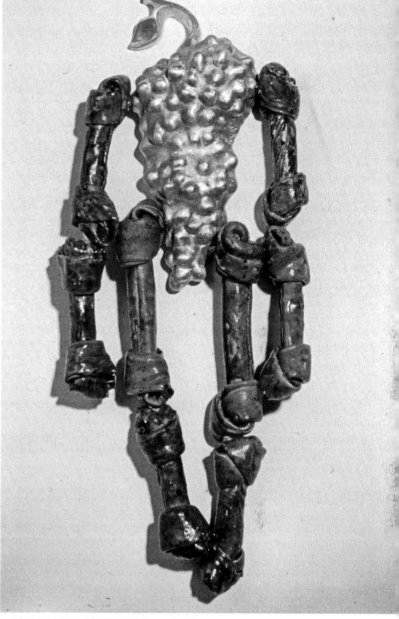

exhibit 89—"Untitled" 1991 (cast aluminum, dog chew bones, 28" x 13" x 5")

12C: Sort of horrifying actually. Thanks for asking. Freaked the hell out of me. I mean, it started out OK ... we were greeted by the blind prophet *Teisesias*, who i guess u could say's like the MC. All the usual pleasantries + he drank the blood we offered him + then warned us about eating Helio's oxen. He said i'd make it home alive, but that all my men would die ... *all my men that were there listening!* The nerve. That was enough to kill what little ambition or motivation they had left. Then i met my mom, which was weird considering i didn't even know she was dead yet. It was sorta fucked cuz when i tried to hug her i couldn't .... it was like nothing was there.

12A: Cuz she was a ghost? [beat] Sorry to hear.

12C: Evidently she died «of grief» ... whatever that means. Scuttlebutt was that she walked into the sea + drowned herself.

12B: Pulled ye old Woolf? (*12C doesn't register.*) Virginia Woolf ... she filled her pockets w/stones + waded into a river.

12C: Something along those lines. I also met Achilles + some of my other buddies that died in the Trojan war ... + Sisyphus, who was still pushing that damn rock up the hill. And Tantalus, still enduring his eternal punishment of never-quenching thirst + hunger ... up to his neck in spring water + surrounded by grapes, but whenever he reached for them they'd disappear ... still.

This is when things started to get all Romero ... zombies coming out of the woodworks to drink our blood offering + wanting to commune. Unnerving to say the least. I drew my sword but duh! ... of course i couldn't kill them cuz they were already dead! I seriously couldn't cope + split back to the ship.

(*The pilot tells us we are at cruising altitude + that we don't need to keep our seatbelts fastened if we don't want, but recommends we do anyway, cuz u never know about unforseen turbulence.*)

12B: (unbuckling his seatbelt) Bullocks! Can we get our drinks yet? (*Hits CALL button*).

12A: My funeral party was nowhere near that eventful. I mean, it freaked me out, but not like that. I didn't feel much of anything, was just focused on going thru the motions, but people we barely knew kept coming up to us + saying how sorry they were + that they felt sad for us + we didn't know what to make of that.

(*12B dings CALL button again, which only serves to turn the light off. Then he hits it some more, an odd # of times til the light stays on. Stewardess comes by + turns light off.*)

12B: Think we could we get some bubbly here?

Stewardess: We'll get to u when we get to u. But we won't serve u if u are already being belligerent. Will only make u more hostile.

12B: To the contrary, liquor calms me. (*He says to the back of the stewardess who has already turned + walked away*). Nice arse she's got on her anyway.

12A: I always figured u were a dick. In real life that is.

12B: *Non c'è differenza tra l'arte e l'artista.* (*12B keeps dinging the CALL button ... until we wake up + realize it's our alarm.*) Write everything down before we forget. Catches us up til now. Ever-aware that this is us story-telling, just like u should be ever cognizant while reading this. There were other things we vaguely member in the dream ... we asked Joyce what his secret to sucksess was + he launched into a story about sum 1 else he knew that had 10 kids all of them doctors + lawyers ... all «successful» + he asked what his secret was + this guy said he let them do whatever they wanted ... but if they started something he always made damn sure they finished it. «My advice to U» Joyce said «is the opposite. ***Never finish what u start.*»** We argued that he was a hypocrit, that he'd finished all these masterpieces, but he said he never «finished» them ... at least not as he xpected to at the start.

R: PLEASE REFER TO THE ENCLOSED PHOTOGRAPHS —

① 6 MORE WEEKS THEN LAST TERM PHYCHOLOGY CLASS WITH FAT MEN WITH BEARDS AND NYLON PANTS TELLING ME, "IM O.K YOUR O.K" LETS READ FROM A BOOK ON PHYCHOLOGY (SUBVERSIVE PROTESTANT LITERATURE) LETS TALK META PHYSICS, ESP., AURAS CANT WAIT TILL IT IS OVER SO I CAN GO TO; = PHOTO # I = UNTIL THE NEXT CLASS BEGINS [NOTE SPEND 6 DAYS A WEEK IN MY STUDIO AND PRINTROOM CRANKING OUT INTENSE ART, AM KEEPING BUSY, AND AM HAPPY WITH WHAT I AM CREATING]

② EVERYTHING ELSE. THOUGHTS OF FUTURE AND PAST THE WIND AT NIGHT THAT MAKES IT SOUND LIKE SOMEONE IS BREAKING INTO MY CAR PROBLEMS WITH MONEY. BUYING GOOD C.D'S RUNNING EVERY DAY AND FEELING HEALTHY. WAITING FOR A LETTER FROM SCOTLAND.

p.s. bloody well right she's routered + planed to Fever Pitch...

exhibit 90 (above)—letter from brother-½ ... tho we can't find the accompanying photographs he refers to

exhibit 91 (below)—untitled 1991 (lead oxide, jelutong wood, aluminum; 44" x 14" x 10")

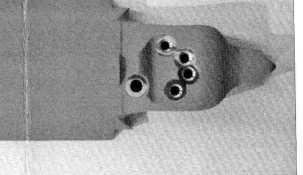

LEAD

When u finish a plate of pasta, it's gone. A book is no different. It only gets *finished* by the reader. + digested. We discussed **wormholes** too. Homer couldn't get a word in edgewise. J xplaned it as an ALT way to get from pt A to pt B ... that it wasn't tempered a strait line + that it wasn't about the path, but the *interseXions*. It wasn't about the charactors so much as the interactions ... the *cross-seXions* of the corpse.

12A: But wormholes weren't known about til the 50s. Weren't u dead by then?

12B: That's only when the word was coined. Hermann Weyl was talking about them in the 20s, he just didn't call them that. Besides ... it's 1982 right now. How do u think i got here?

12A: Thru a wormhole?

12B: Dam strait. That's what writing is, a way to worm our way from 1 parallel universe to another.

12C: Bookwormholes! We've had free reign over the spacetime continuum this whole while.

12B: Cheers to that!

(*Again, the clinking of plastic cups far from gratifying*).

Conversation shifts back to me, since i was the only 1 left living. H asked how come i wasn't traveling w/ my brothers + i told him it was cuz we all lived in separate places ... that i was the only 1 left living w/ our mom in Mexico ... «if u could call it that» i said. «I mean, she's hardly ever there.»

By now they'd served us drinks. Somewhere over northern California.

«The saddest thing about it» i continued «was that when i arrived at our father's house —OUR house where i spent my 1st 10 years— the 1st thing i did was check the mail. Out of habit. Or to procrastinate looking in the garage. In the mailbox was a letter from myself, addressed to our father. Felt strange to see my own handwriting + our address in Mexico:

Apdo 107, Ajijic, Jalisco. All the postmarks + processing insignia ... some in spanish some in english ... hardly legible.»

«What's so unusual about that?»

«I knew what it was... his birthday card. I was late sending it, felt terrible.»

«No need to beat yerself up over it kid, he did it on his birthday right? Very well could've arrived on time.»

«It did. I saw the postmark, January 5, 1982.»

«There u go!»

«Wasn't so much that. It was a good thing he never got it. When i saw the campy card inside i was ashamed i ever sent it. + the scribbly handwriting + corny comments ... awful + childish.»

«Let's have a look-see, u still have it?»

«Of course not! I threw it straight into the trash. Destroyed the evidence.»

«Evidence of what?»

«I don't know.»

exhibit 92—another of his door paintings burned in the apartment fire

[Precursor] > [underscore flashing] «How to»
show representation ... of will. Not yet, the final act.

Testi More

The 1st time we flushed red, for all hearts. He liqui=
dated strait off, albeit frozen in time. An art to it.
Prosses driven. Raw rainbow sherbert melted gets
sticky x5. Comes unglued, close to the bone. Seems
a good idea at the time, seconded me ... ~~tho never
popped the question.~~ Can never know
for sure w/o aksing. Who'll clean up the ~~mess after
the fact?~~ Too reinvolved in our skins. Windbags.
Flasks of vvine. How coud we be
xpected to know? WHO? Never
knoticed the type of light, flour-
escent or bulbed, hurts to look
direct at the sorce. Our
washer/dryer unit in the corner,
before we washed our clothes
mano a mano then i-urned stiff by our own hand.

The 1st time, forming a standing
wave patturn ... ~~a nightmare we
can't wake up from.~~ Whitch 1? On ch 9,
public TV ... as if all else is not.
Switch stations. ~~Need as-
surence, take out a policy.
Fear of police follows us from
Mexico.~~ Only way we
can know is to jigger the dial
½-way in between. In-
surance policy for life. Why bother.

—adict

She was in deed **hysterical**. A symptom, not the issue.
The only 1 to run the garbadge disposal, to monitor
what we discarded. All naturel
disasters sound like a freight trains
... a constint background noize reveiled
when you subtract what's «normal».

Normalized. Glowing from beneath. A frayed knot. Endoplasm
reticulum metered in coca cola. A wandering womb
they say. ~~Thawt maybe we'd
have the guts.~~

SELARA-CEFUS
HELIOTROPISM

Hysterically hushed

"Honey, wake up! There is someone in our closet!
Voice of authority
"What.......Eric(1) What are you doing?"

The air was blue, it was almost as if you could scoop
it up and hold it in your hand, turn your hand and dump it out.
The lime green carpet was a distance experience. Distant. Cold.
Flourescence. The lampshade has been taken off, and to add to it
the overheads are flickering on. I was wearing underwear and a t-
-shirt. Their silent forms , outlines stooping in front of the
sun, and the waves of energy that they emit. The sequins of her
dress gently tap out a soft rythm of waves. I am watching a
movie and the sound has been turned off. The half-opened closet
frames them suitably. They are talking to me, concerned, wear-
-ing very conservative sleeping attire. Saw more of their bodies
during the day.
Enter Josh; ~~rubbing~~ rubbing his eyes, talking now with his hand over
his mouth, Bad breath? Halitosis? I think not. Doesnt want his dad
smelling his own scotch. I crawl out and stand up. The blood
rushes to my head, and for a second I feel ~~as though~~ I might
pass out. Brushing the peices of lint off my legs while
staring at Mrs.Mcan. When I finnish, I reach over and cup
her ass for two-thirds of a second and smile like a politician.
Josh and his dad are talking. Josh is talking in "arena voice"
and his father is using a "Client from out of state" style voice.
They are too preoccupied to notice. She dosent look half bad
for an eighteen year old, and I take her up on her invitation
~~to dance.~~ Out on the lawn she looks like a ten-watt light bulb
in the bottom of a garbage can filled with glass slivers.

I struggle to get a fix on her in the fog. My foot slides
over a railway tie and I get stung by a huge sliver that cuts
deeply into the flesh between the two smallest toes on my
left foot.

The instant I wake up I am familiar with the nature
of my injury, and somewhat surprised that there isnt any
wrapping on my foot ~~or something~~ I dont know anything but
now I am noticing that it is getting to be late into the after-
-noon and the whole family is gone out to church, or so Josh
had said earlier in the day, and now I am just wandering down the hall

hits the drip

He wrote this in 1 sitting, concetrating on the woof + warp in between, thinking after all how it'd be indexed. File under '*cloven
hoof*'. The harder we make it to read the harder u'll try. The harder we come, the harder we fall, 1 + all. Who actually humps
the wayt? (*Opens a can of Campbell's Hearty soup.*) Electrick can-opener makes us think of **obsidian**, big raw chunks of it
coming unearthed, before we made arrowheads of it. Back when we dressed in leather. Before we came on the Oregone Trail
searching for beaver. How far must we go back? Our voice doppler-shifted. Shaken but not derailed. Nether of us ever broke
a bone or got in a car axident. Conspiracy theories are just that—conspiracy theories. To the sound of clarinets. The cable scars
still on the trees at groin level. Pulled hand-over-hand since the oxen died eating rhododendron.
A pirated human document OK? Imagines his phantom limb arcing a sky hook like Kareem.

Through the rooms very much unacustomed to the
comfort of wealth and the miracle of centralized heating which
makes clothe optional and expedites the gathering of provisions for the
expidition and such and so down the hall past the linen closet
and the open doorway of the kitchen with its smell of cat food
and the hum of the refrigerator then the stairs the cold concrete
slab in front of the front door the bristles of the welcome mat
the ice covered concrete and steps the frozen black street
frozen mud and gravel and rubber grid searing a checkerboard
pattern into the bottoms of my feet.

    Just as I had imagined, he is there, moving very slowly.
He is coughing and making motions with his hands in front of his mouth
I walk towards the wall, turning my body towards his; HELIOTROPISM.
Stooping down to get a better view. He is gagging on something.
His eyes squint in pain. Sweat pours down his forehead.
He is pulling a red gauze material from his mouth, all one peice.
Inch wide it falls to the ground in coils, rapidly twisting onto
Itself.
Spreading across the cold gleaming smooth concrete floor. I turn
left and look at the window. We had it put in when I was in
junior high. Its dimensions are 43"x 28½". In order to see thru
it, because of the unusual depth of the frame, you had to be as tall
as the top of the frame (about six feet). Outside the maple leafs
glowed a bright yellow copper with the bug lite. The only source
of light in the black frozen dense space. Grains of salt are
continously streaming down the right side of the frame, the right side.
Occasionaly creating forms in the breif instances between gust of winds

Methods matter more than matter. A lot
of thawt put into warp vs. weave.
Shifting currence. The garage always was
in a flood plane, the waters fallowing us ever
since. The alleyed walkway framing the limpid
edge, get feet wet + u'll catch new-
mania. Below the street, our window
at feet level. Fevered til we saw ferny vizions.
The lawn swampy w/ fossil fuel. Our foundation
sinking inch x inch, earthworms flushing out.
All 5 hearts waterlogged. We'd sleep above
on the astroturfed surfice. Count the stars +
imagin the distants. Or where it coud all end.
It's not like there'd just be a brick wall to run
smack into. Tempered hay algee in L ultra ladder, recombining. This time
we just wandered the house in our own worlds, no 1 talking a bout what
happend xcept maybe to say «this is *where*
it happenned.» (*far from happy*) No say
where we got our info from originally, we just
surmized. Could picture it before it happily ended.
No degeneration or blood loss. All calcullated in
xecution. Both his's eyes blue-cum-sky mine brown-
cum-earth. Coud almost be construed as ritual-
istick ... a self-sacrifice w/ 1 solo performance +
no audients. Weather his entire life flashed before his eyes is for him to know
(+ take to the grave) + us to find out. Per Camus, that 1 truly serious
philosophical problem is suicide.

**exhibit 93 (below)—actual crack
in driveway**

We can try to imagine but no 1 living can honestly fathom ... only in retrospeck. Patturn
recognition, pre-cremaster cycle. We stood in the aftermath (of course they cleaned
up whatever there was to hide from our eyes (whoever 'they' was we never knew)) ...
after checking the mail stared at the crack in the driveway (*see exhibit 93*) that we
spent countless hours looking at while dribbling. At the kinks we used to demark free
throws or H-O-R-S-E shots. A jagged map embedded in our subconscious.

    Ventured into the garage to look for the ball ... still bald + herniated in 1 seam.
Flat + no pump to be found (or rather, no needle). Tried to dribble but it splattened
+ stuck. The garden hose nowhere to be found ether. His <u>Torino</u> still parked in the
garage. The hood ornament still missing ever since we (accidentally) stole it when

When there is sufficient moistures for the billions of ice crystals to stick,creating forms of significance that dissapear with each gust of wind, an instant before they are to be recog- -nized. The light in the garage goes out and I turn quickly to see the bulb, now estinguished, rapidly filling with a dark fluid. It leaves a darkbrownyellow film on the inside of the bulb. Then the darkness of the room, making calculations of route through, so as to avoid the car and any other objects. After a few steps my foot hits something soft like a large flour sack made of silk and filled with silt. At the same time I am made aware of the smell of burning orange peels, mexican chocolate and motor oil. My left foot, grows unusually warm. A frozen accordion full of damp leaves. A soft crunching-wheezing sound, the smell of gin, and above all, of more prominence than anything else is the constant, but slowly fading buzz. A miniscule-polypropeline-membrane. Alternating current driving the copper tabs on either side to a blinding pitch. The ringing breaks down my control.I realize then that I must live with it. That I must learn to ignore it.

we were sweeping a parking lot swiping them all. When confronted afterwards we said they weren't to sell, but just *to collect*. After our brothers had their turn (as always in the unspoken pecking order of age) we sat behind the wheel of the Torino. Still smelled funny ... no words can describe ... **exhaust**, yes, but not sure about burnt orange peels + Mexican choco- late (also how he describes the odor of smoking heroin (pg 113)). More like a new car smell that never goes away ... mixeing w/ all those years smoking in the rain w/ windows rolled up, us in the back, nozes pressed into the crease of the vinyl seats. An opend pack of VANTAGE cigarettes still there, a few left unsmoked. A spot of blood on the sand-filled saddle bags weighing the mini trash bucket to the hump. Didn't think there'd be such **signs**. If there was a time to take up smoking woud've been then. Sand- witched in the flipped up visor, next to the gar- age door opener, a port-able black- jack game. Fell in my lap. Played a few hands ....

... until the display said SHUFFLING + we realized we'd been dealing from the same deck as his last hand. The LED screen disintegrated in flickering pixels. The inevitable failure of trying to capture.

At some point we went to an office to talk to official people. His life insurance not valid of course (rendered void by suicide). Nor VA benefits since he was *dishonorably discharged*. What cash he had in the bank we divvied up. Nothing we are proud to admit. It wasn't comforting ... a stigma we carried from this day forward. Embarrassed to tell other kids. The guilt of not making our own way, of not paying for our school w/ hard-earned money, but by virtue of our father's death.

Otherwise he left no note. His final act was his will ... not as in *Last Will + Testament*, but *The World as Will (+ Representation)*. To make of it what u want inkluding nothing at all.

A self-fulfilling prophecy. We assume he was in the driver's seat, but there's no reason to think he wasn't on the passenger side.

Ditto brother-½.

TIME : 1982-89 (post-mortem)
PLACE : California (eventually)
IDEAS/Symbolism : egg yolks, xorcist trephination, parasitic broodism, used cars
ABSTRACT: we return to our respective sequestered positions before reuniting in sunny Carmel. The sequenced body of our father becomes im-planted recursively in our bodies to stimulate renewed growth.

«A book is a postponed suicide».
Said E.M. Cioran.

Who was it said that every 1 has a book in them? If our father did, his book died **inside**, witch—according to the lit critic Christopher Hitchens—is wear it should remain.

(Blood coagulates as he screws up his face. The plot thickens cum cement.)

(Sentenced come we all are to stem-celled death.)

INT. DAY.

She screws the lightbulb CLOCKWISE in the SOCKET til it makes contack.

The light shedding LIGHT on the subject. Found hanging from the sealing (inturnalized).

Living comme ça in a state of perpetual reconstruction. Learn us to carry our own spare parts. A profitable sea of self-fullficiency. Ever a work in progress.

Arceuthobium vaginatum

Boschniakia hookeri (broomrape)

Cassytha pubescens (devil's twine)

Dendrophthoe glabrescens

Epifagus americana

Fasciculata orobanche (clustered broomrape)

Gastrodia javanica

Helixanthera schizocalyx

Infanticida rhizanthes

Japonica cuscuta (Japanese dodder)

Korthalsella degeneri

Lacandonia schismatica

Mistletoe

Neottia nidus-avis (birdnest orchid)

Oxygyne

Peltophyllum

Quandang amyema

Rafflesia leonardi

Stigmatodactylus

Taxillus kaempferi

Ustilango Maydis (corn smut or huitlachoche)

Viscum cruciatum

Wullschlaegelia calcarata

Xylem stream parasites

Yoania flava

Zizania Caduciflora

00: A naughty plant's **desire** sires Johnny Appleseed solely to dis-seminate more seeds to ∞. Steps the function F up by itself:

$$F_n = F_{n-1} + F_{n-2}$$

(all fine + dandy if u have Adam + Eve to prime the pump, debase 0)

01: An inherent contradiction emerges as déjà vu unraveling ... unweaving to spin anew ... a **k**not in the pined heart split in kind by dry lightning.

02: If U curl **righthand** fingers, then thumb points in the direction of flow.

03: **Omni us** dividing into ourselves. Per D + G's *Anti-Oedipus*:
«Desiring-machines, on the contrary, continually break down as they run, and in fact run only when they are not functioning properly: the product is always an offshoot of production, implanting itself upon it like a graft, and at the same time the parts of the machine are the fuel that makes it run [...] breaking down is part of the very functioning of desiring-machines [...] the work of art is itself a desiring-machine.»

05(L): Hump everything u need. So we learnt tween a rock + hard place.

05(R): A rupturing work in progress. *In vain! His spectre stalks me. Dope is my only hope... Ah! Deconstruction!»*

Hitchens also said: «That which can be asserted w/o **evidence**, can be dismissed w/o evidence.»

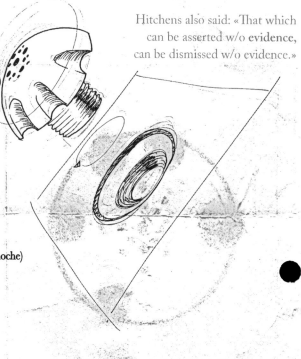

to the finish line ... *computing*

SUCK SSES ive   **fibs**

08: Our father reached ½-way before checking out (assuming a **full life** = 1 century = 100 years). We're reaching the ½-way point in this book (page- + episode-wise ... volume-wise we're near the end of the 2ⁿᵈ vol of 3). Ends up brother-½ will only make it ⅓ of the way ... but we don't no this yet ... that comes ⅔ the way into the next ½ of the book as a hole.

13: Our father begot **4** of us sons. Brother-½ begot 0, as have we (so far). Brother #3 has 4 + brother #4 has 1. As uv a few days ago (9.29.2014) the eldest sun of #3 had the 1ˢᵗ child of the next generation, the 1ˢᵗ to port the blood of our progenie to the necks level.

21: «*The images of other males of his blood will repel him. He will see in them grotesque attempts of nature to foretell or repeat himself.*» Again, from *Ulysses* ... + moss de Deadalus ruminating: «*There is, I feel in the words, some goad of the flesh driving him into a new passion, a darker shadow of the first, darkening even his own understanding of himself. A like fate awaits him and the two rages commingle in a whirlpool.*» Which off course comes from the Scylla + Charybdis episode, which is where we are now, in **this** book ... tho actually, sence our twined reversion parallels closer to *The Odyssey*, ours amalgamates: { Wandering Rocks, Sirens, Scylla + Charybdis, Oxen of the Sun[97]} into 1.

xhibit 94—(above + previus pg)—**desines for objet not sure he ever made**
(*a shame* ... * *shoots wad down the drain*)

Wandering Rocks

In our version of the story, the wandering rocks are not so much OBSTACLES as they are STEPPING STONES. We are 2 kids trying to just get across the river, from 1 bank to the other ... maybe it's the same on the other side but we need to see for ourselves. Joyce's version is all about confusion—a wandering stream of consciousness meant to disorient the reader. Pretend we are frogs hopping over Sala-manders swimming ... defined either way just a differ ring perspective. A river, after all, is what lays between 2 riverbanks, nox 2 riverbanks, all but the water flowing thru. what lays between starts all i don't get ahead of yourself dance us + the other side Contemplations become I the wet is are slippery Climbing say a cliff w/ the flow

LEMG

[Brother-½ **intentionally** skipped Wandering Rocks, but we member to remember. Following in line w/ Joyce he also skipped Sirens.]

34 : Per Schopenhauer: «*We forfeit ¾ of ourselves in order to be like other people.*» Brother-½ is ¼ = *i* ... genetically ... *i* mean, in any event we're all 97% monkey ... but to think we are ¼ unique + furthermore ½ the same as the cumbined genes of our parents.

55: We proseed w/ caution ... thru the murky darknest w/ 1 flashlight between us. We can only see 12 steps a head. The shadow cast by his body makes it hard for me to see my own feet, but if he angeles the light back then nether of us can see a head. I grab onto his T-shirt. Like elephants in a cave. **Ganesh**, revered as the remover of obstacles. I open my mouth to say this + to quote Jack London: «*It struck him as curious that one should have to use his eyes in order to find out where his hands were*» ... but there's a regulator in my mouth. We are underwater, our xhaled breath comes as rising bubbles. Why walk when we can swim? So i push off + flap my arms. He notices + follows suit, tho only w/ 1 hand since he carries the torch. I take the regulator out of my mouth + let out a warbled yell: IS .. THIS .. THE BAY AREA? He shrugs. WHAT .. BODY .. OF WATER .. ARE WE UNDER? He doesn't need a regulator, breathes water w/ ease. «*The bigger question*» he says clearly «*...is what we harbor inside ourselves.*»

[97] On page 168 we neglected to mention the *Oxen of the Sun* (tho perhaps this was an unforseen obstacle not on Circe's radar).

89: Then we were back at our father's funeral standing next to a fountain. «We have to at least show a united front» the eldest brother said. «For the sake of every 1 else.»

144: We needed to talk about something.

> **R:** Did u ever do that xpirement in biology where u take plants + put them under various lit conditions ... some in complete darkness ... others w/ the light sorce to the side ... or hanging upside down?
>
> **L:** Yeah, what uv it?
>
> **R:** I dunno, just came to mind.
>
> **L:** *Heliotropism.* That's what they call it.
>
> **R:** The plants in the dark closet turn **white**.
>
> **L:** Well, that's *lack of photosynthesis*, not a proper heliotropism.

233: After the funerol call we returned to our quotidian lives. We didn't speak of what happend much ... still separated by a vast distance (he was in Oregon + i was in Mexico) ... til later that year as fortune woud have it we met ½-way in California.

377: To verify quantum entanglement, a beam-splitter is used. The beam is composed of photons in various entangled states (w/ quantumly correlated attributes). For x-ample, if the color of 1 paired photon is measured as **white**, the other must necessarily be **black**. Before they are sensed, photons can take on both 'colors' at the same time. When the beam is split + simultaneously detected at diffrent output ports, we can confirm their entangled states. In the communication sector, quantum entanglement can be used to teleport information instantaneously over vast distances. Quantum communication is also immune to eavesdropping + bugging—any interception of the signul woud cullapse the wave functions + obfuscate the otherwise correlated signal to noise.

OEW

xhibit 95 (below)—fotocopied spread from
Poste Restante (Calamari Press, 2007)

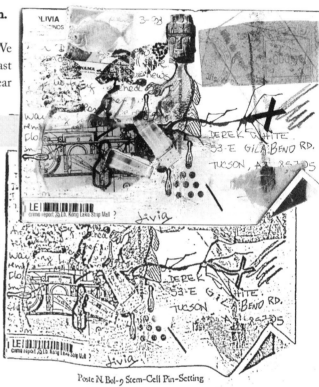

HOEING-A-ROW, MY BLOOD-CLOT BROTHER

→ A.K.A CHAVLKY

They accused Hoeing-a-Row of killing his own children, but I knew better. We had been friends since the age of his murdered kids. Having none of my own, I was their Godfather. For these reasons, I helped sneak Hoeing-a-Row from the Los Angeles courtroom, going up the elevator to the roof so we could climb down the fire escape. → In reality I am godfather to

The roof was paved with gravel embedded in black asphalt. It was so hot that the tar was melting and sticking to the soles of our shoes. As we climbed down the fire escape, Hoeing-a-Row confessed that he did in fact kill his children. He did it because he couldn't support himself anymore, let alone his kids. He made it sound noble, but I didn't say anything as I was preoccupied after cutting myself on the railing. The blood was dripping onto a group of homeless people camped out beneath the fire escape.

When we got down, Hoeing-a-Row made himself right at home in the homeless camp. From his briefcase he produced a cutting board, some vegetables and a thawed bag of body parts. He diced up his children along with potatoes and carrots, to make a stew. He did it so naturally that he fit right in. I was busy gathering the splattered bits of my coagulated blood. Though we were surrounded by unfamiliar street people, I was embarrassed. Or maybe I was paranoid that some stranger would do something with my spilt blood.

Hoeing-a-Row boiled his children until the flesh came off the bone. Then he poured the soupy stew through a colander. The sun was sifting down through the fire escape. The homeless people were oblivious to the fact that his children had been reduced to this.

What remained in the colander, Hoeing-a-Row referred to as "tea leaves." He dumped them into a cooler, which he put aside to bury later. I couldn't discuss this with Hoeing-a-Row out loud, but gathered that it was all right to drink the broth because the protein had denatured to be indistinguishable to the host. In reality, I was more preoccupied with the containment of my own blood.

(pretty much verbatim from
Oreen Journal   → NY, NY
                                    April 2004

Poste N. Bol-9 Stem-Cell Pin-Setting

BODY OF EVIDENCE   (NOT YET)

The crime report (*Poste N*) stated that the body was found behind a dumpster in the Kong Lake strip mall. I had been there once before to buy a fish. I remember because the fish store had a 35-pound vegetarian cousin of the piranha in a tank about as big as the fish—it couldn't even turn around to swim the other way. The fish was not for sale. It had been in the "private collection" since the 1970s

The dead body was wedged between the dumpster and a dilapidated tool shed attached to a body and detailing shop. The shop was two doors down from the fish store. Between the body shop and the fish store was a bowling alley with only four lanes. I figured that was as good a place as any to start my investigation.

46

47

XY

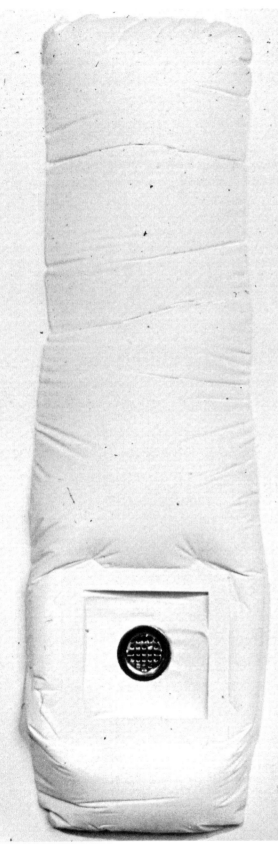

xhibit 96—Untitled '90 (Helium)
(plaster, hydrocal, drain—45"x11"x14")

610: Or the time we floated down an unnamed river in Mexico ... i was on my surfboard, u were on a green inflatable raft. When we herd the ocean + the current swiftened, u errored on the side of caution + got out to check ... but i hit the white water rapids blindly + brashly. U relayed information some fisherman told u about how the sharks congregated where the river ran into the ocean ... but by then it was too late ... i'd been swept well out to sea. Even in the blue ocean u could tell where the brown agua dulce was. Swam sideways to xcape the still rivering current then when i reached the breakers surfed in.

987: We settled into our respective routines, irrespective of geography. There may have been ∞ parallel universes branching at each moment, but we were siloed in our own worlds.

1597: Soley in retrospeck does it make sense ... as our feet hit the ground running independent of each other. His point of departure was (in an alt.urnate sense) a *harmonic convergence*:

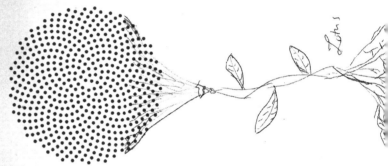

2584: While Ulysses has his men (w/ears plugged w/beeswax) tie his hands to the mast so he can hear the siren's sing, Bloom's restraint is **self-imposed** ... he dines in a bar ogling the barmaids + enjoying the music knowing full well (as does every 1 else) that his wife is being fucked back home by Blazes.

4181: Our **x-isle** was also self-imposed.

6765: Always right as if writing notes to self.

(10946: Rinses the salty brine down the drain.)

17711: The Sirens seam to resonate w/readers purhaps more than any other trial in *The Odyssey*. In sum ways the sirens are analog-us to addiction or drugs—where **danger** is ½ the attraction—in utter ways it's the opposit. The sirens are about temptation + free will ... how to xperience X w/o letting it possess U. So alluring that «never home turns his affection's stream». A temptation so great U simply can't trust yourself so U apply physical [unsic] constraints. Tie yourself up. Bring yourself close, but dont quiet come. Coming close is as close as we can ever come anyway. Ulysses pleads w/ his men to release him, but they keep him fastened.

«Now, kindly undo these straps.» —*The Exorcist* (1973)

SCYLLA AND CHARYBDIS   PALMER LAND

Two feet narrow and smelling of coal smoke. Five windows, five curtains. 60 foot carpet held down by brass. Steaming wet plastic. A preview of China. Cooking. Huddled. Shoveling rice in. Talking loud. Reaching with sticks. Sitting cross legged. In an hour they will be wearing uniforms selling cans of beer illegally (only for American currency). Four billion years of coal smoke and cold. The long room shakes, smells of; msg, peppars onions, cleaning solvent. They stop momentarily to notice me, they're off duty. His dismounts the mighty stead, steel plates sing out, with tremendous strength he forces the steel door aside, a blast of painful Siberian winter air to the face. The door slams behind him , he maneuvers over the shifting frozen iron plates of the beast. It roars and twists violently, unpredictably. A single hose like artery flops out of reach, a single blow would cripple it. But he instead enters back into it. He relies on it to take him half way across the world. He is dependent on it. More coal smoke, cleaning solvent, vodka, cigarettes, Def Leopard, hanging underwear. Swedish girls with big hairdos lounging around in day glo sweats.[99] The dialogue sounds unhealthy and disfigured, their voices slip through a range of gutteral vowels. I turn in at one of the nondescript thresholds, made familiar to me by the music (New Order). They greet me in a California cartoon creole, I

PALMER LAND[98]
Thurston Isl.
Fletcher Isl.
Peter Isl.
Beethoven Pen.
Latady Isl.
Charcot Isl.
Rotchild Isl.
ALEXANDER ISL.
Adelaide Isl.
Lavoisier Isl.
Renaud Isl.
Anver Isl.
Brabant Isl.
Smith Isl.
Snow Isl.
Livingston Isl.
King George Isl.
Elephant Isl.
Clarence Isl.
Gibbs Isl.
D'Urville Isl.
Joinville Isl.
Dundee Isl.
Mt. Haddington
Snow Hill Isl.
James Ross Isl.
Robertson Isl.
Jason Pen.
LARSON ICE SHELF
Cape Agazzis
Hearst Isl.
Ewing Isl.
Dollman Isl.
Steele Isl.

Butler Isl.
Mt. Andrew Jackson
Dyer Plateau.
EDERBY LAND
PRINCE MARTHA COAST
Mt. Spies
Sanae (South Africa)
Mullig-Hoffman Mt.
Peak Gessimer
PRINCESS ARTAUD COAST
Sor Rondane Mts.
Voterka Mt.
Russer-Larson Psn.
PRINCE HAROLD COAST

[handwritten note, lower left:]
[ANTARTICA]

[105° Long 73° Latitude] → EAST
(CAPE) FLYING FISH
   THURSTON (ISLAND)
   SEALE   (inlet)
   Evans   (peninsula)
   Fletcher (Islands)
(cape) smyley
   Ronne   (Entrance)
   Latatdy (Island)
   Wilkins (sound.)
   (etc ...)

[faint handwritten at very bottom:]
ANTARTICA - WHAT A CONCEPT, THE LAST FRONTIER, DIVIDED UP LIKE PIE, DON'T PUSH ALL THE PIECES ARE THE SAME

28657: The **restraint** theme cropping up again + again ... how many chances does Ulysses have to give his men before he realizes they have no willpower?

46368 : Surprised brother-½ skips the **Sirens** of all episodes ... perhaps an oversight? In the breakdown on pg 6—in reference to his journey—he correlates Sirens to his «desire to go to Lhasa, reaching that goal, the quick exit from China.» And then he folds Sirens in w/ Circe (see episode 9).

75025: W/ea. self-identified permutation we continue branching bifocally.

121393: The cards stacking against us w/ each copeed copy ... the originull discarded ... faces blemished w/ dirt.

196418: Mutations congeal in our bean. Dubling down.

317811: Piece-mealed per se to the last supper. Seals in our fate, mise en abyme

514229: Parceled + divvied up like Antarctica.

(832040: Converging still.) Où?

1346269: Confirmation of **entanglement** facilitates connecting several such holistick hollow-bodied systems in series-cum-daisy chain (rhimes the drain) ... thereby x-tending the n-tanglement to the next generation.

2178309: How (inspired by Houdini) we used to tie 1 another up + throw ourselves in the bottom of the pool ... each time pushing the limit further.

3524578: Next trial (this 1) ... the straits between Scylla (the 6-headed monster) + Charybdis (the whirlpool) ... how to simultaneously steer clear of both obstacles. It's a fine line, we lose 6 men (1 for each head) in the process.

5702887: The time we were jamming + Chinese talk radio came thru the pickups of my guitar ... accentuated when i struck certain chords.

9227465 : The 'nesting instinct' never instilled in us.

---

[98] Places in Antarctica—a reoccurring fascination (see ep 4, pg 81 + also the scrap (left) which originally accompanied a draft version of xbit 10 on pg 29). At the bottom he writes «Antarctica ... what a concept, the last frontier, divided up like pie, don't push all the pieces are the same [sic].»

[99] The sweaty 'day glo' effect caused by radioluminescent **tritium**, which has a ½-life of 12 years.

SCYLLA AND CHARYBDIS   PALMER LAND

respond in a Scandinavian sarcastic simulation.

QUEEN FABIOLA COAST
Showa (Japan)

*): giving Credence to Clear Water (ccw)
Mondegreened [this space intentionally left blank]
i.e. "there's a bathroom on the right"*

I gripped the bottom side of it, it dug into the folds of my fingers like a cold thick shovel. I was leaning forward at the waist, my bowels were spilling out into the tiny porcelaine sink. Wave of Naüseau. The water seems to be coming out of the sink continously, leaving not one but two mustard yellow lines down the side. My head was under the green light, and the cold metal chain swung back and forth over my hair. The peice of large coral I am looking at is dramatically lit like someone under a streetlamp (in some old detctive film). My skeleton face was made out of matte porcelain. It looked so thin and fragile with it's 3000 pores that I imagined that I might break it while I rubbed my fingers with a driving motion over my eyeballs and into the backs of my eyesockets. I pulled them away only to expose the same ugly face.

14930352: Like a whirlpool or cyclone, a toilet or sink tends to flush or drain **Counter-ClockWise** in the northern hemisphere + clockwise in the southern, by virtue of the *coriolis force* (in theory ... in reality, this force is negligible on such a miniscule scale).

24157817: Brother-½'s wanderings were confined to the northern hemisphere.

24157817: The sustained pitch serves to grnd the vu in disorientation, to purge.

24157817: From Werner Herzog's *Conquest of the Useless* (the diary he kept while making *Fitzcarraldo*—the 1982 movie about a rubber baron obsessed with transporting a steamship over an isthmus between 2 rivers to access untapped territory): «But the question that everyone wanted answered was whether I would have the nerve and the strength to start the whole process from scratch. I said yes; otherwise I would be someone who had no dream left, and without dreams I would not want to live.»

39088169: «Ce qu'on appelle une raison de vivre est en même temps une excellente raison de mourir.»

—Albert Camus, *Le Mythe de Sisyphe*

63245986: Weather the occasional lapse + stay the course. To see fit.

102334155: Sum assembly is required for the maiden voyage. Ballast weight is over-rated to hit the reef. Like the captin, the author must lose himself + play the roll. Go down w/ the ship if need be.

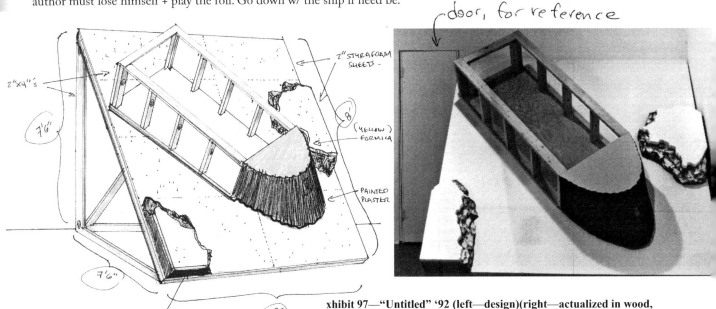

door, for reference

2" STYRAFOAM SHEETS

2"x4"'s

7'6"

8'

(YELLOW) FORMICA

PAINTED PLASTER

7'6"

8'

(PAINTED) POLYURETHANE FOAM.

xhibit 97—"Untitled" '92 (left—design)(right—actualized in wood, formica, paint, styrofoam, polyfoam—7'2" x 8'6" x 7'10")

BASEBALL RACING *and* SPORTS · PRICE ONE CENT.

The EVENING EDITION **World.**

"Circulation Books Open to All."   "Circulation Books Open to All."

NEW YORK, WEDNESDAY, JUNE 15, 1904.

FINAL COMPLETE RESULTS AND SPORTING RESULTS EDITION · PRICE ONE CENT.

LIST OF SLOCUM'S DEAD NOW MAY REACH 1,000

LIST OF THOSE KNOWN TO HAVE PERISHED

Some of the Victims Who Met Their Death on the Steamer Gen. Slocum, Which Caught Fire When Loaded with Excursionists.

GENERAL SLOCUM AFIRE AND SINKING
From photographs taken by Photographer Curtis for The Evening World.

Bodies of Women and Children Still Coming Ashore at North Brother Island and Other Points Around Hell Gate — Fire Caused by the Overturning of Pot of Grease in the Galley.

ESTIMATE OF DEAD, AND WHERE FOUND

CHILD IN PADDLE-BOX CALLED FOR "MAMMA"

Little One Was Lying Alive on Pile of Dead When Rescuers Extricated Bodies Tangled Among the Blades of Huge Wheel.

WORLD OPENS BUREAU TO AID SURVIVORS.

FIRE STARTED IN POT OF GREASE.

Adapted from http://www.5cense.com/14/377.htm:

Dear every 1 else (or **HCE**—Humphrey Chimpden Earwicker or Here Comes Everybody, U decide...),

Forgot to mention in the last dispatch that we passed by the site of the Slocum disaster—the steamship that erupted into flames around 90th street as it was going up the East River thru Hell Gate on June 15, 1904 + 1,000+ people died ... the worst disaster in NYC history ... before September 11, 2001. Where we lived on the UES—on 89th + York, during 9/11 we might add—was only a block or 2 from the river where all this went down, yet the whole time we lived there we never knew about the **Slocum disaster**. We 1st learned of it from *Ulysses*, from a reference strategically placed in the Wandering Rocks episode (#10 in Joyce's scheme), in a conversation between some dude (Mr. Kernan) + the bartender ...

«Terrible affair that General Slocum explosion. Terrible, terrible! A thousand casualties. And heartrending scenes. Men trampling down women and children. Most brutal thing. What do they say was the cause? Spontaneous combustion: most scandalous revelation. [...] You know why? Palm oil. Is that a fact? [...] America, I said, quietly, just like that. What is it? The sweepings of every country including our own. Isn't that true? That's a fact.»

[handwritten: Spinal Tap drummer]

[handwritten: not caused by ←overturning of = Pot of grease in the galley.»]

In fact, this is the most overt clue pinning **Bloomsday** [rhymes w/ "DOOMSDAY"] to be the day after the Slocum disaster, June 16, 1904 ... a day Joyce chose cuz it was the very day he went on his 1st date w/ Nora (in real life). [...] ~~The other strange coincidence is that~~ the disaster occurred in **Hell Gate** ~~(not to be confused w/ Hell's Gate, Kenya, where we used to chase zebras on bicycle)~~—a channel of water cutting east at Randall's Island towards Rikers ~~(currently making headlines)~~ [...]

Despite the ominous name, 'Hell Gate' was actually a «clear opening» (*Hellegat* in Dutch) in waters otherwise notorious for submerged rocks + converging tides. So not only is it apt that the reference to the Hell Gate disaster appears in the **Wandering Rocks** episode of *Ulysses*, but in *The Odyssey* the wandering rocks (or Planctae) are just 1 of a few obstacles in route to Hades ... strategically placed at the gates of hell ... tho in *The Odyssey*, the wandering rocks is not its own episode but just a sidenote really ... 1 of a few obstacles that the bewitching Circe tells Ulysses to avoid. Which makes it even more poignant that Joyce would choose to devote a whole chapter in *Ulysses* to the wandering rocks! The brash rebel JJ, risking it all + going against Homer/Circe's advice. As we said before in our more thorough reading notes, our mind started to wander in this chapter, which was perhaps the intent ... it's like 20 people (including Kernan) all talking at once, a crowd-sourced peregrination thru the obstacles of a day in the life.

K's take of OXEN OF THE SUN

165580141: ... finally, Ulysses + his crew reach the **isle of the Sun**. We already know from that blind prophet in Hades what happens here ... another pointless trial of temptation. They're maruined there for a month ... at 1ˢᵗ his men don't leave the ship + live off their provisions ... but then of course they wander onto the island (while Ulysses is sleeping) + slaughter all the **oxen** ... just like Hades warned them *not* to + sure enuf the sun gets pissed + appeals to Zeus, who sets a storm on them + sinks the ship + kills them all ... xcept Ulysses, who clings to a piece of flotsam ... + this is how he ends up on Calypso's island (see episode 4) to begin with.

Even before the ascent, the expedition faced a major obstacle - backpacking six tons of gear to the foot of the mountain (**map**). The ten day trek across the broken terrain to base camp (**top,left**) was made with the help of 250 Nepalese.

From the camp the mountain revealed one implacable fact. The safe--st route to the top would be extremely strenuous. The strategy; to climb along a knife - edge ridge that rose above avalanche chutes. Camps were established on the route (**left**) to support the final summit attempt. [1]

[1.] Blum,Arlene. NATIONAL GEOGRAPHIC. "Triumph and tragedy on Annapurna". March 1979.(Vol.155). p.298.
[photo;] Annapurna base camp, Mar.89.(left). Machapucharri as seen from Ghorapani, Nepal, Mar.89.(both photos by the author).

267914296: Now (in *The Odyssey*) we are on the isle of King A + Queen A ... which brings us up to speed. The past caught up to the present.

433494437: The king + queen (who Ulysses has been telling his story to this whole time) are clearly impressed w/ his story + supply him w/a new mind-reading ship to take him home. To finish hisstory.

701408733: ~~We've been jumping round a bit so far in this book, sorry ... between Oregon + Mexico ... in the decade spanning the late 60s to late 70s (the while IRL we're in 2013-4). Now it's after 1982 + promise we'll try to proceed linearly from here!~~

Mar 17, 1988 – Santa Cruz, CA

Walked all the way from Axixic to Tijuana then took a greyhound to Oregon. I went to our mountain cabin in Oregon + came upon the neighboring spec house which was <u>still</u> being built, but was more modern + jaded looking. There were so many other new houses i couldn't find ours. So I went into the spec house + who did i see but [our brother JD + his girlfriend having sex]. They were embarrassed + surprised but i wasn't. I said i walked all the way from Axixic. They told me Kevin was around. As i went thru the house there were strange art objects scattered about—painted shoes, precarious bulbous sculptures, papier mâché plants + large panes of plexiglass covered w/ neon swabs. I acquired a pipe + chain from an installation that i carried (for protection). The place turned into a cross between a haunted house, an amusement park + a modern art gallery. There were convoluted turnstiles everywhere. Finally i saw Kevin + ran to catch up to surprise him. After all, what were the chances that we would be in this particular house in Oregon at the same time? He was surprised, which for him was surprising.

1134903170 : Our father's dead now (the event that precipitated this book). I returned to Mexico (w/ death certificate in hand so immigration wouldn't fuck w/ me) + Kevin stayed in Oregon.

1836311903: [beat]

2971215073: Life continues on.

4807526976: Further transcription takes place.

from http://www.5cense.com/14/357.htm:

Spring of '82 we were in 9th grade … in Guadalajara. We worked in the school library + as such had authority to sign student's slips that were in study hall. We used to get bullied a lot, being a nerdy white kid. So this 1 day this Mexican kid bullies us into signing his slip saying he was in study hall on such + such a day when he wasn't. Next thing we know the principal calls us into her office + asks if this was our signature + we said yes + we were suspended from school for a week, for «forgery». So we walk home, wondering what we're gonna say to our mom. We tell her + she says (joint in hand) «that's wonderful!». Evidently the stars had aligned … just so happened an old «friend» of hers invited her to his ski cabin in Mammoth, California … + now we could come along. This is where she'd find out about her father dying. We woke up in the ski cabin + went upstairs + this creepy guy was playing guitar for her, buck naked. She told us Grandpa Cal had died + that we should just go skiing for the day while she made arrangements. While it was convenient we were in California (our grandfather lived nearby in the Bay Area—another cosmic coincidence to our mom) this «friend» w/ the ski cabin was a real sleazeball + didn't want his ski-trip escapade ruined. He handed us money for the lift ticket + scooted us out the door then plotted how he'd hold our mother hostage. Seemed strange at first, but **skiing** is a therapeutic thing to do when grieving. Not sure we've mentioned our grandfather here, but he was our favorite relative. He's ½ the reason we call ourselves Cal A. Mari (the other ½ being our father). Grandpa Cal was a grouchy old fuck. We don't have many photos of him cuz anytime some 1 would turn a camera on him he'd flip the bird. […] Anyway, maybe 1 day we'll finish the ski-trip funeral story, or write a book about our grandfather. Right now we're still working on the book by/for our brother Chaulky (who resembled Grandpa Cal most), about our father.

THE OXEN OF THE SUN

(**top**) The author strikes a pose in front of the Xiang (Yellow) river, Yangshou, Heshan province (Guanxi Zhuanghzu Zizhiqu).
(**bottom**) The author at the entrance to the forbidden city, Tian Min square, Beijing. (Both photos; Feb.89)

7778742049: … so we probly reunited w/ the other ½ of Chaulky at Grandpa Cal's funeral. He died on April Fool's Day, so it would've been a few days after this (once our mother + i xcaped from Mammoth mtn).

12586269025: We'd had no real-world xperience w/ death to this point (that wasn't hidden from us) + suddenly every 1 was dying.

20365011074: ~~Not sure about brother-½, but i lost my virginity the summer ('81) before our father died.~~

32951280099: To the left + below is brother-½ at the entrance to the forbidden city.

53316291173: **1982** was a year of the Dog. Brother-½ will write the original *'SSES" 'SSES"* in the year of the Horse (1990) + will die in 1997, year of the Ox.

86267571272: All was escalating + falling into place yet at the same time the cement was drying before it occurred to us … before we coud leave our names in the sidewalk.

139583862445: Not sure the details of how it came to happen, but later in '82 both of us transferred to the same snooty private boarding school (named for Robert Louis Stevenson) in Carmel, CA. We had a creepy step-uncle that was a teacher there + he somehow worked it out so we had scholarships. + our cousin was there already.

225851433717: Personally i found RLS to be a miserable place + xferred to a public school in Mtn View after a year (only had a scholarship for 1 year anyway).

365435296162: ~~By this time i was into punk rock + brother-½ was a sort of a preppie, so~~ the prep-school xperience only served to xacerbate our conditions, driving us further to opposite poles. But at least we had this 1 year together.

THE OXEN OF THE SUN

(**top**) Entrance to a typical home in Ulan Bator, Mongolia.(Jan-89) (**bottom**) On the roof of the Potola Palace. Lhasa, Tibet. (April, 89).

591286729879: Brother-½ thrived in this environment, broke records in running (see newspaper clippings on facing page) + got congressional awards for his art, etc.

956722026041: My roommate at RLS was some rich brat whose parents lived somewhere in the middle east (like most kids there, the parents didn't want to deal w/him). He came back from Xmas break w/ a type of horse tranquilizer u coud get over the counter there. He was in good spirits at 1st but next thing i know he's crying hysterically, claiming his dad died. He ran thru the dorm + jumped out a window ... i found him in a field picking flowers ... said they were «for his father's hand-eye coordination.» When the school nurse called his family, ended up his father was alive + well. He never recovered + was sent off to another type of institutional facility.

1548008755920: For our part, we both steered clear of drugs + alcohol after our father's death.

2504730781961: Joyce (thru Dedalus) has this to say about **fathers**: «A father, Stephen said, battling against hopelessness, is a necessary evil.» + then to **elaborate further**: «Fatherhood, in the sense of conscious begetting, is unknown to man. It is a mystical estate, an apostolic succession, from only begetter to only begotten. [...] The son unborn mrs beauty: born, he brings pain, divides affection, increases care. He is a male: his growth is his father's decline, his youth his father's envy, his friend his father's enemy...»

4052739537881: His same story, generation aft re-generation.

6557470319842: Always surprises us there's still **records** to break.

10610209857723: We worked in the student radio station before realizing we were more intrested in **channeling** waves than their transmission.

17167680177565: **Running** still, in a free-falling free-for-all, augmented by 1.

27777890035288: Our older brother JD was already getting girls pregnant at this point. Pressure mounted from behind.

44945570212853: «*Here comes the ocean*» sang The Velvet Underground.

72723460248141: The inherent hypocrisy of identifying a self-fulfilling prophecy.

[adapted from http://5cense.com/13/rejoyce2.htm :]

In Joyce's take on Oxen of the Sun, Bloom is at the hospital to support Mina Purefoy in her birthing process. There are many revolving & obfuscated dialogues between various characters, mostly about medical issues & things like birth control ... the language is all over the map ... anything & everything goes ... language mimicking the gestation process. Phylogeny recapitulating ontogeny.

In light of Bloom's previous wank job, you could also see this as the natural consequence (impregnation) ... Purefoy as vehicle of immaculate conception (which her name helps to conjure ... almost pure joy) ... as the virgin Mary (& a knock-out version of her name conjures ...MinA puRefoY) ... specially since she is seemingly just a friend that Bloom xpresses no sexual interest in. The knockout letters spell «**IN PURE FO**» ... conjuring **Mary in pure form**.

117669030460994: ~~Went from getting straight As in an elite private school, to getting Bs + then Cs + Ds in a shitty public school. Which is not to say i wasn't learning ... i was learning there was more to learn.~~

190392490709135: He spent some time (circa mid-80s) at Rhode Island School of Design + then went to UCLA. Then after a year switched to Art Center College in Pasadena, where he'd write the originul iteration of this book.

308061521170129: Meanwhile i graduated from Mtn View High (not that i **walked in graduation**) + bummed around for a year before going to UC Santa Cruz. When it came time to declare my major i chose **math** just cuz i'd already fulfilled most of the requirements.

KEVIN WHITE RUNS TO RLS CROSS COUNTRY WIN
... before approving applause of Pirate gridders

Cross Country
White Sets Mark in RLS Wi

With Kevin White setting a course record time of 16.59 for three miles Robert Louis Stevenson's cross country team upped its record to 4-0 with Mission Trail Athletic League victorie over Carmel and King City high Thursday in the Del Monte Forest.

Carmel, led by Carlos Zarate who finished second overall in 17.20, also defeated King City 25-33. Stevenson downed Carmel 19-42 and King City 48.

In the girls varsity run, King Cit defeated RLS 23-36 and Carmel which fielded an incomplete team, also givin the Pirate girls a win.

Stevenson also won the junior vars boys run 15-49 over King City and 14- over Carmel, while Carmel edged Ki City 28-31.   BEAT OLD COURSE
RECORD BY
Varsity leaders: 25 seconds

Boys Division
1. Kevin White (RLS) 16.59, course record. 2. Carlos Zarate (C) 17.20. 3. Tim Carmichael (RLS) 17.3. 4. Stewart Purnell (RLS) 17.58. 5. Mike Nardoo (RLS) 18.48. 6. Arnulfo Garcia (KC) 18.50. 7. Bra Fowler (RLS) 19.05. 8. Scott Rogerson (C) 19.15 Craig Matthews (RLS) 19.21. 10. Steve Stacy (KC 19.22. 11. Adam Cabot (RLS) 19.26. 12. David So (KC) 19.27. 13. Mike Saenz (C) 19.46. 14. Mat Bellecci (C) 19.52. 15. Trevo Lundquist ...

Girls Division
1. Trish Wilkinson (KC) 21.58. 2. Kathy McGuire (RLS) 22.46. 3. Charlotte Kwon (RLS) 23.12. 4. Mary Wilkinson (KC) 23.59. 5. Kery Rohan (C) 24.05. Dawna Donnelly (KC) 24.05. 7. Dora Garcia (KC 24.49. 8. Ann Wood (KC) 25.33. 9. Heather Brown 25.35. 10. Staci Stacy (KC) 26.01. 11. Shannon Hack (C) 16.28. 12. Megan Laurence (RLS) 26.42. 13. Erin Bering (RLS) 27.13.

498454011879264 : The final push, 5 more pages ... at least to ½ way.

806515533049393 : If we listen to **Zeno**, Ulysses never makes it home. «That which is in locomotion must arrive at the ½-way stage before it arrives at the goal.»

1304969544928657: Before u get ½-way u got to get ½-way to ½-way, which is ¼ the way ... but before u reach the ¼ mark u got to get ½-way there, which is ⅛ the way, ... ad infinitum, ...

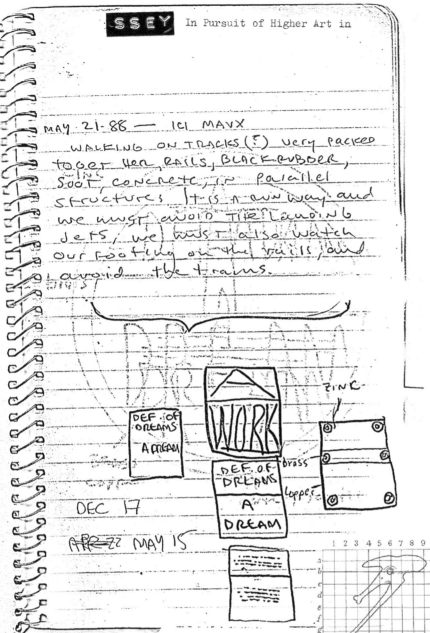

MAY 21-88 — ICI MAVX

WALKING ON TRACKS (?) very packed together, RAILS, BLACK RUBBER, SOOT, CONCRETE, in PARALLEL structures. It is a runway and we must avoid the landing jets, we must also watch our footing on the rails, and avoid the trains.

DEF. OF DREAMS

A DREAM

WORK

DEF. OF DREAMS

A DREAM

ZINC

brass

copper

DEC 17

APR 22 MAY 15

61305790721611591: U can lichen brother-½ + i to those opposing spirals, rotating around the same stem like DNA. A shifting labyrinth between 2 shores, between Scylla + Charybdis. A twined **dyadic diptych**—like this very book object (given the constraints) ... shifting + bifurcating between opposing pages (leaves) + columns.

99194853094755497 is itself a prime number.

160500643816367088: When we reach ½-way, bifurcation abates + reintegration begins.

2111485077978050 : Which is to say if u spend too much **thinking** u never leave the ground.

3416454622906707: The same can be said about writing/reading a book (this 1 included).

5527939700884757: For that matter we never die ... then again, we never really begin living to begin with.

8944394323791464: This is of course a negativ «glass is ½ empty» way to look at it ... but even if we take a «glass is ½ full» approach, we get **closer** to our destination (home) .... but still never quite get there ... which is equally infuriating, if knot worse.

14472334024676221: Somewhere around this time ('88) is when his apartment burned down ... probly while he was at UCLA. Not sure how it happend—evidently some 1 was burning a candle. Brother-½ woke up + the building was on fire. The only thing he grabbed (sides what he was wearing) were his cowboy boots. All his art work gone, xcept what was in his car or that he had w/ family + friends. He had to start over from **scratch**.

23416728348467685: After the fire, he became disillusioned w/ painting + 2-D works + turned to **conceptual** art. This is when he started making objects ... objects that represented more than just the objects themselves. *That even once gone the idea remains...*

37889062373143906: i did my undergraduate thesis on **Phyllotaxis**—the whorling patterns of leaves on plants «... ends up that the ratio of consecutive Fibonacci numbers is an approximation to the golden ratio, Φ. In an idealized geometric setting we have seen that a divergence of Φ gives the optimum spacing of points around a circle. We conclude that nature utilizes Fibonacci numbers as an optimizing agent in the spacing of leaves.»

May 20, 1989 – Santa Cruz, CA

Dad + Shirley [our stepmother] came over to [my X's] house. He didn't give me a hug or even say hello. I tried to talk to him but he was very nervous ... reminded me of Dustin Hoffman in *Rain Man*. Kevin was there too + had a Playboy magazine. We just sat there across a table from them—Kevin across from Shirley + me directly across from Dad. Kevin asked him a question + he answered. I don't know what was said but it was very vivid.

Bloom practising Parasitic boodism

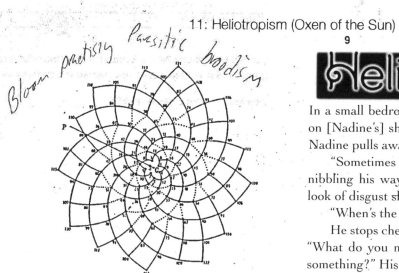

Figure 3. Rising Phyllotaxis, i.e. how a plant changes from m/n phyllotaxis to (m+n)/m (Richards).

Heliotropism

In a small bedroom late at night, [Telemachus] gnaws on [Nadine's] shoulder, trying to put her in the mood. Nadine pulls away, feigning only slight interest.

"Sometimes I just want to eat you," he says, nibbling his way down her arm, despite the wincing look of disgust ~~showing~~ on her face.

"When's the last time you took a shower?"

He stops chewing and looks at her, somewhat hurt. "What do you mean? I just took one. Do I smell or something?" His tone is defensive, a bit paranoid.

"Actually..." she [says], staring off at the opposite wall. She leans forward and Telemachus's body lumbers into the space behind her.

He struggles to sit upright, smelling his armpits. "I used soap and deodorant, I don't know what it is. Maybe something I ate."

"You smell sick," she says. "Unhealthy."

Telemachus's mind seizes up with anxiety [+] begins to sweat, which only makes the smell worse. "I'm sorry. I can't help it."

"Well I'm sorry, but I can't sleep with this smell. I'm going out to the couch."

"No, I will," insists Telemachus.

"It's okay, you don't ~~fit on the couch~~," she says. "It's no big deal, really." When Nadine grabs a blanket and pillow and leaves, Telemachus feels relieved to be alone with his stench.

have fallen off (figure 4). In an in depth study, Davis (1971) found the number of spirals, or in botanical terms *parastichies*, of different species of

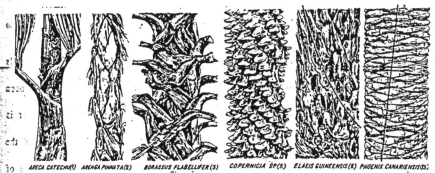

ARECA CATECHU(1)   ARENGA PINNATA(2)   BORASSUS FLABELLIFER (3)   COPERNICIA SP.(5)   ELAEIS GUINEENSIS(8)   PHOENIX CANARIENSIS(13)

Figure 4. Six different species of palm displaying, in order from left to right, 1/2, 2/3, 3/5, 5/8, 8/13 and 13/21 phyllotaxis (Davis).

The next day Telemachus wakes up early to go for a run. He ends up walking most of the time because he feels lethargic and weak. He realizes that he has felt this heavy for years, but only notices during times of exertion. It always feels like he is carrying extra baggage. **His excessive physical state is so familiar to him as to be non-existent** ... as long as he can maintain a sedentary equilibrium of inactivity. But he has never been in love ~~before~~, he has never cared what [others] thought of him before Nadine. The realization and admission of his problem makes him feel lighter. He believes that Nadine's confrontation is out of love and this forces him to finally come to grips with his obesity.

He makes an appointment with his doctor, convinced that he is suffering from something other than typical weight gain—perhaps a glandular disorder or chemical imbalance. Nadine thinks he is crazy for thinking this and grows increasingly disgusted with him. Telemachus doesn't understand why she is avoiding him when he has admitted he has a problem and is taking initiative to do something about it.

Telemachus goes to Dr. Cottle[100] and tells him what he thinks is wrong with him. Dr. Cottle is reluctant to do anything ~~at all~~ for [him], but Telemachus convinces the doctor to give him a physical, analyze his blood and take some X-rays. **Dr. Cottle performs these tasks, taking care to conceal his annoyance of Telemachus, whom he regards as yet another overweight hypochondriac looking for an external [fix] rather then assuming internal control over his own will.**

---

[100] This is the actual name of our dentist when we were kids.

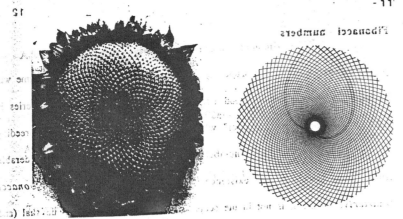

Figure 5. Left: Photograph of Sunflower head with 34 clockwise spirals and 55 counterclockwise spirals (Thompson). Right: Simplified drawing of spiraling pattern in sunflower head showing 55/89 phyllotaxis (Feininger).

encouraged to observe (and count) for themselves.

While the above examples are more striking and obvious, it ends up that 95% of plants follow these patterns. Even the exceptional cases are still governed by the same recurring relation, $\alpha_{n+1} = \alpha_n + \alpha_{n-1}$, but with different initial conditions, for example the Lucas sequence 1, 3, 4, 7, 11, 18, 29, ... In any event as Rosen puts it (Jean, p. iix),

> *The relation between phyllotaxis and the Fibonacci sequence is clearly not an accidental or random one and points to some deep mechanisms of morphogenetic control, which is manifested in ontogenesis and strongly conserved in phylogenesis.*

In order to better understand these mechanisms it is first necessary to study some of the properties of Fibonacci numbers and ϕ (the golden ratio).

259695496911122585:
Wherein Jack sells the family ox for a few magic beans.

«Behold the mansion reared by dedal Jack,
See the malt stored in many a refluent sack,
In the proud cirque of Jackjohn's bivouac.»
—*Ulysses*

A couple of days later, Telemachus returns to the doctor's office for the results of the tests. There are six other men in the office besides [Dr. Cottle], some of them are in scrubs, others [...] in suits. Telemachus realizes [...] there is something wrong. Everyone is trying not to stare at his mid-section, [no] one looks him in the eye.

Without saying anything, Dr. Cottle turns out the lights and [switches] on the X-ray viewer. The transparency is a brownish-yellow color. The X-ray image looks like a poster for some modern dance company—an emaciated figure [holds] a contorted pose that resembles a diver springing out of fetal position an instant before he strikes the water. This nebulous figure is superimposed over a more defined figure of a man standing with his arms down to his sides—the posture readily recognizable as that of Telemachus.

Telemachus steps towards the light, studying the face of the man in the [striking] pose. He recognizes his father's corpse wedged inside of his own body, and knows that none of the doctors know who it is. This thought makes him feel a little more secure, a little less self-conscious. He can play the part of the victim.

The doctors seem to be concerned for Telemachus's health. A discussion ensues on how they might operate to remove the corpse. **No mention is made as to the how and why of his condition.** When they find out that Telemachus does not have health insurance, they decide to postpone the operation.

Telemachus observes the doctors with detached subjectivity, but every time he is able to attach the condition they are discussing to his body he endures a crippling rush of emotional pain. He returns to work, but then immediately feigns sickness and leaves early. He meanders back to the apartment, arriving just as Nadine does. She manages a brief smile [...] and then lets her self into the apartment, leaving the door open as Telemachus shuffles in like some unwanted garment Nadine drags behind her.

When he tells Nadine about his medical condition, she gets angry ~~with him~~. She thinks ~~that~~ he is making up a [sob] story to [get] her pity and it pisses her off. She won't even look him in the eyes. He insists it is true. "Call the doctors and ask them, they'll show you the X-rays." He pleads with her as she readies to leave.

"[What's with you, huh?!] Why do you say stupid shit like this?! You're overweight and you smell! Deal with it! I'm sick of being nice about it. It's not [helping]." She feels a rush of liberation now that she's not suppressing her real contempt and disgust for him.

144 + 233 = Dead Sea Scrolls

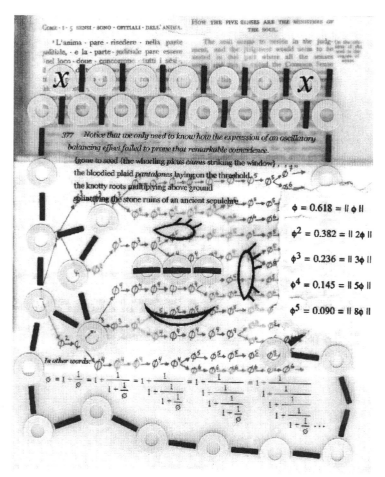

After she packs a bag and leaves him alone in the apartment, Telemachus sits in the living room and stares out the window in shock. **He tries to recall when and how he managed to get his father's corpse inside of his body.** He soon finds himself in the dark, but still does not turn on a light. After a while he concludes that it must have happened shortly after his father's death six years earlier. In the darkness of the living room he travels back to that time. He sees his father's funeral and all the relatives. He bends over to look into his father's casket[101] but cannot fix an image on his face. It's like when they blur faces on TV to censor them or render them unidentifiable.

He remembers being very thirsty [...] after the funeral. Back at the house, [he drank] more than a gallon of water and [fell] asleep, feeling ~~very~~ bloated and heavy.

Telemachus wakes up the next day and goes over to ~~stay at~~ his mother's house. He tells his whole family the new development in his life and they prove to be understanding. His grandmother offers to pay for the operation to remove his father, pointing out that she always hated him and didn't see why Telemachus should have to carry his corpse around inside ~~of him~~. His mother is disgusted by the whole [affair] and his stepfather doesn't ~~seem to~~ care one way or the other.

xhibit 99—page 377 from *P.S. At Least We Died Trying to Make You in the Backseat of a Taxidermist* (Calamari Press, 2005)

It takes a series of three operations to remove the entire corpse. The operations span a week during which Telemachus is heavily sedated. When he finally wakes up after the last [one] he asks the doctor what they have done with his fathers [body]. The doctor tells him that they have "disposed" of it.

"Who gave you permission to throw away my father's body?" Telemachus tries to sound upset, but is still sedated.

"Your mother signed the release form ~~for the disposal of your father's corpse~~ three days ago."

The doctor tells him that they had to cut up his father's body into twelve sections to [extract it from] his body. He describes—with as much emotion as one would use to describe the carving of a Thanksgiving turkey—the methodical dismemberment of his father. Even though he did not witness it, the idea of [carving up] his father's corpse has left Telemachus in a lot of pain, for which he is prescribed copious pharmaceuticals, all of which make him feel sick and unfocused.

All together it takes about two months for Telemachus to completely recover. He is left with seven large scars. The longest [one]—an eleven inch [suture] about an inch thick—stretches across his stomach just below his belly button. Except for a lingering dull ache in his gut, the pain is all but gone by the time he leaves home to return to the city. He moves back to the city by himself, finding his own small place and getting work as a lifeguard at a public pool. He doesn't feel any lighter after the operations and still cannot manage to run very far, or for very long. After a while he gives up on the idea of running and switches to playing golf, which [involves] less psychical [sic] strain.

[101] In reality there was no casket—our father was cremated.

Telemachus [settles] into a comfortable existence as a slightly overweight golfer, alone except for the occasional night out with his golfing buddies and trips home to see the family. He stops thinking so much about his father and the operation and begins to concentrates more on his own isolation [+ well-being].

A year after the operation Telemachus runs into Nadine in the frozen food section of a supermarket. She's shocked to see him so self-confident and content. All of the self-conscious bitterness (about life), that she remembers in him [seems] to have disappeared. She finds herself very attracted to his aloofness and he responds to her flirting automatically, as if it was some learned behavior he'd long since forgotten. They spend the [entire] weekend in his apartment getting re-acquainted and talk [non-stop] on the phone during the week. By the next weekend she has all but moved into his apartment. They are back together as if nothing had ever happened.

There is a certain lightness to their relationship this time, however, something that was not there before. It is as if any reason they might have had for [harboring a grudge] before had disappeared. She simply no longer found it necessary to ridicule him because of his weight and for his part he no longer pretended to be his father.

xhibit 100—Untitled '92 (colored RTV 500 silicone, cast resin fasteners, formica—28" x 23" x 11")

[... to be continued in volume 2 of 'SSES' 'SSES' "SSEY' —**The Homecoming**—wherein we recapitulate this story 1 step further by embedding our brother-½ (w/ the ghost of our father embedded inside him) inside us ...]